DOCTOR WHO

THE FALL OF YQUATINE
NICK WALTERS

Published by BBC Worldwide Ltd,
Woodlands, 80 Wood Lane
London W12 0TT

First published 2000
Copyright © Nick Walters
The moral right of the author has been asserted

Original series broadcast on the BBC
Format © BBC 1963
Doctor Who and TARDIS are trademarks of the BBC

ISBN 0 563 55594 7
Imaging by Black Sheep, copyright © BBC 2000

Printed and bound in Great Britain by Mackays of Chatham
Cover printed by Belmont Press Ltd, Northampton

*For Paul Leonard Hinder, without whom I would never
have got to Dellah, Sweden or Yquatine*

Acknowledgements

The Fall of Yquatine *owes its existence to the following people:*

Steve Cole, for liking the story in the first place
Justin Richards, for all his help during the writing and editing of this book
Jac Rayner, all at BBC Worldwide, and everyone on the Celestis discussion group
Paul Leonard and Paul Vearncombe, for reading the first drafts, handy scientific and military advice, encouragement and friendship
Becky Waghorne, for extremely quick read-through duty, and girly perspective
Lawrence Miles, for starting the whole thing off with Interference
Paul Cornell, for The Shadows of Avalon
The Bristol SF Group and Bristol Fiction Writers

And, while I'm here, hello to all my friends and family, and thanks to all the people I don't know who read and enjoyed Dominion.

– Nick Walters

Law and Chaos, the two processes that dominate existence, are equally indifferent to the individual. To Chaos, Law destroys; to Law, Chaos. They equally create, dictate to, and destroy the individual.

- John Fowles, *The Aristos*

I thought I might help them understand
What an ugly thing to see

- Michael Stipe

Contents

Part Four: As Long as Your Luck Holds Out

The Yquatine Calendar

The planet Yquatine in the Minerva System has an elliptical orbit which bestows it with long summers and short winters. The Yquatine year has 417 days: 10 months of roughly 42 days each:

Spring:
Stormstide
Petalstrune
Cicelior

Summer:
Sevaija
Jaquaia
Lannasirn

Autumn:
Perialtrine
Shriveltide

Winter:
Forlarne
Ultimar

Part One
You Can Run, but You Can't Hide

Chapter One
'What the hell am I doing here?'

Arielle felt as if the city of Yendip was trying to absorb her into itself. Caught up in a surging throng, she stumbled past a Kukutsi foodstall, bubbling pots sending wraiths of steam into the air. Next, a street café spilled out into the road, a tangle of chair legs, limbs and conversation. A sound system had been set up in the middle of the road, tiny speakers darting through the air like dozy bees, exotic dancers of several species cavorting amid the crowd.

Arielle felt drunk on the variety, each new sight, sound and smell making her laugh, gasp, choke or simply gape in astonishment. She wanted to stop and look but the crowd wouldn't let her. She had no choice but to half-walk, half-stumble down the street, past rows of biscuit-coloured stone dwellings from which more people poured, swelling the tide.

And it was *so hot*: her face ached from squinting against the dazzling sunlight and her feet were baking inside her boots. She grimaced. Stupid to wear the things, but her sandals were somewhere inside one of the couple of dozen packing cases cramping her small room back at the university. There had been more than enough time to unpack – her course didn't start for two weeks – but she had arrived early so she could catch the Treaty Day celebrations.

'Hey, girl, whatya *doing*?'

Fixing her expression into a mask of disinterest, Arielle looked over to the side of the street. A trio of male humans were lounging against a trestle table heaving with bottles. They all wore the fox-faced look of drunken lust.

She'd come here, partly, to get away from this sort of thing. But maybe there was no escaping it. She was what she was, wherever she went.

She smiled sweetly at them and raised her hand in the universal gesture of 'go mate with yourself'. Unfortunately, her dignity was totally compromised as, in the next step, she stood on a bottle which skidded from under her feet and sent her flying into the arms of the nearest reveller. Which just happened to be a huge Adamantean. Arielle gasped as the being clutched her to itself to break her fall. It was like being mauled by a statue.

'I'm all right, really,' she said.

The Adamantean nodded. 'Mind how you go,' it intoned, the words banal in its deep, rumbling voice.

The collision had shocked Arielle, and she suddenly felt lost and homesick. Maybe best to go back to her room, unpack properly, send a message to Boris –

She frowned, marshalling herself. That was the old Arielle. The dutiful Arielle who never questioned anything, who did what the family wanted. Who was going to work for Markhof Mining Corporation. Who had died that day she'd looked in the mirror and seen a stranger.

The street began to level out, and presently Arielle found herself in a wide open space. The crowds thinned out, and a welcome breeze wafted through her sweat-damp T-shirt. This must be Founders' Square, she thought, remembering the map in the university prospectus – supposedly the very site where the colony ship *Minerva* had landed over two hundred years ago. It was obviously a focal point for the celebrations – the three-pronged jade obelisk in the square's centre had been festooned with flags and bunting which stretched from its tips to the eaves of the buildings at the edge, rather robbing them of their dignity, Arielle thought. There were stalls and games and entertainers, and excited children running about *everywhere*. Chaos. Cheesy organ music wafted over it all.

A couple of deerlike Eldrig trotted past. They hooted at her and she realised she'd been staring. They were the first of their kind she had ever seen up close. They were beautiful, their dun skins shining with perspiration, their hooves tapping on the flagstones.

Behind them, trying to grab their flicking tails, was a rather uncharacteristically merry-looking Saraani clutching a bottle of beer. Drink. Now that was an idea. Maybe that would steady her nerves. She remembered Boris telling her where all the best bars in Yendip were – in a place called Pierhaven, on the seafront.

Arielle found it without too much trouble. The esplanade, with its frontage of swish hotels, was impressive, and the sight of the sea took her breath away, but once more she had no chance to stop and look as she became swept up in a crowd. She overheard the name 'Pierhaven' a few times so she kept her head down and folded her arms, trying to make herself inconspicuous, and let the crowd take her along the seafront towards a sprawling wooden construction which staggered out into the sea on countless wooden legs.

Arielle hung back, waited for the crowd to thin out, and then pushed through the doors. Neon light and blaring music assaulted her senses, and as she walked deeper in she felt the beginnings of panic; muggings were common in Yendip, she was new here, she had no weapons. She hid in the crowds for safety, befriending a small blue-skinned Ikapi woman who told her a bit about the place. Pierhaven was a maze of dusty passageways and rickety wooden walkways which led to innumerable bars, cafés, tattoo parlours, shops, trance dens, clubs, brothels and the like, all arranged haphazardly so that you were always stumbling upon some seedy establishment or other. Some were open to the sky, others enclosed under awnings. The floor beneath varied alarmingly from wooden slats to rope bridges, metal gangways clearly salvaged from wrecks, and circular wells open to the sea in which people swam or fished. It was the sort of place you could lose yourself in and Arielle could see, among the brightly clothed revellers, the sagging faces and shabby clothes of drunks.

Arielle turned to her new friend to comment on this, but she wasn't there. Probably slipped into some bar or other. Arielle suddenly felt vulnerable, so she ducked inside the nearest tavern. It was crowded and noisy – lunchtime on Treaty Day had to be one of the busiest times of the year – and Arielle had to push herself towards the bar. She leaned her elbows in sticky spilled beer, trying to look casual and unconcerned, her heart hammering away. She couldn't see any bar staff, and masses of hands, pincers and feelers were waving money and hollering for attention. Arielle began to have second thoughts. Perhaps she should come back another day.

Then she caught sight of her face in the mirror behind the bar.

The face that stared back at her wasn't her own. It was beautiful – pale, smooth skin, gleaming golden-brown hair, big brown eyes, an elegant nose and perfect lips. Even after four years, it still gave her a shock to realise that she looked like this. That she was beautiful.

'What is your pleasure, madam?' came a rasping, lisping voice.

Arielle jumped. A tall lizard-like figure with bright yellow eyes stood before her. It had pale, sand-coloured scales, a narrow, birdlike face, and wore a tight-fitting leather jerkin. It was – Arielle had to think for a second – an Izrekt.

Arielle spoke in Minervan, the common language of the System. 'A bottle of Admiral's Old Antisocial, please.'

The Izrekt hissed and drew a forelimb to its chin. 'Anti-sssocial I do not have.'

Arielle was disappointed – she'd wanted to try Admiral's, it was the favourite drink of a heroine of hers. It didn't matter. 'Erm, well, whatever, then,' she muttered.

The Izrekt cocked his head to one side. 'You new here? This first time on planet?'

Arielle nodded. How did he know? 'Yes, I'm a student, came early to see Treaty Day.'

'Interesting, very! What subject?'

Arielle glanced nervously around. He didn't seem to notice the clamouring throng of customers waiting to be served. 'Xenobiology, mainly.'

The Izrekt smiled, showing double rows of tiny teeth. 'Well you came to right planet! Welcome to Yquatine, and welcome to my bar. Name is Il-Eruk.'

13

Arielle took his small, clawed hand in hers. 'Arielle Markhof. Um, any chance of a beer?'

Il-Eruk gestured to the bottles on the shelves behind him. 'Anthaurk Ale, I recommend.'

Arielle shrugged. 'OK, Anthaurk Ale it is.'

Il-Eruk nodded politely and moved towards the bottles. Arielle noticed tiny wings sprouting from a hole in the jerkin. He swung round, an open bottle in his forelimb, head cocked to one side.

Arielle took the bottle and sipped. It had a strong, peppery taste which seemed to shoot right up her nose. She gasped. 'And I have to drink a whole bottle of this!'

She became aware of a silence around her. She turned around slowly, to face four tall, top-heavy figures. Arielle recognised them instantly – Anthaurk. Their homeworld had been invaded by the Daleks and the surviving Anthaurk had settled in the Minerva System about a hundred years after the humans. There had been two years of war, before the Treaty of Yquatine had ushered in a peace that had lasted a century. Not the sort of people you wanted to annoy.

'And what is wrong with our ale?' growled the tallest and fiercest-looking Anthaurk.

'Nothing,' said Arielle, in Anthaurk. 'Just takes a little getting used to.'

The Anthaurk hissed and its wide mouth opened, revealing rows of tiny, sharp, white teeth and a glistening purple tongue the size of a small snake. 'So, you abuse our language as well!'

Arielle backed against the bar, realising she was in a lot of trouble. These creatures were obviously out for a fight and unlike humans they didn't care that she was a woman, beautiful or not.

Il-Eruk waved his forelimbs in agitation. 'No trouble, I want!'

The Anthaurk glared at him. 'Stay out of this, Izrekt!'

It reached out and grabbed her arm. 'Humans should leave all things Anthaurk alone.'

'Let go of me!' Arielle hissed, suddenly angry with the alien. 'Are you stupid? The tax on Anthaurk Ale is helping to prop up your economy and you should be grateful that people like me are trying it!'

The other Anthaurk hissed with hilarity and clapped their gloved hands. Arielle hoped this would defuse the situation, but the grip tightened.

The Anthaurk's face darted closer to hers, in a fluid, snakelike movement. 'You presume to know our affairs?'

Arielle recoiled, despite her respect for aliens; its breath stank like rotting meat.

'Let her go, Elzar.'

The voice came from behind her. An Anthaurk voice. Arielle twisted round. Another Anthaurk stood at her shoulder, disapproval etched over its scaly features.

Elzar grimaced. 'Let me have my sport, Zendaak.'

The newcomer bared his teeth in anger. 'Let her go! I will not tolerate this!'

Elzar's red eyes widened. Obviously this Zendaak had authority over him, and in his drunken anger he'd forgotten. Until too late.

Elzar let her go and bowed his head. 'I am sorry, Commander.'

Arielle rubbed the life back into her arm. She bruised easily – especially since the surgery – and there would be an ugly purple mark there tomorrow.

Zendaak towered over her. Like his comrades, he was clad in the uniform of the Anthaurk military: a close-fitting leather garment adorned with piping and shoulder pads, inlaid with swirling patterns. From the wide collar of the uniform rose the neck, a thick, sinewy trunk supporting the curved, snakelike head. Zendaak's scaly skin was a dull orange and across the eyes was a band of darker skin, from within which two red eyes burned like embers. The mouth was wide and the nose was just a double vertical slit. Around the top of the head was a crown of stubby black horns. Zendaak's limbs were thick and powerful, muscles rippling under the tight-fitting uniform. 'You must be punished, Elzar.'

'Yes, Commander.'

Arielle gulped. She had the horrible feeling she was about to witness an evisceration at the very least.

Zendaak fixed Elzar with a stern glare. 'It seems you cannot take the ale, while this mere human –' he waved a clawed hand at Arielle – 'can.'

Arielle took instant umbrage at being called 'mere' but she decided to play along and raised her bottle to Elzar.

Zendaak hissed. 'As punishment for such an act of violence on Treaty Day, you will not be permitted to attend the function tonight.'

Arielle almost laughed aloud, but Elzar looked even more abashed.

'Instead, you will remain in our hotel suite, and study the Treaty, including all clauses, subclauses and amendments. Hand over your pass.'

Elzar reached into a pocket on his belt and took out a small transparent disc, which he passed to Zendaak.

Zendaak took the pass, his lips parting in a grin wide enough to bite your head off. He proffered the disc to Arielle. 'Perhaps you would like to attend in his place?'

There were hisses of outrage from a few of the Anthaurk, laughter from others, and Elzar bared his teeth in a grimace of shame.

Arielle took the disk and smiled her loveliest smile at Zendaak, wondering what this 'function' was. She looked at it. Blue holotext shimmered before her eyes:

You are cordially invited to
the Palace of Yquatine
on the evening of the 16th of Lannasirn 2992
to celebrate the
ninety-ninth anniversary of the signing
of the Treaty of Yquatine

Arielle stared at it. This felt like a dream. She heard the Anthaurk stomping off and when she looked up again she was alone.

She took another sip of Anthaurk Ale. Not bad, on second tasting.

She looked at the invitation again. She couldn't, surely?

Then she smiled. Why not?

Arielle leaned back in the seat of the hover-taxi, relishing the comfort and trying not to think of the expense. It was dusk, and Yendip was coming alive with lights. Fireworks bloomed in the sky, and the music and revelry went on seemingly without end. She had unearthed the least creased of her frocks – a pale-blue strapless thing – and found some court shoes. Her mind was a soufflé of panic and excitement. At this function she'd get to meet aliens from all over the Minerva System. She couldn't imagine a better start to her studies. All she had to do was concoct some plausible cover story – her good looks would do the rest. She hated herself for using her beauty in this way, but it was foolish not to use it. Like having a superweapon or a passport to anywhere.

Yendip lay on the eastern coast of Julianis, the largest continent of Yquatine. It boasted a large, busy harbour, from which the town stretched westward until it met Lake Yendip, formed countless millions of years ago when the land masses rose and cut off the body of water from the sea. Hills rose in a crescent on the landward side of Lake Yendip, effectively forming the boundaries of the town, though small villages straggled up and down the forested valleys.

They left the town and skimmed across Lake Yendip. It was a beautiful evening, the placid waters reflecting the lights of the town, vessels drifting to and fro, the starry, dark-blue sky, the hills rising in the distance, dotted with buttery yellow light. On those hills sat the University of Yquatine; one of those lights indicated Arielle's hall of residence. She tried to work out which one, but soon gave up. There were so many.

In the middle of Lake Yendip there was a flat, disc-shaped artificial island, which supported the Palace of Yquatine and its gardens. The Palace of Yquatine, seat of government not only for Yquatine but for the entire System. Never had Arielle thought she'd be actually going inside it on her first night on Yquatine. She tried to contain her excitement as they approached the island, the towers of the palace rising before her like immense blue sheets of ice.

The console of the taxi gave a few bleeps as they were scanned. Arielle held her breath, and took out the invitation. What should she do, wave it in the air? The palace security systems were renowned for their ruthless efficiency and Arielle fully expected to be fried to a crisp that very second.

But no. A wrinkle appeared in the sky in front of them, and a tingly feeling ran over her whole body as they passed through the portal opened in the force field for them.

She was in.

And there before her was the Palace of Yquatine. It was fairy tale itself. It stood in the centre of acres of gardens, floodlit statuary and illuminated fountains. Glow-spheres hovered in the air, lighting the way for the taxi. The palace looked as though it had been made from a sheet of blue-green silk laid across a bed and tugged upwards by invisible fingers – the walls were smooth, opaque, and they seemed to ripple and flow like water. It was an incredible feat of architecture. Man-made beauty, just like her own.

Arielle paid the fare and disembarked. The taxi hummed away. She sighed, a heavy feeling in her chest. Well, she was here now. No going back. She lifted up the hem of her frock and trotted up the steps, acting as if she did this sort of thing all the time. The reception droid scarcely glanced at her pass. Once past the force field that was it, she supposed.

Inside, Arielle was welcomed by a smooth and smiling palace official and shown into a high-ceilinged circular room, with a balcony offering views of the island and lake, tables groaning with food, floating drinks droids, and crowds of humans and aliens dazzling in their diversity.

A feeling of sheer social vertigo overtook her. Once again she was sixteen, clumsy and shy. She remembered – in time to quell her panic – that she was a tall, attractive woman. She could do just about whatever she wanted. She smiled at nothing, filled her head with a simple tune, scanned the room for Zendaak.

She saw him, on the far side of the room, and made a beeline for the Anthaurk commander. There were half a dozen other Anthaurk flanking Zendaak so closely that she had to squeeze past them.

'Hello,' she said, smiling up at his snakelike face. 'Thought I'd take up your... offer...'

Her voice tailed off and she froze. Zendaak's face showed no sign of recognition – in fact he looked totally hostile. 'I'm sorry?' he hissed.

'The tavern,' she prompted. This was a bad idea. 'Elzar, remember?'

'Oh. Yes, I remember.' He sounded totally uninterested.

'What is this, Zendaak?' hissed an elderly Anthaurk leaning on a wooden staff.

Arielle flashed it her best smile, and felt an arm on her bare shoulders. Zendaak was ushering her away. 'Excuse me. I have affairs of state to discuss.'

Suddenly Arielle was facing a wall of unsmiling Anthaurk guards.

Great.

She backed away from the Anthaurk. It had been a mistake coming here. She'd been just part of Elzar's punishment. Zendaak's politeness had been nothing to do with her, just a means of embarrassing his subordinate. She'd been used.

Suppressing her anger, Arielle circled around the room. She soon found herself gazing in awe at the diversity of alien life gathered under the glittering crystal ceiling. For the first time, she felt safe – here, her beauty meant nothing. That was one of the factors that had drawn her to Yquatine – in a multispecies environment, it wouldn't matter how she looked. Beauty is in the eye of the beholder, and if the beholder was alien they might even find her ugly. The thought was refreshing and exciting.

So she passed among them, unremarked upon. A herd of Eldrig, their jewelled antlers towering above the crowd. A couple of insectoid Kukutsi, their black carapaces gleaming in the soft light. In one corner, a silver-grey diamond shape rotated slowly in a self-generated field. An Ixtricite – or a representation of one. She hadn't quite got a handle on them yet. Rorclaavix, tiger-like beings in shining golden armour. They seemed rather drunk. And there were yet more she didn't even recognise. Yquatine itself was home to two hundred different species, and there were nine other planets in the system, all but one of them heavily colonised. And she'd come here to study them all. She was going to have her work cut out and a pleasurable thrill ran through her at the prospect.

An ovoid shape drifted towards her, bearing a silver tray in its manipulation field. Its voice was plummy and slightly haughty. 'Would you like a drink, madam?'

Arielle took a goblet and sipped: a full, fruity red wine. Château Yquatine, famed export of the Yquatine vineyards. Better not drink too much and embarrass herself, she decided.

Now she was used to the novelty of the situation she wished she could find someone to talk to, enthuse with about her pet subject. She began to feel self-conscious, hot and bothered. Perhaps some fresh air would help.

Outside, on the balcony, she felt a bit better. The view was entrancing. The lake seemed to glow with a blue, inner light, and the stars of the System fascinated her. On her homeworld you couldn't see the stars unless you left the planet.

She stayed there for a long time, not wanting to go back inside, letting the wine fill her head, despite her earlier decision. Alcohol always made her emotional and she succumbed to conflicting feelings of elation at what she had done, and homesickness for what she had left behind. She kept muttering, 'What the hell am I doing here?' and laughing quietly to herself.

'There she is.'

Arielle spun round. The palace official who had welcomed her earlier had come out on to the balcony. He wasn't smiling now, but pointing at her. Beside him was a palace guard, in full traditional uniform – big hat, ornamental breastplate and all.

'Can I see your pass again please?' When he wasn't smiling the palace official had a cold, inhospitable face – shiny orange-tinted skin, yellow hair and cold blue eyes.

Arielle put the goblet back on the balustrade and proffered the invitation with a lurching feeling in her stomach. She should have known that something like this was going to happen. And in all the excitement she hadn't got round to preparing a cover story.

'Where did you get this?' the official snapped.

Arielle met the man's gaze defiantly. 'An Anthaurk gave it to me. Commander Zendaak.'

The official blinked. Then he smiled. 'I think you had better come with me.'

The palace guard had already unholstered his blaster.

'Look, I'm telling the truth. I met him in a bar in Pierhaven.'

The palace official clearly didn't believe her. He didn't even seem to be responding to her extraordinarily good looks. Probably too dedicated to his duty. Either that or he was a droid. 'I'm going to have to ask you to leave.'

Arielle pointed back towards the hall. 'If you don't believe me, ask Zendaak!'

The official ignored her. 'Come with me.'

'What's going on?'

The voice came from the entrance to the palace. Arielle looked past the guard. There stood a tall, handsome man in a black jacket inlaid with gold insignia.

He was instantly familiar, and Arielle tried not to scream as he walked slowly towards her.

His portrait hung in the lobby of the University of Yquatine. There was a statue of him in Founders' Square. His face was even on her credit card. He was Stefan Vargeld, the Marquis of Yquatine and President of the Senate of the Minerva System.

Arielle backed away, her hands meeting the cool roughness of the balustrade.

The guard and the official snapped to attention. 'An impostor, sir,' intoned the official.

Arielle heard the official explain the problem, but she didn't hear the words. She was staring at the President. His portrait didn't do him justice at all. It didn't show the smile playing around his eyes.

President Vargeld waved his underlings away. There are probably smart weapons concealed all over the palace, thought Arielle. One word from the President and she'd be vaporised.

He walked over and leaned on the stone balustrade beside her. Close up the jacket looked gaudy, the buttons and epaulettes overelaborate. She could tell by the set of his shoulders that he hated wearing the thing.

'I should have you thrown out.' His voice was warm and soft, but he sounded deadly serious, as if he was going to chuck her off the balcony.

Arielle tried to keep her voice steady. 'I was telling the truth. Zendaak did give me the pass.'

President Vargeld turned to face her. His eyes were suddenly cold. 'You expect me to believe that?'

Arielle's knees turned to water. 'No, but it is the truth.'

His eyes searched her face. 'Who are you?'

'I'm a student.' His eyebrows rose at that. 'Honest truth.' She blurted out everything that had happened to her that day.

When she'd finished, the President smiled. 'You've had quite a day. What's your name?'

'Arielle. Arielle Markhof.'

President Vargeld smiled and extended a hand. She took it. It was warm and soft and the touch of it sent a thrill right through her body to the soles of her feet.

'I knew about you already. Zendaak told me. He said you spoke Anthaurk like a native, seemed perfectly at home among them.'

Another effect of her beauty, she thought – even in the direst straits, her face refused to show fear. 'I'm here to study them. As well as all the other races in the System.'

He laughed. 'Well you've certainly got your work cut out.'

He'd put words to her thoughts as if he could read her mind. She shivered. 'I'm interested in appearances. How perceptions affect who you are.'

She realised she was still holding his hand. She let go. She should be feeling self-conscious, but something in his manner made her feel right at home. It was as though he was someone she'd always known. He wasn't looking at her as men usually did, their eyes feasting on her beauty. He seemed to see the real Arielle, the gawky, shy, clumsy kid walking around in the body of an ultramodel.

He leaned towards her. He couldn't be far away from his twenties and here he was, the ruler of a star system. If her parents could see her now...

'Look, I have to make a speech in a minute,' he said conspiratorially. 'How about joining me at my table afterwards?'

Arielle gulped. 'Why?' she blurted, instantly regretting it.

'Well, because I'd like to know someone like you. Someone who, on their first day on Yquatine, can infiltrate a diplomatic function with such ease.' He smiled boyishly, his blue eyes twinkling. 'You've just got to be worth knowing.'

Arielle smiled back, despite the cheesiness of the line. Still, she'd heard worse.

'I'll see you later.' He strode back inside.

Arielle gave a little wave, and watched him go. 'I must be dreaming,' she muttered to herself, then went inside.

President Vargeld made his speech, and it was very well received. Another Treaty Day, another year of peace. There was something about taxation of trade routes and a slightly gloomy note about overpopulation, but Arielle didn't really notice. She was looking at President Vargeld, trying not to pass out at the sheer funk of what she was doing, and mentally composing a letter to her brother Boris.

Later, at the end of the evening, when most of the other guests had left, President Vargeld and the student stood once more on the balcony, close together, their hands almost touching on the stone balustrade. They talked – about their lives, their hopes and dreams. They watched ships take off into the sky. They heard the low cries of the creatures from the lake. They laughed, they drank wine.

And then something terrible happened. They fell in love.

Chapter Two
'She'll probably never trust you again'

Fitz pointed to the orange stuff. 'What did you say that one was again?'

The vendor, a giant beetle-thing, waved a pincer. 'Devilled mud-maggot in gruntgoat cheese sauce,' it gurgled.

Fitz wondered if the alien was joking. He smiled. 'Sounds groovy. I'll have a shellful.'

The vendor chirruped its approval and scooped out some of the stuff into a shell-like tub. Fitz took a tentative taste. Blimey. Like Stilton mashed up with kippers.

'Not bad,' he lied as he handed over a crumpled bundle of notes to the vendor. 'Keep the change.'

'Come on,' said Compassion, tapping his arm. 'The Doctor's waiting, probably.'

She turned and strode off through the marketplace, the hem of her black cloak swirling around her legs. Fitz sighed and followed her, carrying the tub of devilled mud-maggot. He badly needed a smoke to purge the taste of the stuff. That or a beer. It was hot – the height of summer, apparently. The market buildings were clay domes, like upturned cups scattered randomly on the dusty ground, painted gaudy shades of yellow, blue and pink, inlaid with mosaics, decorated with flashing signs and flags and curtained doorways. The place wasn't crowded; in fact it was decidedly threadbare. The Doctor had told them that today was the centenary of the signing of some treaty or other, and Fitz had been expecting a carnival of Mardi Gras proportions, but when Compassion had disgorged them into the streets of Yendip, it had been into a decidedly muted atmosphere. There were a few street performers, the odd drunken reveller, but that was all. This had annoyed the Doctor, as he had planned to blend in with the crowds. Fitz had suggested that they may have landed on the wrong day. Compassion had stated proudly that she was no rickety old Type 40 and had total control over where and when she was going. This had made the Doctor frown, and look strangely embarrassed.

Fitz broke into a sweat as he followed Compassion's cloaked figure through the market. She walked bloody fast and probably wasn't sweating. TARDISes didn't have sweat glands, or any other glands, or skin in the normal sense, reflected Fitz. Probably didn't even need to wee. That was a thought – was there a toilet somewhere within her depths? Fitz boggled at the thought of performing his bodily functions inside her body.

His need for beer rose sharply.

Fitz came to a breathless halt beside Compassion. She had stopped at the edge of the market, where the ground sloped downwards to a river bordered by open grassland and intricate, well-tended gardens. Most of the traffic of Yendip was airborne, passing high above at leisurely speeds. The only vehicles Fitz had seen on the ground were a tricycle thing ridden by what looked like a blue octopus, and a strange, hovering sedan chair. This lack of ground traffic made for a clean and beautiful city, and the more Fitz saw the more he thought he'd like to wind up in a place like Yendip. Each building seemed to be of a different design and made from a different material, but all tended to blend into a pleasing whole, and most things appeared to be constructed to please the senses. 'Utilitarian' and 'functional' probably weren't even in the Yquatine dictionary.

Compassion's face was hidden beneath a black hood and her arms were folded. She looked like the Angel of Death. Most unseasonal in this baking heat.

Fitz felt extremely uneasy in her presence. 'Nice planet this, eh?'

No answer.

She was supposed to be able to change her appearance – in fact, the Doctor had told her to, to help evade their enemies – but Compassion had been reluctant. She'd seemed afraid of her new abilities, wanted to keep her usual appearance for comfort. The cloak and hood were a compromise measure.

'Any idea where the Doctor is?'

Compassion stretched out an arm, pointed. 'He's in there.'

Fitz looked across the river, where a large dome of blue-green glass sparkled in the sunlight. 'How can you tell?'

'A TARDIS and its tenant are linked in ways that a human could never understand.'

Tenant. The Doctor would love that. 'Are you trying to make me jealous?'

She didn't reply, just started walking down a serpentine path towards the river. Fitz chucked the shell of yuk into a nearby bin and followed Compassion as she crossed a wrought-iron bridge which led towards the dome. The height of an office block, it seemed to be made of rotating triangles of glass, held together by some strange force. Fitz could actually see through the gaps to the cool green interior. His curiosity roused to the fullest, Fitz followed Compassion through a pair of automatic crystal doors. Inside, sunlight filtered down through the twinkling glass, soft ripples falling over every surface, just like being underwater. Mellow music tinkled away at the edge of Fitz's hearing. Above them stretched a network of balconies and walkways, lined with stalls, shops, cafés and bars.

Even though it was the thirtieth century, Fitz recognised a shopping centre when he saw one. It somehow seemed more incredible than the flying cars, weird food and the head-spinning cacophony of alien life. 'Amazing, but comforting.'

'It's called Arklark Arcade,' said Compassion.

What a mine of information. Fitz had clocked what looked like a bar beside a fountain but Compassion had already set off in the opposite direction, heading for a tiny place sandwiched between a Fizzade stall and a body-beppling clinic. Fitz grinned at the sign above the door: in old-style lettering, Lou Lombardo's Pan-Traditional Pie Emporium. Fitz's stomach rumbled. Now this was more like it!

Inside, the place was done out in green and white tiles bathed in wince-making fluorescent lighting, a painful contrast to the rest of the arcade. It stank of chips and the air was heavy with steam. It reminded Fitz of the pie-and-mash shops he used to frequent in Archway. Small universe. He couldn't help smiling.

He walked up to the counter with Compassion. Fridge units lined the walls, bearing an unbelievable quantity and variety of pies. Formica-topped tables stood down the middle and jazz music issued from tiny speakers. Three customers, two young chaps and a rather foxy chick in presumably retro hippy gear, sat at one table tucking into plates of pie and chips. And mushy peas. Why the Doctor had wanted to come here, God only knew. He was leaning on the counter, a plastic cup of tea steaming at his elbow, chatting away to a large man in a white coat and green apron.

'Ah, there you are,' he said, on seeing Fitz and Compassion. He looked preoccupied. 'Do try to keep up. United we stand, remember.'

Compassion reached up and pulled down her hood. Her eyes flashed. 'I haven't detected any temporal activity in the area.'

Fitz couldn't help staring at her. Was she subtly different, somehow? Her face thinner, the hair darker? Was her TARDIS-ness taking her over, changing her into someone else?

'Yes, yes yes.' The Doctor stepped towards them, reaching out and putting a hand on each of their shoulders. 'We're safe for now. But I know the Time Lords. They're horribly devious.' His grip tightened slightly. 'We want to be alert all the time, don't we?'

'Yeah,' said Fitz, leaning forward to whisper in the Doctor's ear. 'Doctor, what are we doing in a pie shop?'

The Doctor smiled. 'Aren't you hungry?'

Fitz remembered that he still was. 'Now you come to mention it…'

'Who's your friend?' said the man behind the counter in a soft yet deep voice.

'Oh sorry, introductions,' said the Doctor. 'Fitz, Compassion, this is Lou Lombardo, an old friend.'

Lombardo leaned on the counter. His face was round and glistening in the fluorescent light. Rather like a pie, thought Fitz. He had thinning auburn hair and there was a delicate, epicurean quality to the set of his lips and his thin nose. 'Compassion! Now that', he said, 'is an interesting name.'

'My name is not important,' said Compassion, turning abruptly away.

The Doctor frowned. 'What's up with her?' he muttered, motioning for Fitz to keep an eye on her.

'I thought this was meant to be a day of celebration,' said Fitz.

'Treaty Day', said Lombardo, 'usually is. Not this year, though. Trouble with the Anthaurk. People don't feel like celebrating.'

Fitz walked up the counter and started fiddling with a chip-fork dispenser. 'Anthaurk?'

The Doctor waved a hand. 'Big snaky things, great architecture, short tempers.'

It wasn't like the Doctor to be so dismissive, thought Fitz. Something must be bugging him. 'What trouble?'

The Doctor clearly didn't want to get involved. 'Local difficulties, they'll sort themselves out.'

Lombardo winked at Fitz. His eyes were small, the lashes pale, almost white, and there was a blue tint to his eyelids. Eye shadow? 'Aye lad, not to worry. I'm in a party mood even if no one else is.'

Fitz grinned back at him queasily. Was this some sort of come-on? 'Ri-ight.'

Lombardo straightened up. He was tall, much taller than the Doctor, with a barrel-shaped chest and long arms. 'Right!' he said, nodding at Fitz. 'It's the bloody centenary today, and no one feels like celebrating. Too scared of Anthaurk attacks. All the tourists have left, everyone's cowering in their houses watching the news. Well, not me!'

The Doctor was practically hopping from foot to foot. 'Can we...?' he almost squeaked, waving to the back of the shop.

Lombardo tapped his lips with a fat finger. 'Oh, er, right.' He took the chip-fork dispenser away from Fitz and hid it behind the till. Another wink. 'Come this way.' He ushered the Doctor behind the counter.

'What's up?' asked Fitz.

'I've, er, got something to discuss with Mr Lombardo. I'll be back in a moment.' So saying, the Doctor dodged behind the counter and followed Lombardo into the back of the shop through a clattering bead blind.

Fitz glanced at Compassion. She was staring past him. Or was she staring inside herself, at her console chamber, her corridors and forests and whatever else lay in her depths?

He cast about in his mind for something to say, but what could you say to a talking, walking TARDIS? At last he settled on, 'What's this Treaty all about, then?'

Compassion's eyes seemed to shift focus. 'The Treaty of Yquatine was signed in the Earth year 2893 (Common Era) by the major sentient species of the ten planets of the Minerva System after a short period of intense warfare with the Anthaurk, dispossessed reptilian race, who arrived in the System in 2890, taking over the planet Kaillor and renaming it New Anthaur. Since the signing of the treaty there has been exactly a century of peace. Many other races have come to settle in the System and its central planet, Yquatine, is the jewel of the System, representing –'

Fitz held up a hand. 'Enough, all right?'

Compassion blinked, there was the briefest of smiles. 'Sometimes I amaze myself. Do I amaze you?'

'Yeah, baby, you're totally shagadelic.' Fitz sidled away and inspected the pies on the shelves, half listening to the chatter of the customers. His stomach rumbled. Might as well take advantage of the location. Before him were set out, wrapped in cellophane imprinted with a rather unsettling logo featuring

Lombardo's grinning face, rank upon rank of steak-and-kidney pies, cheese-and-onion pies, Scotch eggs, sausage rolls, vegetable patties, pizza slices, samosas, wedges of quiche, even what looked like Cornish pasties.

Fitz took down a pork pie, laughter welling up inside him. 'Talk about the English abroad,' he said, turning back to Compassion, brandishing the pie like a trophy. 'Here I am, interdimensional wanderer, on the most culturally diverse planet I've ever seen and –' he paused from dramatic effect – 'I'm going to eat a *pork pie*.'

The people at the table stared at Fitz as if he was mad.

Compassion's eyes glittered.

'Oh, come on,' said Fitz, unwrapping the pie. 'It's still you, isn't it?'

Compassion pouted. 'Yes and no.'

Fitz blinked. Images flickered before his eyes. The dark console chamber, the walkways, the gnarled, black console. The forest, his room on the dark side of Compassion's interior. He shuddered. All inside – inside *her*.

He took a bite of the pie. Things could get seriously Freudian if he wasn't careful.

There was a clatter of bead curtain and the Doctor reappeared, alone this time. He strode over to them, rubbing his hands together. 'Time to go!'

'Already?' Fitz pointed at Compassion's waist. 'Is there a food machine in there?'

Compassion glared at him.

The Doctor smiled. 'Now there's an idea.' He raised a finger and pointed at Compassion's head. 'Ding-dong! Avon calling!'

Compassion smiled, covered her face with her hands, and then opened out into a glowing, white doorway.

Fitz dropped the pie.

A clatter of chairs, panicked swearing from the customers.

'Come on, come on!' hustled the Doctor.

Fitz stepped towards the doorway, everything flashed

painfully white, and then and he was… *inside* Compassion.

'I'm never, ever, ever gonna get used to this,' he groaned, rubbing his eyes.

They were in the console chamber, standing on the metal walkway above the churning blue milky stuff beneath. The console still looked to Fitz like a cross between a malevolent spider, an oil rig and something you glimpse in nightmares. 'So, where to now?'

The Doctor bounded up to the console, his hands flicking over switches. He called to Fitz over his shoulder. 'Where to, indeed? Who knows?'

And then the Doctor took something from his pocket. Fitz caught a glimpse of a metal box with flickering lights in the top and two silver prongs poking out of the back. As Fitz watched, the Doctor plunged the thing into the console. There was a shower of blue sparks, and black liquid spurted on to the Doctor's coat.

Then came a voice. Compassion's voice. It came from all around Fitz and from inside his head and sent him quivering to his knees. She was screaming, a sound of hurt and fear.

'*What are you doing? Get it out of me! Get it out!*'

The tallest tower of the Palace of Yquatine rose like sheets of silk into the Yquatine sky for almost two kilometres. Near its top was the Senate Chamber, a circular glass bubble encased in a web of force fields. From the bottom of the bubble a cylindrical shaft extended towards the centre. On top of this shaft was a podium, on which President Stefan Vargeld stood, hands gripping the railing, his face haggard, looking much older than his thirty-three years. Behind him sat palace officials, tapping away at their keypads, recording every nuance of the Senate meeting. Radiating out from this central hub like the spokes on a giant wheel were eight arms, ending in smaller podiums on which stood the senators and their aides from each of the other inhabited planets of the Minerva System.

President Vargeld spoke, his voice ringing out across the Chamber. 'Senator Zendaak, I urge you once again to call off your attacks on the trade routes in your sector.'

Zendaak stood, arms folded, the personification of defiance. 'Urge all you like.'

President Vargeld raised his arms and indicated the other senators. 'The entire Senate condemns your actions. For the sake of System unity, for the sake of peace, you must call off the attacks.'

Zendaak's red eyes fixed President Vargeld like lasers. 'Remove the sanctions on our world.'

Mutters from the other senators. Senator Fandel of Luvia swore, and shot a glance at President Vargeld. Luvia was a small world, almost totally inhabited by humans, and since the war there had been a coldness between the Luvians and the Anthaurk. The current crisis had sharpened that coldness to outright hatred.

'We see no point in these disagreements,' boomed a voice. This came from Senator Rhombus-Alpha of the Ixtricite. A holographic representation of the crystalline gestalt, it revolved above its podium, its smooth surfaces reflecting the overhead lights.

'Neither do we,' hissed Senator Okotile, a beetle-like Kukutsi.

President Vargeld had expected this. The Ixtricite kept themselves almost totally aloof from Senate affairs, seeming only to keep a weather eye on things from their crystal planet of Ixtrice. The Kukutsi, as leaders of the insect-dominated world of Chitis, trod more or less the same line.

The President took a deep breath, thinking carefully about what he was going to say next. 'Nonetheless, they must be resolved. If they aren't, the situation could escalate. The Anthaurk have been hitting the Adamantean and Luvian trade routes. I have managed to persuade Senators Krukon and Fandel not to take any retaliatory action, but, if the Anthaurk persist in their attacks, I will have no choice but to take condign action.'

It was a roundabout way of making a declaration of war, and the effect on the Senate was electric. Fandel's eyes positively gleamed with bloodlust.

Senator Krukon, the Adamantean, simply stared at President Vargeld, his entourage of two Ogri glowing with golden light behind him. Krukon trusted the President and had a lot to be grateful to the Senate for in the terraforming of Adamantine. The last thing the President wanted to do was let them down. If they had to fight the Anthaurk, the Adamantean fleet would be a valuable asset.

There was a smirk on Zendaak's thin lips. President Vargeld got the feeling that this was what he was after. War. Well, now he'd got it.

'There is one thing that can be done to avert this war,' said Zendaak.

President Vargeld allowed hope to flutter in his heart. Was Zendaak going to back down?

His next pronouncement quashed all hope of that. 'Dissolve the treaty.'

There was a general hubbub. Senators Juvingeld and Tibis exchanged worried glances. Juvingeld was an Eldrig, a cervine quadruped from the ice world of Oomingmak. Tibis was a Rorclaavix, a tiger-like creature clad in gold neck chains and flowing robes, from the jungle planet of Zolion. The only two sentient indigenous species in the Minerva System, they had both benefited from colonisation while keeping their cultures intact, thanks to the provisions of the treaty. Its dissolution was the last thing they wanted.

The only person who looked the least bit pleased was Senator Arthwell of Beatrix. It stood to reason. If there was a war the spaceyards of Beatrix would once again be at full capacity.

Krukon brandished a blue-jewelled arm like a mace. 'I say if they want war, we give it to them!'

President Vargeld fought to retain order. 'Senator Krukon, I won't permit such an outburst in the Senate Chamber. Please think before you speak.'

Krukon leaned on the railing of his podium, a scowl on his grey face. 'Very well, but we must take action. Now.'

President Vargeld drew in a breath, ready to make his final appeal. His heart was heavy and his legs felt weak. He was tired. He wanted to get away from the Senate chamber. Not everyone can carry the weight of the world, let alone an entire solar system. 'I called this extraordinary meeting on Treaty Day – on the *centenary* of Treaty Day – to remind us all of what we signed up to. We signed up to sovereignty for each planet and species in the System.'

Zendaak snorted.

'But we also signed up for the greater good of the System. So that we could help each other in times of crisis.' His eyes were on Zendaak as he spoke.

Zendaak's voice was calm and level. 'The assistance you want us to give violates one of the prime provisions of the treaty.'

President Vargeld ignored this. 'We signed up to independence from the Earth Empire. We signed up to free trade. We signed up to mutual aid, famine and disaster relief. We signed up to technology transfer and cultural interaction and I think most of you will agree we have had undreamed-of successes in these areas.'

Nods and mutters of agreement, and a power salute from Senator Tibis.

President Vargeld leaned forward. 'Most importantly, we signed up to peace.'

Silence.

'Very moving,' hissed Zendaak. 'But just words.' He turned away, beckoning to his two aides.

'Where are you going?'

'Back to my people. To prepare.'

The arm supporting Zendaak's podium extended towards an opening in the shimmering wall of the chamber, which swallowed it like a mouth taking a particularly bitter pill. President Vargeld saw Zendaak step into the elevator, then

Zendaak's podium returned to its position, empty.

The gaze of some twenty beings – senators and aides – rested upon the President. Waiting for him to speak. As often before, the responsibility of his position felt like a pressure in his chest. He forced himself to relax, staring at the golden glow of the Ogri. The situation could still be saved. Diplomacy and calmness were the order of the day. 'Any other business?' he said, aware of the banality of the phrase.

Senators shuffled, aides whispered.

'There was the matter of the latest survey of Xaxdool,' boomed Rhombus-Alpha.

Xaxdool was the largest planet in the System, an uninhabited gas giant, subject to endless surveys and tests. Trust the Ixtricite to bring that up. It seemed like a monstrous irrelevancy. 'I think we can safely leave that until this present crisis is over.'

The other senators nodded their assent.

'What are we going to do about the Anthaurk?' said Krukon, gesturing at the empty podium.

President Vargeld gritted his teeth. Now he could be seen to stand firm, show real determination. 'We stand against them.'

There were murmurs of agreement.

President Vargeld felt light-headed, and there were tears in his eyes. For the first time in a hundred years, war was coming to the Minerva System. But his tears weren't for the coming hostilities and the sorrows they would inevitably bring. His tears were for Arielle.

Fitz was on his knees, jamming his fingers in his ears, trying to blot out Compassion's screams. It was one of the most terrible sounds he had ever heard. Like someone being slowly put to death. The stuff below was churning and heaving like a stormy sea and the whole TARDIS was shuddering like a convulsing animal.

Fitz couldn't stand it any more. He leapt up, launching himself at the console, where the Doctor hung on, both hands around

36

the metal box, which was now fully embedded in the console. In Compassion's flesh.

He grabbed on to the Doctor's shoulders. 'What are you doing to her?' he roared.

The Doctor's face turned to his. It was set in a grimace, features blurred by the juddering. 'I didn't know! I didn't know it would *hurt* her –'

Compassion's screaming reached an almost unbearable crescendo. Words formed out of the chaos. *'Get out. Get away from me.'*

Then suddenly they were falling, down into dizzying whiteness. Fitz filled his lungs with more breath to scream and – slap!

His hands made contact with cool, smooth, green and white tiles. The pie shop. He groaned and writhed about, his body stiff and bruised. He sat up. The Doctor was sitting cross-legged on the floor, his hands over his face. There was no sign of Compassion. The hippie kids were staring at him, but he couldn't raise a jolly quip or even a smile. Compassion had vanished. Dematerialised. Gone. What the hell had the Doctor done to her? Had he killed her? Had the Time Lords planted some posthypnotic command in the Doctor's mind? The devious gits.

Fitz scuttled across to the Doctor, full of questions. 'Are – are you all right?' What else was there ever to say in situations like these?

The Doctor took his hands away from his face. His eyes were wide, shadowed, his cheeks pale. 'Fitz, I'm a fool.' He started to get to his feet. 'I should have told her what I was doing.'

'You should have told *me* as well,' said Fitz. 'Then I'd have some idea of what the hell you're talking about.'

'Yes, yes, erm, yes.' Wearing a distracted look, the Doctor strode out of the pie shop, Fitz following close behind.

The Doctor was shouting as he ran. 'We've got to find her. Fortunately, she's still on Yquatine.'

Fitz caught up with the Doctor in the middle of the iron

bridge, where he had stopped, and seemed to be sniffing the air. 'Yes, she's still in Yendip. The Randomiser won't grow into her for a while yet.' He stared into the river, his eyes suddenly wide. He grabbed Fitz's arm, his voice hushed. 'She might even reject it!'

'Sod it, Doctor!' cried Fitz. 'Listen to me. I'm not a TARDIS, or a Time Lord: I'm just a bloke. I'm not telepathic: I need things explained. So tell me what you did to Compassion and what the hell a Randomiser is.'

The Doctor's face creased, he instantly looked very sorry. 'Oh Fitz.' He looked down at the river. 'Where are the ducks? There really should be ducks.'

Fitz looked at the river, waiting for the explanation, giving the Doctor time. The water below was crystal clear and unpolluted; Fitz could see the pebbles and stones on the river bed, tiny shoals of fish punctuating the ripples, dark clumps of weed waving like a mermaid's hair. The river was wide and stretched towards the horizon, towards the lake. Boats glided up and down. In the distance, Fitz could see the next bridge. A couple stood huddled together upon it, mirroring their own position.

At last the Doctor spoke. 'A Randomiser is a simple circuit that can be linked into TARDIS guidance systems. It sends the TARDIS on a random journey into the vortex. Not even I would know where we would be going.'

'Nothing new there,' muttered Fitz.

The Doctor smiled sadly. 'Well, I made one once, when I had to evade an angry and powerful enemy. So I thought it would be just the thing to give the Time Lords the runaround. Unfortunately, Compassion didn't agree.'

'You spoke to her about this?'

The Doctor nodded. 'While you were in your room.'

Fitz tried not to think about his room.

'She thought she could evade the Time Lords on her own.' He smiled. 'She may be totally unique, but she's still growing, still learning. And while she's learning she's vulnerable.' The Doctor slapped the railing of the bridge with his palm. 'A Randomiser was the only answer.'

'So,' said Fitz. 'That's why we came here. How, in the name of all that's funky, did a pie man come to have one?'

'I knocked one up myself when I was younger, out of components in the TARDIS. Couldn't do that with Compassion, so I came here.' He looked at Fitz with a twinkle in his eyes. 'There's more to Lou Lombardo than meets the eye. Apart from selling the finest pies in the galaxy, he's also a dealer in black-market temporal technology, among other things.'

Fitz decided to let that pass. 'So you got a Randomiser off him, and just – well – stuck it in her?'

The Doctor looked pained. 'It was for her own good.'

Fitz couldn't look at him. Perhaps it was because he wasn't human, perhaps it was the stress, but the Doctor had really messed up this time. The words 'violation' and 'rape' swam through Fitz's mind. It was all too horrible. The Doctor couldn't have known the effect: he would never do anything to hurt his friends. He could be a clumsy sod at times, though. 'Doctor, you've hurt her, and scared her. She'll probably never trust you again.'

The Doctor's mouth turned down at the corners and he stared at his shoes. 'I must remember she's a person as well as a TARDIS.' His eyes met Fitz's. 'We have to find her. I have to apologise. I've seriously miscalculated. But Fitz, it's not going to happen again.'

'We'd better get looking, then.' The pain in the Doctor's voice made Fitz feel uneasy and slightly embarrassed.

The Doctor pointed. 'There – over there by that barge!'

Fitz whirled round, expecting to see Compassion floating down the river. He couldn't see anything. 'What?'

The Doctor was grinning. 'Ducks. I told you!' He grew suddenly serious and intense. 'We'll split up, it'll be easier that way.'

'Doctor –'

But the Doctor was already running away, across the bridge.

'Meet you back at Lombardo's in an hour – no more, no less.'

Fitz watched him go. How was he going to find Compassion, in a city this size? Unlike the Doctor, he didn't have a special link to her. He squinted across the gleaming water but he couldn't see any ducks.

Chapter Three
'We want to get out of here, and quick'

President Stefan Vargeld walked into the lobby of his private chambers, shrugging off his coat of office. Damned thing was so bulky. Tradition demanded that he wore it, didn't mean he had to like it. Franseska stood up from behind her crescent-shaped desk as he entered.

'As you were,' he said.

She sat, but kept on looking at him.

He felt like hurling the coat into the furthest corner of the room – quite a feat, as this would have meant throwing the heavy garment twenty-five metres – but he checked himself, and hung it on the stand by the side of the door.

There was an ache behind his eyes. He hadn't slept much recently. And there – one of the gold buttons was coming loose. As he touched it, it fell, bouncing on the marble floor and rolling under a cabinet. The President sighed. He looked over at Franseska. She was smiling, her hands folded over her keyboard.

He couldn't help but smile back. 'Well, if that's the worst thing that happens today, I'll be a happy man.'

He walked over to Franseska's desk. She was a small, dark-haired Yquatine woman in her mid-twenties, with pale skin and large brown eyes. She'd been his personal assistant for two years now. 'Anything for me?'

'The usual,' said Franseska. She had thin hands and moved with economy and precision. 'Proposals for the development of the Amerd Archipelago, a report from the installation on Ixtrice...'

She tailed off as he raised a hand. 'It can all wait,' he said. 'I'm going to relax. For probably the last time in a long, long while.'

He went to walk past the desk.

Franseska stood up. 'One more thing.'

There was a pleading look on her face. He knew what was coming. Franseska's brother was a pilot in the Minerva Space Alliance. He met her gaze squarely. 'Yes, Franseska?'

She was suddenly nervous, aware that he was President and she a mere secretary. He hated it when that happened, so he smiled. 'It's all right. You know you can talk to me.'

Franseska smiled and seemed to relax, then shook her head, averting her gaze. 'The Senate meeting. How bad, I mean… what…'

President Vargeld cut in. 'You want to know if there's going to be a war. Well, so does the entire System. That's why everyone's stuck inside in front of their media units instead of celebrating.'

Franseska nodded, biting her lip. 'They're going to want to know sooner or later.'

President Vargeld sat on the edge of her desk. 'I'm going to make a public broadcast, but not until I'm absolutely sure. And, though right now things look grim, I'm sure I can turn it around.' He smiled at her again, watching her face soften. 'You know me. I can talk my way out of anything and, though I can't rule it out, I'll do everything I can to prevent a war.'

Franseska sat down, looking much more relieved.

'Can I go now?' he asked. Franseska laughed. 'See you later.' President Vargeld walked across the lobby, under the pink glass dome in the centre and through into his private rooms.

He walked over to the tall bay window which overlooked the gardens. The afternoon was maturing, long and hot – perfect Treaty Day weather – and droid gardeners toiled, watering, weeding and tending. Just like his job, really. Tending the needs of the System, while the individual planets got on with their own business. The flowers didn't really need the droids – they would flourish, weeds and all. The System was a well-tended, weedless garden. Until now.

The presidential apartments were at the rear of the Palace of Yquatine, overlooking the gardens, the lake and the hills beyond. He'd inherited them from the previous President, Ignatiev. He'd been living here for five years now, and it still didn't seem like home.

Which was a pity, because all his life he'd aimed to be President.

The Vargelds were one of the founding families of Yquatine, and they came to prominence when President Marc de Yquatine, the last of his line, died at the turn of the century. De Yquatine had drawn up the treaty and presided over the early years of peace with the Anthaurk. He was a popular leader, a humanist and a visionary. In his wake followed a string of leaders, not all of them human, and the Minerva System had flourished. During this time the Vargeld family took over the rule of Yquatine. Stefan's father and his father before him had been Marquis of Yquatine, following on seamlessly from the de Yquatine family.

It had always been assumed that the young Stefan would succeed his father as Marquis. He had a passionate interest in history and at a young age had garnered all the facts about the Minerva System – the life of its founder, Julian de Yquatine, the specifications of the colony ship *Minerva*, the names and dietary requirements of every species in the System. He'd gone through school with flying colours and went to the University of Yquatine. He'd done a stint with the Minerva Space Alliance and then entered politics, becoming a councillor of his home town Farleath, gradually gaining power. He didn't think himself ambitious – though his enemies certainly did – and he viewed his progress as a natural course of events, like a strong current flowing through him. He became Marquis when he was only twenty. He took the rule of an entire planet in his stride, tackling it with relish. This was during the rule of President Ignatiev, an unpopular Luvian politician who had angered the Anthaurk and brought the System close to war. Stefan had stood against him in the elections of 2988, and won by a landslide. At the age of twenty-eight, he became President of the Minerva System.

He sighed. It had been easy, at first. He'd taken it all in his stride, coped with the endless demands of presidency. The people loved him and said he was the best President since de Yquatine. His enemies said he was too young, but he'd proved himself time and again. He'd smoothed over the Rorclaavix–Adamantean incident, and the strikes on Beatrix were a thing of the past, thanks to his negotiation skills. He found politics and diplomacy remarkably easy: all it took was common sense and honesty and he couldn't understand the dreadful, self-destructive knots certain people tied themselves into –

– *Arielle* –

He closed his eyes, forcing the thought of her from his mind. Had to concentrate on the moment, on the job in hand. He knew, deep down, that he was just a bureaucrat. A droid tending the flowers. And now the weeds were growing, threatening to strangle the flowers.

Could the Anthaurk have been planning this all along? Signed the treaty, only to use the peace to prepare for war, and now, after almost a century spent assembling their war machine in secret, preparing to strike?

He couldn't believe it. If it was true, then the Treaty of Yquatine was a lie. Treaty Day was a lie. The presidency and the Senate and the entire political network were just an incubator for the Anthaurk war machine.

President Vargeld was breathing hard now, panic clutching at his heart. He wasn't a worrier by nature: he was a practical man. That was worse in a way. He knew in his bones that there was a war ahead, and there was nothing he could do about it. History was about to convulse, and here he was bang in the middle of it.

President Vargeld went to a drinks cabinet, opened a bottle and poured out a stiff measure of brandy. He tried to enjoy the peace – soon he'd have to meet the other senators again, prepare for war. It would be a virtual conference: most of them had departed for their home planets, wanting to be there if anything happened.

If. It was almost a certainty. What a Treaty Day!

He sipped the brandy, but it tasted sour and did nothing to calm him.

With sudden force, the image of Arielle returned. Her face, the way she carried herself, as though she had no idea of the effect she had on men. The first and only woman he had ever truly loved in his busy life. He swore, angry at himself, ashamed that his feelings for her were ruling his life. But, if war came, she'd be caught up too, and he'd never have the chance to win her back. His mind went back to Treaty Day last year, when they'd first met. How ironic that it had been Zendaak who had invited her to the ball. He had that to thank the Anthaurk senator for at least.

He walked over to his comms console, ordered it to call her comms unit. The screen blinked for a few seconds, and then a computer voice said, 'Sorry, the other unit has been programmed to receive no incoming messages.'

Damn her. She was deliberately avoiding him, hiding herself away on Muath. He often thought he understood aliens better than women. Perhaps, even, women *were* a separate species. The banality of the thought made him smile.

At least there was something he could do about Arielle. Something he should have done weeks ago, before he got mired in the war situation.

A musical yet insistent chiming rang out. President Vargeld turned, muttering a curse. Franseska's face appeared on the screen above the door. He felt the muscles in his stomach tighten, but he tried to keep his voice light and friendly. 'Yes, Franseska?'

Franseska's voice was shaking. 'Senators Krukon and Fandel want to know if they can begin preparing their fleets. The captains of the Minerva Space Alliance want to speak to you urgently. The media want you make an announcement now. There are riots in Mertown and Ellisville. And Aloysius Station reports an Anthaurk battle fleet on the other side of the border.'

President Vargeld closed his eyes. It had to be now. He opened his eyes and fixed Franseska with his most presidential look. 'Tell Krukon and Fandel yes. I want their fleets here within the hour. Tell the captains of the Alliance the same. Ignore the media. Tell Aloysius Station to prepare for battle. I don't want any Anthaurk ships crossing the border. And Franseska?'

She noticed the pause. 'Yes, sir?'

President Vargeld downed the rest of his drink. What he was

about to do was madness, especially on the eve of war. But he had to do it. For Arielle's sake. 'Prepare my personal Nova-fighter.'

The Doctor hurried through the marketplace, dodging people and beings, haring round corners, knocking over a pallet of fruit, stopping to apologise and then having to run away from the irate vendor, falling over a small child who burst out crying, standing on the toe of a very old and irate Draconian, getting called a ponce by a group of drunken humans, generally causing total chaos wherever he went, but getting absolutely nowhere in finding Compassion.

He stopped to catch his breath. He was in an octagonal plaza, the floor of which was a mosaic depicting humans and aliens linked together in an endless wheeling dance. Their cavorting forms looked to the Doctor to be mocking, cajoling, as if they had spirited his friend away.

The Doctor knew that Compassion was here, in this city – he could sense her Artron signature – but that was as specific as the feeling got. His hearts ached. He had to find her, had to apologise. He could still put things right, he had to believe that. Why couldn't he find her? Maybe the bond between them wasn't strong enough yet. 'Or perhaps we're not telepathically compatible,' he murmured at the mocking faces in the mosaic.

Still ten minutes or so until he was due to meet up with Fitz again. Better keep the rendezvous, didn't want to lose Fitz as well. What was it with companions? It was almost as if some unseen force travelled with them, delighting in making sure they always got lost. Still keeping his eyes peeled, he walked slowly back towards Arklark Arcade, keeping his eyes open for Compassion or Fitz. He crossed the bridge, waved to the nonexistent ducks, and entered the Arcade. His heart sank as he approached Lombardo's shop. He'd been secretly hoping to find Fitz and Compassion waiting for him. A happy reunion, a rushed explanation, and off they'd go. But, no.

Lou Lombardo looked up from behind the counter as the

Doctor entered. Despite everything, the Doctor grinned hugely. What *was* Lou wearing? A costume even his sixth incarnation would have balked at. He'd changed out of his overalls and apron and now sported an eye-dazzling silver shirt open almost to the navel, revealing curls of ginger chest hair and a clutch of medallions. Mirror shades completed the image. He slid them up on to his gelled hair as the Doctor approached.

'Hello, Lou – any sign of Fitz?'

'Hello, Doctor. No, haven't seen him.' Lombardo's moon face was wearing a frown of concern. He came out from behind the counter and put an arm around the Doctor. 'Hey, I was worried about you. Last I saw, you were pegging it out the door.'

The Doctor nodded sadly. 'Yes, I'm afraid my little plan backfired.' He frowned. 'Or is it *mis*fired?'

Lombardo stood back from the Doctor, his small brown eyes widening in concern. 'Oh, bloody hell. That Randomiser circuit blew up, didn't it?'

The Doctor shushed Lombardo. 'No no no, there was nothing wrong with it. Probably. It was Compassion – she rejected it.'

'Where is she now?'

'I don't know.'

Lombardo took off his shades and started polishing them on a scrap of tissue. 'Christ. I'm sorry. But you know me, I'm no tech-head, I just buy and sell the stuff.'

'It's not your fault. It's mine.' The Doctor fiddled with a tube of multicoloured plastic straws. It was now high time that Fitz was here. 'Why are you dressed like that?'

Lombardo struck a disco pose, one hand pointing at the insectocutor on the ceiling, the other to the green and white tiles on the floor. The Doctor noticed that he was wearing dark-green leather trousers and cowboy boots. 'I'm shutting up shop. Going clubbing. Sod the war, I'm going to enjoy myse–'

His words were cut off by a terrible sound from outside – the roaring crash of breaking glass.

The Doctor was at the door in an instant. A few metres away lay a matt-black egg-shaped capsule, the size of a barrel, covered in foot-long spikes, half embedded in the floor of the arcade. Shards of glass tinkled down from a hole in the ceiling above. Several people had stopped, staring at it. The Doctor ran at them, waving his arms. 'Get away from here!' he yelled. 'Run!' He had no idea what the thing was, but it looked decidedly nasty and ready to explode. As he watched, grey tubes began sprouting from it like obscene putty fingers. Black gas began to issue from the tubes with a hiss.

'What the Merry Hill?' Lombardo was beside him, fiddling with his medallions.

The black stuff was spreading slowly across the shiny tiles. Too slow for any effective gas, and the Doctor couldn't detect any fumes. It looked somehow alive.

There was a whistling sound from above, another crash. The Doctor instinctively covered his head with his arms and backed away towards the cover of the pie shop. An upward glimpse through his fingers – the ceiling was a smashed-open mess; he could see the sky, dotted with black ovoid shapes. From them, smaller shapes were falling, as fast and as thick as hail.

There was no way past the gas, which was encircling them, rising up towards the ceiling. And then a smell hit the back of the Doctor's throat, as though tarry fingers had shoved inside his mouth. The Doctor could hear choking and retching from beyond the black wall of gas.

'We want to get out of here, and quick,' said the Doctor, hustling Lombardo back to the shop.

'The sewers,' gasped Lombardo. His eyes and nose were streaming. The Doctor was OK but then he had a superior respiratory system. 'There's a way into them out back. I use it for – you know – special deliveries.'

Lombardo led the Doctor behind the counter, through the storeroom with its humming freezer units and into a bare, concrete room piled high with boxes and bags where the Doctor had purchased the Randomiser, barely an hour ago.

Lombardo was wrestling with a drain cover in the corner, and the Doctor bent to help him prise it loose. It came free with a heavy clang, and Lombardo swore as it caught his fingers. The Doctor let his friend go down first, casting a fearful glance over his shoulder. The black gas was rolling into the shop, its movement obscenely leisurely, as though it knew there was no escape, not even underground.

With an anguished thought for Fitz and Compassion, the Doctor followed Lombardo into the darkness.

President Vargeld sat in the bubble-shaped cockpit of his personal Nova-fighter as it soared out of the atmosphere of Yquatine. It was a small, dart-shaped ship, most of the rear half taken up by powerful ion engines, most of the front half by weapons arrays and scanning equipment. Monitors in the cockpit took care of the blind spots. When the fields were activated the fighter was invisible to all but the most sophisticated of scanners. President Vargeld didn't want anyone to know about this mission. It was too personal. If word got out, then his presidency would be in jeopardy.

Ahead, he could see the tiny moon of Muath, one side a blinding white crescent lit by the sun Minerva, the other side blackness blending into surrounding space. He could just make out the domes of the university's installation, and the half-completed domes of the Powell Industries site.

He tried to raise Arielle's personal comms unit again. No response. He programmed the flight computer for low orbit, checking that all the scanners were on line. As he neared Muath, he began to notice something. Something that shouldn't be happening. The grey disc of Muath was darkening, as though becoming obscured by clouds

And then, suddenly, the small moon disappeared.

President Vargeld jerked forward in his seat, his breath seeming to solidify in his body. Almost blindly his fingers tapped the controls in front of him, activating the long-range scanners. He glanced down at them, seeming to see the figures as if from far away. They made no sense: Muath was still there, but he couldn't see it. As if it had been swallowed by shadows.

'What the hell –'

Then the cockpit went dark, as if something had come between his ship and the sun. He craned his neck and looked out of the top of the bubble.

Blackness. No stars, no sun, just a blackness that hurt his eyes, made his head throb. He looked wildly around. There were *shapes* everywhere, sliding across the stars, shutting out the light of the sun. It was as if giant hands had cupped his ship in black fingers. What was this? A new Anthaurk weapon?

President Vargeld felt a terror rising within him, a terror of the unknown. Hands shaking, he set course for a small shard of visible star-speckled space and cranked the ion engines right up.

The little fighter shot towards the narrowing gap, and President Vargeld yelled, an animal sound of fear and defiance. The starfield almost filled his forward vision when the surrounding blackness shifted and the ship glanced against something solid, throwing President Vargeld against the console. He gasped as everything danced around him, the fighter flipping out of control. Stars and black fingers and the blinding inferno of the sun spun around him in a sickening kaleidoscope. His insides knotted with dread as he realised that he was spinning away from Muath, towards the sun. Unless he did something soon he'd enter the sun's corona and burn up. He grabbed the navi-rod with both hands, fighting to bring the ship under control. But there was something wrong: the little ship wasn't responding, her engines dead.

As he spun away towards the orb of the sun, the President looked back towards Yquatine. And what he saw made him forget that he was going to die, burned to nothingness.

What he saw was a swathe of ships, arrayed in a vast arc around the planet. They were featureless black ovoids, their size and number impossible to determine. And they were closing in on Yquatine. Already the blue-green disc of his home planet was being obscured by the invaders, like a swarm of flies crawling over a petalfruit.

Of Muath, there was no sign.

He should have been thinking of the millions of people who were probably going to die, but he could think of only one.

One who may already be dead.

Arielle...

Chapter Four
'In a few hours, nothing will be left alive'

In the end, Fitz didn't find Compassion. Compassion found Fitz.

He'd wandered aimlessly at first, back through the marketplace and town until he'd come out on to the seafront. It reminded him of the places he'd been as a kid – Brighton maybe, or Weymouth – but everything was on a much grander scale, the buildings gleaming and seamless, and most striking of all there was no litter. It all looked so perfect, so serene, that Fitz momentarily forgot his quest and crossed the road to look at the beach. He'd taken in the view for a few minutes, marvelling at the yachts and cruisers moored in the harbour and at the rippling green expanse of ocean, before he remembered he was supposed to be looking for Compassion.

He'd started wandering along the pavement beside the beach, unable to keep his eyes from the sunbathers, even though many of them weren't even human. He'd rarely seen such a variety of alien life – tentacles, flippers, feelers, all crowded the beach; here, at least, were people determined to have fun. When he did eventually clap eyes on a pair of naked, female, human breasts it felt like coming home, and he'd had to restrain himself from breaking into a round of hearty applause. He was contemplating a bevy of bipedal dolphin-like creatures, splashing and laughing at the water's edge, wondering if they were humans who'd decided to become dolphins or dolphins who'd decided to become human, when a hand clamped down on his shoulder.

He turned. It was Compassion, her face still hidden beneath her hood. 'Fitz, we have to get away from here. Something bad is coming.'

Fitz was relieved to see her. 'Where have you been? Are you OK now?'

Compassion shook her head. 'No. Come on, we have to leave.'

Then Fitz saw something out of the corner of his eye. Something falling. There was a splash from out at sea, a few shrill cries from the dolphin creatures. People were getting up, pointing at the thing that was bobbing in the sea.

Fitz shaded his eyes. A black spiny object, for all the world like a mine. As he watched, more of them fell out of the sky with eerie whistling shrieks.

Fitz pointed. 'Is that what you mean?'

Compassion nodded. 'Yes.'

A flicker of movement above. Fitz looked up. And gasped. The sky was black with oval shapes, blotting out the sun, dappling the white sand with shadow. From them the spiny things were dropping like seeds, whistling and splashing into the sea. Now black gas was surging out of the objects in the sea, spreading incredibly quickly as if it was replicating within itself, rolling over the top of the waves, heading for the shore. People were screaming, climbing over the sea wall, pushing past Fitz and Compassion. The dolphin creatures ran past, chirruping and squeaking in agitation.

Fitz stared at the black gas as if hypnotised. 'What is that stuff?'

'Some sort of gas, but there's something more. Something –'

'The Doctor,' cried Fitz. 'We gotta get back to the pie shop.'

'We'd never make it,' said Compassion.

It was true. Now the entire seafront was a thick mass of black, as if a thundercloud had fallen to earth, and it was surging up the beach towards them. Fitz watched as someone fell, further along the shore, their cries abruptly cut off as the black cloud rolled over them.

'Time to go,' said Compassion, and turned herself into a doorway.

Fitz felt oddly detached. It was almost as if he'd been expecting this.

Then it began to rain.

A drop landed on the flagstones before Fitz. It hissed angrily, burning a tiny crater in the concrete.

Acid rain?

Fitz gritted his teeth, closed his eyes and dived into Compassion.

Everything went white and –

Fitz fell –

And then there was solid ground beneath his feet.

Fitz opened his eyes. He was inside Compassion, in the console chamber.

'Acid rain,' he muttered, looking up at the roofspace with fearful eyes. If he'd stayed out just a second longer...

The roofspace was Compassion's scanner, and Fitz had a grandstand view of the attack – if it was an attack. It seemed more like a natural process – or nature gone mad. The sky was dark with the black shapes, the air gleaming with rods of acid rain. Fitz could see the outlines of the buildings on the esplanade visibly softening as the acid ate into them. The façade of a large hotel began to melt, its balconies crashing down into each other, human and alien figures thrown clear, their bodies steaming as the acid went to work on them. Everywhere at ground level, the black stuff, rolling along the streets, rising up in obscene hammer-headed clumps, like a sea monster rearing its head.

Nothing made of flesh and blood could possibly withstand it. Bile forced its way into Fitz's mouth and he swallowed. He tried not to imagine what the acid would do to all those people, all those beings. The streets would run with blood. People would see their loved ones eaten away, faces sluicing from skulls, before their own pain became too much.

Compassion's voice, flat, emotionless. 'They're surrounding the whole planet. In a few hours, nothing will be left alive.'

Fitz slumped to the floor, totally stunned by the speed and devastation of the attack. He spoke, his voice cracking. 'Take us out of here.'

Compassion's voice rang out again, this time a hoarse, desperate whisper. 'Get this thing out of me first.'

Fitz was too stunned to focus on her words. 'What?'

The voice took on a rough, urgent edge. 'The Randomiser. Quickly!'

Fitz got up and approached the console. He didn't want to go near it – it was like the spider in the corner of the bedroom, the darkness at the top of the stairs. He forced himself, swallowing, the sour taste of bile still tainting his tongue. The silver box of the Randomiser was still embedded in the console. And it was changing: black tendrils, like plant roots, were twining up from the console, wrapping themselves around the metal box.

Fitz hesitated to touch it. He remembered what happened before, when the Doctor had tried to remove it. 'It'll hurt.'

'Do it.'

'Are you sure?'

'I don't want it in me. I want control!'

Fitz felt a pressure inside his head. It was getting hard to breathe, for some reason. He was safe in here – or was he? Why was it so hard to breathe? Was Compassion proof against the acid? The old TARDIS had been indestructible, so the Doctor said – but look what had happened to that!

Fitz spun round, peering agitatedly into the roofspace, anxious for signs of acid. But he couldn't damn well *breathe*. His hands clawed at his throat and he felt sweat break out on his forehead and down the middle of his back. 'Compassion,' he wheezed. 'What's happening?'

No longer a whisper, her voice rang loudly in his ears, making his head throb. 'I've stopped the oxygen supply. I'll only restore it if you get that thing out of me.'

Fitz sank to his knees. 'You'll – kill – me!'

'Help me.'

Fitz's vision was beginning to blur. It wouldn't be long before he passed out. He had no choice. He staggered to his feet, fell on to the console and grabbed the Randomiser with both hands. It felt as solid as rock. Black ooze was congealing where the box joined the console. Fitz was sweating freely now, the breath rasping in his throat.

He really had no choice.

He grabbed the Randomiser at both ends and twisted, hard.

Compassion screamed, the TARDIS lurched and Fitz staggered away from the console, sinking to his knees, hands scrabbling uselessly at his throat, stars flashing before his eyes and his head pounding, pounding, pounding in time with his struggling, hammering heart.

The Doctor followed Lou Lombardo along a dark, dripping sewer tunnel. He had to bend low to walk, and the stench was not pleasant. He forced himself to forget about Fitz and Compassion, at least for the moment, and concentrate on the situation in hand. Which was largely unknown. Down here, he couldn't know what devastation was being wreaked above ground. He tried not to think about it.

Lombardo seemed to know where he was going. His silver-clad back bobbed before the Doctor's eyes, the torch beam questing ahead. The Doctor smiled. Lombardo had obviously had recourse to this route many times before.

After what seemed like an age of cramped-up crab-walking, they stopped. The slimy rungs of a ladder hung on the wall to their left. The Doctor estimated they must have walked at least a mile, maybe two.

Lombardo turned round. His face was pale and sweating in the torchlight. 'This leads to one of the underground hangars of Yendip spaceport.'

The Doctor was thinking. 'This spaceport. Commercial or military?'

'Commercial. Why?'

The Doctor clapped his hands. 'If we could get our hands on a battleship or a fighter at the very least, we'd have more of a chance. It would be better shielded and armed.'

Lombardo shrugged. 'Any port in a storm.'

'Shhh!'

The Doctor grabbed the torch from Lombardo and put his hand

over the end. He felt Lombardo grab his arm.

'What is it?'

'There's something in here with us.'

From further along the sewer, there was a slow, laboured shuffling. The Doctor squinted into the gloom. 'No giant rats on Yquatine, are there?'

'Hello?' called a female, human voice.

The Doctor relaxed, shining the torch at the two figures approaching.

'Thank the Gods,' said the woman. She was supporting a tall, gaunt man in a green tunic. His arm was a melted, fused mass, and his eyes were rolling. 'We thought we were the only ones left alive.'

The Doctor and Lombardo helped the couple. The woman was small, middle-aged, with short steel-grey hair and an intelligent, lined face. The man was tall and gaunt, with long white hair tied in a ponytail.

The Doctor felt relaxed, confident. This was what he was used to. Saving people. 'I'm the Doctor, this is my friend Lou Lombardo.'

The woman extended a hand. 'Naomi Vohner. This is my husband Thom.' A brief, tired smile. 'I know you, Mr Lombardo. The pie shop in Arklark Arcade?' Even though she was being formal, putting a brave face on things, the Doctor could see the worry in her dark-brown eyes, the tension in the set of her mouth.

He examined Thom's arm. The flesh on the forearm was being eaten away, as if by acid. He was delirious with pain.

'What happened?' said Lombardo.

Naomi told them, in a weary, matter-of-fact voice. One of the spiny capsules had landed in their garden, and they had gone to investigate. When more of the things had started to land, and the black gas had begun to emerge, they had decided to escape underground. Not before acid rain had begun to fall, catching Thom's arm as he pulled the drain cover over their heads.

The Doctor set his mouth in a grim line. Again, he tried not to think of what could be happening to Fitz and Compassion.

'We need painkillers,' said the Doctor, looking up at Lombardo and Naomi.

Lombardo shook his head. 'We have to get to the spaceport, get out of here.'

The Doctor spoke to Thom. 'Can you hear me? Can you climb that ladder?'

Thom made no sign of having heard him.

'We're going to have to leave him,' said Lombardo.

'No,' said the Doctor and Naomi in unison.

Lombardo looked embarrassed. 'Well, OK – we'd better move, then.'

The Doctor smiled reassuringly at Naomi. 'Just follow us and do exactly as I say.'

They climbed up the ladder, Thom progressing slowly, and emerged into a dusty, ill-lit tunnel, festooned with spiders' webs. Naomi was staring at Lombardo's silver shirt and medallions.

The Doctor turned to Lombardo. 'Where now?'

'We're in a subsidiary service tunnel. Used for maintenance access. There's a ship docked not far from here.'

Lombardo started down the corridor. The Doctor followed, ushering Naomi and Thom after him. Soon they arrived at a circular access hatch. Lombardo tapped in a combination and the hatch swung open.

The Doctor frowned into the dim corridor revealed. 'What sort of ship is at the other end of this?'

Lombardo grimaced. 'Freighter. Large, bulky and powerful. Like me after a few pints.'

They filed down the access tube. The sonic screwdriver made short work of the airlock.

Lombardo eyed the device greedily. 'Always wanted one of those. You'll have to give me the design specifications. If we get out of this.'

'I'll give you more than that if we get out of this,' said the Doctor, ushering him on board.

Lombardo ducked inside, winking at Naomi. 'Promises, promises!'

They made for the flight deck and the Doctor lost no time in strapping himself into the pilot's seat and powering up the ship's systems. He could make out the darkness of the hangar through the forward screen. 'Find the medical supplies,' said the Doctor. Lombardo nodded and headed for the rear of the flight deck.

Naomi strapped Thom into a spare seat and then did the same for herself.

The Doctor brought the ship's systems fully on line, and there was a gradual hum as power built up. Lights snapped on outside the ship, illuminating a sloping runway ending in a pair of massive doors.

'Have you ever flown one of these before?' said Naomi, staring doubtfully at the Doctor's frock coat.

The Doctor smiled. 'No, but I'm sure I'll pick it up as I go along.'

Lombardo returned carrying a small red box.

'Any painkillers?' said the Doctor hopefully.

Lombardo nodded, and passed a small hypodermic to Naomi.

Naomi was holding Thom's good arm. 'Don't worry, we're getting out of here.' She injected him but he didn't even seem to feel the pinprick.

'We certainly are,' said the Doctor grimly, sending the signal that would open the doors.

'We hope,' muttered Lombardo as he settled himself into the copilot's seat.

A crack appeared between the massive portals. A crack through which thick, black gas began to pour, slowly, but then more quickly as the gap widened.

The Doctor and Lombardo stared.

'It should be daylight outside,' whispered Lombardo.

The doors had opened fully now. A churning black wall was surging towards them.

The Doctor locked eyes with Lombardo. 'We have to go. Now!'

The ship glided forward, and the Doctor cranked the engines up to full power – insanely dangerous, as the ship was still in the hangar, but there really was no choice. A giant hand pressed him back in his seat as the ship plunged into the black cloud.

The Doctor steered the ship upwards into what should have been the blue Yquatine sky.

But everywhere was blackness.

The control panel began to flash with warning lights and there was the urgent bleep of several alarms.

'What's happening?' cried Naomi.

'Oh, hell,' said Lombardo. 'Whatever that stuff is, it's eating into the hull. We're losing integrity, fast!'

The floor began to shake under the Doctor's feet. The ship was breaking up around them.

The Doctor stared grimly at the forward screen. Surely they had to break through soon. Surely.

From behind him, he could hear Thom, whimpering in pain. Naomi's voice, trying to reassure but shaking in fear.

Lombardo's usually calm tones began to rise in panic. 'We'll never make it off the planet. We're not going to make it!'

Chapter Five
'Woman trouble?'

Fitz lay face down on the grating, the time-stuff a blue blur beneath him. Mad, angry thoughts buzzed about his brain like wasps. *Killed by a TARDIS! We're supposed to be on the same side! Bloody cow!* The pressure in his chest grew into a bursting, stabbing pain – and then diminished. A cool breeze slid over his sweat-slicked face and he gulped in sharp, stinging lungfuls of air. He sat up, doubled over in agony, his breath tearing in and out of his body, thankful and amazed that Compassion had restored the air supply. It took a minute or so for his heart to stop hammering, and, when he felt almost normal again, he stood up, leaning on the rail. 'Compassion?'

No answer, just cool currents of air curling around his body. His shirt was plastered coldly to his back and he shivered. Was Compassion dead? Had he killed her? Had the acid somehow got into her?

'Compassion!' he yelled, his throat aching with the effort. His voice echoed off the walls, and as the echoes died away he became aware of a distant thud-thud, thud-thud, like subterranean machinery. Compassion's heartbeat? If so, she was still alive.

He approached the console. He operated the screen control using the switch he'd seen the Doctor use. The roofspace cleared to show a view of Yendip harbour. Boats sailed serenely about their business, and traffic floated in the clear, blue sky.

Fitz blinked. 'Wha…'

There was no sign of the black shapes or the black gas. Everything was picture-postcard normal. Perhaps Compassion was showing this image because the reality was too horrible to portray.

'It's sealed.'

The voice was a haunted-house whisper and it made Fitz jump, starting his heart racing again. He put a hand to his chest. Wasn't he too young to have a heart attack? 'Compassion?'

'It's becoming part of me.'

Fitz looked down at the console. The Randomiser casing had turned almost completely black. He hadn't succeeded in shifting it an inch.

'It's becoming part of me,' Compassion repeated in a ghostly singsong. 'Why did he do this?'

'Well,' said Fitz, gesturing around the darkened chamber. 'To protect you.'

The grating shook under Fitz's feet and Compassion screamed. '*I do not need protection!*'

'All right, all right!' Fitz grabbed on to the console gingerly. It felt rusty and barnacled, like something washed up from the sea. 'Look, we'd better find the Doctor.'

'The Doctor isn't in this time zone.'

Fitz frowned. What was she talking about? His head ached and his throat felt as if he'd swallowed a cheese grater. The gloomy console chamber made him feel jumpy. The roofspace still showed the same peaceful view. He badly wanted to get out of Compassion, in case she tried to kill him again or went mad or something. But he couldn't be sure it was any safer out there than it was in here. 'Is that really what it's like outside?'

Silence.

Then a flash of light, a falling sensation in his guts and he was standing next to Compassion on the esplanade, overlooking the sea. Fitz shaded his eyes against the bright sun, squinting up into the sky, trying to stop himself from trembling. There was no sign of the attackers. 'What happened?' he said nervously. 'Did you, er, knock them all out somehow?'

Compassion had her hood down, and seemed unaffected by the acid, her red hair ruffling in the breeze. 'They won't arrive for –' she frowned – 'fifty-eight days.' She turned to Fitz, smiling. 'We've escaped.'

Fitz remembered what she'd said about different time zones. 'Oh no. Compassion, *when* are we?'

'When you tried to remove the Randomiser, I went into temporal spasm. I time-jumped into the past. To the first of Jaquaia, according to the local calendar.'

Fitz boggled. He felt the sudden urgent need for a cigarette. He hadn't smoked in what seemed like ages. He patted his pockets, but apart from an old rusty penknife and a gnarled hanky they were empty. 'Temporal spasm?'

Compassion smiled slowly and raised her fist in a crushing movement. 'If I twisted a certain part of your anatomy, you would literally jump in space. The same thing happened to me, only in time.'

Fitz let it sink in for a bit, and then an image of the Doctor's face flashed before his eyes. 'The Doctor! Where's the Doctor?'

Compassion shrugged, staring out to sea. 'Still in the future. On Treaty Day, the sixteenth of Lannasirn. Helping to fight the invaders, presumably.'

She started to walk off.

Fitz was suddenly angry at her lack of concern. 'We've got to go back – forward – and help him!'

Compassion shook her head, a slow smile spreading across her lips. Then she turned and walked away.

A few minutes later, they were walking in silence together along a stone pier which ran out into sea from the harbour, straight as a needle. Looking back, Fitz could see the whole of the harbour, the strip of white beach, the town stretching back to the distant forested hills. There were a few airships moored along the pier, translucent boarding tubes gleaming in the sun. It all looked so peaceful. The elegant shapes of the boats in the harbour, the hotels on the esplanade, the airships in the sky above. As Fitz looked they turned in his mind's eye into dark ovoids, raining death.

Fitz stopped walking. 'OK, stop.'

They were almost at the end of the pier. Compassion regarded him with disdain.

'We can't just sit back and let the Doctor, and this whole planet –' he made a sweeping gesture towards the town – 'suffer!'

Compassion pouted, and walked on to the end of the pier, which expanded into a circular stone platform, in the centre of which was a little metal tower with a spiral staircase. Compassion climbed up, her cloak scuffing on the railings.

Fitz followed, trying to fight down his feelings of exasperation and anger, telling himself she wasn't human any more, she probably didn't realise how badly she was treating him. Just like the Doctor sometimes. Well, great.

There was room for only the two of them at the top. Cool place to take a girl, thought Fitz, shivering in a sudden fresh breeze. He looked back: the pier stretched to the mainland, the water on either side rippling, giving Fitz the unsettling sensation that they were moving. Very pretty, but now wasn't the time for sightseeing.

He grabbed Compassion's shoulders. Her body felt disconcertingly human, pliant yet firm. 'We're going to help the Doctor.'

She shook him off. He remembered the console chamber, how she was prepared to kill him, even if it was out of panic, and he was suddenly scared of her.

She smiled, her lips parting to reveal small, white teeth. How deep is the veneer? wondered Fitz. How far down do you look human? How long before the black metal takes over? 'The attack won't happen for over a month. We're perfectly safe until then.'

Fitz felt as if she was missing the point. 'But the Doctor isn't.'

She looked at him as if he was a child. 'He's as safe as we are.' She raised her arms towards the sky. 'So why not enjoy the peace while it lasts?'

A flock of sea birds swooped and dipped in the distance, and Fitz saw that she was right. They were in no danger now. The Doctor wasn't even in this time stream, this reality.

But he couldn't shake the feeling that he ought to be doing *something*. He couldn't shake the feeling that the attack had just happened. His blood and his bones remembered it, even if his mind told him that he was quite safe. Illogically he fully expected the sky to darken at any moment. 'I don't have your sense of perspective,' he muttered.

Compassion shrugged. 'That's a pity.' Then, with a wheezing, groaning sound, she faded away.

Fitz looked at the space where she had been for a full minute, half expecting her to return. 'This had better be a very, very bad joke,' he muttered through clenched teeth. But she remained not there. Just a gap in the air.

The wind had sharpened, and Fitz suddenly felt very cold. He hugged himself, rubbing his arms with his hands. He looked back along the pier towards the town, and waited. Then he looked out to sea, where a pleasure cruiser was knifing through the waves, and waited. He stared into the sky as the shadow of an airship passed over him, and waited.

Eventually his self-acknowledged low reserve of patience ran out and anger burst through his body. He drew air into his still aching lungs, and yelled into the sky. 'Come back, woman!'

'What are you doing, mister?'

Fitz looked down. A small child had climbed up the spiral steps, and now stood hanging on the railing, one hand gripping a blue-green stick, clearly a sweet of some kind.

Fitz smiled sweetly at it (he couldn't tell if it was a boy or a girl). 'Go away, kid. I'm the nutter your parents warned you about.'

The kid laughed, a squeaking, bell-like sound, revealing a blue-green-coated tongue.

Fitz's smile abruptly vanished. On Treaty Day, the kid would be dead, melted away by the acid rain. Not even a body left behind. And, he realised, there was nothing he could do about it. He couldn't reach the Doctor, and he had no idea where Compassion was. He also had no money and nowhere to stay, and he knew no one on the planet.

He ruffled the child's blond hair. 'What's your name?'

The child laughed again. 'You're a nutter!'

'You're not wrong, kid,' muttered Fitz. What could he do? Scoop up this child in his arms, hope that Compassion turned up? It was ridiculous. How far would he get before he was arrested? It was so stupid, so senseless, that he began to laugh.

The child laughed back, and offered Fitz the blue-green stick.

Fitz declined. He leaned nearer. 'Look, kid, I dunno if you can understand me – uh, what's your name?'

'Lorena.'

So it was a girl. 'Look, Lorena, this is very important. When Treaty Day comes, you've got to be off this planet. Go and visit your granny –'

'Treat day!' trilled Lorena. 'Treat day! Presents!'

Fitz sighed. Useless, pointless. How could he expect a child to understand? Far better to warn the authorities. And, oh God, here come the parents, their faces hard with suspicion, eyes hostile.

'Well, goodbye, Lorena.'

Fitz ignored the angry questions of the parents, and climbed down the spiral stairs, walking slowly back along the stone pier, reluctant to leave the place in case Compassion returned. But deep inside, he knew she was gone for ever. She'd spread her wings and flown away, leaving him – and the Doctor – in the lurch.

What the hell was he going to do? Warn the authorities about the attack on Treaty Day? Then what could they do – evacuate the planet? He didn't even know who the attackers were – were they these Anthaurk guys? And would the 'authorities' listen to him? They'd more than likely lock him up.

If only he knew somebody in Yendip.

Then Fitz remembered: he did know somebody. Or, rather would, in the future, in his past.

He set off at a run for Lou Lombardo's Pan-Traditional Pie Emporium.

* * *

The Doctor tried to be the calm at the eye of the storm, concentrating on maintaining a straight course. Lombardo had overcome his panic and was rerouting power from all nonessential systems to the engines and the force fields – which weren't that powerful, this being a commercial freighter. The Doctor estimated – hoped – that they'd last long enough to hold off the corrosive clouds. If they could keep up speed they might survive. But it was no good. They weren't going fast enough. The bulky ship wasn't built for speed.

Naomi started screaming something about Thom but the Doctor couldn't let himself be distracted. He had his head in his hands, calculating, muttering formulae under his breath. He came to a conclusion and sat back in his chair.

'We've got one chance,' he announced.

'Well that's better than no chance,' mumbled Lombardo.

The amount of energy used to maintain the fields just might, if diverted to the engines, give them enough power to break through. It was an insane risk, but there was no other choice. 'Lou! Patch through the power from the fields to the main thrusters. Now!'

Lombardo gaped. 'You must be joking, y'tart!'

'Do it!' yelled the Doctor.

Muttering curses, Lombardo flicked a relay. There was a sudden surge of speed and a simultaneous tearing, screaming sound which made the Doctor grimace. The console exploded in a shower of sparks and the Doctor and Lombardo covered their eyes.

'Escape pods,' yelled the Doctor, freeing himself from the pilot's harness. The ship rolled and yawed and everyone was thrown to the floor. The Doctor grabbed a chair support with one hand, finding Naomi's with the other.

'Look!' she cried, pointing at the forward screen. The Doctor yanked his head round. A half-gasp, half-laugh escaped him.

The screen showed a vista of stars. They'd made it.

'Whahey-hey!' cried Lombardo in surprised relief.

The ship lurched again.

The Doctor scrambled to his feet. 'This ship's very badly damaged. We want to find the escape pods, and fast!'

He helped Naomi and Lombardo to get up. The ship was flying blind, its guidance systems eaten away. If the corrosive gas reached the power core, kaboom. 'Come on! We haven't got much time.'

Lombardo lifted Thom up. His eyes were open, his features slack.

Naomi shook her head, hands fluttering to her face. 'Oh, no. No, no, no.'

Lombardo laid Thom back down. 'Come on, love,' he said gently. 'We've still got a chance.'

'I'm not leaving him!' cried the woman, struggling from the Doctor's grip and scrambling over to the body of her husband.

The Doctor swallowed hard, bending over Thom. He had to make sure. After a few seconds checking, he was sure. Thom was dead.

He turned to Naomi. They really had very little time before the ship broke up. He held her face with both his hands, making eye contact, speaking patiently and calmly. 'We have to go *now*.'

There was an explosion, frighteningly near, and smoke belched through the doorway.

The woman's brown eyes were like glistening pools. 'I can't leave him.'

'Naomi,' said the Doctor gently. 'He's gone. You have to save yourself.'

'Come on!' urged Lombardo, halfway to the door.

'You'll thank me for this later,' said the Doctor, grabbing Naomi around the waist and dragging her from the flight deck. 'I hope.'

A short, cramped corridor led to the circular escape-pod bay. Lombardo yanked open the hatch of the nearest pod. The ship shuddered as a series of explosions rocked the floor beneath their feet. The Doctor bustled Naomi forward, and Lombardo manhandled the weeping woman through the hatch.

The pod interior was cramped and barrel-shaped with recesses in the walls. The Doctor strapped Naomi into one recess. She did nothing to resist, just hung there limply, heaving with sobs, her face wet with tears.

Once the Doctor had strapped himself in, Lombardo hit the LAUNCH button. The lights in the pod flickered madly, and there was a sickening, lurching sensation as the pod was ejected from the freighter.

The Doctor craned his head to look out of a tiny porthole. He caught a glimpse of the freighter – a bulky, functional, charmless vessel streaked with years of use – before it exploded in a silent burst of white light.

'Hold on!' he cried.

The shock wave hit them and they all cried out as the pod was buffeted like a seed in a hurricane. The turbulence didn't last long, and the control panel bleeped as the pod started sending out its SOS.

'That was a close one,' said the Doctor, failing to sound even remotely cheerful. 'A lucky escape indeed.'

Lombardo smiled thinly above his double chin, but there were hollows under his eyes.

Naomi just hung there in her harness, staring at nothing.

Fitz slid the note towards the sandy-skinned reptilian barman. 'A glass of the strongest thing you have, please.'

The barman crumpled the money up in a three-fingered claw. That had been Fitz's only piece of luck so far today: finding the banknote. He had no idea how much it was worth; judging by the alien barman's reaction, and the change slapped down on the bar before him, not much.

Beside the change, the barman slid a tall glass towards Fitz. It looked like gravy. Dark lumps stirred within its depths.

Fitz frowned at it.

'What is this?'

The barman had a rasping, slightly strangled-sounding voice.

'Oomingmak honey-brandy. Sledgers rely on it during long, cold winter drives.'

'Sounds just the ticket.' Fitz took a sip. God! It burned like... acid. He grimaced at the unwelcome thought.

The lizard thing nodded. 'You like?'

Fitz tried to speak, could only gasp. 'Yeah... I... like.'

The barman wandered off to serve other customers. Fitz took another sip. He needed to get drunk, very drunk, because his situation just didn't bear thinking about and alcoholic oblivion would provide a welcome, if temporary, retreat from reality.

After leaving the stone pier, he had walked back to Arklark Arcade with visions of somehow enlisting Lou Lombardo's help. The Doctor hadn't told him much about Lombardo but he was clearly a pal of the Doctor's, which meant he had to be useful to know. Hell, he could even be a Time Lord, with a functioning TARDIS.

As Fitz had crossed the bridge to the Arcade, he'd realised that he couldn't speak to Lombardo, couldn't even let the man see him – because Lombardo hadn't recognised Fitz in a month or so when he'd met him for the first time.

Fitz took another long gulp of the drink, remembering how the rest of that afternoon had progressed.

He remembered leaning on the railing of the iron bridge – the very railing he had leaned/would lean on with the Doctor – and working it all out. If he did approach Lombardo now, then Lombardo would have recognised him on Treaty Day. But he hadn't, so he couldn't have. So, if Fitz did approach him now, he'd be seeding a mighty fine time paradox which could cause much more damage than any alien attack.

So not only did Fitz have to avoid Lombardo now, he'd have to make damn sure he didn't accidentally bump into him during his time on Yquatine. The same thing applied to warning the authorities. If he did, and they listened to him, and they managed to somehow prevent the attack, then he'd never have come back in time to be able to warn them, which had been a result of the attack in the first place. Or had it? It was his fiddling with the

Randomiser that had brought them back. But it was the attack that had caused him to take refuge in Compassion.

Cause and effect stacked up like four-dimensional dominoes with Fitz stumbling around in the dark trying not to knock over any of them.

Another sip of brandy. He could feel it loosening his mind, his thoughts beginning to freewheel, his emotions getting stirred up. He remembered being close to tears on the bridge, trying to work it all out. The sensible thing would seem to be to warn the authorities – after all, don't the timelines always sort themselves out? Perhaps, in the future he'd just escaped from, the authorities had been forewarned by him but were unable to act. But on the other hand – and this was the real bugger – what if the attack had been *because* of his warning the authorities?

It was enough to drive him to drink. So here he was.

He'd decided not to do or say anything to anyone about what he knew would happen on Treaty Day. It was the safest bet. Like it or not – and he definitely bloody didn't – the attack had to happen. It had already happened: that part of the future was solidified like concrete, waiting for the present – and Fitz – to catch up with it. It was part of history – Fitz could hear the Doctor saying this – and there was Nothing He Could Do About It.

The glass was almost empty now and Fitz was beginning to feel a bit better. There was a warm glow in his stomach and a floaty feeling in his head.

So, he had decided on the bridge, if he couldn't do anything about the attack, he had to find Compassion and get out of this time zone. And so he'd spent the whole afternoon and early evening searching for her. In her long black cloak and hood, she'd be easy to spot. But a planet is a big place. When you're searching on your own, on foot, even a town like Yendip is a big place. Eventually, fatigue and hunger had overcome him and he'd sat on the edge of a public fountain, washing the sweat from his face and gulping down mouthfuls of clear cold water. He'd given up then, figuring that he'd wait for Compassion to find him.

She better had, before Treaty Day. He didn't want to be around to meet his past self or the black shapes in the sky.

It was then that his luck had changed – of sorts. He'd found the banknote, and then a place called Pierhaven, which extended over the harbour and contained loads of cafés and bars. He'd bought some food, and then come to this tavern. Il-Eruk's Tavern, the glowing orange sign had said.

And there he was going to stay until booze blotted out the horror of his situation. Until he forgot how Compassion had so casually abandoned him, the bloody cow.

He shoved the pile of change back across the bar towards the barman, who he'd come to realise was Il-Eruk, owner of the tavern. 'Another one of those, please.'

Il-Eruk poured him another. 'Man with a lot on his mind, you look like.'

Fitz managed a tired, woozy smile. 'Yeah, well, you know…'

Il-Eruk winked a yellow eye. 'Woman trouble?'

Fitz grabbed the full, tall glass gladly. 'You're dead right, mate.' He took a long, satisfying sip. God, was he going to get ratted! 'Woman trouble.'

Chapter Six
'Don't ask me, I'm just the pie man'

The escape pod carrying the Doctor, Lou Lombardo and Naomi had drifted far from the orbit of Yquatine, heading slowly inwards towards New Anthaur, sending out its SOS. The Doctor tried to keep everyone's spirits up, but they were in a defenceless little pod in the middle of a war, so he had a hard time of it. Being unable to steer the pod, it was likely that they would make planetfall on New Anthaur, the home of the enemy. If they weren't either rescued or killed beforehand. It all depended on which side noticed them first.

To take their minds off the situation, the Doctor and Lombardo were discussing pies they had known.

'I remember once on Everdrum,' said the Doctor, 'I was invited to the King's coronation. They'd baked an enormous pie! When they cut it open a horde of rebels burst out and assassinated the King.' He sighed. 'And I was *hungry*.'

'I'm an old-fashioned guy in some respects,' said Lombardo. 'In my opinion you can't beat a good old traditional steak-and-kidney pie.'

The Doctor was keeping his eye on Naomi, who hadn't spoken since the destruction of the freighter. The inane chatter had a purpose, to keep a blanket of normality wrapped around the woman. He nodded enthusiastically at Lombardo. 'It's the portability of pies that endears them to me. You can eat them on the beach, running for a bus, up a tree –'

All off a sudden they were bumped about in their harnesses as though the pod had run aground. Pies forgotten, Lombardo regarded the Doctor with fearful eyes.

'What's happening?' said Naomi in a voice shaking with fear.

The bumping smoothed out and the Doctor grinned broadly. 'Tractor beam!' he said brightly. 'We're being rescued.'

Lombardo had craned his head round to look out of the pod's

73

single tiny porthole. 'No, we're not – we're being captured. That's an Anthaurk ship.'

The Doctor noticed Naomi's eyes harden at the mention of the Anthaurk.

'There's loads of them out there,' declared Lombardo. He turned back to the Doctor. 'Anthaurk battle cruisers!'

The wrong side had found them. 'Well, if they were going to destroy us they'd have done it by now.'

There was a jolt, which knocked the breath out of all three of them and the hatch began to open.

Naomi's eyes widened in terror. 'We can't let them get us!'

'We haven't got much choice,' said the Doctor.

The hatch opened fully, to reveal the helmeted head and armoured shoulders of an Anthaurk commando. 'Out!' it hissed.

The Doctor emerged from the pod, followed by Lombardo and Naomi. They stood in a long, low hangar with a curved, ribbed ceiling. Stubby, blunt-nosed Anthaurk assault ships lined each side of the hangar.

The Anthaurk commando gestured with its weapon, a bulbous-looking, knobbly blaster. 'This way.'

Suddenly, Naomi threw herself at the alien, hands scrabbling its ribbed and ridged armour, screaming obscenities. It brushed her aside casually.

The Doctor pulled her away, muttering soothing words, as the alien gestured again.

'This way,' it repeated, adding almost as an afterthought, 'You will not be harmed.'

They stumbled after the huge alien. It didn't even bother to look back to see if they were following.

Naomi looked terrified, and Lombardo was doing his best to mask his fear, but the Doctor was instantly relaxed. 'We're in no danger here,' he whispered to his companions.

Naomi looked at him as if he was mad. 'Yes, we are!'

'No, he's right,' put in Lombardo, waving at the assault ships. 'We're on an Anthaurk battle cruiser crammed with weapons of mass destruction. Of course we're in no danger!'

The Doctor sighed. Lombardo's sarcasm could be wearing at times. 'Trust me,' he said, indicating the Anthaurk commando. 'There's something odd about this. They've just wiped out an entire world – why take the trouble of bringing us aboard now?'

'We're prisoners,' said Lombardo glumly. 'They're probably going to torture us.'

They were taken from the hangar along a series of tunnel-like corridors and shown into a bare, dimly lit cell in which sat or lay a few dozen other humans and creatures. Only a few looked up as they entered, and they didn't seem to notice the incongruity of the Doctor's frock coat or Lombardo's disco gear. Lombardo and Naomi slumped against the wall, while the Doctor flitted from being to being, checking injuries, offering words of comfort or advice, and gathering information.

He went back to Lombardo and Naomi, his face grim. 'These people are from ships that were leaving or nearing Yquatine when the attack happened. Some of them said the ships appeared from nowhere. I didn't know Anthaurk technology was so advanced. Lou, tell me what the dispute with the Anthaurk was about.'

'Don't ask me, I'm just the pie man,' moaned Lombardo.

The Doctor knew that his friend was much more than that, but he didn't question Lombardo further. He looked shattered, the muscles on his face slack, his eyes staring blankly from deep hollows.

A silence fell. Everyone was wrapped up in their own inward-looking shell of grief. The Doctor could feel their sense of numb shock, of disbelief. Of wanting to know what had happened to their homes and loved ones, but not knowing whom to ask. He'd noticed a few of them staring at him, eyes pleading, as they'd entered. But he was as much in the dark as they were. He wished he'd done his homework, looked up the future history of Yquatine before he'd brought Compassion and Fitz here. He'd been here a few times before to see Lou Lombardo, had attended President Vargeld's inauguration, and knew all about the planets and races of the Minerva System. But the future was unknown. Something as large as a full-scale attack on Yquatine wouldn't have been hard to miss, and he could have avoided this whole mess. Well, it was too late now.

The floor shifted beneath them. The Anthaurk ship had changed course.

'Do you think they're taking us to New Anthaur?' said Naomi.

The Doctor nodded. 'Almost certainly.' A little human girl came up to him. She had curly blonde hair and dark eyes. Her face was streaked in dirt, her eyes red from crying.

'Hello,' he said. 'What's your name?'

'Lorena,' said the girl, in a small, lost voice.

Lou Lombardo stared out of the window at what lay before them. Then he turned to the Doctor. 'Well, that's not New Anthaur.'

The Doctor was staring, too, taking in the beauty of the structure. 'No, it certainly isn't.' It was quite a feat of engineering. A giant crescent shape, a gleaming sickle in space, with entrance ports dotted along the concave side. Ships were streaming back and forth, mostly Anthaurk battle cruisers and assault ships, but the Doctor recognised a few of Adamantean design. 'What is it?'

'Aloysius Station. We're on the border of Anthaurk-Yquatine space. Built just after the treaty, to keep an eye on things, make sure the Anthaurk didn't try anything.'

The Anthaurk ship flew into the arms of the station, and soon the Doctor, Lombardo, Naomi, Lorena and the other prisoners were walking along a wide corridor with a view of space. They ended up in a large, open hall, flanked by terraces. There were people everywhere – wandering around looking lost, resting, being tended to, eating, talking. The Doctor scanned the crowds for Fitz and Compassion, but there was no sign of them.

Lorena tugged at his hand. The Doctor looked down at her, smiling sadly. She had left Yquatine with her parents on Treaty Day because of the rumours of war. Their ship had been attacked, and she'd become separated from her parents, bundled into an escape pod, and picked up by the Anthaurk in much the same way as the Doctor and his friends had been

Now she was asking where her parents were. 'Oh, I'm sure they're around here somewhere,' he told her. He felt sad, but not overly worried. Children had remarkable reserves – they were born survivors. It was the adults you had to worry about.

The Doctor turned to the adults. Lombardo was fingering his medallions nervously, and Naomi looked old, tired and confused.

The Anthaurk commando had taken his helmet off. His broad, snakelike face looked down at the Doctor, red eyes burning. 'You will remain here.'

There were other Anthaurk in the hall, guarding the exits, but some were tending the wounded. There were also a number of human soldiers, the personnel of the space station, the Doctor guessed. They were being far less tolerant than the Anthaurk. The Doctor watched as a scuffle broke out between a human soldier and an Anthaurk.

Naomi and Lorena had gone off in search of food. The Doctor looked after them. 'I hope they're going to be all right.'

Lombardo was looking around the hall, frowning. 'I wonder if any of my chums made it.' He sighed. 'Probably not.'

The Doctor had that feeling in the soles of his feet, a feeling that told him that he was dying to have a good nose round. 'Lou, will you look after Naomi and Lorena? I'm going to see if I can find out what's going on.'

Lombardo winked. 'Aye, OK. Doctor?'

The Doctor turned. 'Yes?'

Lombardo reached out a large, pale hand. 'If we don't meet again, good luck.'

The Doctor took his hand. He was dearly regretting ever buying the Randomiser from Lombardo, but the man couldn't be blamed for supplying the goods. 'Thank you for all your help, Lou.'

Lombardo embraced the Doctor and patted his back. The Doctor felt his breath in his ear. 'Just you look after yourself. I know you, always getting into scrapes.'

'I will,' said the Doctor into Lombardo's shoulder. 'And I'll let you have the blueprints for a sonic screwdriver.'

He felt Lombardo's body shake as he laughed, and they

separated. With a last wave and a smile he turned and walked from the hall, trying to fight down the horrible feeling that he'd never see his friend again.

The Doctor wandered unhindered for a while. Everywhere was the same – distressed refugees, chivvying Anthaurk troops. He stopped to help when he could – a man with a broken arm, an Adamantean suffering from acid burns, an Eldrig with a torn ligament. He was helping, but only on the periphery. He could spend days wandering around, tending the wounded and reassuring the frightened, entertaining the kiddies and charming the women. In fact, he would quite like to. But he had a duty. He had to get to the bottom of things.

He made his way towards the upper levels of the station, where he guessed the control centre would be. There were fewer people the higher he went, fewer Anthaurk guards. Eventually he came to a long corridor, so brightly lit that he had to squint. 'Why do they have to make it so bright?'

The corridor was lined with Anthaurk troops. Their helmets covered the whole of their broad heads. There was a grille for the mouth, and a dark, curved visor for the eyes. At over seven feet tall, they were an intimidating sight, but the Doctor refused to be intimidated. He simply walked along the middle of the corridor, towards the interesting-looking double door at the far end, hands behind his back, whistling tunelessly.

As he'd expected, two guards crashed into his way, like a pair of doors slamming shut.

The Doctor stopped before them, staring up at their visors. 'Let me pass.' The guards didn't move. 'Look, there's a very important meeting going on in there and I'm late.'

They could have been statues for all the notice they took of him.

The Doctor took his sonic screwdriver from his pocket. 'You're not going to like this.'

Before the guards could raise their weapons the Doctor flicked a switch, setting the frequency to that which he knew would be painful – though not damaging in any permanent way – to Anthaurk ears.

The guards dropped their weapons and sank to their knees. The Doctor nipped round them, and walked up to the double doors. To his surprise, it wasn't locked, and he pushed it open.

He found himself in a large circular chamber, the floor of which bore a stylised motif of the Minerva System. Ranks of seats stretched back towards the domed ceiling. Light came from globes set into the walls, and at the far end, dominating the room, was a large circular window which showed an impressive view of space, the arms of the crescent-shaped space station just visible.

There was a lectern on a dais before the window, and upon this stood a proud-looking Anthaurk in a wide-collared uniform and scarlet cloak. The seats were crowded with a ragtag mixture of aliens and humans. All of them seemed to be speaking, or shouting, at once.

The Doctor smiled. Of course. The Minerva System Senate, or what was left of them.

The Doctor walked into the middle of the makeshift Senate chamber and roared for silence.

Silence fell, satisfyingly quickly.

The Anthaurk's eyes latched on to the Doctor. 'What is this?' He had a look about him the Doctor had seen countless times before. The moment the Doctor saw him he knew he would, before long, be ordering the Doctor's imprisonment, or execution. Oh well.

'You mean, *who* is this,' said the Doctor calmly. 'Well, since you ask, I am the Doctor, and I am here to help you. All of you.'

The Anthaurk waved an arm. 'Guards!'

The Doctor began to talk, quickly and earnestly. 'Before you bang me up, listen to what I have to say. You –' he pointed at the robed Anthaurk – 'are guilty of a terrible and ghastly act of genocide!'

There were mutters of agreement from the senators and their aides.

The Anthaurk walked up to the Doctor. 'That is not true. We are involved in a rescue operation. As I keep trying to explain to the Senate, something else has invaded Yquatine!'

'Ah.' This was an unexpected development – or a diversionary tactic. 'Well, who?'

'Yes, who, Zendaak?' cried a short, stout human in what looked like Victorian garb.

Zendaak turned and hissed at the man. 'That is what we are trying to find out!'

The Doctor pointed at all the surviving members of the Senate. 'You all think the Anthaurk are responsible?'

There were mutters of assent from the Senate. An Adamantean stood, bejewelled arm pointing at Zendaak. 'They *are* responsible, no matter what this vile snake says!'

The Doctor called for silence again. 'Zendaak, no doubt you have been denying this.'

Zendaak cocked his head, keeping one red eye on the Doctor. 'Vehemently, yes. We may have had... disagreements with the Senate, but we were not preparing to attack.'

'What about the attacks on our trade routes?' bellowed the Adamantean.

'That was a direct result of the sanctions imposed on our world. And, for your information, we were going to call them off!'

The Adamantean remained standing. 'At the last Senate meeting, you were on the point of declaring war!'

Anthaurk guards had appeared at the Doctor's side, hissing angrily. Their aural cavities must be ringing, reflected the Doctor. They'd be very angry. He'd better be very careful.

Zendaak addressed the Senate, spreading his arms wide, as if he was willing them to trust him. 'I was on the way back to Yquatine to negotiate peace, when this attack occurred.'

The Adamantean wouldn't let up. 'On the way back with a full battle fleet!'

Zendaak folded his arms. 'It is an Anthaurk custom.'

The Doctor sensed that the truth was here somewhere but it was going to take a lot of teasing out. 'And instead of negotiating a peace you found yourselves picking up the pieces after an attack on Yquatine?'

Zendaak nodded, letting out a hiss. 'Yes.'

The Doctor beamed. 'Brilliant! So now we're all chums and we can work out what really happened to Yquatine, then?'

'I still think this is an Anthaurk trick.' The man in Victorian dress again. 'I do not trust Senator Zendaak.'

'And you are?' said the Doctor.

'Senator Fandel, Luvia.'

'Oh, hello,' said the Doctor, walking over and shaking the senator's dry little hand. He cocked his head at Fandel. 'You may be right. But you may be wrong. There's only one way to find out. Trust *me*.'

Fandel glared at the Doctor.

'It will take more than trust. I need proof before belief,' came a gravelly voice. The Doctor turned to see a stout, barrel-shaped humanoid, silver eyes glinting from beneath a jewelled brow. The Adamanteans were a silicon-based life form, whose adopted homeworld, Adamantine, served as a refuge for others of their kind.

'You'll get proof, Senator…?'

The Adamantean inclined his massive head. 'Krukon.'

'You'll get proof,' he said again, watching Zendaak. 'Either way.' He was itching to get down to Yquatine. He looked around the makeshift Senate chamber. Heated discussions had broken out between the senators and their aides. The Doctor recognised most of the races – the Eldrig, the Rorclaavix, the Kukutsi – and there was a hologram of a rotating crystal hovering at the back of the banked circle of seats, watching over all. The Doctor frowned. What was it? Oh yes – an Ixtricite. Combined crystalline gestalt of the Krotons, the Rhotons and the something-else-ons. How nice. All living in perfect harmony with each other.

But something was bothering him, or rather the absence of something – or, more accurately, some*one*. 'Where's President Vargeld?'

'The President is missing, Doctor,' said Zendaak evenly.

'So who put you in charge?' said the Doctor.

Zendaak smiled. 'Circumstance,' he said smoothly. 'The Minerva System is an a state of emergency. The Anthaurk fleet was the only cohesive force in operation near Yquatine at the time of attack. It is only natural that I should take charge at the time of crisis.'

There was an outcry. Krukon rose to his feet, bellowing. 'You were the only cohesive force because you were going to *attack* Yquatine!'

Fandel's face was white with fury. 'Such insane arrogance! We should eject you from the Senate.'

A voice boomed from the back of the hall. 'This squabbling is irrelevant.'

The Doctor looked up at the rotating crystal, which pulsed as the Ixtricite spoke. 'We must ascertain what has happened to Yquatine.'

'That's the wisest thing I've heard since coming in here,' said the Doctor.

'But who leads? Who makes decisions?' appealed Zendaak.

'Hardly you!' shouted Fandel. 'Do you want to start another war? The Luvian fleet is prepared for battle!'

'As is the Adamantean,' rumbled Krukon.

'And the Kukutsi,' rattled a beetle-like insectoid creature.

'I hardly think starting a war will help matters,' said the Doctor coldly.

Zendaak glared at them. 'Very well,' he said. 'Until the crisis is over, we work together.'

'Oh, good good good!' cried the Doctor loudly, clapping his hands. He walked up to the podium in front of Zendaak, where he alone had noticed a little light flashing. 'What's this mean?'

The muscles across Zendaak's face twitched, his mouth curving downwards as he glanced at the podium. His eyes met the Doctor's. 'The first pictures from our reconnaissance ships.'

It had been six or so hours since the attack.

A 3-D image of Yquatine appeared abruptly in the centre of the chamber.

Or what had been Yquatine.

Everyone gasped in shock, and even Zendaak took a step back.

The Doctor's jaw dropped.

Where the planet of Yquatine had once been was a mass of blackness, its surface teeming and boiling like a thunderhead.

Part Two

But at Least You Can Run

Chapter Seven
'I want something removed from me'

Beatrix was the eighth planet of the Minerva System, and, you could say, its heart – but not a heart full of goodness and love. More like a satanic, mechanical heart, churning its way around the sun, its blasted surface masking what went on beneath. Beatrix boasted no equivalent to the Palace of Yquatine, the sticky jungles of Zolion, the crystal caverns of Ixtrice, the labyrinthine stone cities of the Anthaurk, or the endless ice plains of Oomingmak. There was not a single remarkable feature on its airless, barren surface. But without Beatrix the Minerva System might well have fallen to the Anthaurk in the war. Beatrix was the industrial centre of the System, home of the best-equipped spaceyards, the largest industrial concerns, the most intensive mining facilities, and innumerable factories churning out everything from weapons of mass destruction to radiation shielding. The economic argument was sound enough: if you were going to have one you were going to need the other.

Beatrix also boasted the harshest penal institutions, a thriving black economy and a booming trade in prostitution – all species and tastes catered for, however depraved or bizarre. An ugly, brutal world, its population almost entirely made up of factory workers, prisoners, prostitutes, addicts, the lost, the desperate, the abusers and the abused. It was almost as if Yquatine, with its serenity, beauty, tolerance, learning, culture and breathtaking sea views, had somehow spawned a twisted, black-hearted twin.

Beatrix City was sunk into a crater left by some aeons-old meteor strike on the western hemisphere. Here lived the majority of the population, the families of the workers, and the lowlifes previously mentioned. The most expensive apartments were those that protruded above ground, around the rim of the crater.

Sick, grubby daylight could be glimpsed through the windows of these dwellings. Below them, the levels descended for two thousand metres, becoming more seedy and dangerous the deeper you went.

Compassion had picked up all this from the Beatrix medianet. She knew it was a dangerous place. She also knew that there was someone here who could help her. She hoped.

She slunk along the subterranean streets of level D39, footsteps echoing on the dirty concrete, wondering if there was some way of making herself invisible. That would save her a lot of trouble. She came to what must once have been a retail area, but all the outlets were boarded up with sheets of metal, mad and threatening graffiti scrawled all over their surfaces in luminous green paint. In the centre a dented metal cowling ran down from the cobwebbed ceiling and below it was some sort of pit. Compassion walked over and leaned on the railing surrounding the pit, taking care not to put too much weight upon it, looking down into a deep, seemingly endless shaft. Water fell from some cracked pipe or other, a baleful, metronomic drip-drip-drip. Compassion smiled. The place reminded her of herself, of her insides.

She had a quick look inside her console chamber. All seemed well, apart from that cursed Randomiser.

Returning her gaze to outside, she stepped back from the railing, considering. The trouble was, she'd gone down ten levels too many. Petersen was on Level D29. But the lift had dropped past D29 and stopped at D39, from where it had refused to budge. She toyed with the idea of using the vortex to get back to D29, but she had no experience of short hops and she wasn't sure what the Randomiser would do. It had allowed her to get to Beatrix, but would it allow her to go anywhere else? It wouldn't matter, anyway, once she'd found Petersen.

She looked up the shaft. Sick, weak light some distance up, at the next level. More life signs. A foul-smelling breeze caressed her face. There was a ladder, rusty and grimy, but it looked sturdy enough. She leaned out and up, grabbed hold of lowest rung, and began to climb.

Ralf Petersen had been looking forward to this all day. Ever since he'd taken the message in his luxury Level A2 apartment that morning, he'd been suffused in a delicious glow of pleasurable anticipation. That was how he'd put it to Lashana, his latest mistress, anyhow. Suffused. Rarely did a client offer such a large amount for what appeared to be a very simple piece of surgery.

He'd dressed, looking out of the picture window at the lights of the apartments on the other side of the crater – wondering as always if anyone was looking back at him – eaten a light breakfast prepared by the tall, blonde and smooth-skinned Lashana, and then repaired a faulty servo-unit in her ankle, which he'd damaged during the previous night's activities. Ralf Petersen preferred to take artificial lovers. He knew far too much about the human body to be able to like it or trust it, let alone love it. Knew far too well how biological processes determined temperament. He'd never been able to handle women, except in the crudest manner, and so Lashana and her kind had been his bedmates since his teens.

One day, he often promised himself, he'd get himself an artificial body. Not while he was still fit and fully functional, but when his body became old and ruled by a deteriorating mind and distressing bowel movements. Maybe he would start with a cybernetic arm or leg, or something to increase his stamina. Not that Lashana ever complained. She was programmed not to.

Anyhow, he checked his face in the mirror – neat, short grey hair, trimmed moustache, a face of dignity and authority – programmed Lashana with her daily duties, checked that his blaster and other weapons were fully charged and set off for his office down on level D29.

He'd set up on D29, dangerously close to the line separating what passed for civilisation on Beatrix from anarchy, mainly because the rent was cheap, but also because no one ever came around asking awkward questions. His offices were spacious, airy and always clean and tidy. He made sure of that. He enjoyed watching the surprise on his clients' faces as they came from the vandalism and oppression of the corridors of D29 into a fragrant, pastel-hued room with attendant pot plants and gentle music tinkling away in the background. It served a practical purpose, as well as amusing him. It helped his clients relax.

The first couple of appointments that day had been particularly uninspiring. A mineworker who'd wanted improvements to his respiratory tract – a common one that, as Petersen ruthlessly undercut the official Beatrix Health Service fees. Then a professional brawler who'd wanted bionic implants and a holographic tattoo removed. Then an exotic dancer who wanted her middle breast enlarged. All mundane, the usual traffic of Petersen's trade. He'd booked them all in for surgery and downloaded their deposits briskly, almost impatiently. He'd had a quick lunch and now he sat awaiting his mystery client. The woman who'd given only her first name, Laura. The woman who'd offered him ten thousand credits for his services.

As the minutes ticked away he wondered if it was a trick.

He had enemies and maybe one of them had come for revenge. He wasn't particularly worried – there was enough concealed weaponry in his office to instantly vaporise any would-be assassin. You had to be careful in Petersen's line of work.

At the appointed time, the intercom bleeped. Petersen kept no secretary, relying instead on automated systems. True, they broke down sometimes, but they'd never deliberately betray you or try to filch credits from your account.

Petersen leaned forward over his patinated softwood desk and pressed the intercom button. He spoke, his voice a deep, reassuring baritone. 'Ralf Petersen.'

The intercom crackled. 'Laura. I have an appointment.'

Petersen raised his eyebrows. Something about her voice. Not fear or trepidation, no – it sounded as if she had something to hide. Petersen was used to this. 'Good afternoon, Laura. The door is open. You may enter.'

He imagined her pushing open the heavy security door, walking along the narrow corridor to the door of his office. He switched on the monitor. It showed the image of a red-haired woman in a black cloak. A leap of excitement. Something about this woman seemed special, out of the ordinary, quite apart from the enormous sum she was offering.

Scans revealed no concealed weapons, so Petersen pressed the button that unlocked the door to his office. As it opened Petersen rose from his chair, as he always did. He extended his hand towards the pale-skinned woman who entered his office. 'Please, sit down.'

She sat. Petersen began the usual spiel, watching her. He couldn't help but be intrigued. Her eyes were dark, but he couldn't tell what colour they were. Were they brown? Dark green? Even purple? Interesting.

She held up a slender hand, interrupting his spiel. The nails were short, the fingers long. 'I know what you do.'

Her voice didn't sound Yquatine, it almost sounded Old Earth. An Empire agent? Petersen's pulse quickened.

'You perform surgery on those who pay you enough. Biomechanical enhancements. Cybernetic replacements. You have wide experience with many species. That is why I am here. I believe you can help me.'

Petersen steepled his hands under his chin. 'That depends on what you require of me.'

Laura's lips tensed, and her eyes flickered downwards, as if she was trying to make up her mind. Then she turned her dark gaze on him, and whispered, 'I want something removed from me.'

She was obviously trying to unsettle him. Petersen wasn't having any of it. 'What sort of something?'

'A growth.' She pronounced the word as if it was the filthiest thing she could imagine. The word hung in the air between them. He could almost see it, shining, swelling, *wrong*, ringed with scarlet, complaining flesh.

Petersen felt a twinge of pity for the woman. She must be ill, or crazy, or for some reason unable to go through the usual medical channels. He'd seen it all before, and never usually let it bother him. But this time… 'All right, I'll book you in for an examination.'

'There is no need for an examination. You will perform the surgery now.'

Petersen stifled a laugh. She was obviously crazy. 'How can I perform any surgery without examining you first?'

And then she had smiled for the first time – a bright, breezy smile that contrasted wildly with her manner since she'd stepped into his office. 'I'll show you!'

So she did.

And Petersen screamed.

Less than half an hour later, Petersen had put together a medikit, donned a sterile cloak and gloves and was prepared to go inside Laura to perform the surgery. His hands where shaking and he badly needed a drink, but underneath his fear there was a sense of excitement. After the initial shock of seeing her head turn into a glowing white doorway, he had bombarded her with questions. Who was she? What was she? She'd refused to answer any of them. All he knew that was that she wanted something removed from inside her. Which meant *going* inside her. He'd taken a bit of convincing, but when Laura had downloaded her ten thousand credits into his account he had decided to go along with her. He'd cancelled all his afternoon appointments and switched on the answer machine, and now he stood before her.

She had a slight frown above her eyes, searching his face. He'd seen the expression before, on countless clients. The fear, the need for reassurance. 'You know what to do?' she said.

Petersen nodded. He hadn't felt this nervous, or this excited, for years. 'Yes, I know what to do.'

She smiled her breezy out-of-place smile, and then her head opened out into a glowing white doorway.

Taking a deep breath, Petersen stepped forward.

There was a second or so of total disorientation, then a sickening lurch, like being in a plummeting lift. And then he was standing on solid ground. He looked wildly around, clutching his toolkit, fighting down the yell of fear that threatened to burst from him.

He was standing in a gloomy chamber, cool air pressing on his skin. Blue light flickered down from somewhere above, and below, through a metal grille, cloudlike matter broiled and churned. Directly in front of him, in the centre of the chamber, was a tall column of black, spiky machinery, rearing up into the dark, vaulted ceiling.

'Holy Mother of God,' he whispered. 'What are you, Laura?'

Her voice came from all around him, making him jump. 'Walk towards the console.'

The console. That thing in the middle of the chamber. Petersen's mind was whirling, trying to cope with what he'd stumbled upon. He wasn't shy to admit that this was totally beyond his experience. His mind settled on one thing: she had to be artificial. An artificial woman. But *what* an artificial woman! Made Lashana look a shop-window mannequin. And he was right inside her. Whatever happened, he had to hold on to Laura, help her, explore her depths. As he fumbled in his toolkit for his laser scalpel, he realised that this was what he'd been born for, what his whole life had been leading up to.

'The black rectangular extrusion. Remove it!'

Petersen looked down at the console. There was the black box Laura had spoken of. Lights pulsed dimly under the blackness. Not exactly the glistening cancerous growth he'd imagined, but it had the same aura of incongruity. He could tell it wasn't meant to be part of her.

He activated the laser scalpel, and made the first incision.

A shriek of pain made him stop. He looked up at the vaulted ceiling. 'What is it?'

Her voice was thick, distorted. 'It… hurts.'

He waved a hand. 'Maybe… painkillers?'

There was a distant rumble. 'Painkillers are no good to me! Continue.'

Trying his best to keep a steady hand, Petersen reapplied the scalpel.

This time the scream was deafening, and the floor shook beneath him. He fell, dropping the scalpel. It slid through the grating to be swallowed up by the stuff below.

Suddenly, Petersen was scared. He was out of his depth, out of anyone's depth. An image of Lashana flashed into his mind, her plastic face smiling. 'Let me out. I'm not going on.'

Laura's voice was huge and terrifying. '*You must continue!*'

He let out a strangled, terrified cry. 'I can't – my scalpel!'

'*Get it out of me! Get it out!*'

The whole chamber was shaking, and Petersen clung to the grating, screaming. 'Let me go!'

Her voice rose to a crescendo, a wordless tumult of sound which blocked out his own yells. The floor tilted beneath him. Petersen felt himself falling, falling, towards something dark and massive and churning, sparks flying and pistons pumping with a deafening screech of tortured metal.

There was a sickening crunch and suddenly Petersen couldn't feel anything below his waist. He spun round, in time to see a black hammerhead thundering towards his head. He let in a breath to scream, and –

Compassion stood in the pastel-tinted office, staring at the mess on the floor that had once been a man.

She hadn't wanted to kill Petersen. She hadn't even known she was doing it. When he'd tried to remove the Randomiser, the pain had consumed her, sent her mad, and she'd taken Petersen deep within herself. Down somewhere beneath her great dark heart there was a gear chamber busy with massive cogged wheels and gleaming shafts. She didn't know what it was for, not yet.

She let herself out of the office, and wandered around the filthy streets of Beatrix City, feeling numb. She'd killed a man. She'd almost killed Fitz. She recalled his face, mouth open wide as he fought for air. No, she hadn't meant to do it! The Randomiser hurt her, wasn't part of her, she had to be rid of it.

As she slipped along the slimy walkways of the lower levels of Beatrix City she realised that none of it would have happened if the Doctor hadn't inserted the Randomiser in her. The Doctor had hurt her, perverted her new nature, made her kill.

She pressed herself against a cold concrete wall, water dripping on to her skin – her outer plasmic shell.

She couldn't believe he had meant to do that. After all they had been through, it just didn't make sense. She calmed herself, concentrated on the moment. Useless to submit to fear and despair. She was – she should be – beyond such emotions. Logic should be her guiding principle now. And logic told her that she was stuck with the Randomiser for the time being. Any attempt to remove it ended in disaster. Maybe, then, there was a way to work with the Randomiser – bond with the circuit, so that it activated only when *she* wanted it to. Maybe. She needed to test her abilities, grow stronger. She needed some sort of project.

There was one that immediately suggested itself. In some fifty days, Yquatine would be invaded, and totally destroyed. The Doctor and Lou Lombardo had spoken of the reptilian species, the Anthaurk, as the aggressors. Perhaps, then, it would be a good idea to try to prevent the attack. Alter the timelines, save a planet. The Doctor would approve. She could do it, she was sure. She was Compassion, more than human, more than a TARDIS. She could do anything.

Chapter Eight
'You said Yquatine is gonna be... destroyed'

Fitz woke with a bastard behind his eyes. He opened them to see... feet. Everything was too bright and there were feet everywhere, walking up and down a stone wall. Wait – must be lying down. Wall must really be ground. Now then, these feet: brown, shapely female feet in strappy sandals. Nice. Hairy male feet in strappy sandals. Not nice. Booted feet, feet in weird things that looked like miniature spaceships. Hooves, even. Fitz stared dumbly at this slapping, tip-tapping, trotting procession, waiting for his brain to catch up. The sight of a pair of bare brown female legs brought him nearer to his senses and he raised himself up on one elbow, wincing as a fiery pain sparked down his spine. His mouth was dry and his face felt as if it had been *kneaded*. He ran his hands through his hair. It was matted and dusty. He realised gloomily that he was at the start of one mother of a hangover which would only get worse as the day progressed.

He sat up, looked around. He was sitting on a low stone bench. Must have slept there all night. That explained the pains in his hips, back and shoulders. The bench was on a wide walkway at the edge of a large area of open parkland, with the usual fountains and statues and stuff. How he'd got here God alone knew. The last thing he remembered was joining in a singsong with a group of drunken tourists at Il-Eruk's Tavern. He'd sung the song about the turnip fish. And hadn't he tried to chat up that blue-skinned woman? And hadn't he thrown up? He looked down at his white silk shirt. It looked clean, but suspiciously rumpled. The image of himself, naked, splashing in a fountain with the blue-skinned lovely flashed into his mind. He allowed himself a smirk of satisfaction. Must have been a good night, then.

He squinted across the park towards a group of lithe reptiles playing some sort of game which involved throwing a hooting ball over a silver net. Yeah, a good night. If only he wasn't stranded on a planet that was going to be totally destroyed.

Much later, Fitz was back at Il-Eruk's, spitting feathers. It was mid-afternoon, and the place was shady and deserted, pleasingly cool. There were hardly any other customers, just a couple of dedicated alcoholics and a couple mauling each other in a dark corner.

Fitz walked up to the counter, and slapped down his remaining coins. 'What will that get me?'

Il-Eruk cocked his head to one side, spread his arms and lisped, 'Precious little.'

Fitz's stomach growled. He felt as hollow as a punctured football. Food was probably a better idea than booze. 'Have you got anything I can eat?'

Il-Eruk clicked his claws against the top of the bar. 'I have selection of pies?'

Fitz nodded. 'That'll do.'

'What would sir prefer? Cheese and –'

Fitz cut him short. 'Anything. I'm very hungry.'

Il-Eruk brought Fitz a pasty. The porky face of Lou Lombardo leered out at Fitz from the wrapper. Fitz's heart sank at this unwelcome reminder of his temporal troubles. He scoffed the pasty eagerly, as Il-Eruk watched.

'Bad day?'

Fitz nodded. 'You can say that again.'

'Bad day?'

Fitz ignored him. It had been a spectacularly bad day. He'd been to Yendip Spaceport, intending to stow away on the first ship off planet, only to find the place tight as a tin of beans, security and surveillance everywhere. Something to do with strict immigration controls, he wouldn't wonder. On a planet where so many alien species mixed and mingled the authorities had to be careful. And so Fitz had resigned himself to the fact that he was stuck on Yquatine with no money and nowhere to stay.

His mind returned to the present. Il-Eruk was still hovering nearby. 'But you had *good* time last night?'

Fitz nodded. 'Mmm.'

Il-Eruk leaned on the bar. 'I can tell when man is really having good time. Eyes see distant place, man is generous with money. Good for business!'

'Well that was the last of my money, mate,' mumbled Fitz.

Il-Eruk blinked his bright yellow eyes. 'That is my point. You *not* having good time last night. You getting drunk to mask *bad* time. Not wise.'

'Tell me about it.'

Il-Eruk straightened up and let out a curious whistle. 'I am telling you about it.'

Fitz waved a hand. ''S a figure of speech.'

'I see many alcoholics in here. They start like you, masking bad time with drink. Soon, life *is* drink.' He spread his arms wide and licked his beak. 'But what can I do? I run bar, I sell drink, I not force people to drink.'

Fitz grinned. A barkeeper with a conscience. 'Yeah, I don't want to go down that road,' he said. Then an idea struggled into his befuddled mind. 'You're right: I was getting drunk deliberately last night; I *am* having a really bad time.' Time for another lie. He put on his most wretched voice – he didn't have to try too hard. 'My woman's left me, I've got no money and I wanna get home to see my folks. I don't suppose you've got any jobs going? Or know of anyone who's got any jobs going?'

Il-Eruk picked up a glass and began polishing it. His long, beaklike jaw opened in a yawn, showing rows of tiny teeth. 'You lucky. My main bar guy Luke just done runner. Woman trouble again!'

Fitz tossed his head. 'Pah! Can't live with 'em, can't kill 'em, eh?' It seemed at once bizarre and perfectly natural to be swapping sexist banter with a giant bird-faced lizard.

Il-Eruk leaned towards him. 'You got experience?'

A few weeks behind the bar of the Mother Black Cap in Camden

Town in the sixties had given Fitz all the bar experience he would ever need. 'Oh yes,' said Fitz. 'I've worked behind bars on countless worlds.'

Il-Eruk's eyes narrowed. 'You got CV?'

Fitz put on his most plaintive voice. 'Yeah, man, but it's, erm, on my computer, and my woman took that along with the rest of my stuff!'

Il-Eruk seemed to consider. 'OK. You join my team. Behind bar, yes? You no meaty enough for bouncer. Trial period, mind.'

Great, thought Fitz – a piece of luck at last. 'And, uh, could I stay here as well?'

Il-Eruk considered. 'You sleep in Luke's old room, have to clean out first. Luke lazy in that area.'

'Great. Thanks.' Fitz extended a hand and Il-Eruk took it. 'It's a deal. My name's Fitz Kreiner.'

'Zaqisk Il-Eruk Iskel'patrut.'

It sounded more like a choking fit than a name but Fitz smiled politely. He sank back on to the bar stool, allowing himself to relax. The prospect of the days ahead seemed like a holiday. Work in the tavern, then get the hell off Yquatine before the invasion, find the Doctor and save the universe again.

Il-Eruk was still hovering. 'Something you said last night, bothering me.'

Fitz swallowed the last of the pasty and brushed flaky crumbs from his jeans. He was wondering how the alien would respond if he asked for an advance. 'Yeah?'

Il-Eruk leaned across the bar, his beaked face inches from Fitz's own. His breath stank like gone-off tuna. 'You said we all doomed. You said Yquatine is gonna be… destroyed.'

Bugger. The drink must have loosened his tongue just that little bit too much. 'Yeah, well,' he bluffed, 'well we are, aren't we? It is, isn't it?' He whirled his arms above his head, playing the spaced-out hippy. 'I mean, eventually, all the planets in the System will crash into the sun. I'm talking millions of years, man! Must have been something in the drink, making me see the cosmic scale of things.'

Il-Eruk stood back from Fitz, his beak open, rocking on his heels.

Damn! thought Fitz. That little performance has probably cost me my job. Well at least the future's safe.

Without taking his eyes from Fitz, Il-Eruk poured a short measure of whisky for them both. 'This on the house.'

Fitz smiled with relief. 'Thanks.'

They sipped in silence for a while, Fitz mentally berating himself for his drunken lapse and promising himself it would never happen again.

Il-Eruk put down his empty glass and emitted a hissing, cackling wheeze. 'Fit, I was wrong about you. You not just got woman trouble.' He tapped the side of his narrow skull with a clawed finger. 'You got deep, deep mind problems.'

Chapter Nine
'Take me back'

The Doctor stood in the observation gallery, the metal rail cool on his hands as he leaned and watched the Kukutsi ship glide smoothly into the spacedock. It was a sleek horseshoe of smooth chitin, dotted here and there with chocolate-brown bumps. It was beautiful, and probably alive in some sense, the Doctor guessed, linked to the insect minds of its pilots.

As soon as the space doors closed and the atmosphere had normalised, suited figures ran towards the ship. A hatch swung open in its side, like a beetle's carapace.

The Doctor gripped the rail harder. He wanted to be down there, where the action was, but the Senate had confined him to the civilian parts of the station, pending an investigation into who exactly he was. He didn't blame them: an entire planet had been destroyed, they were bound to be suspicious of strangers, however nice and helpful they were. Same old story. So he'd decided to play along with them, take a back seat for a while, lie low until he discovered the truth.

Several Kukutsi scuttled from the skip, their feelers waving in agitation. Human soldiers boarded the ship, followed by two medical orderlies in grey and yellow suits. Six guards took up flanking positions on either side of the hatch. A door opened in the far side of the hangar. Senator Krukon appeared and ran over to the ship.

Things were happening. The Doctor stepped away from the railing.

An armed trooper barred his way. 'And where do you think you're going?'

The Doctor could see the boredom in her eyes, the resentment of being tasked with guarding him. He gritted his teeth. 'Nowhere.'

His guard smiled. 'Thought so.' Her rifle hung loosely from a shoulder strap. No doubt in less than a second it could be brought to bear on him. She was a stout young woman with short-cropped brown hair and a pale, freckled face. She wore a sleek grey uniform with black piping and insignia, big boots and black gloves, and she carried a slim, silver-barrelled rifle. She was quite piggishly unfriendly – all he'd gleaned from her was her name and rank: Trooper Bella Otterley, Minerva Space Alliance.

The Doctor smiled back at her. Maybe she'd respond. People often remarked upon how good-looking he was, though he had no idea how it worked. 'What's on that ship?'

Trooper Otterley didn't take her eyes from the activity below. 'They picked up a damaged fighter. It was going to crash into the sun.'

The Doctor was intent once more on the scene below. Senator Krukon was standing, hands on massive hips, watching the entrance to the ship. The Doctor was beginning to lose his patience. Damaged fighters crashing into suns – this had all the hallmarks of a Fitz Kreiner misdemeanour. He glanced over his shoulder at Trooper Otterley's unsmiling face. 'Any survivors?'

Her voice hardened. 'I'm afraid that's classified.'

'Yes, I understand, you're only doing your job.' He turned back towards the observation window, muttering. 'I only wish you'd let me do mine.'

His eyes narrowed. One of the orderlies was backing out of the Kukutsi ship, easing a gurney down the ramp. The Doctor couldn't see its occupant, because the guards blocked his view. The other orderly emerged, guiding the trolley across the hangar. The first orderly stopped and spoke to Senator Krukon. Then the whole procession set off towards the hangar exit.

Then the Doctor saw who was on the gurney. Not Fitz, or Compassion. A male human in a spacesuit, with dark hair and aristocratic features.

The Doctor smiled at Trooper Otterley. 'Er, I think I've just gained access to some classified information.'

She actually smiled back, obviously pleased that her President was safe. 'It will soon be common knowledge anyway.'

The Doctor watched the Kukutsi scurrying across the carapace of their ship. He frowned. 'Wonder what he was doing zooming towards the sun.'

Senator Zendaak strode through the disgusting bright white corridors of cursed Aloysius Station, his skin tingling as though tiny parasites were burrowing beneath the scales. He hated this place and what it represented. He had spent many nights on New Anthaur, on the stone ramparts of the Imperial Citadel, staring up at the bright star that he knew was Aloysius Station. That shining point represented compromise, defeat, acceptance. It had goaded him through his career, from his initiation into the Inner Circle to his rise to role of senator, representative of his species on the Minerva Senate. Goaded him through the years of planning this campaign. It had shone, blind and unknowing, as the Anthaurk battle plans had developed, as the mighty Anthaurk Battle Fleet had grown and grown. Eventually, after a hundred years of cloying, insufferable peace, the Anthaurk had been ready to assert themselves once more upon the galaxy, their fleet massing on the border.

The black ships rained down their scourge upon the planet of his enemies.

Zendaak could still see the disc of Yquatine in his mind's eye, clouded with the strange blackness which almost seemed like a living thing. The other senators had been mortified – all those millions of lives, lost, snuffed out as easily as a candle flame. That weakling Doctor's face had crumpled like an eggshell with grief. Fools.

He reached his quarters, slipping gratefully into the dark, cool interior. It was a makeshift arrangement – all artificial lighting removed, Anthaurk candles and incense placed on drape-covered furniture.

Zendaak sat before a desk which was covered with the cloaks

of his fathers. A small globe rested on a pile of smooth pebbles in the middle of the desk. Zendaak passed a hand over the top of the globe and an image flickered on to its surface. The face of an old, wizened Anthaurk, its skin dull brown, its eyes deep-set. It spoke, its voice wheezy and thin with age and impatience. 'Developments, Zendaak!'

Zendaak saluted. 'Grand Gynarch, the others do not accept our leadership.'

The Grand Gynarch considered. 'That was to be expected.'

'So what of our plans now?'

The Grand Gynarch leaned forward. The image of her face distorted, became convex. 'Start sending our ships down.'

Zendaak frowned. 'Is that wise, O Gynarch?'

The ancient Anthaurk bridled. 'You dare question my orders!'

Zendaak immediately realised his mistake. 'No, Gynarch, I was just speculating –'

'This is not a time for speculation. It is a time for action.'

Zendaak could sense one of his leader's tirades coming on. He sat back and assumed his most reverential expression.

She leaned back, the image of her face returning to normal. 'A hundred years, we have waited. I was a hatchling when the humans of Yquatine beat us down. They are now no more. It seems that the wait has been worthwhile.' The Grand Gynarch waved at Zendaak. 'Now away and do my bidding.'

Zendaak saluted again. 'Yes, Grand Gynarch!'

The face vanished from the sphere.

Zendaak stared at the rows of devotional candles on the altar beyond. Could the Grand Gynarch be right? After two humiliating defeats – first the Daleks, then the cursed Yquatine humans – could the Anthaurk be returning at last to their rightful place as conquerors?

Take me back to the time before it happened

A piano picked out a lonely, descending series of notes, like a funeral march, or a tune produced falteringly by a sentimental drunk. Slow. Deliberate. Endless. Hopeless. Going round and round and never back. Because you couldn't go back, only forward.

Take her back to the place before it happened

The notes became points of light, like stars. Were they stars? Or were they flakes of skin on black silk sheets? There were hundreds of them, thousands, accumulating, spreading, more and more and more. Because you couldn't reverse entropy, only accelerate the process.

Take us back to the time and place before it happened

The white flakes now outnumbered the black. There were only a few points of black left. That was good, wasn't it? Because the black stuff was evil – as if it could be that simple! The black stuff was what had snuffed out –

'Take me back!'

He sat up in the bed, eyes open, seeing nothing but bright white light. It hurt his eyes. He squinted.

In the *bed*?

Hands on his arms, pushing him gently back down to the cool softness of the pillow.

The *pillow*?

He could see properly now. There were figures around the bed, heads angled down towards him. His head felt soft, like the pillow. Floating.

A voice, a female human voice. 'Welcome back, Mr President.'

'Franseska?'

But Franseska was dead. There was no way she could have escaped. Her brother in the Space Alliance had probably survived her. President Vargeld groaned.

'Mr President?' The speaker was a tall, crop-headed female doctor with a serious face.

'I'm here,' he said. He tried to smile, look presidential.

'You're suffering from concussion, and slight radiation sickness. You'll be OK, but you need to rest.'

Then President Vargeld noticed the senators, standing in a ring around his bed. Fandel, Zendaak, Tibis, Krukon, Okotile, Juvingeld.

Zendaak.

President Vargeld lunged for the Anthaurk senator, a roar of rage scouring his throat. Hands tried to press him back to the bed, but his anger made him strong. He actually managed to slip his hands around Zendaak's throat before they sedated him.

The Doctor was bored and impatient and he was beginning to lose his temper with Trooper Bella Otterley.

More ships had docked, and he'd watched as they'd disgorged their occupants, refugees from Yquatine. Now a slablike Adamantean ship and a rather primitive-looking rust-coloured Rorclaavix cruiser sat alongside the Kukutsi vessel.

The Doctor rather liked spaceships. He used to keep a notebook detailing all the different types and classes he'd seen, but that had gone west along with his old TARDIS. And now wasn't the time for spaceship-spotting.

Trooper Otterley was holding forth against the Anthaurk. 'We should have kicked the bastards out of the system after the last war. Shifty-eyed lizard scum. Do you know they eat their own babies?'

The Doctor had had enough of such unimaginative, racist bilge. He was profoundly repelled by this glimpse into a closed, nasty, prejudiced mind. Still, it wasn't all her fault: she was probably trained to hate the Anthaurk. Anyway, it was about time he was rid of her. He had to get himself involved with things.

He walked up to her. 'I'm afraid I find your attitude very sad.'

She looked him up and down in clear disgust. 'What are you, an Anthaurk apologist?'

'No, I'm merely open to all sides of the argument and I don't like to jump to conclusions.' He fished in his pocket. Ah, there they were. Desperate measures, but... 'Would you like a jelly baby?'

She looked at the proffered sweet with a sneer. 'You're crazy.' A flicker of interest in her cold blue eyes. 'Who *are* you?'

He popped the sweet into his mouth. A green one. Nice. 'No, who are *you*?'

She scowled and raised her rifle. 'Don't try anything stupid.'

The Doctor never let his eyes leave hers as he spoke. 'What are you, twenty? Brought up on, let me see, Beatrix. Probably an orphan. Joined the army because you wanted to belong to something.'

Trooper Bella Otterley let out a long breath. 'No, no, no, and no. I'm twenty-nine, I grew up on Luvia, my parents are tax inspectors and I joined the army because I like uniforms, big guns and spaceships.'

The Doctor smiled his widest and most unnerving smile. 'Big guns, eh?'

He held her gaze, stepping closer, closer, aware that the rifle was pointing at his midriff – and when he was close enough he reached out and grabbed the end of the rifle, jerking the barrel up towards the ceiling. 'That's not a very big gun!' he yelled.

'Hey!' cried Trooper Otterley. She fired once, a laser bolt sizzling towards the ceiling.

The Doctor gave her a shove, tripped her up and ran from the observation gallery, closing the door after him and fusing the lock with his sonic screwdriver.

Panting with relief, he hared off along the corridor. Hopefully things would be in too much disarray for anyone to notice him. Realising that haring along would draw unwelcome attention to himself, he slowed to a stroll, stuck his hands in his trouser pockets and walked off casually, humming a song about a man who often dreamed of trains, looking for somewhere to poke his nose in.

President Vargeld was alone with his thoughts of Arielle.

Memories of her crowded in on him. He remembered her eyes, her watchful, wary eyes. They were dark brown with large pupils. Mysterious eyes, enchanting eyes. She had always seemed to be on the lookout, keeping a barrier between herself and the outside world. He remembered when they'd meet, and her eyes would lose their watchful expression, her gaze would soften and welcome him into her. It was like visiting a private world they shared together.

He remembered the night he was cast out of that world. It had been the night he'd asked her to marry him. She'd looked horrified at first, as if he'd confessed to some crime or perversion. Then her eyes had grown distant, watchful again, and she'd refused him. And then... then he had felt cast out of paradise. He so badly wanted to be back there, in that special place they'd shared. He wanted to see her, to call her name and for her to turn around, surprised, her face lightening with a smile and her eyes, her beautiful eyes –

He choked back a sob, a hard feeling in his throat. And then a crushing feeling of guilt. He had seen his home planet destroyed, but he had thoughts only for Arielle. The idea that she was still alive, somehow, somewhere down on Muath, tormented him to the exclusion of all else – duty, responsibility, a sense of proportion. He thought of his family, his mother, father and sister in the big old house at Farleath. They were certainly dead, like everyone else on Yquatine. Why couldn't he feel anything for them?

He stared up at the ceiling, waiting for his mind to slow down and settle. Waiting for his sense of duty to assert itself.

But he settled instead on Arielle.

It was no use. He knew what he had to do.

Take me back

He sat up. He was in a private room, windowless and warm and safe, with guards on the outside. But he was feeling better now. He stood up. Still a bit light-headed, and with a sick feeling in his stomach. But fit enough. Surely he could go now. Hell, he was President, he could do what he liked.

He found his clothes in a cabinet by the bed. He smiled grimly. His coat of office was still on Yquatine – what was left if it –

which meant he had to wear his pilot's uniform, a more practical and damn sight more comfortable outfit. He dressed quickly.

The Doctor held his frowning forehead against the cool glass of the viewport. A fleet of six Anthaurk ships were heading out, spiky slabs bristling with weapons, the glow of their engines receding like fireflies against the vast night of space. Yquatine was out there somewhere, its boiling blackness invisible, shrouding it from view.

The Doctor turned away, feeling the usual slow burn of anger that came when he was confronted with acts of genocide. Whatever the Anthaurk had used to destroy Yquatine, it had been totally devastating. Now they were going to check on their handiwork. Well, maybe it was time he got down to the stricken planet himself.

He hurried away from the viewport, intent on finding Lou Lombardo. He'd been a useful ally in the past, and it would be good to have him around.

As he rounded a corner, he collided with someone in a black and silver uniform.

The Doctor stepped back, gushing with apologies which stuttered to a halt when he realised who he'd bumped into.

The President.

He looked ill, his face pale, unshaven, forehead shining with perspiration. His eyes were pale blue under dark brows, and they had a distant, distracted look. 'Who the hell are you?'

'I'm the Doctor,' said the Doctor. 'I was at your inauguration.'

President Vargeld looked at him blankly. 'I – I don't remember…'

Of course. He'd been someone else back then. Oh well. The Doctor smiled and extended a hand. 'Nice to meet you again.'

The President's hand was hot and clammy. The Doctor leaned in for a closer look at his eyes. 'Are you all right?'

President Vargeld shook the Doctor's hand away, made to shove past him. 'Out of my way.'

The Doctor grabbed his arm. 'Where do you think you're going?'

President Vargeld pulled away. 'I've got to – get back – find her.'

'Find who?'

The President blinked. 'Arielle.'

The Doctor had never heard the name before and said so.

'She's on Muath, she's still alive, I know it.'

Muath was Yquatine's sole satellite, a small moon with a few scientific installations. 'You've got to get back... so you were on Muath just before the attack started?'

President Vargeld shook his head. 'No, I was on my way there to see Arielle, try to talk her round.'

'And your ship got damaged, plunged towards the sun.' He patted the Yquatine leader on the back, making him stagger. 'You're lucky to be alive!' Then he caught the President's gaze, held it. 'What did you see out there?'

President Vargeld grimaced, shook his head. 'Things...'

The Doctor widened his eyes, trying to see into the man's mind. 'Be more specific.'

'Black... things...'

'Anthaurk ships?' the Doctor prompted.

The President looked away. 'Those bastards.' He began to panic, trying to push past the Doctor. 'Out of my way! I've got to find her!'

He shoved past the Doctor and staggered away down the corridor.

The Doctor stared after him, thinking furiously. The best thing would be to get the poor man back to sickbay. But no. He'd seen something. Better to go with him now before he got bogged down in Senate meetings and bureaucratic whatnot.

He caught up with the Yquatine leader. 'Let me come with you.'

President Vargeld stopped in his tracks. 'Why?'

The Doctor stepped up to him. 'I want to know what happened to Yquatine. And so do you. Let me help you.'

The President nodded. 'OK. Follow me.'

They picked the pride of the station's fleet: a stealth ship manufactured in the spaceyards of Beatrix. A thirty-metre-long needle, its shining hull reflecting the chilly white lights of the spacedock, fitted with powerful ion engines and the most advanced shielding techniques yet developed. There had been a bit of bother at the spacedock, but the station staff really had no choice but to sign the ship over to the President.

Now the Doctor and Stefan Vargeld sat side by side in the cockpit as the ship lanced out from the crescent of Aloysius Station. The President seemed more relaxed, more in control now that they were spaceborne.

'So, you were at my inauguration,' said President Vargeld. 'Still can't remember you. Who exactly are you?'

'A traveller,' said the Doctor. 'And a friend.'

President Vargeld still looked unsure, but didn't ask any further questions. This suited the Doctor fine.

After a few hours of uneventful travel, during which the President filled the Doctor in on some aspects of Minervan history, they neared Yquatine. The Doctor gazed at the black sphere. Was it his imagination, or had it grown larger?

'Muath,' said the President, pointing.

A smaller patch of darkness was orbiting the main mass of Yquatine. President Vargeld guided them towards it. The Doctor flicked switches on the console, bringing all the shields on line.

The small beclouded moon grew larger and larger in the forward screens until it blotted out the stars. And then they were in total, solid blackness which billowed against the screen like oil.

President Vargeld was staring at it, mesmerised.

The Doctor studied the readout in front of him. 'Seems to be some sort of dense gas, composed of highly toxic and corrosive elements. Traces of sulphuric acid, phosphorous and, er, substances this ship's computer has never heard of.'

The President worked the controls, still staring.

The Doctor realised how unstable he was, how dangerous it was bringing him here. Perhaps a dose of reality might help.

'You know there's very little chance of anything surviving out there,' he said gently.

'I'm taking her in to land,' said the President. His voice was flat, devoid of emotion.

The Doctor had planned on taking samples of the atmosphere, not landing. 'I wouldn't do that if I were you.'

'Why not?' snapped the President.

Warning lights began to flicker on the console. Some of the stuff was penetrating the shields. 'Because I don't advise it,' retorted the Doctor. 'The shields aren't going to hold for much longer.'

'We're landing. I must find her.'

'Listen to yourself! You're not rational. We can't land here!'

'I'm doing it, whether you think I'm being rational or not.'

'There's no point in throwing your life away,' said the Doctor slowly and calmly. 'We just take a few samples and then leave.'

'Whatever,' muttered the President, intent on guiding the ship slowly down through the churning atmosphere.

The Doctor sighed, and let him get on with it. With zero visibility President Vargeld had to rely on sensors, and the Doctor didn't want to distract him in case they crashed. There was a bump as they landed and then the President unstrapped himself and went to the back of the ship.

The Doctor followed. 'You're not going out there!'

President Vargeld was already donning a spacesuit. 'I most certainly am.'

The Doctor grabbed him by the shoulders. 'Listen to me! There's nothing out there but that corrosive black gas. Nothing can survive in that! If you don't believe me, check the computer!'

The President's eyes widened, as though he'd just seen something horrible over the Doctor's shoulder. 'She's dead. Oh, she's dead.' His voice broke with pain, and then the tears came.

The Doctor held him as he cried, his body shuddering with sobs. He was trying to form words, but the Doctor shushed him. He knew the man had to let out all his sorrow. Humans were frail things, especially their minds. They weren't built to cope with the true nature of the universe, which wasn't unfair or malignant, but something much worse: indifferent, taking no heed of individual suffering. It was something the Doctor had learned at a very early age.

Vargeld's sobs subsided and the Doctor sat him against the wall, legs akimbo, hands useless in his lap. 'Listen, we have to get out of here.'

The President nodded in resignation. 'She's not here.'

'But something is.' Giving the man a reassuring pat on the shoulder, the Doctor went back to the cockpit, intending to ready them for immediate take-off, but something on the console caught his eye. 'Now that is interesting. I wonder if it's meant for us.'

He went back to where Vargeld sat on the floor, for all the world like a life-sized broken Action Man. 'We're not leaving just yet. Something's happened outside.'

President Vargeld looked up, hope glimmering in his eyes. 'Someone's out there?'

The Doctor shook his head. 'No. There's a convexity of clear-ish air around the ship. It's still pretty nasty – a human couldn't breathe it – but I'll be OK. I think something wants me to go outside.'

Vargeld got to his feet. 'I'll go.'

'No no, you're human,' said the Doctor, steering him gently back towards the cockpit. 'Rather too human, it seems. Suit up and stay in here – then you can rescue me if things go pear-shaped. Which hopefully they won't.'

Vargeld nodded and began to don the spacesuit stored behind the pilot's seat.

The Doctor was glad he'd trusted his instincts and come on this madcap mission. He had a feeling he was about make a key discovery. 'Right. I'm all set.'

The President's eyes were evasive, inward-looking. He sounded embarrassed. 'Look, Doctor, I'm sorry about cracking up just now. Must be a side effect of the medication.'

'Don't be sorry,' said the Doctor. 'Just make sure you pull me in if there's trouble.'

* * *

The Doctor stepped out of the airlock on to the rocky surface of Muath. An acrid smell, like burning rubber, crept into his nose and mouth. He was standing in a dome of relatively clear air, at the edges of which the black gas broiled and heaved. The beams of the ship's lights shone over his head and were swallowed up by the blackness.

The Doctor coughed, putting a crumpled hanky over his nose and mouth. He could have used one of the spacesuits, but he figured that, if the sentience behind the black gas – and he was certain there was one – had gone to the trouble of making things tolerable for him, he'd meet it halfway. And he hated spacesuits – clumsy, confining things.

He walked a few metres over the grey, dusty ground, taking long, loping steps in the low gravity. He took the hanky away and bowed theatrically, waving it. 'Well, here I am,' he said. He looked around. Still the black stuff roiled and he realised that if it suddenly decided to collapse around him he wouldn't stand a chance. Best not to think about that. 'It *is* me you want to see, isn't it?'

To his left, a section of blackness bulged inwards and detached itself from the main mass. It floated towards him, a wraith of black smoke, trailing grey tendrils.

The Doctor reached out with his mind. Yes – there was intelligence, of sorts. Nebulous, indistinct, but the thing approaching him was definitely a sentient being. Whatever the Anthaurk had used to conquer Yquatine, it was highly advanced.

It bore down on him soundlessly. He felt its smoky edges brush his skin.

He backed away, towards the ship, recoiling from its caresses. 'Now this is nice, but we haven't been introduced.'

And then, suddenly, the cloud creature surged all around him, closing like a fist around his body, crawling into his nose and mouth, choking him. The Doctor fought against it briefly, but it was too strong. His lungs filled with the thing, his vision clouded and darkened, he tried to scream. And then consciousness slipped away.

Chapter Ten
'I've just got to get off this planet'

After a week or so of living in the city of Yendip, Fitz had settled into a kind of routine.

He would rise a few hours before lunchtime and swallow a bit of breakfast, either alone or with Il-Eruk, who habitually rose at some frightfully early hour. Then there would be a few hours of cleaning and tidying. There were three lichenous wooden rooms below the bar, only a few metres above sea level – a store room, a pantry and a square, low-ceilinged kitchen. All trod a greasy line between cleanliness and filth, and it was Fitz's job to maintain this seedy equilibrium. When things were quiet down below Fitz could hear the lapping of the waves around the struts of Pierhaven. It always made him feel precarious, as if the whole tavern was about to plop down into the deeps.

It was the main kitchen that occupied Fitz the most. Gleaming pots and pans and a worrying number of knives hung from a giant creaking wooden construction which occupied the centre of the room. An ancient, grimy electric oven crouched against the far wall, years of grease baked hard on to its dull metal surfaces. There was also a freezer big enough to ice a bison, a cold store full of alarming things wrapped in plastic, and a dishwasher that looked to Fitz like the torso of a decommissioned battle-droid. There was more: toasters, blenders, coffee makers, food mixers, all of a similar age and dubious safety. Il-Eruk often spoke of upgrading his cooking appliances but there never seemed to be the time or money.

Usually Fitz would grab a bite to eat after his cleaning duties, and begin work serving behind the bar. The tavern was open from just before lunchtime until whatever hour Il-Eruk pleased – there didn't seem to be any licensing restrictions in Yendip – and Fitz sometimes worked all through the night. Apart from the bouncers, who seemed to turn up only when they liked – Il-Eruk obviously being too scared to impose set working times upon them – there were only two other staff. Val, a tall, busty and flirtatious woman of 'a certain age' who kept giving Fitz the glad eye, and Zabulong, a rather nervous alien which looked like a light bulb with about twenty arms and legs. It was good at clearing tables but absolutely useless behind the bar. Fitz would have thought it able to serve loads of customers at once, but many limbs and one rather skittery brain were a recipe for broken glass, spilled beer and hurled abuse. Fitz often covered for both Zabulong and Val, who was always taking sick days, but he didn't mind. He needed to earn as much money as possible in order to buy himself off this doomed world.

He tried not to think of the coming invasion, or what may be happening to the Doctor, or what would happen to the people he'd come to know – Val, Il-Eruk, Zabulong, Lou Lombardo, the regular customers in the tavern – and beyond them the millions of innocents in Yendip and all the other towns and villages of Yquatine. But at night, when he lay exhausted in his tiny room, back and arms aching from pulling endless pints, he often found he couldn't sleep for thinking about the black ships, the acid rain. One thought preoccupied him: an illogical fear of the attack coming now, despite the certain knowledge that it wouldn't happen until Treaty Day. He would eventually fall into a fitful, sweaty slumber, only to arise irritable and drained. Often he drank to help himself sleep, and this only made him feel worse.

When he had a few hours to himself, he would explore Yendip, visiting the libraries and museums, building up a picture of Yquatine and the Minerva System. The more he learned, the more his heart sank at the grim future that awaited Yquatine. Fitz tried to hide behind his customary shield of cynicism, but it didn't work. He would walk along the shore of the lake and gaze across at the Palace of Yquatine, torn with awe at the serenity and beauty of Yendip. Or on one of his rare free evenings he would brave the stiff sea breeze and walk the length of the stone pier (he still half-heartedly hoped that Compassion would reappear there) and gaze back at the yellow lights of the town spread out along the dark humped coastline, faint sounds of music drifting over the lapping waves. He'd become filled with a numb sorrow, an almost overpowering sense of impotence. This whole town, this whole *planet*, was going to come to an end. Forces beyond his control were cranking slowly towards war. The feeling would soon change, as the wind whipped his hair into his face and flapped his cheap imitation-leather jacket against his body, to one of guilt. His pot of money was growing, slowly but steadily. He would be getting off Yquatine in a few weeks. Abandoning it to its fate. He'd given up trying not to feel too bad about it.

One night, Fitz was having a particularly hard time. A crowd of Anthaurk had taken over one corner of the tavern and were proceeding to get noisily and rowdily drunk. Fitz and Val were kept busy attending to their every whim. They continually demanded the most exotic drinks and the most obscure foodstuffs, in the rudest and most provocative manner possible. Fitz tried not to let it get to him, tried not to show his fear of these seven-foot lizards with their snakelike faces and blood-red eyes, but he could see and hear Val becoming more uptight by the minute, almost visibly swelling and reddening, her bosom quivering like a trapped animal in her tight top. Il-Eruk, usually quite a mellow individual, took pride in his culinary abilities and so was not pleased that the Anthaurk sent back almost everything he prepared for them. Fitz could hear the swearing and clanging from the kitchen as Il-Eruk vented his anger on pots and pans.

As Fitz pulled another foaming glass of ale, Val thrust her face near to his. 'The bastards!'

Fitz placed the drink on a tray alongside seven others. 'What have they done now?'

She averted her head as he picked up the tray. 'Nothing.'

Fitz carried the tray over to the table, ignoring as well as he could the crusts and other detritus hurled at his head, and put it down quickly, stepping back as clawed hands reached across. He overheard a snatch of conversation: they were trying to work out how much money it would take for an Anthaurk to have sex with a human female, and the conclusion was that there wasn't enough money in the universe to persuade them to perform such a disgusting, degrading act; and the best – no, the only – thing to be done with such a 'sagging, pallid beast' like Val was to boil her alive and feed her to the troops.

And they looked like they were seriously contemplating it.

No wonder Val was pissed off. No wonder the Anthaurk had started a war. It seemed the natural thing for them to do. Fitz could hardly imagine them playing croquet or going to concerts or even sitting down quietly with a book. Here, in his place of employment, was an ugly mob of the creatures that would destroy Yquatine. It was all he could do to contain his anger and fear.

Fitz retreated behind the bar with Val, feeling quite well disposed towards the woman. 'Well at least they're spending money,' he said, wiping his beer-sodden hands on a grimy towel.

'Wish they'd go and spend it somewhere else,' muttered Val through clenched teeth. She had a flat, predatory face, with widely spaced eyes and a full-lipped mouth the size of which actually scared Fitz. She had masses of dyed red hair and wore short skirts and spangly tops, clearly blissfully aware that she was several decades past the suitable age for such attire. She reminded Fitz of the mother of the girl who worked in the greengrocer's down the road from where he grew up. She'd had a crush on him as well.

Fitz knew why their boss tolerated the rowdy Anthaurk, even though Il-Eruk's race, the Izrekt, had colonised Kaillor before the Anthaurk had claimed it for their own, even though the Anthaurk had slaughtered thousands of Izrekt and forced the refugees to live on Beatrix, Zolion or Yquatine: 'They're good for business. Think how much they've spent already, and it's early yet.'

'They're poor tippers, though,' said Val, taking a sip from a tall glass of something blue and strong. You weren't meant to drink on duty, but Fitz wasn't about to grass her up.

'True enough,' agreed Fitz.

Il-Eruk bustled in from the kitchens. The skin on his neck was taut and his eyes were gleaming. 'If they don't like it this time, then my patience is at an end.'

Fitz smiled and took the proffered dish, a lime-green fruity concoction. He'd noticed that the more agitated Il-Eruk was, the clearer and more precise his speech became.

He carried the dish over to the Anthaurk. There were about a dozen of them, their orange scales gleaming like jewels in the subdued lighting.

Fitz laid the dish down at the head of the table.

An angry hiss. 'You expect us to eat this?'

No, I want you to smear it over your knobbly reptile arses, Fitz felt like saying. He steepled his fingers and adopted tone of mild servile concern. 'What appears to be the problem, sir?'

The Anthaurk dipped a claw into the stuff, and tasted. He spat it out, all over Fitz's apron. Fitz clenched his teeth and counted to ten.

The Anthaurk stood up, swaying slightly. He was a good two feet taller than Fitz. His red eyes glowed. 'Your food is excrement, human. *You* are excrement!'

Fitz wasn't about to start a fight with a seven-foot drunken reptile. 'I'll get you another,' he said, turning away.

A claw snared the collar of his shirt and yanked him backwards. 'Hey!'

The Anthaurk grabbed Fitz by the lapels and hefted him off the ground. 'I insulted you, human. What are you going to do about it?'

'Akhhh,' gasped Fitz. The other Anthaurk had all risen, glowering, clawed fists bunched. The bouncers hadn't turned up tonight. He was on his own. He was paste.

'Put him down.'

The voice was female, and it came from behind him.

116

'Put him down,' it said again. And then it said something in a hissing, clicking alien tongue.

The drunken Anthaurk let Fitz go with a grunt. He dropped to the ground and crawled to the nearest chair.

Val appeared, all fluttering hands and shrill concern. 'Are you all right, love?'

Fitz looked up. The drunken Anthaurk was looming over a tall, slim woman in a purple tunic and black trousers. She was gabbling away in the creature's own language. As Fitz watched the Anthaurk raised its hands in a gesture of resignation and stomped back to his comrades.

The woman smiled, looking very pleased with herself, and came over to Fitz. Fitz blinked. She was incredibly attractive, and she walked with an economic, wiggle-free gait. Val muttered something beneath her breath, pouting with jealousy.

'Are you all right?' said his rescuer, raising perfectly sculpted eyebrows over big brown eyes. She had incredible hair, like honey and spun gold, which fell in tresses down her back. She brushed a strand away from her face and blinked at him.

Fitz knew he was grinning all over his face but he couldn't help it. Female beauty did strange things to him, especially when it was of this calibre. 'Well, I am now, baby!'

She rolled her eyes. 'Oh, please.'

'Sorry,' muttered Fitz, suddenly embarrassed. 'Still a bit shook up.'

The woman flashed a brief smile. 'That's all right.'

Val was staring over at the Anthaurk. 'Whatever did you say to them, love? They're all meek and mild now.'

Fitz straightened his collar. Much as he was enjoying having two women fussing over him, he wished Val would leave him alone with this gorgeous specimen. 'What *did* you say to them?'

She sat down on a chair next to Fitz. 'Oh, I just reminded them that twelve to one is hardly the sort of odds for honourable warriors.' She waved a pale, fine-boned hand. 'They're suckers for all that honour-and-glory stuff, even when drunk.'

'Well, I don't know how to thank you.' But he did. 'Val, be a star, bring us a bottle of Château Yquatine.'

Val narrowed her eyes towards Fitz and leaned in towards him. She smelled of gin and cheap perfume. 'I see your little game.'

'Oh, go on,' said Fitz through gritted teeth. Then he turned to his rescuer. 'Fine wine for –' He leaned towards her. 'What's your name?'

'Arielle.'

'For Arielle.' He knew he was deliberately winding Val up but she'd been getting a bit touchy-feely of late and this should put her in her place.

'All right. Seeing as you saved his scrawny neck and more importantly prevented any damage to the furniture, this is on the house.' Good job Il-Eruk was still working – or most probably sulking – in the kitchen. Val minced off, muttering under her breath, returning with a slender blue bottle with a thin neck and two glasses, which she plonked down on the table between them.

Fitz watched her go with some relief. Arielle had watched this little performance with detached amusement; her mind was clearly on other things.

Fitz poured the wine, enjoying the trickling glug of the dark ruby liquid. 'My name's Fitz Kreiner, intergalactic man of mystery currently down on his luck and working behind a bar.'

Arielle smiled distantly, sipping her wine. 'Arielle Markhof, first-year xenobiology student, currently sitting in a bar wondering what the hell to do with her life.'

This sounded extremely interesting. Fitz took a sip of wine, but then duty called – the Anthaurk started demanding more ale, with a perceptible degree of politeness. Within half an hour they upped and left for another bar, but more parties arrived and Fitz was kept busy, able to glance at Arielle only once in a while. She sat on her own, drinking from the bottle of Château Yquatine, avoiding the glances of the male customers. She looked as if she'd been stood up or chucked, but even in despondency her face was quite something. The angles of her cheekbones, the tilt of her nose, the refined pout of her lips, combined to stunning effect. If Fitz had been asked to design the perfect woman, Arielle would pretty much fit the bill. And there was something else: she carried her beauty casually, unadorned by make-up, uncaring of the loose strands of hair that fell over her face. Every now and then she'd toss her head so it all flew back into place. The way she did it was natural, without affectation, as though she had no idea how *damn sexy* she looked.

Val tried to take no notice of her, but Fitz could see a desperation in her eyes, a coldness towards him.

'Not jealous, are you, Val?' he joshed.

'She's young, she's beautiful, and you're already half in love with her.' She looked at him, her brazen manner abandoned, suddenly an ageing and lonely woman. 'Of course I'm jealous, you prat.'

Fitz smiled back at her. So often had he thought of her as a figure of fun, when he even thought of her at all. He whispered in her ear, 'I'll make it up to you.'

She put her hand on his shoulder. 'Promises, promises,' she said sadly, and went off to clean the ashtrays. She left shortly afterwards, claiming a bad head.

When things had quietened right down and looked like staying that way, Fitz went over to Arielle and sat down opposite her. He'd been thinking all evening of how to approach her and he'd decided the best angle was the friendly, sympathetic barman. 'You look like someone with something on their mind.'

She looked wary, as though she resented his intrusion. 'For all you know, I could be something with someone on my mind.'

Touché. 'So what's a nice girl like you doing in a place like this?' he said with a self-conscious swagger in his voice.

She ignored the cliché. 'Getting drunk to forget.' She waved a hand at him. 'You don't want to know.'

'I tried that once,' said Fitz, knowing it was more like every other night. 'Doesn't work.'

She sighed, and half sagged over the table. Her hair descended in a golden fall. 'I've just *got* to get off this planet.'

Fitz boggled. He felt like crying. So do I! Let's go, baby! But he managed to stop himself. 'Love affair gone wrong?'

She glared at him. 'Does it show?'

Fitz shrugged. 'Lucky guess.'

Arielle leaned back in her chair. Her movements were slow and leisurely with wine, her eyes seeing distance. 'Then yes, you're right, love affair gone wrong.' She frowned. '*He's* the problem. He's so bloody childish and clingy, he won't let go. Every time I go away he makes me feel guilty.'

Fitz couldn't blame him: who'd want to let a beauty like Arielle go? 'Why do you have to go away?'

'I would have thought that was obvious. I'm studying xenobiology. There are hundreds of races in the System, so…?

Fitz nodded quickly. 'Ah, I see.'

'He only likes me for the way I look, has no interest in my inner life, or the reason I came here in the first place. But the worst thing is, he's totally restricted my life on Yquatine. My friends are his friends. All the other students shun me because they think I'm having such a great time with Stefan.' She sighed, and held out her glass for more wine. 'All I do is study, and go to functions and visits with Stefan. I'm in the papers all the time. Can't go anywhere without some fly-camera zipping around me like a damn insect. This is one of my few places of refuge. Nobody here cares who I am.' She let out a sigh of exasperation and took a long glug of wine. She smiled at Fitz. 'Sorry. I tend to go on a bit after I've had a few.'

Fitz already hated this bloke. What right did he have to treat her this way? 'No problem,' he said. 'I've been through a few relationships in my time,' he added – to show his credentials. 'And I bloody hope I've treated my ladies better than that!'

She smiled at him. She actually smiled! 'I'm sure you have,' she murmured.

This was the green light for Fitz – or at least it had been, once. Now he wasn't so sure. He didn't particularly want to get involved. Not now, so soon after Filippa. But Arielle had said she wanted to leave Yquatine. And she was extremely attractive and friendly. 'You should chuck him,' he said casually, fiddling with the stem of his wineglass.

'Chuck him?' Arielle's eyes widened as though this was the first time she'd entertained the idea.

'Yeah!' said Fitz, mustering all his self-righteousness. 'I wouldn't stand for being treated the way he treats you.'

Arielle's face had darkened. 'Do you know who he is?'

Fitz shook his head.

Arielle leaned conspiratorially towards Fitz. 'Stefan Vargeld.'

The name was obviously meant to mean something. Was it some Yquatine pop star? 'Who is...?'

Arielle looked insulted. 'Oh, come on!'

Fitz ran his hands through his hair. 'Look, OK, but I've only been here for a week.'

She banged the table with the side of her hand. '*Everyone's* heard of him!'

'I'm from outside the System,' wailed Fitz.

Arielle rolled her eyes, a gesture Fitz was beginning to recognise as characteristic. She spoke in a slow, duh-duh voice. 'He's the Pre-si-dent of the Min-er-va Sys-tem.'

Politics had never been his strong point. 'Oh. Blimey. Well I hope he treats his constituency better than his woman.'

'I'm not "his" woman,' said Arielle irritably. 'And, oh yes, he's very good at his job. Very popular. Slick Stefan.'

'It doesn't matter who he is, he can't treat you that way.'

She banged the table again. 'I know!'

Il-Eruk began calling from the kitchens.

Arielle gestured towards the bar. 'Duty calls.'

Damn! He leaned towards Arielle. 'Anyway, you gonna take my advice? Get shot of the Pres?'

Arielle frowned. 'I dunno. It's late and I've had quite a bit to drink.' She stood up, pushing her chair under the tabletop.

'Fit!' came a rasping voice from the bar.

'Coming!' yelled Fitz, following Arielle to the door. 'Come here again tomorrow night. Drinks on the house,' he whispered, glancing over his shoulder. 'Let me know how you get on.'

She eyed him appraisingly from beneath a raised eyebrow. 'I might take you up on that.'

With that she pushed through the clattering doorway and into the rickety wooden corridors of Pierhaven.

Fitz watched her go, wondering if he should have offered to walk her home, wondering if he would ever see her again.

He did see her again. The very next night. She came in very late, wearing a figure-hugging red dress, and a frown the size of Scotland. By the way she floated up to the bar Fitz could tell she was the worse for drink.

'How did it go?' he asked gently.

Arielle's beautiful face bunched up, reddened, and she shouted a word that silenced the bar and made Fitz gasp in horror.

He wordlessly poured her a glass of whisky. She downed it in one go. Then she burst into tears.

All the customers had turned to look at her.

Fitz turned to Val, whose face suggested she had just popped the sourest boiled sweet in the universe into her mouth. 'So, yer girlfriend's back,' she growled.

'Val, take over for a sec. I need to speak to her.' Fitz turned away before Val could protest, and, taking the bottle of whisky, ushered the compliant, weeping Arielle to a private booth on the far side of the bar.

She sat opposite him, shoulders slumped, face wet with tears. Fitz wanted to reach over and hug her. Crying women always made him feel guilty and upset as though somewhere down the line it was all his fault.

Clearly not so, in this case.

Fitz hated this President guy for bringing her to this state. He'd seen him on the news earlier that evening. He looked a right smarmy git. He guessed Arielle didn't want to know his opinion of her lover, but instead needed cheering up. 'Good swear back there,' he said.

Her brown eyes flicked up at him, and down. There was the briefest of smiles.

Fitz began to feel uncomfortable. Should he tell her how great she looked in that dress? He remembered her litany of hate. 'He only likes me for the way I look.' Probably not. He settled for an uninspired, 'What happened?'

She spoke, not looking up at him. 'He took me out for a meal. Well, not out. At the bloody palace. He bloody proposed to me.'

Silence. The whole world seemed to recede to just him, the woman in the red dress, the whisky on the table and the blue-green curtains of the alcove. 'Go on,' prompted Fitz.

'I turned him down. And I told him I never wanted to see him again.'

'How… how did he take it?'

She looked up at him then. Her eyes were like two golden jewels, bright, unattainable. 'He went mad. Violent. He scared me.'

Her hands reached out across the table. Fitz took them. He noticed a bruise starting to bloom on her forearm, the imprint of gripping fingers clearly visible.

He quickly looked up at her. Through choking sobs, she was saying something Fitz couldn't quite make out.

'What? What is it?'

She let go of his hands, wiped the tears away from her eyes. 'I did it. I'm free of him! Free of him.'

Fitz felt shell-shocked. He'd never had someone take his advice with such devastating effect.

She didn't want to go back to her rooms at the university that night, in case the President tried to contact her, so she slept in Fitz's room. Fitz slept in the kitchen, in the baleful presence of the dishwasher, the oven and the refrigerator.

The next day, Fitz got the morning off to help Arielle sort out her life. They left the tavern early and breakfasted together in the town. It was a bright, clear Jaquaia day, and Yendip was as serene and beautiful as ever.

Arielle didn't speak much over breakfast. She asked Fitz about his life, and he spun some tale about coming to Yquatine to find his fortune, and ending up working in Il-Eruk's Tavern. She accepted what he said without further questions.

After breakfast, as they walked along the esplanade, Arielle came to a decision.

'I'm leaving Yquatine,' she said as she gazed out at the wide green ocean. 'Today. Within the hour.'

Fitz stood beside her, trying to act casual, unconcerned, while his guts knotted and his heart pounded.

Now was his chance. He had to go with her. But how? What could he say? Could he tell her about the coming darkness?

She knew the President. She might have some sense of duty left, although she didn't love the man. She'd want to warn him, if only for the sake of everyone else on Yquatine. Fitz felt the colour drain from his face. Couldn't he warn the authorities? Let them deal with it? Pass on the responsibility? He was tempted, for just a moment, but then his doubts returned, headed up by the biggest and blackest of them all: *what if the mere act of warning the authorities was the trigger that set events rolling towards the future he'd seen?*

No. He couldn't. He had to think of something else. But his brain refused to help.

Something tickled his fingers, and he looked down with surprise to see Arielle's hand, finding his. He looked at her. Her face had a tight, concentrated look of worry. 'Fitz, all I have is the clothes I stand up in, and my credit card. I've packed some cases, they're back in my rooms. I can't go back there: I know Stefan, he'll have his people out looking for me.' She glanced over her shoulder, but the coast was apparently clear. Her hand squeezed his. 'I'm going to ask you something important. Can I trust you?'

Fitz nodded. 'Yeah. Yes, you can.'

Her eyes took on a veiled, distant look. 'You're not doing this just because you fancy me? Because if you are, then I'll do it on my own.'

'No, no, Arielle. I want to help.' Curse it! Why did his voice sound so insincere?

'And I also want you to come with me, away from Yquatine. Help me get away.'

Fitz almost laughed aloud. 'OK, I will.'

She shook her head. 'But your job...'

Fitz grabbed her shoulders. 'Oh, balls to that! Look, I'll go and get your things, square it with Il-Eruk, and meet you in Founders' Square in an hour.' Now that he was actually going to get off the planet, he couldn't wait.

She looked surprised but pleased. 'OK.' She handed over a plastic card. 'The key to my room. There's a case on my bed. It's all I need. Grab it and get out.'

Fitz took the key. 'I'll be as quick as I can.' He tried to look trustful and dependable as he walked away. He waved at her until he couldn't see her red dress through the crowds any more.

Fitz picked up Arielle's case without incident. There was no one watching her rooms – the only people around were a gaggle of young female students. Fitz did not allow them to distract him.

He'd used a hover-taxi to get up to the university, which was some distance from the town. And from the university to Il-Eruk's Tavern, where he'd gathered all his money and possessions, and stole away with a gutful of guilt. He'd got the rest of the day off, after some argy-bargy with Il-Eruk. Zabulong would have to cope behind the bar; Fitz had pitched it as a learning experience for the lightbulb-headed alien.

Fitz had no intention of returning. He would never see Il-Eruk again. He would never throw his arms up in exasperation over Zabulong's incompetence again. He would never feel Val's sly hand on his arse again. All three would die in the coming invasion. These were the facts Fitz carried away with him as the hover-taxi whisked him towards Founders' Square. Why couldn't he have warned them about the invasion? It was cutting him up inside. He swore that he was through with time travel. After this escapade it was all going be strictly linear for Fitz Kreiner.

And anyway, Arielle may not be there. She may have decided not to trust him. He could hardly blame her: they'd only just met. She may have left Yquatine on her own, or even reconciled things with the President. Then he would have to go back to the tavern. He may still be on Yquatine when the balloon went up.

And, more immediately, he may be stuck with a colossal cab fare.

But Arielle was there, and she looked worried. She ran up to Fitz and actually hugged him.

'I thought I'd made the stupidest mistake of my life, trusting you,' she murmured into his shoulder.

He laughed. 'Well, thanks!'

She kissed him. On the cheek, but it still made him go weak at the knees. 'You've just restored my faith in human nature.'

Fitz muttered something about paying off the hover-taxi but Arielle shook her head. 'We're going to need that to get us to the spaceport.'

Fitz nodded dumbly. So this was it. He was leaving Yquatine.

With the President's girlfriend.

They boarded the taxi and were whisked off to Yendip Spaceport, where the space cruiser *St Julian* awaited them in all its ceramic and chrome majesty.

Chapter Eleven
'I don't know if I believe you'

President Stefan Vargeld stumbled down the short corridor from the cockpit to the airlock, clamping on the helmet of his suit. The padded shoulders bounced off the instrument-lined walls. Hands trembling, he spun the airlock release valve. The inner door opened with an efficient sigh and he slipped through before it was fully ajar. He hesitated before punching in the code that opened the outer door, but only for a moment. The Doctor was in trouble and needed his help.

The outer door hissed open, retracting smoothly into the hull. Framed in the doorway was the Doctor, prone on the rocky ground a few metres from the ship. All around him was a wall of black cloud that looked ready to crash down in an instant. Again, the President hesitated. He was feeling weak and light-headed, and his limbs felt heavy and tired. Must be the medication wearing off. Legs shaking, he ran to the Doctor and hefted him up with ease in the low gravity. He carried the Doctor back towards the ship and through the airlock in one rush of movement, which made his chest heave and his breath mist the faceplate of his helmet. He unlocked the helmet, let it bounce to the floor, and half carried, half dragged the Doctor to the cockpit, where he let him slump in the copilot's seat.

No time to examine him. President Vargeld hit the switch that brought the fields on line and initiated the take-off sequence. Soon they were zooming up through the dense, dark, unnatural atmosphere of Muath. The shields were holding, but only just. The President concentrated on keeping the ship going, trying not to think of Arielle, smothered and corroded by the black gas.

Soon the ship was free of the black substance and soaring out into space. He looked over at the Doctor. He seemed to be sleeping peacefully. A sense of relief surged through President Vargeld's body, followed by a crushing wave of tiredness and grief. He had just seen Arielle's tomb, the rocky moon of Muath wrapped in its cocoon of foul, choking gas.

President Vargeld leaned back in his seat, setting a course for Aloysius Station.

A few hours later, President Vargeld stood in the sickbay, looking down at the figure of the Doctor. He lay under a single white sheet, monitoring equipment pulsing at the head of the bed.

It was his fault that this man now lay in a coma, hovering just this side of oblivion. His madcap mission to Muath had endangered his life. He'd been a fool to think that Arielle could survive that stuff, whatever it was.

A medical orderly trod softly up. 'Mr President?'

President Vargeld turned round. 'Yes?'

'They're waiting.'

The President groaned. A Senate meeting had been convened on his return to Aloysius. It was the last thing he wanted. But he had no choice. Presidential responsibility was challenging, rewarding, even fun, in times of peace, but in wartime it frightened him.

He looked back at the Doctor. His face was so serene, picked out in the soft blue lights of the sickbay. He looked like a poet or an artist, and his clothes – they looked like something a Luvian would wear, something from Earth's distant past. Not for the first time, President Vargeld wondered who the hell he was. Now his mind was free of the effects of the medication, he could think rationally once more. Where had this Doctor come from? Who was he?

And what had he seen on Muath?

Something that proved Anthaurk culpability, he hoped.

'Well, you won't be telling anyone your secrets for a while,' whispered the President sadly. Then he turned and accompanied the orderly out of the sickbay.

* * *

On the bed, the Doctor's eyes opened.

They were shining, jet-black.

Then they closed again.

President Vargeld let the accusations and counteraccusations fly like arrowheads across the makeshift Senate chamber. He just stood there, taking his example from Senator Rhombus-Alpha, whose glowing form rotated slowly at the back of the room. It was fortunate that all but one of the Senate had survived. All had been en route to their homeworlds at the time of the attack. All but Senator Arthwell, who had remained on Yquatine, opting to communicate with her homeworld from the palace.

He heard Senator Fandel call out that the Anthaurk must have developed a superweapon. He heard Senator Krukon demand to know what had happened to the Anthaurk ships that had gone down to Yquatine earlier that day.

It was still Treaty Day, the President realised. It was very late, barely an hour left, but for that hour it would still be Treaty Day. He almost felt like laughing. What use the Treaty of Yquatine now, when where was no Yquatine? What use this bunch of squabbling senators? With Yquatine gone there was a hole at the centre of the Minerva System, and it would be some time before the shock hit home, and some considerable time before they could all work out what to do. Right now he knew that the best thing for them to do was go away, contemplate, wait for the realisation to hit home.

At length, he decided enough was enough. He was tired, it had been a long day, he wanted to get to his quarters and sleep. He clapped his hands for silence. 'Gentlemen, gentlemen!' The senators all grew silent. 'As you all know, I have returned from an expedition to Muath.'

'Ah, yes,' hissed Zendaak, mouth curving in a sly smile. 'Your unauthorised, secret mission –'

'I am the President,' he cut in. 'For me, there is no such thing as unauthorised!'

Zendaak continued unabated. 'And who is this mysterious

"Doctor" who accompanied you?'

President Vargeld met his scarlet stare unflinchingly. 'What's happened to the ships, Zendaak? The battleships you've sent down to Yquatine? How many was it – six? That's a lot of Anthaurk lives.'

Zendaak's face fell, and he turned his head down to look at his claws clasped in his lap. His voice was sepulchral. 'We lost contact with them two hours ago. None have returned.'

That meant nothing. They could be down there, establishing a base, preparing defences, anything. 'That's what you say, Zendaak. To be honest, I don't know if I believe you.'

Senator Krukon's voice rumbled out over the assembled Senators. 'I say this is an Anthaurk ploy!' The Ogri beside him glowed belligerently.

'As do I!' yelled Fandel. 'Those ships are still down there.'

Senator Tibis roared.

They all started shouting again.

President Vargeld rubbed his itchy, tired eyes. 'And on it goes,' he mumbled to himself.

He only hoped the Doctor would come out of his coma soon. Maybe he had all the answers.

Chapter Twelve
'We have reached a turning point in our great history'

A month before the fall of Yquatine, the Grand Gynarch was looking out over her still relatively new world. New Anthaur was a planet of hot sand and stone cities. A world of ochre and yellow and orange, of dust storms, of an intricate and efficient irrigation system, of towering gnarled totems to the six hundred Anthaurk deities. Home to two million Anthaurk, the descendants of the survivors of the Dalek attack on the Anthaur homeworld over a century ago, testament to a rigorous and intensive breeding programme.

The Grand Gynarch often feared the return of those screeching metal carapaces. Their harsh yells still haunted her dreams. She had been very young during the Dalek war, and though she hadn't seen any of the creatures at first hand she'd heard their voices, screaming in insane rage and frustration as her mother's craft made good its escape. It was the first thing in her life she could remember. Later, when she was older, she'd studied the images taken by assault craft, and found that the Daleks looked comical, hardly able to pose such a potent threat. She had been almost disappointed. But then she'd spoken to the survivors of the Dalek attack on Anthaur, heard their whispering voices, fragile with fear. That fear had found its way into her heart, too, and its voice was that of a screeching machine.

The Grand Gynarch shook her head, trying to rid herself of such thoughts. She stood, clutching her blackwood staff, on the tallest tower of the Imperial Citadel. The single sun – she could never get used to that – was low in the sky. It was soon time for the Inner Circle. It was important, this one. She was going to make a pronouncement that would change history.

She gazed over at the pyramidal cities on the horizon. They

matched almost perfectly the holograms she'd seen of Old Anthaur. Her people had striven for a century to make this world like their old one.

The Grand Gynarch, oldest of the Anthaurk and bearer of some three thousand children, had been a mere hatchling when she first came to this world. She had no memories of the brief but bloody war with the humans, of the signing of the Treaty of Yquatine. She knew only of the century of planning and construction. She had personally overseen the construction of the Imperial Citadel, laid the first and last stones herself. You would have thought such a leader would have abandoned thoughts of war, become reconciled to living in peace with the other species in the Minerva System.

But the Grand Gynarch possessed something other than memory. Something stronger, more permanent. She possessed the bloodline of the Gynarchs, which stretched back for millennia, back into the murky history of the Anthaurk homeworld. She possessed the beliefs and the attitudes of thousands of Grand Gynarchs before her. Anthaurk supremacy, over all. Nontolerance of other races. Even the Daleks, the living embodiment of such a creed, hadn't weakened this resolve. On the contrary, the Anthaurk defeat had strengthened their determination to conquer all. For the Grand Gynarch, when she was young and learning about her race's history, had found out that the Daleks weren't mechanical creatures as she had first thought. There had been something organic inside those screeching carapaces. They had once been humans. Just like the settlers of Yquatine.

To her mind, that meant that the noble Anthaurk race had been beaten twice by different evolutionary stages of the same species.

Knowing this, she would never have signed any treaty with the humans. But she had been so young. Her mother, the previous Grand Gynarch, had signed the cursed Treaty of Yquatine, knowing full well that it was an act of betrayal, but having no choice in defeat. After the signing, her mother had ritually sacrificed herself to Hiss'aa, Goddess of War and Venom. And thus the current Grand Gynarch, red eyes blinking, young scales shining in the hot sun, had been thrust into the limelight.

And then had begun the Century of Waiting.

Now it was almost at an end.

The sun sent a shaft of light through the jewel embedded in the end of her blackwood staff. The light diffused, spreading out around the Grand Gynarch like a robe of beaten gold.

It was time for the Inner Circle to convene.

The Inner Chamber was a crude bowl cut into the side of a mountain, open to the sky, rough seats carved into the crumbling sides. It was meant to represent the volcano from which the first of the Gynarchs had crawled, spitting and hissing, only to be half blinded by the twin suns of Old Anthaur. The recreation wasn't perfect: New Anthaur had only one sun, but there was little that could be done about that.

The Grand Gynarch stood, as custom dictated, right at the bottom of the bowl. This may seem demeaning, but the Inner Chamber was constructed to funnel sound down towards the bottom, so the Grand Gynarch could hear and see all.

She thumped her staff on the stone plinth on which she stood, and spoke, head raised, gazing at the three hundred members of the Inner Circle. 'We have reached a turning point in our great history,' she said. 'Certain events are coming to pass which will force us to act – force us to imprint our will upon this System!'

Cries and hisses of assent.

She gestured to her right, where Zendaak sat. Young Zendaak, member of the Minerva Senate, her eyes and ears. He possessed almost as much zeal as she. 'Zendaak brings news of the latest heresy the Senate wish to force upon us.'

Zendaak stood up, his arms akimbo, his chest puffed out. 'People of New Anthaur! I have recently attended a Senate meeting during which the matter of overcrowding was discussed. Apparently, this System is such an attractive, desirable place that hundreds of beings of all species are descending upon it. During the last hundred years, we have seen the arrival of the Adamanteans, the Ixtricite and, most of all, more and more humans.'

Three hundred Anthaurk hissed in sibilant hatred. The Grand Gynarch bared her teeth. She'd taught them well.

Zendaak continued. 'The other races have bred and spread throughout the System, so that now there is little room for any more.'

'Tell them what the Senate propose, Zendaak!' cried the Grand Gynarch.

A silence descended on the Inner Chamber. Zendaak's voice was a tight, concentrated hiss of hatred. 'They propose that we give up our sacred lands for colonisation.' Silence. 'They say that we have space enough for millions of others. This is directly against the treaty we signed a hundred years ago!'

The Grand Gynarch was pleased. Although hated, the Treaty of Yquatine had at last tripped up the humans. One of its clauses guaranteed autonomy for each planet in the System, and noninterference by the Senate. Except in an emergency. Well, to the Grand Gynarch, there were other ways of dealing with overpopulation. Mass exterminations, sterilisation, exile. Zendaak had proposed all these, but the faint-hearted Senate had voted unanimously against him.

The Inner Chamber erupted in calls for action. The Grand Gynarch let them have their shout. Then she thumped her staff three times, and silence descended. 'At last, we have a reason to commence hostilities.'

Zendaak raised his fists in the air. 'War!' he cried. The Inner Circle took up his cry.

The Grand Gynarch thumped her staff again. 'People! We must be cunning. We must be seen to be the injured party in this. We must use the treaty as a weapon against the Senate. We will start by attacking the trade routes, goading the Senate into action against us. And, when they do, we can attack in full. After decades of preparation, our battle fleet is ready.'

Three hundred pairs of red eyes stared down at her.

'We attack on Treaty Day.'

Thunderous applause.

As it tailed away, a lone voice spoke out. 'I do not think we should. We should try to live in peace.'

The Grand Gynarch swung round, locating the speaker.

A female Anthaurk three rows back had stood.

'Who speaks?'

'My name is M'Pash, Grand Gynarch.'

The name was not familiar. The Grand Gynarch stepped down from her plinth, hobbled towards the dissenter, ignoring the knifing pain in her hips. 'You say we should live in peace?'

'This is heresy!' cried Zendaak.

The Grand Gynarch held up her hand for silence. 'Let M'Pash speak. I need to know how an Anthaurk of the Inner Circle could arrive at such a decision.'

If M'Pash felt intimidated, she didn't show it. 'It is for the best. A hundred years ago, we had no choice but to surrender to the humans. We were few, our ships in bad repair.'

'And now we are many, with the finest fleet in the System,' put in Zendaak.

'True,' said M'Pash, nodding. 'But consider: we would not only have to stand against the humans, but the Adamanteans, the Kukutsi, the Rorclaavix, the Eldrig – the combined might of the Minerva Space Alliance. Need I go on?'

'We have developed weapons,' said the Grand Gynarch. 'Weapons of mass destruction.'

'And so have the others.'

'Ours are superior!' cried Zendaak, showing admirable faith in Anthaurk technology.

'Even if they are, we would still lose.' A pleading tone had entered M'Pash's voice. 'Even if we strike first, and hard, on Yquatine, with our most terrible weapons – weapons which rain instant death from the skies – we will suffer terrible retribution.'

The Grand Gynarch had heard enough. This was dangerous talk.

'You misunderstand, M'Pash. It does not matter if we lose. We cannot continue with this compromised existence. War is a way of life for the Anthaurk, as you should well know.'

'Then it is the wrong way of life!'

The Grand Gynarch felt her bloodlust stirring, heard the spirits of her ancestors hissing in her ears. This M'Pash must be silenced, lest she infect the Inner Circle with her heresy. 'Take her away!'

Guards broke formation at the arched entrance to the Inner Chamber and moved towards M'Pash. She just stood there, arms by her sides, staring at the Grand Gynarch. She allowed the guards to take her down the stone steps, out and away. The Grand Gynarch looked forward to blinding and torturing her later. But she would have to defer that pleasure. There was a war to plan.

M'Pash let herself be manhandled along the stone corridors of the Anthaurk citadel. There were no windows; flaming torches were driven into the sandstone walls at intervals, casting shadows like bats' wings. Presently they came to an archway which led on to a long, narrow walkway high above the ground. At the other end of this was an ugly grey tower, rearing up from the ground like an excrescence from deep within the planet.

The top of the walkway was covered in grit and dust, which M'Pash's booted feet ground and crunched, and a low parapet ran along each side. She couldn't take her eyes from the tower. She knew full well what it was, though even a visitor to New Anthaur (not that the Anthaurk ever allowed any) would be able to discern its purpose from its appearance. Its rough grey stone walls, slitlike windows like wounds, the smell of despair wafting across the walkway all told M'Pash that, once through inside that grey tower, she'd never be coming out again, not alive anyway.

She couldn't allow that.

So she spun round, hands outstretched. 'Stop.'

Such was the command in her voice that her escorts actually obeyed, their tall figures framed against the pale yellow sky.

Then they snarled and levelled their guns at her head.

M'Pash stepped back nimbly. 'I wouldn't be too hasty: the Grand Gynarch wants me alive for interrogation.' She looked over the edge of the walkway, the blocks and pyramids of Anthaurk citadel spread out like a map below. It was a very long way down. 'She won't be too pleased if one of you kills me.'

They weren't impressed by this tactic, judging by the angry impatience in their red eyes. 'Move, dissident!'

'Very well.' M'Pash started back towards the tower. They were almost halfway across the walkway by now. Her mind was furiously calculating distances and rates of acceleration, her body was tensing, knotting itself up in preparation.

The only sounds were the crunch, crunch, crunch of booted feet and the low moaning of the wind.

Then M'Pash made a decision, and relaxed.

Before her guards could react, she dashed to the side of the walkway and threw herself over the parapet.

Chapter Thirteen
'This isn't the way I was made'

Fitz couldn't take his eyes away from Yquatine. It was beautiful, a blue-green pearl laid on the black velvet of space. That and a thousand other clichés crowded his mind, but none of them could do justice to the spectacle. He took a good long look. It was probably the last time he'd see it, before... before... He rubbed his eyes, and groaned. Fatigue had joined forces with his permanent sense of crushing guilt and he badly wanted to sleep. He hated himself for running away. Oh yes, cowardly, craven Fitz, doing what cowardly, craven Fitz is best at. He was safe, but Il-Eruk, Val, Zabulong, probably even the Doctor, were all doomed. And, beyond them, millions of others he had never met, never would meet. A planet full of teeming life. Gone. How could he cope with such foreknowledge?

Arielle came to stand by him. 'You're looking very nostalgic for a place you've only known for a week.'

Fitz could hardly bring himself to speak. 'Yeah, well. It's a nice place,' he sighed lamely.

She looked out of the viewport at the receding planet. 'I'm just glad to be away.'

She'd changed out of her red dress, and was now wearing a practical costume of dull green trousers with lots of pockets, boots, and a shapeless grey tunic. Even in that, she was still drop-dead-and-come-back-as-a-zombie gorgeous. She'd tied her hair so that it hung in a long ponytail down her back. Now she was away from Yquatine she seemed more relaxed, but there was a resolute set to her mouth, a worried frown around her eyes, and she kept glancing nervously around, as if she expected Presidential aides or even the President himself to appear.

Fitz's stomach rumbled. Food was probably a good idea. It might even make him feel better about himself. 'Let's get something to eat.'

Arielle nodded her consent and they made their way to the restaurant.

The *St Julian* reminded Fitz of an ocean liner: it had similar levels of comfort and décor, airy lounges with space vistas, sumptuous rooms, bars, restaurants, swimming pools. Loafer's heaven. Arielle had no immediate plans other than escape from her former lover. The *St Julian* was heading for Luvia, Zolion and Oomingmak, a tour of the pleasure spots of the System. Fitz had no immediate plans at all, but that was nothing new. He was just glad to be away, and with Arielle.

Things were a lot easier when you were in the company of a gobsmackingly beautiful woman. The crew treated Arielle with deference, even servility. Fitz couldn't help thinking that if he was on his own he wouldn't have been able to swing the luxury cabins they'd obtained. Right in the nose cone of the ship, as far forward as you could get.

The restaurant was all trellised archways, parasols, fountains, plants, soft music and android waiters in white tuxedos. Fitz couldn't work out if it was sincere or a pastiche. Some sort of surround-3-D effect turned the ceiling and walls into a summer sky, complete with little fluffy clouds. As Fitz sat opposite Arielle at one of the less conspicuous tables, he began to relax. And with food inside him, he began to feel a lot better.

He was just turning his mind to planning what to do next when Arielle said, 'Do you find me beautiful?'

She said it as though she was referring to something other than herself, such as a painting or a piece of music.

'Um,' said Fitz, trying to work out what she wanted him to say. He gave up on that and told her the truth. 'Yes. You are quite fantastically attractive.'

She rolled her eyes and sighed. 'Everybody does. Everybody human, anyway. That's the problem. It's not me.'

This sounded terribly precious to Fitz. With all the suffering in the universe, were her looks all she was worried about? 'We can't help the way we were made, baby.'

She gave him a direct, intense look. 'That's the point. This isn't the way I was made.'

Oh, God, did she use to be a man – or worse? 'What do you mean?'

She took out her wallet and slid something across the tabletop towards him. He picked it up and looked at it. It was a photo of a girl in her mid-teens. She had a rather gawky face with masses of brown hair, a large nose and a lopsided smile. Not exactly ugly, not exactly pretty. The sort of girl who could possibly grow into an attractive woman, but the bets were off. She was looking past the camera at something, head half turned, there was a wall behind her, out of focus, festooned with pictures or posters.

Why was she showing him this? Who was this? Her sister?

Then Fitz realised. He looked from Arielle to the picture and back again. 'It's you,' he whispered.

His heart seemed to sink to his boots. He could see the ghost of the girl in the photo in Arielle's face, in her eyes. He tried to speak, but he couldn't say a word.

She took the picture from his hands and slipped it away. Her eyes had grown distant, as though she was sitting alone. 'Yes,' she said, in a small voice. 'The old me. The real me.'

'You look… so different.'

She was staring at him, her eyes wide, intense. 'I don't know how I'd look now if it wasn't for the surgery.'

His hand found hers. He hated hospitals, and the word 'surgery' set his teeth on edge. He wasn't sure he wanted to hear what she had so say. 'What… what was wrong with you?'

'Nothing,' said Arielle. 'I was totally healthy in mind and body. Trouble was, I was ugly. Gawky. Big nose, uneven teeth, stubby little fingers.' She let go of Fitz's hand, splayed her long, well-manicured fingers out on the table. 'That all changed because of my mother.'

Realisation dawned on Fitz. 'She made you have cosmetic surgery?'

Arielle nodded. 'Facial reconstruction, skin grafts, limb lengthening – the best biomedics money could buy.'

'Why?'

'My parents are rich.' She said it like a confession. 'Father owns Markhof Mining Corporation; Mother is big in the media. Image is all important. I was a disappointment to Mother and like a fool I eventually gave in to her pestering. She kept on that I didn't have to be ugly, that I could be beautiful.'

'Why did you agree? It's what's inside that counts – I know it sounds trite, but it's true.'

'I know that now,' whispered Arielle. 'I was fourteen. I was too meek and mild to be rebellious and I wanted to please Mother. Now look at me.'

Fitz looked at her. He couldn't help wondering what Arielle would have looked like had nature been allowed to take its course. 'Are you happy?'

The question seemed to surprise her. 'Yes, I suppose I am. Despite all this crap with Stefan, I don't want for anything. Why, are you happy?'

Fitz grinned. Happiness was a state of mind that mystified him. Besides which, blind, accepting, conforming happiness didn't suit him. Pessimistic, questioning cynicism was more his style. 'Ecstatic,' he drawled.

Arielle's look grew distant. 'I often wonder what happened to the old Arielle. When I found out that beauty equals power, I turned into a right bitch.' She smiled and squeezed his hand. 'Don't worry, I've adjusted now. Once I got used to the way I looked I decided I wanted to learn more about appearances, how the way you look determines how others think of you, how they treat you. And so I began to research alien species, and human reactions towards them. Ever heard of Professor Hamilton Smith?'

Fitz shrugged. 'No.'

'He was a brilliant man. Published the definitive work on alien–human interaction, centuries ago. It was reading him that made me want to study xenobiology. And so that's why I'm here.'

She frowned, obviously realising where she actually was. 'Or, rather, that's why I went to Yquatine.'

Her life story made sense. Fitz almost envied her.

'There's more to it than that.' She took a sip of wine. 'I thought that if I was among aliens my attractiveness wouldn't matter. I'd be free to study, without worrying how others saw me.'

Fitz nodded. Logical enough – although Fitz found her irresistible, the Adamanteans, Eldrig, Kukutsi and all the others wouldn't pay her a blind bit of notice. 'Of course, not every human male would find you attractive.'

She glared at him. 'I wish. When they designed my face they used computer modelling, based on decades of surveys on beauty and attractiveness. Unfortunately I have the sort of face men usually only see in their dreams.'

From anyone else, this would have sounded like an arrogant boast, but from Arielle it sounded like a complaint.

Arielle was still caught up in her story. 'And what did I do? On my first day here, I met and fell in love with Stefan. Big mistake.'

'In love?' Fitz didn't believe in love at first sight. 'How did you know?'

'It was like a bolt out of the blue – biggest cliché there is, but that's how it felt. It was as if I came here to find him. He completed me... and so on and so on.' She grimaced. 'Now I know it wasn't love, just infatuation. My first time away from home, the wine, the starry night...' She waved a hand. 'I'll not fall for that again.'

She raised her glass and they made a toast to not falling in love at first sight.

What Arielle had told Fitz explained so much about her – the way she carried herself wasn't how beautiful women usually carried themselves, with a knowing, superior air. Arielle was completely natural and unselfconscious. And Fitz was becoming more and more self-conscious with every passing second – watching the way he ate, the way he drank, desperately trying not to fall in love with this woman.

142

Finally, in desperation, he said, 'How are the studies going?'

She pouted. 'Rotten. I'm completing my assignments but I'm not really getting anywhere. Not much to show for almost a year's work.' She sighed. 'Perhaps my destiny doesn't lie on Yquatine.'

Fitz shivered. The only destiny awaiting anyone on that planet was death. 'What do you plan to do now?'

Arielle shrugged. 'I dunno. Could go to Zolion, stay at the university there for a few months. As long as I'm away from Stefan.'

'A man obsessed only with your beauty,' said Fitz.

She looked at him critically. 'How about you? D'you think you could fall in love with me, the real me? I'm bossy. I'm moody. I act a bit superior. But I'm more real than I appear.'

Fitz found himself actually blushing. Fall in love? No! It was the last thing he wanted to do. 'What about our toast?'

She took a long sip of wine. 'That was against love at first sight. The first time I saw you, you were being throttled by an Anthaurk. All I felt for you then was pity.'

He couldn't take his eyes off her, couldn't work out where she was coming from. 'And now?' he said hoarsely.

She flicked a strand of hair away from her face. 'I don't know.'

Bloody typical, thought Fitz, confusion settling on his mind. The first time he'd clapped eyes on Arielle it had certainly been lust at first sight. Oh, crikey. 'Well, I don't know, either,' he babbled. 'I mean, I don't know you, you don't know me.' He paused, thinking back on his travels. 'I mean, I don't even know me...'

Then he thought about Filippa.

He smiled at Arielle. She smiled back at him. 'More wine?' he said.

Compassion, still in her Anthaurk guise, fell towards the ground, completely calm and collected as the planet hurtled towards her. Everything seemed in slo-mo, which was nice. It allowed her to focus her Artron energy, prepare for dematerialisation. The moment she'd leapt, she had reverted to her default appearance with some relief. Looking like other things unsettled her, made

143

her doubt who she was. She only hoped her chameleon circuit didn't get stuck like the Doctor's old TARDIS. The prospect of looking like an Anthaurk for the rest of her existence didn't bear thinking about and anyway she didn't have time because here came the ground.

As the wind tore through her flapping coat, she marshalled her energies for dematerialisation.

But something was happening. Connections were being made, sinking deep into her command circuits.

She had managed to reach New Anthaur with great difficulty: the Randomiser had tried to drag her away into the spiralling whorls of the vortex. She'd fought it, and won – just – but it had skipped her eight days into the future, like a pebble skimming across a lake.

But the Randomiser was fully connected now. She wouldn't be able to dematerialise without it dragging her away to anywhere, anywhen, with no guarantee of ever getting back here and finishing her tampering – or of seeing the Doctor and Fitz again.

The ground filled her vision.

Would she die if she hit? She remembered the Doctor's old TARDIS. That was meant to be indestructible. And it had been totally destroyed.

Then she began to panic, began to scream in anger and fear.

She had no choice.

A second from impact, Compassion focused her energies, engaged her dematerialisation circuits, pulsed pure Artron energy through her time rotor, and the Randomiser took her screaming into the vortex.

Interlude 1
Cloudbusting

The black cloud was very old and had travelled immeasurable distances, but it hadn't lost sight of its objective. It knew what it had to do. It knew little else. Each one of the particles in its enormous, moon-sized volume vibrated with the purpose its Masters had programmed into it. Some particles were there to shield from any type of radiation the spores that the cloud harboured in its dense central mass. Others were there to ensure the cloud remained undetected by even the most advanced of technologies, or to maintain the jet-black coloration of the particles, which absorbed light and emitted nothing. Others were there to catch the solar winds from the suns of the systems the cloud passed through, sailing it through the starless chasms between them. Others were there to reach out into space, to scan for radio emissions, certain types of radiation, the presence of life.

When it had entered this particular system, the scanning particles had almost overloaded with information. There was so much life here that the cloud – or rather those particles within it that performed the function of mind – didn't know where to go first. It hung there, invisible in space, overwhelmed. It had eventually decided to set off in a more or less random direction towards the centre of the system. It was bound to bump into something sooner or later. There was no hurry: it had waited for millions of years already and a little longer wouldn't hurt. Besides which, the fulfilment of its objective would mean the end of its cloud-based existence, and, over the countless years, it had perhaps come to develop particles that enjoyed this state of being.

And so it drifted slowly on towards the centre of the system, its movements leisurely, invisible, inevitable.

Soon enough, it found what it was looking for. Life, encased in an artificial shell, travelling through space at an incredible speed, more or less in the cloud's direction.

The cloud slowed, halted, positioned itself in the path of the oncoming object, its scanning particles busy. Its sentient particles recognised the sleek, smooth object as a 'spaceship', a machine used to ferry organic life between planets. At the speed it was travelling the ship would pass through the cloud in a flash, so it would have only one chance. It was confident. It knew it would succeed. It was what it was programmed for.

The cloud made itself denser, thicker, and activated the spore particles within. They became aroused, potent. As the ship drew nearer they rushed to the point in the cloud through which it would pass.

The ship streaked through the cloud like a bullet through paper. Contact was brief, but it was enough. The spore particles had adhered to the nose of the ship, and, as it sped on its way, they altered the molecules of the ceramic hull, integrating with the basic molecular structure, working their way in a chain reaction towards the interior. Only a few would make it to the artificial atmosphere inside, but it would be enough.

Now, an immense distance behind the hurtling ship, the black cloud, its task completed, activated certain particles that had been inert since its day of manufacture. These particles, ravenous and unstoppable, ate their way through the cloud, consuming the shield particles, the guidance particles, the sentient particles and all the other component particles of the cloud until there was nothing left. Then they, too, sated, withered and died in a final orgasmic flare of energy.

Chapter Fourteen
'You've got a lot of explaining to do'

Fitz lay on the bed in his cabin, lights dimmed, fully clothed, hands behind his head, staring at the ceiling. His head was spinning from too much wine and there was an ache behind his eyes. He felt as though he was being drawn into Arielle's world, as though she'd somehow infected him with her spores.

He laughed woozily. If only she was an alien. She'd be far easier to deal with. But she wasn't, she was a woman – much more complex, much more dangerous.

He swung his legs over the side of the bed and stood up, wincing as the ache behind his eyes intensified to a sharp throbbing. He walked into the gleaming silver and aquamarine *en suite* and splashed water on to his face, trying to clear his mind. A plan was forming, a plan he liked very much, and which he hated himself for liking.

He was going to get away from Yquatine, and take his chances with Arielle. He knew she liked him – that much was clear from the light in her dark-brown eyes – and maybe this was it. The woman who could save him.

And Compassion and the Doctor?

Fitz turned away so he didn't have to look at his reflection, water dripping from his face into the gleaming sink. The guilt was still there, and he knew it wouldn't ever go away. He'd just have to learn to live with it. But what could he do? How could he save the Doctor? How could he change the future without being absolutely sure he wasn't destroying it?

He looked at himself, at his thin face, the large grey eyes, long hair, lips that seemed always to be on the verge of uttering a lie or a facile witticism. Hardly a face you could trust. A face that let people down. Shifty. Cowardly.

Time for truth. Fitz. He knew what he was doing. Running away. So what?

Maybe the Doctor and Compassion would come out of it. Maybe they didn't need him. Maybe they would save the day on their own and come and pick him up. Then everything would be all right. Wouldn't it?

'You can run,' he said to his reflection in the circular mirror, 'but you can't hide. But at least you can bloody well run.'

Then he heard a scream, a shrill female shriek of alarm. He swung round, stepped back into the room. There it was again, coming from the next room. From Arielle's room.

He was at her door in seconds, and without knocking thrust it fully open and stepped inside, calling her name.

She was standing in the middle of the room, her hands over her face, hair falling loosely over her shoulders. She'd taken her trousers off, revealing the shapeliest pair of pins he had ever seen – damn it!

'Arielle?' he called again.

She showed no sign of hearing him.

He walked up to her. Her toenails were perfect, like little pink seashells. 'Arielle?'

He reached out and touched her bare arm.

She snatched the limb away and swung round, a throaty gasp escaping her lips, her eyes –

'What the hell?'

Fitz stepped nearer, narrowing his eyes in concern.

Arielle blinked and smiled nervously, looking at Fitz and the room as if it was the first time she'd set eyes on either.

Fitz's scalp actually tingled. He couldn't be dead sure, but for a moment her eyes had looked totally black, as though her pupils had dilated beyond the limit of her eyelids.

They looked normal enough now, though. 'Are you OK?'

She looked a bit shell-shocked and peaky. She hugged herself, moved one leg so her left instep rested on her right foot. 'Yes, I'm fine,' she said in a husky voice.

Then she collapsed in a heap at Fitz's feet.

Later. Fitz was standing on one side of a wall of smoked glass, and
Arielle was on the other, under a single white sheet, a horseshoe
of medical equipment surrounding her head. Deep coma, the
doctors had told him. They couldn't tell him how long it would
last, or what had caused it.

Typical. The moment he falls in love with a girl, she falls into a
coma. There are easier ways of avoiding a relationship with me,
he thought, caught in a paroxysm of self-pity, anguish and the
usual underlying background radiation of Kreiner guilt.

The next stop was Luvia; they should be arriving in a few hours.
He'd go with her to the hospital, keep an eye on her. At least they
were both away from Yquatine.

But, for Arielle, it might be the end of the story.

He became aware of someone standing close behind him, a tall
reflection in the smoked glass.

Fitz turned round, resenting the intrusion. 'Yes?'

The intruder had a heavy, pockmarked face, black hair and thick
eyebrows, or rather one thick eyebrow, as the two met in a point
above his flat beak of a nose. 'Mr Fitz Kreiner?'

Fitz was instantly on his guard. 'How do you know my name?'
Damn! Why didn't he just say no?

The man smiled, but his eyes remained cold. 'A certain drinking
establishment provided us with all we need to know about you.'

Fitz couldn't imagine Il-Eruk squealing on him. 'Who are you,
anyway?'

The man took a step towards Fitz, his suited body invading his
personal space. 'I work for President Vargeld. I protect his
interests. Make sure nothing untoward happens to them.' He was
looking over Fitz's shoulder at Arielle. He sucked in a breath
through his teeth. 'You've got a lot of explaining to do.'

All the President's men. Fitz wondered why they hadn't been
collared earlier. Then he remembered an unscheduled stop at a

space station a few hours ago. He'd thought nothing of it, nor had Arielle. Pair of idiots.

'I don't have anything to say to you. I've got nothing to do with her condition!' Fitz's voice rose in panic.

Another man had appeared, slimmer and with thinning blond hair, and a dainty but deadly-looking pistol.

'You're coming back to Yquatine with us,' said the first man.

It sounded like a death sentence. 'No I'm bloody not!'

The second man smiled. 'Yes, you "bloody" are.'

Fitz had a moment of sheer panic. They were going to take him back. He wasn't going to escape. Events were closing in on him like a net of steel. 'There's nothing I can say or do that will persuade you otherwise?' he babbled.

The two men exchanged glances.

'No, I don't think there is,' said the first man in a loose, casual drawl.

Then he punched Fitz right in the stomach.

Treaty Day was over. It was now the small hours of the 17th of Lannasirn, a date now meaningless because the planet upon whose seasons that calendar was based no longer existed.

President Stefan Vargeld lay under a single sheet, damp with sweat – he could feel it on his back, behind his knees, under his hair – totally unable to sleep.

If I ever sleep again, I want to dream of her

A mood of detached numbness pervaded his body, and he lay tense, waiting for the shock to hit him. A whole planet and all its people gone, just like that. But it didn't seem real. It made him want to laugh, and that made him feel worse. He recalled his flight to Muath with the Doctor. The way he'd broken down. Lost control. Cried like a kid. Could he blame it on the aftereffects of the medication? Or was he losing it?

If I ever look into her open eyes again

Easy enough to be President when all that concerned you was the taxation of trade routes and interspecies technology transfer policies. He'd probably even have been able to cope with a conventional Anthaurk attack. But this? A whole planet smudged out of existence – not just any planet, but the heart of the System?

He closed his eyes and saw Arielle's face, unsmiling, hostile and closed to him for ever. She wasn't alone. There were people with her – people and beings – the millions of dead. They all wore that distant look she'd had the night he proposed to her. Frightened, but composed. Hurt, but determined. Private, resolved. You're never coming back in here again.

Take me back to the time before it happened
I'll make it all right
I'm President – it's my damn job to make it all right

Then, under the weight of it all deep in the artificial night of Aloysius Station, he cried, and he wasn't a President: he was a kid again.

Too young to be President
Never be able to cope with the responsibility –

He woke up shouting, the tears dry on his face. Must have fallen asleep at last. He winced, rubbed his eyes. His watch told him it was morning.

The day after.

The shock would be hitting home all across the System. The people of the Minerva System would be looking to him for leadership. Now was his chance, his time. He'd make sure the Anthaurk paid for what they had done.

His comms unit bleeped and he spoke through a mouth coated with stale, dried saliva. 'Yes?'

'President Vargeld, sir?'

He rubbed his unshaven face. 'Who else would it be?'

'There's a Senate meeting in half an hour, sir.'

He didn't recognise the voice. Young, nervous, female. An image of Franseska flickered in his mind, and he banished it angrily. 'On whose authority?'

The voice stammered on. 'It's the Doctor, sir. He – he says he's got something important to tell the Senate.'

'The Doctor?' Last he'd seen, the guy had been almost a goner.

'Yes, sir. The meeting's in Laboratory A.'

'How –' But the communication clicked off.

He dragged himself from his bed, ran his hands once again over his stubble and through his stiff hair, and groaned. He washed and dressed and left his quarters. To his surprise, Fandel was there, just about to press the entry coder.

'Fandel?' said President Vargeld. The bright white light of the corridor hurt his eyes.

'Did you get the message as well?' Fandel was virtually hopping from foot to foot. Despite the early hour, he was in full costume – padded waistcoat, long frock coat and fastidiously pressed trousers. 'This is most irregular!'

'Well, we're living in irregular times,' mumbled President Vargeld, yawning as he walked along the corridor beside the Luvian senator.

Fandel was babbling away, illustrating his speech with little jabs of his small white hands. 'The Doctor's emerged from his coma!' he cried. 'A few hours ago, he simply woke up, fresh as a daisy. No ill effects whatsoever! Turns out his coma was self-induced. And now he's called a Senate meeting!'

'He's overstepped his bounds,' said the President. He had to be seen to be in control. 'But we'll see what he has to say for himself.'

He quickened his pace towards Lab A, making Fandel scurry along beside him. He was fully awake now. The Doctor had found something, down on Muath. And it had to be something important – so important that the Doctor had decided to convene the Senate all by himself.

Well. No harm in that, if it produced the desired results. President Vargeld set his jaw, pressing his teeth together until it hurt. He ached to see Zendaak's comeuppance.

Laboratory A was one of three scientific laboratories on Aloysius Station, used for the study of alien diseases, spatial radiation and observation of the sun. Arielle had been up here a few times, mapping the constellations of the System. He'd come with her once. It had been magical. Just themselves, a darkened observatory, and the stars wheeling in the blackness above. What choice did they have in such a situation? They'd made love –

President Vargeld shook his head and swore.

'You all right?' said Fandel.

'Yeah,' said the President. 'Bad night. No sleep.'

'Me too,' sighed Fandel.

They reached the entrance to the laboratory. President Vargeld pushed open the double door and walked into a large, circular room, lined with equipment, Fandel scurrying at his side. In the centre of the lab, an isolation room had been set up, and inside this stood the Doctor, in his clothes, which still looked to the President like some sort of Luvian get-up, hale and hearty as you like. Grey-suited technicians stood nervously by.

All the other senators were already there. Krukon, Juvingeld, Tibis, Okotile, Rhombus-Alpha. All looking at – or facing towards – the Doctor.

And Zendaak, in his scarlet robe, his face impassive.

'Good morning, gentlemen,' said the President evenly. 'Doctor –'

'Ah, now you're here we can begin,' said the Doctor, his voice crackling from speakers set into the ceiling.

Best to ignore this undermining of his authority. Had to stay calm. 'Begin what, exactly?' He walked right up to the glass and fixed the Doctor with a presidential stare.

The Doctor paced around the chamber, waving his arms, his face alight and alive. He didn't look as if he'd just woken up from a coma. 'Down on Muath, I encountered something. A form of gaseous life. It tried to attack me, but I managed to trap it within my respiratory bypass system.' He coughed, holding his chest. 'And I don't want it there any longer,' he wheezed.

Zendaak stepped forward. He was grinning, chin jutting forward, eyes glowing with triumph. 'The Doctor is going to prove Anthaurk innocence!'

'Yes yes,' said the Doctor. 'Now I'm going to release the creature.' Mutters of alarm. 'It will be quite safe in here, never fear.'

The Doctor stood stock still, eyes closed, hands covering his ears, mouth open as if in a silent scream. President Vargeld was reminded of a very old and very famous painting.

Nothing happened for a few minutes, then a throaty rattling came from the speakers.

The senators had crowded closely around the isolation chamber, in various attitudes of fascination, disbelief, or in Fandel's case, scorn. 'What is this conjuror's trick?'

The rattling became thicker, more muffled, and the Doctor's mouth filled with darkness. Suddenly, something leapt from the Doctor's mouth – a streak of black, like a skid mark in the air. It began to curl in on itself, like a comma. It was followed by another, and another, black plumes twisting in the air like snakes.

Fandel, Krukon, Zendaak, Tibis and Juvingeld all invoked their various deities.

President Vargeld stared, mesmerised. The Doctor was standing stock still, eyes closed, as the smoke-snakes curled around him, caressing him. Was this what had happened to Arielle?

Then the Doctor opened his eyes.

They were totally black.

His voice boomed from the speakers, thick and distorted: '*We are Omnethoth. All solid mortals will be dissolved.*'

Part Three

For How Long, Though?

Chapter Fifteen
'If you even call me, it is over between us'

None of the guides Fitz had read, and none of the people he'd spoken to, had ever mentioned Yendip Internment Centre. It was tucked away on a windswept plain beyond the hills surrounding Yendip, an apology of unsightly red-brick buildings clustering in a cracked and weed-strewn concrete compound. Neglected, overlooked, swept under the carpet, it was Yquatine's only prison – though no one used that term. Everyone – police, warders, judicials and 'inmates' – called it the Internment Centre, or simply the Centre. It was as though no one wanted to admit the existence of crime on such an idyllic planet as Yquatine. But exist it did. On a planet where hundreds of species came into daily contact with each other, crime was inevitable.

The Yquatine authorities had come up with an ingenious solution to this problem. Most criminals were sent to one of the maximum-security institutions on Beatrix for incarceration or readjustment – the problem transferred to another planet. Crime took place on Yquatine, but the criminals were rooted out and transplanted like weeds. Yendip Internment Centre was used to mop up the overspill, take care of the least disturbed and less violent type of criminal. Fraudsters, petty thieves, pickpockets – folk who would, on the whole, learn their lesson well and do their time meekly and patiently with their eyes on remission. So the Centre wasn't a dangerous pressure cooker with weekly riots and a history of suicides. But it was still a prison, with its claustrophobia and hopelessness and the sense of endless days with nothing to fill them. A new experience for Fitz.

If he stood on the chair in his cell, he could see out of the barred, semicircular window at the top of the wall opposite the door. He could see the exercise yard with its cracked concrete and weeds. He could see the inner perimeter fence, and beyond that the outer perimeter fence. And beyond that fields so green and a sky so blue that it almost broke his heart.

To this maddening view he would sometimes shout in blind rage. Other times he would stare, feeling nothing, not believing he was here, hoping that he would suddenly wake up. Or he'd try to will himself through the barred window. Or wish that, like Compassion, he could turn into a TARDIS and varoosh himself out of here. It seemed to be the only way, because Yendip Internment Centre was totally escape-proof. The authorities were very keen on preserving the wholesome image of Yquatine. Escaped criminals could make a serious dent in tourism revenue. All prisoners were therefore implanted with nanochips which constantly mapped their movements. These otherwise harmless chips were injected into the lymphatic system, where they spread throughout the whole body. There was simply no way of getting rid of them. There was no escape.

Fitz was in prison, and looked like staying there until – literally – doomsday.

He'd argued all the way in the shuttle from the *St Julian* to Yquatine that he'd done nothing wrong. From Yendip spaceport he'd been taken in a hovercar down a long dusty road across the plain to the Internment Centre. Still he'd pleaded and bargained, but his captors had ignored his pleas. There were two of them – the tall, thickset monobrow and the thinner, almost refined-looking Aryan type. The very sight of them had repelled and terrified Fitz. Men paid to do one thing and one thing only: intimidate, threaten. Stolid, humourless goons.

By the time they had left him in the interview room, Fitz had developed a deep hatred of President Stefan Vargeld, for how he'd treated Arielle, how he was treating Fitz right now. So when the door opened and President Vargeld walked in – goons in tow – it was all Fitz could do to stop himself leaping from his chair and telling the man what a total and complete *wanker* he was.

President Vargeld settled himself in a chair on the other side of the table. Fitz had seen him on newscasts, where he had looked bland and inoffensive, a typical career politician. In the flesh, Fitz found him positively repugnant. For a start, though he didn't look much older than Fitz, he looked a damn sight healthier. He walked with a confident, easy swagger, possessed a flat stomach, wide shoulders and blemish-free skin. He had the manner of a film star, a lazy, relaxed handsomeness, the sort Fitz knew women went all gooey over (he remembered Val going all misty-eyed over a picture of the President). Here was a man who never had to try for anything. So this was what Arielle had fallen for. Good looks and white teeth – was that all it took?

'Doubtless you know who I am.' His voice had the usual Yquatine accent, with an aristocratic twang, and his tone implied threat.

Of course, all Fitz knew about him was what Arielle had told him. Fitz grunted a dismissive response.

President Vargeld smiled coldly. 'And, equally without doubt, you are probably wondering why you have been brought here. I don't care. I don't care what you are thinking or how you are feeling.'

A pause. Fitz took in the closed faces of monobrow and Aryan, the glazed brick walls of the interview room. The place smelled of detergent and Fitz was terribly hungry; he felt hollowed out and sick. He remembered Arielle talking about her former lover, his crass insensitivity. He shrugged. 'The feeling's mutual, squire.'

He'd gone too far and he knew it. When the punch came he was able to duck back, so Vargeld's fist smacked into the side of his jaw. Pain arced through Fitz's skull and his teeth bit down on his tongue, drawing blood.

He stared at Vargeld, more disgusted than hurt. He ruled an entire solar system but he couldn't control his temper. Pathetic – or he would be if he didn't wield so much power.

'I want to know what you were doing with my fiancée. What you've done to her.'

Fitz fought down his sense of panic, swallowing the blood that filled his mouth. He felt shaken, scared. 'I didn't – I didn't do anything to her.'

The President leaned back, sucked in his cheeks. He looked bored. 'I ask again, what were you doing?'

Fitz's only hope was the truth. 'Helping her to escape.'

The President leaned forward, instantly alert once more. 'Escape? From?'

Fitz shrank back, tensing himself for another blow. 'From you.'

The President's face coloured and his hands, steepled on the table in front of him, broke apart and slapped on to the surface. He controlled himself with a visible effort. 'She didn't want to "escape" from me!'

Fitz could see now the type of lover this guy would make – possessive, jealous and dangerous. And as an enemy? Fitz began to shake uncontrollably. This madman could probably have him executed on the spot. His only hope was to try to reason with him. 'Listen, I *was* helping her. She ran away from you, that's the truth! She was – is – scared of you.'

Silence. They stared at each other for a while. No way was he going to let the merest hint of his true feelings for Arielle show. That would probably mean instant death.

At length, Vargeld nodded slowly. 'All right. Let's say she did run away from me. Let's say you helped her get off the planet. So far, so good. So can you explain to me why she is lying in Yendip Infirmary in a deep coma?'

Fitz remembered Arielle, her eyes totally black. Whatever had happened to her, it wasn't anything Fitz had ever come across before. It smacked of something weird and dangerous. 'Is she OK? I mean, have the doctors –'

The President slammed his hand down on the table again. 'She is nothing to do with you! Put her out of your mind for ever.'

'All right, all right.' The last thing he wanted to do was provoke Vargeld. 'Look, I really don't know what happened to her. One minute she was fine, the next she passed out.'

'Whether that's true or not, you still took her away from me.'

Vargeld seemed to marshal himself. 'Were you – were you sleeping with her? Were you in love with her?'

Fitz shook his head, started babbling. 'No, no, I was just helping her. Never even touched her.'

The President folded his arms, his face a cold, unsmiling mask. 'I don't believe you.'

Fitz looked down at his hands in his lap. He'd picked one nail right down to the quick and a crescent of blood was forming on his finger.

The President was still speaking. 'I don't believe you, but until Arielle comes round – if she does – I won't be able to check your story.'

Fitz sniffed, looked up at the President, acutely aware that his fate lay in Vargeld's hands. 'So what are you going to do to me?'

'You're an anomaly. There are no records of you anywhere in the System. You could be a spy for all I know.'

So, political problems. A hint of the disaster to come? Perhaps he should tell all. After all, Vargeld was the ultimate authority. He might be able to do something about it. Fitz opened his mouth to speak. He changed his mind at the last minute. 'I'm not a spy.'

The President smiled. 'Maybe not, but as far as I can tell you have no money and no home. You may as well stay here. It's not bad.'

He was trying to be funny, but the words chilled Fitz to the bone.

Vargeld got up to leave. 'You'll stay here, at my pleasure, until our investigations are complete.'

Christ. It was less than a month until Treaty Day. Doomsday. 'How – how long will that take?' said Fitz through the lump that was forcing its way up his throat.

The President waved a perfectly manicured hand in the air. 'One month, two? Who knows?' He stood up to leave.

Fitz stood up. He'd come to a decision. 'Wait.'

Halfway to the door, the President turned. 'What is it?'

Sod the timelines, he had to get out of here. 'What if I told you that on Treaty Day, Yquatine is going to be attacked?'

The President nodded. 'Then I'd say you were probably right.' He turned, was almost through the door.

'And totally destroyed!' yelled Fitz.

But the door slammed shut behind the President.

Then they came and put him in his cell.

Fitz stared out of the window at the exercise ground, the inner perimeter fence, the outer perimeter fence, the rolling fields and the free blue sky of Yquatine.

He could hardly believe his bloody, *bloody* bad luck.

He'd been home and dry, away from the doomed world, only to be snatched back as if he'd been attached to it with elastic.

No – attached to it by his own stupid desires. He'd gone and fallen for the President's totty, for God's sake! How could he have been so dumb? Now he'd die along with everyone else. And he couldn't save Arielle. That thought hurt worst of all.

There was one hope, one futile, childish hope.

Maybe Compassion would materialise in his cell and rescue him in the nick of time.

Yeah, right. That sort of thing only happened in books.

Stefan Vargeld was the happiest man on Yquatine. Never mind the growing problems in the Senate, his girl was back from the brink of death! He felt like singing. He felt like dancing. He tried to hold the feeling inside until he actually saw her with his own eyes. He drifted through an interminable Senate meeting, parried Zendaak's grievances and the interminable question of the taxation of trade routes. He ached to get away, go to the infirmary to see her. The doctors had contacted him earlier, with the joyous news that she had shown signs of life. She had opened her eyes.

Now, the business of the day over, he walked quickly through the sterile white corridors of Yendip Infirmary, his two bodyguards taking up the rear. If they hadn't been there he'd have burst into song. Arielle's doctor was keeping pace with him.

'She snapped out of it an hour ago and has made an incredibly swift recovery. It was as though nothing had happened.'

The President turned to the doctor, a small, fussy Izrekt. 'Have you any idea what caused it?'

The doctor shook his head. 'All our tests have come up negative – that is, all the tests we've been able to carry out so far.'

'Why can't you do more tests?'

The doctor sighed. 'She's discharged herself. I don't suppose you could persuade her to stay? For more tests?'

The President considered. If she had recovered, that was good enough for him. 'She's checked out OK? No sign of any illness or disease?'

'Yes,' said the doctor, 'but I strongly suggest that she stays for further tests. In fact, I insist –'

The President stalled him with a wave of his hand. 'I'll see what I can do.'

He reached the door of her private ward. Should he knock? He faltered. 'You can wait for me outside,' he told his men. 'And I'll let you know what she says,' he told the doctor.

When they had all gone, he was left alone, facing the door. He let out a sigh of relief. He didn't want them to see the grimace of shame and guilt on his face. Didn't want them to overhear the words he was almost certain Arielle would say to him. Maybe she would hate him; she had every reason to, because he had hurt her. He had struck out at the woman he loved, a rash gesture of anger and frustration. Now it seemed like a lapse into madness, and he didn't understand why he had done it. Maybe to get some reaction, any reaction. He found it hard to reconcile with the intricate politics of the System. He could handle Zendaak and the others, so why couldn't he handle Arielle?

He could barely admit it to himself. He'd behaved abominably and scared Arielle away. And now he was going to put things right. He was going to go in there, apologise; she'd be so pleased to be alive that she'd fall into his arms – he could almost feel the weight of her body against his – and everything would be all right, all right. Hope made him smile, swelled his heart, against the odds.

With a tense hand, he opened the door.

He was surprised to see Arielle standing by the bed, fully dressed, comms unit pressed to her ear.

He stepped into the room. 'Arielle?'

She didn't even look up. A hot flush of disappointment and shameful anger. He spoke again, trying to keep his voice light. 'Arielle?'

She clicked the comms unit off, slid it into her belt.

Her eyes, oh hell, her eyes. Framed with a frown of irritation, shut off from him, as if he was a stranger.

'Arielle, it's me. Stefan.' He reached out for her, but she remained stationary, closed. 'How are you?'

She blinked. Her eyes looked unfocused. 'I am well.'

He walked up to her, but the way she was standing, arms akimbo, prevented him from embracing her. 'What happened on the *St Julian*? What did Fitz Kreiner do to you?'

She moved her head, her hair falling across her eyes. 'Fitz?'

The words came out harsh, ugly, out of control. 'Yes! That guy you were with.'

That stare again. As if he wasn't there. 'Nothing.'

He looked away, feeling crushed, defeated. 'OK. I understand.'

Arielle stepped towards her bed. Should he tell her Fitz was in prison? He noticed she was packing a large case, obviously fetched by the hospital from her university quarters. 'Where are you going?' he said to her back.

She stopped packing, seemed to consider. 'Muath.'

It took him a while to make sense of it. 'What the hell for?'

'The university has a lab there. I'm going to do some work.'

He felt as if he was being pulled in two directions. One side of him wanted to tell her how ridiculous this was, that her place was with him. But the side of him that had loved Arielle, learned her moods and whims and odd sense of humour, told him that they needed some time apart. He knew that the only way to keep hold of this beautiful creature was to let her go, at least for a little while.

'OK. Then after we've both thought things over we can talk, right?' She carried on packing. 'Arielle?' No response. 'For God's sake, woman!' The instant they were out, he regretted the words.

She turned to him, her face still blank. 'I am going to Muath.' Then she paused, and when she spoke again it was as though she had rehearsed the speech. 'Do not follow me there. If you even call me, it is over between us.' She turned to continue packing, then added as an afterthought, 'I'll contact you.'

So there was hope. 'When?'

She considered again. 'When I am ready.'

He nodded. 'OK.' It was the best he could hope for, considering how badly he had acted.

She folded her arms, her eyes glassy, forbidding. 'Go now.'

With a last look at the person he loved more than anyone, President Vargeld turned and left.

Outside, he let out a long, shuddering sigh, and trudged off back to his private car. She would contact him soon, he was sure of it. And then he'd find out what had gone on between her and Kreiner. And until then, the bastard could rot in jail.

Chapter Sixteen
'My need for hot, sweet tea has never been greater'

President Vargeld watched as the Doctor stood in the isolation chamber, eyes black, gaseous snakes writhing around him. He could feel the others watching him, waiting for a response to the Doctor's announcement. Clearly, he had been possessed, down on Muath. Maybe, even, he was behind the whole thing. Maybe he was responsible for the fall of Yquatine.

President Vargeld stepped up to the glass, turning his sudden rush of anger into action. 'Doctor, can you hear me?'

The Doctor opened his mouth and spoke in the same thick, distorted voice. *'We hear you.'*

'What do you mean by "all solid mortals will be dissolved"?'

'All solid mortals will be dissolved.'

'That's not what I meant!' snapped the President.

Rhombus-Alpha spoke up, its representation floating above the chamber. 'How do you mean to accomplish this?'

'The first stage is almost complete. Soon we will expand. Soon we will destroy you.'

'We'll see about that,' said the President. 'Soon *we* will destroy *you.*'

'That is not possi- Arrrgh!'

All at once the Doctor's eyes returned to normal, his hands flew to his throat and he let out a strangulated gargle of pain which poured from the speakers in a surge of distortion.

Medics rushed to the door of the isolation chamber as the Doctor slumped to the floor.

'Stand down!' barked the President. No way was he going to let that thing out into the station.

The Doctor was convulsing, coughing, chest heaving. He rolled on to his back, his spine arched, and a final streak of black gas shot from his mouth, bunching like a tiny thundercloud. The smoke-snakes joined it, forming a loose starfish shape above the Doctor.

Senator Tibis was on his knees, his great tiger-like head bowed, muttering a prayer to one of his gods. Fandel had gone as white as chalk. Okotile was chirruping in alarm, and Juvingeld was stamping his hooves. None of them were any damned good in an emergency, President Vargeld reflected ruefully. He swore as he was barged out of the way by Zendaak.

'What are you doing?'

Zendaak's eyes flashed. 'We've got to get him out of there.'

President Vargeld tried to hold the Anthaurk senator back. 'No, Zendaak! He could still be possessed by that thing.'

With a snarling hiss, Zendaak shoved him to one side.

President Vargeld turned. 'Troopers!'

Space Alliance troopers had been stationed around the edges of the lab and they now sprang into action, covering Zendaak.

Zendaak ignored them, and opened the outer door of the isolation chamber.

If they fired, they'd hole the chamber, let the thing out. 'Hold your fire!'

The gas creature was hovering over the Doctor, its dense, jet-black centre directly above his head, its tapering smoky limbs reaching to the side of the chamber. Its centre was darkening, bulging like a seed pod.

Zendaak walked straight in, waving his arms through the smoky limbs of the creature. It broke up into a diffuse cloud but almost immediately began to re-form. Before it had chance, Zendaak bent down and scooped the Doctor up in one sinewy arm. The President remembered how light the Doctor had been in Muath's low gravity, and was uncomfortably reminded of the great physical strength of the Anthaurk.

Zendaak stepped out of the isolation chamber, the Doctor draped over one arm. 'Put down your guns.'

The creature was flailing about the isolation chamber, re-forming, the black centre emitting clear, liquid drops which hissed as they burned into the floor.

The Doctor was murmuring, head lolling on Zendaak's shoulder.

President Vargeld nodded to the troopers. 'Do as he says, but stay hot.'

Zendaak carried the Doctor round to where President Vargeld stood, the senators in a ragged semicircle around him.

Tibis brought forward a chair into which Zendaak lowered the Doctor. Medics clustered round, scanning instruments busy. 'He's OK,' said one of them in surprise. 'A little shaken, but OK.'

Zendaak nodded curtly. 'Then it is a good job I got to him in time.' He waved a claw at the isolation chamber, where the floor was melting under the acid drops produced by the gas creature. As they watched, the deadly rain thinned out and stopped.

President Vargeld wasn't sure if it was a good job. 'Why did you rescue him, Zendaak? Why did you risk your life?'

Zendaak fixed the President with a narrow-eyed stare. 'He could prove the innocence of the Anthaurk race!'

President Vargeld had expected this. Just about everything Zendaak did was to further the interests of his own species. 'That remains to be seen. We don't even know who he is.'

The Doctor opened his eyes. They were completely normal, a bright blue with a slightly manic light. He groaned, leaned over the side of the chair and vomited on the tiled floor of the laboratory.

'Sorry about that,' he croaked. 'Why are you all staring at me?'

Everyone began shouting questions at him until President Vargeld called for silence.

'I'll tell you all you want to know, but not now,' said the Doctor hoarsely. 'Be in the Senate chamber in half an hour. My need for hot, sweet tea has never been greater.'

Exactly thirty minutes later, refreshed by several cups of Luvian tea, the Doctor stood in the centre of the makeshift Senate chamber on Aloysius, his back to the circular space window. He had the complete and undivided attention of everyone in the room. Great.

'While that creature was trapped in my respiratory bypass system,' he began, ignoring the puzzled frowns, 'I was able to commune with it.'

'Commune?' said President Vargeld, with a suspicious glare. Clearly, he was going to believe only what he wanted to believe.

'Yes, telepathically.' The Doctor could tell that the man thought he was still possessed. The creature had taken him over very briefly, but it wasn't very bright, and certainly no match for a Time Lord mind. 'I know exactly what it is and what it wants.'

'And how to destroy it?' said President Vargeld.

The Doctor pursed his lips. Hadn't there been enough destruction? 'I'll come to that. Now, these creatures call themselves Omnethoth. It's a rather bombastic name, quite meaningless, designed to instil fear. Just like their pronouncement – "solid mortals" indeed!'

'Designed?' rumbled Senator Krukon.

The Doctor loved giving explanations, especially when he had a large audience. 'Yes. Designed. You see, these Omnethoth aren't a naturally evolved, sentient species, though they'd like to think they are. They are – or rather it is – a weapon.'

There were several exclamations of alarm.

'An Anthaurk weapon!' cried Fandel, predictably.

The Doctor wagged a long, bony finger. 'No, no. Despite their rather militaristic bent, the Anthaurk are totally innocent of the destruction of Yquatine.'

Zendaak's lipless mouth expanded in a wide grin. The Doctor almost expected him to say 'I told you so', but apparently the Anthaurk weren't familiar with the expression.

'If you're expecting an apology then you're seriously deluding yourself,' said President Vargeld. 'Before the Omnethoth attack we were on the brink of war!'

'I do not want you to apologise,' hissed Zendaak. 'Just accept the truth.'

There was a dangerous edge to the Anthaurk senator's voice. The Doctor resolved to keep an eye on him. He coughed loudly, to return attention to himself. 'The truth', he announced, pointing at his own head, 'resides in here, if you'd care to listen.'

'We're listening,' grated Krukon, with a baleful glare at Zendaak.

The Doctor continued. 'The Omnethoth were developed millennia ago by a race they call the Masters.' He frowned. 'Terrible choice of name. Anyway, these Masters made the mistake of many ancient races who believed themselves invulnerable. They decided to rule the universe and created a sentient weapon which turned against them.' The Doctor sighed and smoothed his left eyebrow with his little finger. 'Silly billies.'

'So, how did the things end up here, now?' asked the President.

The Doctor shrugged. 'Apparently the Omnethoth died out millions of years ago, but before they did they seeded the universe with colonisation clouds.' He looked at Vargeld thoughtfully. 'Someone on Yquatine must have become infected with Omnethoth spores and drawn the invasion fleet here. Somehow.'

'That doesn't explain how thousands of ships appeared from nowhere,' said Krukon.

The Doctor scratched his chin. 'Yes, well that is quite a mystery. I'll have to commune with the creature again to get to the bottom of it. It looks as though the activation of the Omnethoth happened by chance. Maybe one of their colonisation clouds drifted into the System.'

President Vargeld interrupted. 'You mean to say, Yquatine was destroyed by a product? A sentient weapon, no better than one of our own smart bombs?'

The Doctor nodded gravely. 'Yes. That's more or less the truth.' It was the truth. And it was horrible. Millions had died, millions more would die unless the Omnethoth were dealt with. The Doctor deliberately focused on what he'd discovered, diverting his mind from the phenomenal loss of life.

President Vargeld was staring at the floor. The Doctor walked up to him, full of concern. 'I know how you must feel. I've faced death countless times –'

President Vargeld looked up, his youthful face strained, eyes hostile. 'How can you know how I feel? How we all must feel?'

The Doctor stepped back, mentally admonishing himself. That was a bad bit of counselling: never, ever say 'I know how you feel', even if it was true. It was the last word in patronisation.

'We don't even know how we should be feeling,' said the President in a hoarse, broken voice. 'We've had our heart ripped out. We can't even begin to imagine what the future will be like.'

Rhombus-Alpha spoke up. 'Emotional outbursts are counterproductive – but the Ixtricite must also register our deepest perturbation at this tragic turn of events.'

President Vargeld walked up to Zendaak. 'I almost wish you were the aggressors.' He laughed and clapped the Anthaurk on the shoulders. 'Because we could – and would – have beaten you!'

Zendaak pulled away. 'Don't be so sure of that,' he muttered darkly.

'But instead we have to face this senseless, manufactured thing. Striking us from out of nowhere. By accident.' The last two words were a whisper of horrified disbelief.

Things were getting a bit too emotional. 'By accident', repeated the Doctor, 'is how the universe operates. In the universal whole, nothing is just or unjust. It may only seem that way to us poor individuals. We call it fate or destiny, perceiving patterns where there are none, connecting events, creating our own interpretations of the universe like tapestries of wishes and dreams. The truth is, the universal process has no favourites. The Omnethoth could have struck anywhere. It's just unfortunate for us that it's here and now.'

Senator Juvingeld rose from his seat. 'I do not agree. We Eldrig believe in the prophecies of our forefathers, laid down when our world was young. There is a pattern to everything.'

The Doctor smiled indulgently. 'And have all these prophecies come true? Was this current tragedy foreseen?'

Juvingeld shook his head. 'It depends upon the interpretations of the prophecies.'

The Doctor clicked his fingers. 'There you are, then. With respect to Senator Juvingeld, predestination cannot exist.' Not even for a time traveller like himself, he reflected – his biodata could be and had been extensively rewritten so he wasn't even sure of the past, let alone the future.

Senator Tibis spoke. His voice was deep, growling and sonorous. 'So what you're saying, Doctor, is that shit happens?'

The Doctor let out a long breath, smiled, shook his head wearily. 'Succinctly put, but yes. That's how the universe works. And we have to make sense of it. We –' he spun round, arms wheeling – 'were *made* to make sense of it. It's our purpose!'

'So how can we make sense of what happened to Yquatine?' asked the President in a hollow voice.

The Doctor whirled round. 'The great thing about an indifferent universe is free will. We're free agents –' he nodded to Juvingeld – 'though we don't all realise it. We could choose to let it beat us, let the push and pull of the process tear us apart. Or we could choose to face things positively.'

President Vargeld cut in. 'All this philosophising is very cute but what are we going to do?'

'Well, I'm just coming to that,' said the Doctor brightly. 'I know how to stop them!'

'Destroy them?' said the President.

The look in Vargeld's eyes was beginning to worry the Doctor. 'Let's just say, render them safe. The Omnethoth are a gestalt creature, made up of tiny gaseous particles, tiny spores if you like. They can exist in three states: the gaseous form, which is what is now surrounding Yquatine, and which is lethal to organic life; a liquid form rather like acid; and a solid form, which they use for their ships and probes and whatnot. Only the gaseous form is sentient. Well, it likes to think it is but all it's doing is obeying its programming – spread out, destroy, colonise. But I can change all that. I can reach into the Omnethoth DNA, reprogram them. I'd only have to do it to one attack unit and tell it to reprogram the others. They would then be totally peaceful, and be on their way out of the System to dwell in the emptiness of space quite happily. A unique species of gaseous intelligence… What is it?'

President Vargeld had stepped forward until he was only a metre away from the Doctor. His face was white with anger. His voice was shaking. 'Are you suggesting that we allow this filth, this pollution, to go free?'

The Doctor nodded, slowly. 'It's the only way. Otherwise it'll spread out and take over the whole System. We've got hours at most.'

Ignoring him, the President turned and addressed the Senate. 'Let's take a vote on it, shall we? Shall we do what the Doctor says, or shall we destroy these abominations?'

Every arm and forelimb shot up towards the ceiling. Rhombus-Alpha glowed its assent.

President Vargeld whirled round to the Doctor. 'Pretty unanimous, I would say.'

The Doctor folded his arms. He had expected this. 'So how are you going to do it? Destroy the Omnethoth?'

President Vargeld swept his arm around the room. 'I propose that we reconvene the Minerva Space Alliance. Pool our resources. Bombard Yquatine – the thing that was Yquatine. Blast the Omnethoth into oblivion!'

The entire Senate rose to its feet and cheered, hooted, roared and chirruped raucous assent.

The Doctor put his head in his hands and groaned.

After the Senate meeting, there was a council of war. But before that, Senator Zendaak found time to slip back to his cabin, sit before the desk that was covered with the cloaks of his fathers, and pass his hand over the small globe that rested on a pile of smooth pebbles in the centre of the desk.

The image of the Grand Gynarch appeared almost immediately. 'Developments, Zendaak! It has been long since your last report.'

Zendaak didn't know where to begin. 'I have discovered the nature of the takers of Yquatine, O Gynarch!'

The Grand Gynarch's eyes narrowed. 'Not – not the Daleks?'

Zendaak knew of his leader's obsession with those creatures. He waved a gloved hand and shook his head. 'No, Grand Gynarch, nothing so crude as the Daleks. They are called Omnethoth.'

The Grand Gynarch repeated the word. 'Om-ne-thoth. Thoth is one of the gods! The god of… learning and art?' She shook her head. 'How can such a venerable deity be connected with such destruction?'

'He is not, Grand Gynarch. It's an invented name – its makers were probably ignorant of the wise and holy Thoth. The Omnethoth are a manufactured thing. A weapon.'

'How do you know all this?'

Zendaak hissed. 'A human called the Doctor communed with an Omnethoth he had captured.'

The Grand Gynarch glowered. 'A single human captured one of these creatures? And six Anthaurk ships could not?'

Zendaak shook his head. 'Gynarch, this Doctor is not like other humans. He has a secondary respiratory system. He can put himself in a coma at will, to protect his life. He argues against destiny and asserts all have free will.'

The Grand Gynarch snorted. 'I have heard of such theories. Nonsense – for was I not born to be Grand Gynarch? And are the Anthaurk not destined to rule?'

Zendaak saluted. 'Yes, O Gynarch!'

The Grand Gynarch nodded, satisfied and justified. 'Any word from the ships you sent to Yquatine?'

Zendaak shook his head. 'The Omnethoth must have destroyed them.'

'They will be remembered with full honour and glory.'

The two Anthaurk bowed their heads in silence for a while.

Then the Grand Gynarch spoke. 'The Omnethoth are a weapon, you say?' Zendaak nodded. 'Then we must act with stealth, Zendaak. All is not lost. You must co-operate with this Doctor, gain his confidence. Seem to agree with his views, if necessary. You must try to obtain this trapped Omnethoth and bring it back to New Anthaur. We will divine its secrets, and use the power of the Omnethoth to rule the galaxy!'

Pride swelled in Zendaak's chest. So it was to be. After all this time, the Anthaurk were returning at last to their rightful position as rulers and conquerors.

Chapter Seventeen
'This is just what I've been waiting for!'

Fitz woke up on the morning of the 12th of Lannasirn, after almost a month of imprisonment, with a strange new feeling banging against the inside of his ribcage.

Hope.

He stared at the ceiling with its tracery of cracks and its swirls of paintbrush marks for an unknowable time, letting the feeling swell his heart and send his head floating off into fantasies of freedom he'd never previously dared to entertain.

Then, just before he actually burst into tears of mixed joy and apprehension, he swung out of bed, bare feet slapping on the icy tiled floor, and made himself bend over the tiny sink, splashing water on his face. Cold shock at either end of his body brought him down a little.

He dried his face and beard, got up on the chair and looked out through the window at the inner perimeter fence, the outer perimeter fence and the fields beyond. It was still early, not full light yet, and the sky was deep blue, sprinkled with stars. He pressed his face to the window, trying to see – yes, there it was. He grinned.

Shivering in the cold morning air, which seemed to seep into the stone and tile and brick of the Centre, he slipped on his prison garb – shapeless pale-green trousers and top – and, just as suddenly as it had come, the elation slipped away and he slumped on the bed, head in hands.

After all, his hope might be misplaced. It all depended on whether his number came up. Life was now a lottery. His existence depended entirely on the turn of a friendly card. He tried not to think about it, but it was no good. He got up and paced around the room to stall his rising panic and work out his frustration. What time was it? An hour till breakfast. Then he'd know either way. And then it was either elation or – he stopped pacing – death.

An hour to go.

In Yendip Internment Centre, as with all things Yquatine, species mixed in bewildering variety. The Centre was roughly separated into human, reptilian, insectoid zones and so on, with appropriate gender segregation. Throughout the System's penal institutions, prisoners were often seen as a captive labour force, and in some cases were exploited in the manufacture of various small items – repetitive, tedious work only a few stages above rock-breaking. In the best cases, training courses and avenues of study were thrown open to prison populations. Yendip Internment Centre fell in the latter category – manual work was on offer for those who wanted it, but the main occupation of the Centre was translation. Translation of texts from Adamantean to Kukutsi, from Kukutsi to Eldrig, from human to Draconian and so on. With a huge pool of captive aliens and humans who weren't going anywhere for the foreseeable future, the Internment Centre was ideal for such a laborious, labour-intensive task. At the heart of the Centre was the Translation Room, a great big oblong space of dusty air, dirty skylights, rows and rows of shelves, and desks arranged like a schoolroom, with inmates tapping away at terminals.

Fitz had volunteered for a translation job, but they soon realised he was bluffing, and transferred him instead to the library, where he stacked shelves, stamped books, disks and datachips, and largely read. He couldn't read anything other than Yquatine English, which was weird enough. Every sentence contained a word that was new to him and the grammar seemed overelaborate. There was a common System language, Minervan, which the various races of the System used to converse, and Fitz put himself to learning that, but it was slow going.

As for the evenings, Fitz lounged in his cell, using his portable entertainment centre, reading, or just lying on his bed doing nothing. He'd sampled Yquatine cinema, a very stylised, interactive experience which had left him more confused than entertained. He'd also tried the literature of the System and developed a taste for Adamantean poetry. It reminded him of the old Norse sagas he sometimes used to read on bleak winter days in Archway. He'd tried some contemporary Yquatine novels but they left him completely lost – he didn't have the cultural capital to understand them, and felt adrift in their thin pages and closely packed text. And he couldn't find any pornography. Was it outlawed, in these enlightened times? In the end, he'd decided that he was glad that books – real, paper books you could read in bed and use to prop up wobbly tables – still existed a thousand years in the future, even if he couldn't understand them.

He never socialised with the other prisoners – except at mealtimes when contact was inevitable – not wanting to make another friend he was going to lose in the attack. He withdrew into himself, becoming absorbed in his work to the point of brain death. He knew he was going to die, but it was as though it was going to happen to somebody else. He felt oddly relaxed about things. It scared him, and sometimes he'd wake in the night, screaming: Where are you, Fitz? Where's the old you? The you who would be scheming and skiving and trying to escape and being best muckers with Mr Big and smuggling in tobacco and pornography from the outside? Where are you? Where have you gone?

It was this death, the death of his old self, the snuffing out of the spark of his personality, that would have him crying into his pillow in the small hours. Not his impending, inevitable actual death and the deaths of countless others. The death of Fitz Kreiner, Intergalactic Man of Mystery.

In this way Fitz wallowed in near-catatonic self-pity for almost a month. It wasn't entirely his fault – like any internment centre worth its salt this one kept its inmates' water supply laced with personality suppressant drugs, just to be on the safe side.

And then, one day, it all changed.

* * *

Fitz had been sitting opposite Sorswo, a thin, sour-looking man of indeterminate age, and the closest Fitz had to a friend in the whole place. At meals, Fitz rarely looked up, keeping his eyes focused on the book splayed open in his lap, mechanically spooning the tasteless, rubbery food into his mouth. He was reading a book about the life of Julian de Yquatine, and he was quite getting into it. He'd frowned in irritation when Sorswo had started speaking to him, his sonorous voice a semitone higher than usual. But, when he realised what the man had said, he all but dropped the book to the red-and-blue-tiled floor.

He looked up slowly. Sorswo was smiling – a sly expression, hooded eyes beneath arched eyebrows.

'Sorry, what did you say?'

Sorswo's eyebrows inched a little higher. 'I merely asked you if you were going to volunteer.'

Fitz swallowed a glob of foodstuff. 'What for?'

Sorswo pointed to the cobwebbed, vaulted ceiling. 'They're asking for volunteers to go – up there.'

Fitz frowned, looked to where Sorswo's bony finger pointed. Nothing but cobwebs. Fitz hated heights. 'No bloody way, I'm not cleaning that muck off – they can put me in solitary before I do that!'

Sorswo laced his fingers together and chuckled a dry little chuckle that seemed to come from deep within him. He was a tall, cadaverous fellow with short, curly black hair and a beard flecked with white. He was in for some tax fraud which he'd explained to Fitz one day. It was of such labyrinthine complication and so steeped in alien financial jargon that Fitz had quickly developed a headache. Sorswo had a dry sense of humour which Fitz could identify with, and he never seemed to let anything surprise or faze him. 'I don't mean the ceiling. I mean beyond the ceiling.'

Fitz finished his meal and pushed the bowl aside, suddenly loath to talk to Sorswo. The man was in one of his playfully obtuse moods and was probably setting Fitz up for an elaborate joke only he, Sorswo, would get.

Sorswo smiled satanically. 'Well, are you going to volunteer?'

Fitz decided to throw it back at him. 'Are you?'

'I already have,' said Sorswo, sitting back in his chair and stretching his arms. 'If my number comes up I'm off to the moon,' he said through a languid yawn.

Fitz had half risen from his chair, planning to go back to the rec room to finish the de Yquatine book, but on hearing this he sat back down and leaned across the table, suddenly extremely interested in what Sorswo had to say. 'The moon?'

Sorswo nodded. 'Some company's setting up on Muath and they're such a bunch of misers that they're planning to use the cheapest form of labour there is.' He pointed a finger at his thin chest. 'Us. Me, hopefully.'

Fitz's mind raced – or rather tried to. His mental processes were so sluggish these days. It boiled down to: if he went to the moon he could cheat fate, escape the fall of Yquatine. 'How – how can I volunteer for this?'

Sorswo waved a hand. 'Go and see Dakrius. He'll take your name and they'll draw lots at breakfast tomorrow.'

Dakrius was the officer in charge of their section, a stout, uncompromising Adamantean. 'Why do you want to go?'

Sorswo scratched his nose. 'Oh, just for the variety. Gets so dull in here. It's been ten years since I've been in space.'

Fitz was already out of his chair, intending to visit Dakrius in his cavelike office.

'Where are you going in such a hurry?'

Fitz leaned over the table. 'I'm going to volunteer, of course. This is just what I've been waiting for!'

That had been yesterday. Dakrius had solemnly taken his name and told him that the thirty successful volunteers would be shuttled to Muath the day after the draw, pending a medical to verify their fitness for the task.

The medical. Fitz looked at his pallid face in the mirror. Somehow, he'd put on weight. He felt flabby and lethargic. There was still the best part of an hour to go before breakfast, and Fitz spent the time stretching his muscles and sweating like a bastard doing improvised, panicky exercises.

Soon the hour was up. Fitz washed his face and sweat-soaked hair. Nothing he could do about the damp patches under his arms. Oh well, he'd just have to smell.

At the appointed time the door to the cell automatically clunked open and Fitz walked out on to the walkway and down the stairs to breakfast.

The mess hall was long and narrow with three rows of tables along its length and prison guards pacing up and down keeping an eye on their charges. You were meant to sit at an allotted space according to your cell number, but a certain amount of moving about was overlooked as long as you were discreet about it.

Fitz sat down opposite Sorswo.

Sorswo waved a hand in front of his nose. 'You're particularly ponglorious this morning, friend. What *have* you been up to?'

Fitz grinned. 'Sweating. A lot.'

The food was usually served by scuttling Kukutsi cooks, but that morning there was a delay. Dakrius appeared on the walkway above, his glittering frame reflecting the harsh overhead lights. His voice rumbled out along the mess hall, echoing off the stone walls. 'No doubt you are all awaiting the results of the lottery,' he said. 'Some of you will be going to Muath this afternoon. There are, sadly, no other prizes.'

There were a few laughs and shouted comments.

Fitz exchanged glances with Sorswo. The man's dark-brown eyes were tense, the brows pulled down, wrinkling his high forehead. 'Get on with it, you silicon-based swine,' he muttered, just loud enough for Fitz to hear.

'The following human prisoners have been selected to join the working party on Muath: Seth Jayd, Fitz Kreiner, Rufus Sorswo...'

There were other names, but Fitz didn't hear them. He leapt up from the bench. 'Whoo-hoo!' he yelled.

A guard stepped forward and shoved him back down into his seat.

Sorswo had broken into a grin which split his beard in two. 'Well, my friend, it looks like we're going to have the pleasure of each other's company on this little excursion!'

Fitz felt light-headed and giddy with relief. 'Bloody hell. This is the first lottery I've ever won!'

Chittering Kukutsi cooks appeared behind clattering trolleys bearing bowls of morning slop.

Fitz tucked in, grinning inanely. 'Do you know how I feel?' he said between mouthfuls. 'Over the moon!'

Things were looking up. The old Fitz was starting to emerge, slowly – bit by bit – but surely.

Later, back in his room, Fitz could hardly contain himself. He laughed, he shouted, he cried, not caring who heard. Not caring that they thought he was mad to be so elated over doing a bit of work on the moon. They didn't know what he knew. They didn't know they were all going to die and he was getting out of here!

A moment of guilt. Should he tell them? Tell them that, in a few days, Yquatine was going to be destroyed? No – if he did, they would probably take him off the work detail, send him to the psychiatric wing. Then there would be no escape and he'd die along with the rest of them.

He walked up to his window. It was a beautiful Yquatine summer's day. Even the blighted exercise ground looked cheery: small weeds had pushed their way through the cracks and produced bright spots of colour, welcoming the sun.

The sight both cheered and depressed Fitz. Hell, this was driving him bloody crazy! Total Cassandra complex, only worse. The Cassandra of legend was doomed to know the future with not a soul believing her. Fitz was doomed to know the future and dare not tell anybody in case he brought about that future.

He looked at the small weeds as they drank in the sun. For the first time in weeks, he thought of Arielle – really thought of her,

her long honey-coloured hair, the way she'd roll her eyes, the photo of her as a teenager. If she was still in her coma she was as helpless as these plants, rooted in the Yquatine soil, unable to move. He couldn't help the tears and he let them flow freely down his face.

Interlude 2
Eternal FEAR

Compassion was doomed to travel for ever, never going where she wanted, never knowing where she would materialise next. She would never see the Doctor or Fitz again.

After escaping the Anthaurk, she'd tumbled through the vortex, not knowing what to do. She hadn't accomplished anything on New Anthaur. She'd tried to make the Anthaurk see reason, tried to turn them away from war, but it was in their blood. They were a species so steeped in warfare that to Compassion it was a miracle that there had been a century of peace in the Minerva System. She shelved all thoughts of testing her powers, trying to alter the future. That would have to wait. Her main priority was the mastering of the Randomiser circuit. She had to gain control.

She quickly found that this was going to be extremely difficult, if not impossible. The Randomiser was now so deeply embedded that she couldn't enter or leave the vortex without activating the foreign circuit. When dematerialising, it would drag her into the vortex, already trying to send her to some random destination. If she acted quickly enough she could momentarily cut power to all her circuits, including the Randomiser, and she could drift in the vortex for a while. This seemed to be the only way to temporarily bypass the thing, and it was dangerous, frightening – like dying for a brief, fleeting moment – but it was the only way she could prevent herself from being dragged screaming to an unknown destination.

And so the space-time vortex became her only place of refuge. Some refuge. Drifting in the vortex wasn't pleasant, or maybe she wasn't used to it, or maybe only nonsentient TARDISes could stand it, which was why they were nonsentient. It was as though her eyes had been scooped out and replaced by a million kaleidoscoping mirrors. She could stand it only so much, so she had to materialise somewhere. But every time she tried to set co-ordinates, begin to focus her mind and energies on the task, the Randomiser would kick in, wresting control away, taking her to a destination chosen blindly from an infinity of possibilities. She'd find herself thrust to the rear of her own mind, relegated to the back seat, while the Randomiser took control.

And so she'd find herself in the middle of a situation she'd immediately have to deal with or escape from. Or sometimes just some slab of rock in space, but the Randomiser seemed annoyingly attracted to inhabited planets and dangerous situations. The first trip after New Anthaur had taken her to a smoke-choked trench in the middle of a war zone, shells exploding frighteningly near, splattering her cloak with mud. She'd got out of that one quick – Focus, Engage, Artron surge, Randomiser (not that she could control the last). Then, a jagged, hurtling, airless asteroid. No point hanging round there, so FEAR. Then in the middle of a board meeting, the congregation of suits and haircuts all gaping at her as she materialised in the middle of their great big shiny table. How embarrassing. FEAR. Then somewhere dazzlingly bright and hot, where incredible creatures like flower-headed lions in armour plating reared up over her. FEAR. Then on a damp grassy hillside, having her face licked by a giant singing butterfly. Nice, for a while. But then, FEAR.

And other places, other times, with no control over where she was going. The maddening thing was she knew there must be a way to bypass the Randomiser. It was, surely, supposed to work in conjunction with her, so that it would activate only when she wanted it to. Surely the Doctor didn't intend an endless, crazy flight through Time and Space with no idea where he was going next. That was madness. There had to be a way around the Randomiser, but she was too new, she didn't know enough about herself, to be able to find it. And maybe she never would. She'd done everything she could to expunge it, but every time she touched it she drowned in pain.

Once she'd found herself in a human child's bedroom at night. A small room with a bunk bed, festooned with football posters and cluttered with toy cars and games. She'd watched the little boy sleeping, so peaceful, so innocent, so free, wondering what it was like to mother a child. She'd remained there for quite a while, until reluctantly consigning herself once more to the infinite golden throat of the vortex. FEAR.

And so she flew through the vortex again, growing ever more desperate. Maybe, if she travelled for long enough, she'd eventually bump into the Doctor or Fitz, or someone who could help her. But that may not be for centuries, or longer. Until then, FEAR, FEAR, FEAR, FEAR, FEAR, FEAR.

Chapter Eighteen
'We don't need your help any more'

The Doctor and President Vargeld stood on the observation deck of Spacedock One and watched as the ships prepared to leave for Yquatine.

'I still think this is a bad idea, you know,' said the Doctor gently.

'Say that again and I'll have you locked up,' said the President lightly.

The Doctor glanced at him. His jaw was set, resolute, his gaze fixed on the departing fleets. 'You don't trust me, do you? Why is that?' President Vargeld didn't move or speak. 'You think I'm still in the thrall of the Omnethoth, don't you? Well, I'm not.' He sighed. 'You have to believe me.'

'I don't trust you because I don't know you.' The President turned to face the Doctor. 'You say you were at my inauguration, but I've checked. No one matching your description was there.'

The Doctor scratched his nose. 'Yes, well…'

President Vargeld continued. 'You turn up from nowhere, and swan around acting like you're in control. Well, I'm in control.' He pointed at the departing ships. 'I'm taking action.'

'Well, it's the wrong action!' said the Doctor hotly. His voice became earnest. 'Let me try out my theory on our captive Omnethoth.'

'Station scientists are carrying out their own tests,' said the President smoothly.

The Doctor folded his arms. 'Yes, well that's very nice, but I could do in minutes what would probably take them weeks.'

A half-smile twisted across Vargeld's face. 'We'll see.'

Something moved at the edge of the Doctor's vision and he turned to see a fleet of Anthaurk ships speeding into the night, departing from a spacedock further along the crescent of

Aloysius. Even they had agreed to help in the bombardment of Yquatine, all hostility apparently forgotten. Or so it seemed. The Doctor was keeping a watchful eye on the Anthaurk – for all he knew, it could have been they who had discovered the Omnethoth, found out what it was and used it as a weapon. They were a fiercely militaristic race. It was a possibility.

'You know, I've been thinking,' said the President, half to himself, 'about what someone said to me, a month or so ago. Something about Yquatine being attacked, destroyed. It's been bugging me. How did he know?'

The Doctor watched the Anthaurk ships recede into invisibility, Vargeld's words floating about the edges of his perception. Something about them set alarm bells ringing.

As if in a daze, he turned to the President, grabbing his arm. 'Who told you that?'

The President pulled away. 'A prisoner.'

The Doctor waggled his fingers in front of the President's face, as if trying to tickle the words out of him. 'Tell me more!'

The President's youthful face grew hard, truculent. 'What?'

The Doctor put on his most disarming smile and most relaxed, casual manner. 'Sounds interesting, I mean. Someone being able to tell the future like that.'

President Vargeld remained noncommittal. 'Maybe it was a lucky guess.'

Oh, open up, man! The gravity of the situation – the possible damage to the timelines – made it impossible for the Doctor to relax. 'Maybe, but this could be very, very important. Please, I need to know more. What was his name?'

President Vargeld's look hardened. He clearly had no love for this prisoner. 'His name was Fitz Kreiner.'

The Doctor felt as if he had been rooted to the spot by a shaft of ice. A picture was forming in his mind, like a half-remembered nightmare. Something he would rather not face. He rubbed his hands together, trying to regain his composure. 'Fitz Kreiner is a friend of mine. Where is he now?'

'A friend of yours?' Vargeld looked at the Doctor sharply, his voice suddenly hoarse with anger. 'You're telling me you were mixed up with what he did?'

'Just tell me where he is now!' bellowed the Doctor.

'He's nowhere now.'

The Doctor feared the worst. 'What do you mean?'

'I mean that as far as I know he was still in Yendip Internment Centre on the day of the attack. He would have died along with everyone else.'

Vargeld sounded pleased. The Doctor closed his eyes. Another companion gone. Hope was a stupid thing. The glimmer of light at the end of the tunnel that was either the oncoming train or the torturer returning for a another session. He opened his eyes. 'What was he in prison for?'

'He kidnapped Arielle. Took her away from me. I never found out what was really going on.' A sigh between clenched teeth. 'Suppose I'll never know.'

Arielle. The President's girlfriend, the one they'd gone to Muath to look for. The Doctor tried to put Fitz out of his mind, concentrate on the situation. He was getting nearer to the truth, he could sense it. 'What was she doing on Muath?'

'Why should I even be talking to you?' muttered Vargeld. 'You should be telling me what Kreiner was doing with Arielle!'

The Doctor walked right up to the President. 'Fitz is – was – a good man. I cannot believe he would kidnap your fiancée. There must have been a reason. Maybe he was helping her.'

A shadow seemed to pass over the President's eyes. 'That's what he said.'

The Doctor looked into his eyes. He was getting something from the man, an inkling of his relationship with Arielle – he was clearly hiding something. 'Listen, I want to help you. Talk to me, tell me what happened. It isn't as simple as you're letting on. Arielle left you, didn't she?'

Stefan Vargeld's shoulders sagged. He nodded wearily.

'It was the night I proposed to her.'

The Doctor moved closer to Vargeld, alert for any sign of the breakdown that had overcome him on Muath. He sometimes forgot how much pain human relationships could bring. 'You don't have to tell me if you don't want to,' he said gently.

President Vargeld looked haunted by the ghosts of the past. He talked in low, confessional tones, seeming to forget that he didn't trust the Doctor, eager for someone to talk to. 'It was all so simple, at least that's how it seemed to me. I loved her, and she – well, I thought she loved me. That night, I asked her to marry me. She refused and I couldn't take it. I'm not proud. I acted terribly. When she tried to leave, I stopped her, grabbed her, threw her about. I – I hurt her.' The last three words were an incredulous whisper, the choked hush of a man unable to face his actions.

The Doctor didn't know what to say. 'So, she ran away?' he prompted at last.

The President nodded. 'Yes. She went away with this Kreiner character. I sent my men after them to bring her back, but it was too late. Arielle was in a coma.'

The Doctor knew Fitz well enough. Perfectly understandable for him to assist a damsel in distress. The only odd bit was the coma, but he put that aside for now. 'You kept Fitz imprisoned out of jealousy. You thought he was having an affair with Arielle.'

President Vargeld grimaced. 'I don't like to admit it, but yes.'

The Doctor folded his arms. 'But she recovered and went to Muath. That's why you went looking for her.' Another part of the picture, of the nightmare, was becoming clear.

President Vargeld looked weary, much older than his three decades. 'Yeah, she recovered. She wouldn't speak to me, though. She went to Muath – God knows why – and forbade me to contact her. She was going to come round, I know it! But it's too late now.'

The Doctor remembered their feverish dash to Muath. How the whole moon had been engulfed in the black Omnethoth gas. How the President had been crushed by the realisation of Arielle's death.

And now the man was responsible for keeping Fitz locked up while the Omnethoth had scoured Yquatine bare with their chemical arsenal. The Doctor tried to contain his anger. 'You kept Fitz wrongly imprisoned. You bent the law because of your love for Arielle. Do you think you're fit to be President?'

President Vargeld walked right up to the Doctor. 'Someone has to do it.'

The Doctor turned away. 'You're just a politician, not a human being.'

The remark hung in the air, and the Doctor immediately regretted it. It was a facile observation and completely untrue. Stefan Vargeld's failings were all too human.

The President broke the silence, his voice thick with emotion. 'That time in the infirmary, when she was packing for Muath. She was so cold, so distant. Not like the Arielle I fell in love with. She said she'd call me when she was ready. She never did. That was the last time I ever saw her.'

Another part of the picture became clear and the Doctor actually gasped aloud with the knowledge it brought. Arielle's coma. The only odd bit. Muath enveloped in black gas. The Doctor's mind raced, trying to process the information. 'When she recovered, you say she was acting differently?'

'Yes,' said the President. 'But that's not surprising, on account of what I –'

The Doctor interrupted. 'When she woke up, did you see her eyes – were they normal?'

The President frowned. 'You don't mean you think… she was…' His voice tailed off, and realisation dawned on his face.

The Doctor nodded grimly. 'She could have been the carrier of the Omnethoth spores. Do you know what she was doing on Muath?'

President Vargeld shook his head, ran his fingers through his short black hair. 'No, she never returned my calls, and I was busy with this Anthaurk business. This is crazy: how *can* she have been responsible for all those ships?'

The Doctor was pacing up and down. 'I don't know, I don't know, but it would be a huge coincidence if Arielle was nothing to do with this.'

'I thought you said the universe operated in a random way.'

'Yes yes, events happen randomly – but their consequences follow a logical order. If I throw a stone into a pond, that's a random act, but the ripples are a direct, logical consequence.'

President Vargeld put his hands over his face, clearly trying to control himself. 'I can't accept this – it's bad enough that Arielle is dead but now she's the cause of all this?' His voice had risen to a shout.

The Doctor went up to him, trying to calm him. 'I may be wrong. It may not have been her. It may have been someone else.' A dark thought struck him. 'It may even have been Fitz but he wasn't the one in the coma.' The picture was now more than complete, more than 3-D: Compassion had taken Fitz back in time – maybe that was as far as she could go, because of the Randomiser – and Fitz had somehow taken up with Arielle. Gone off on this cruiser. Encountered the Omnethoth cloud. Caused the fall of Yquatine.

The Doctor calmed himself. No, that wasn't right. Poor Fitz, it wasn't his fault. If it hadn't been Arielle then it would have been some other unfortunate.

The Doctor realised that President Vargeld had come up to him. 'Are you OK?'

The Doctor nodded. He could be angry with the President, but there was no point and more importantly it would be wrong. President Vargeld had been weak, that was all. Not evil, not even slightly mendacious. Love and jealously had guided his hand. The Doctor could forgive that – it was human – but he could never fully understand it. What was it like to be in love – and then to have that love taken away? Was it like losing a TARDIS? Was it like losing a friend? Fitz was dead, but so were millions of others. The Doctor could grieve for him now but then he'd be as weak as the President, allowing his feelings for one person to take precedence over his duty to the whole. The universal process is indifferent to the individual. He blushed as he recalled those words, spoken by him only hours ago. How hollow, how patronising they sounded now.

'Fitz was a good, good friend. I'm sorry he stole your girlfriend.' The Doctor smiled weakly. 'He was always one for the ladies.'

'And you?' asked President Vargeld, almost smiling. 'You dress like a Luvian bon-viveur.'

The Doctor looked into the President's eyes. They were blue, like his own. Indeed, if the Doctor cut his hair short and grew stubble – something he was glad not to have to do – then they'd look remarkably alike. Almost like brothers. The Doctor blinked. 'I do have another friend,' he whispered. 'She was on Yquatine with Fitz. Her name is Compassion.' Another flicker of fickle hope. 'Any sign of her?'

'Compassion? I'd remember a name like that.' President Vargeld shook his head. 'No. Just the guy Fitz. Look, I am truly sorry. We've both lost someone. I think that means I can trust you now.'

So Compassion could still be out there – anywhere. What if the Randomiser had kicked in? She'd never gain control without his tuition. It was all his fault, then. If he'd not fitted her with a Randomiser she would not have taken Fitz back and he would never have met Arielle. 'Can you excuse me, please? I want to be alone for a while.'

Their eyes met for an instant. The Doctor saw the hurt in his own eyes reflected in those of the Yquatine leader.

With a sad smile, President Vargeld left the Doctor on the observation deck, alone.

More alone than he could remember feeling for a long, long time.

The Doctor walked through the corridors and walkways of Aloysius Station, prey to a turmoil of emotions. He'd evaded the guards – he was still meant to be confined to the civilian areas of the station – and was looking for Lou Lombardo. He needed to see a friendly face. He so badly wanted to see Fitz again and spout spurious technobabble to confuse him, so badly wanted to see Compassion and stop her pain, that he kept seeing their faces in the crowds of people milling about the station.

Compassion. The thought of her almost hurt worse than the death of Fitz. He'd wanted to save her from the Time Lords, stop them taking her away from him and – there was no nice way to say this – raping her, using her to breed a race of TARDISes to fight their war. Horrifying, horrible, the thought revolted him to his core. And what had he done? Panicked. Inadvertently violated her. How could he have been so insensitive?

As he wandered around Aloysius Station looking for Lombardo, as he spoke to more and more people, he began to get a glimpse of an entire solar system stifled with shock. The population of an entire planet had been wiped out, almost instantly. The result was, initially, numbness, then a vast, unchecked outpouring of grief. Aloysius Station was full to capacity. Offerings, gifts and flowers clogged the lounges and public areas. The many religions of the System – and with the variety of the species there were very many – had all come to Aloysius to preach and proselytise. The only Yquatine natives to survive were those off planet at the time of the attack. People visiting relatives or away on business or holiday, people working on other planets, students, troopers in the Minerva Space Alliance. Those who could had come to Aloysius, to be near their homeworld. Though primarily a trading and military station, Aloysius had become a shrine.

Many believed the Anthaurk were responsible. The station showed signs of pitched battles between humans and Anthaurk – scorch marks on walls, dried blood, damaged fittings, cordoned-off areas. The news services were broadcasting the Doctor's findings but it would be hours still before the word Omnethoth replaced the word Anthaurk as a name of vilification for the survivors and mourners of Yquatine.

At last, after a good few hours walking, the Doctor found Lombardo. He wandered into a spacious café-bar area, where people and beings crowded round the large screen at the far end. A familiar shape was perched on a stool by the bar, a large glass at his elbow.

The Doctor rushed up to the figure. 'Lou!'

Lombardo turned round, frowning, but on seeing the Doctor he broke into a wide grin. 'Hey, Doctor! Good work!'

The Doctor and Lombardo hugged. The Doctor could smell the beer on his friend's breath. He'd clearly been drinking a lot. Well, if it helped. 'What do you mean?'

Lombardo indicated the screen. 'The news is full of your exploits on the moon. You found the bastards responsible and now we've all joined up to finish them off.'

'I admire your optimism.' The Doctor pulled up a stool and sat next to his friend.

Lombardo shot him a puzzled frown. 'What's up with you? Victory is at hand, my dear.'

'I have a bad feeling about this,' muttered the Doctor. But then he was having a bad feeling about everything.

The news report intercut between a reporter on an orbital platform near the dark mass of Yquatine – far too near, the Doctor thought – and the phalanx of ships moving into position around the planet.

'The combined firepower of the Anthaurk, Kukutsi, Rorclaavix, Adamantean, Eldrig and human ships is easily enough to take out a planet,' the reporter gabbled excitedly. The picture cut to a shot of three silver and rust-red behemoths coursing through space, nacelles and gun ports gleaming cruelly in the light of the sun.

'These are the latest battleship marques straight from the spaceyards of Beatrix – Endurance-class ships fitted with the newest and most powerful planet-crackers and photon projectiles.'

Whoops, cheers and applause from those gathered around the screen.

The Doctor was silent, chin on hands, brooding.

The screen showed the ships lining up in position, warheads primed. All at once, blinding lights flashed from the ships as they rained their destructive firepower upon the remains of Yquatine. In formation, bomb ships swooped, delivered their payloads and screamed back out into space.

The atmosphere was incredible. People were cheering, leaping up and hugging each other as if they had already won.

The Doctor was virtually the only one watching the screen. He saw the beams and bombs vanish into Yquatine's dark mantle. There was no flash of light, nothing.

'Nothing's happening,' said the Doctor.

Everyone crowded around the screen.

The fleet hung in space, impotent above the swirling blackness.

'The Omnethoth must have neutralised the bombs,' whispered the Doctor.

People groaned and turned away from the screen.

The Doctor rose to leave. Perhaps now, the Senate would listen to him.

A hand grabbed his sleeve. 'For the love of God!'

Lombardo was staring in horror at the screen.

The Doctor gasped.

Directly below the fleet, something was happening on the surface of the Omnethoth. A section the size of a continent was billowing outwards, bulging like a distended stomach. The ships began to come about, preparing to fly away from Yquatine but before they could complete the manoeuvre the belly of black gas exploded out into space, releasing churning tendrils of Omnethoth matter, reaching out like clutching fingers. The fleet was totally engulfed.

There was a fizz of static, then the scene changed. The reporter stood against a panorama of space, babbling, clearly terrified.

The Doctor stood up, sending his stool clattering against the floor. 'They're too close. They're too close!'

The reporter was screaming now. There was an explosion off screen, the reporter ran off camera and then – static.

Silence, apart from a muted sobbing.

The Doctor felt numbed, appalled. One more tragedy. 'I tried to warn them,' he whispered.

Lombardo's face was blank, his eyes distant. 'What?'

'I tried to tell them there was another way.'

Lombardo grabbed the Doctor by the shoulders. His voice was cracked, panicky. 'Well go back and tell them again!' he cried.

The Doctor walked into the Senate chamber, vowing not to say, 'I told you so.' He might have done once, but he was too old for that sort of point-scoring. Hundreds more people had died needlessly. He had to make sure it wouldn't happen again.

'Ah, Doctor,' said the President.

There was a gleam of triumph in his eyes – or was it madness? Had this latest setback unhinged him totally? 'Glad you could make it.'

'Well, I wasn't doing anything else,' said the Doctor lamely.

A 3-D image of Yquatine occupied the centre of the chamber and the attention of all those within. It was a shocking sight: the planet had grown noticeably, the mantle of Omnethoth matter adding considerably to its girth. Muath had been completely dissolved, absorbed into the main mass. The churning black surface seemed totally unaffected by the recent barrage. Yquatine had been turned into a giant war factory. The Omnethoth were busy preparing more ships. Soon they would launch into the System and destroy every planet within it. It was what they were programmed to do.

'Well, your attack has failed,' said the Doctor. 'And we haven't got long before the Omnethoth expand into the rest of the System. I think you're ready to listen to me.'

'Think again,' said President Vargeld.

The Doctor ignored him. 'Right!' he said, rubbing his hands together. 'I'll need a small, well-shielded stealth ship.'

'Be quiet, Doctor!' The harshness of Vargeld's voice stunned the Doctor into silence.

'I'm only trying to help,' he mumbled, feeling in his pocket for a jelly baby.

'We don't need your help any more,' sneered Fandel.

The Doctor popped the jelly baby into his mouth. Green again! 'So what are you going to do?'

President Vargeld pressed a control on the dais and the holo of Yquatine faded away. He turned to address the Senate, and the Doctor, who had taken a seat on the steps leading up between the seats.

'We cannot destroy these creatures by conventional means,' began President Vargeld. 'Anything we drop into their mass is simply neutralised.'

The Doctor tried again. 'So you want me to try my theory? Reprogram the Omnethoth into peaceful creatures?'

President Vargeld shook his head. 'No, Doctor. Nothing but the total destruction of the Omnethoth will satisfy us now.'

The other senators voiced their agreement.

The Doctor sighed, exasperated and irritated. 'But you've *tried* that. And look what happened.'

'We have found another way,' said the President. 'Senator Rhombus-Alpha?'

The blue-white diamond shape of the Ixtricite senator floated into the centre of the chamber. 'I have made a study of the Omnethoth. They are animated by a form of electrical energy. An ionisation field could disrupt the delicate balance of electrons within the Omnethoth, neutralising their controlling intelligence and dispersing their structure.'

President Vargeld grinned. 'And it works. We have already tried it on the one we captured.'

The Doctor looked up sharply. 'What?'

'It was totally destroyed.' The President walked up to the Doctor, hands behind his back. 'Did you know they could be destroyed by this means?'

The Doctor stood up, squaring his shoulders. 'Well, since you ask, yes.'

A mutter of disquiet ran around the Senate chamber.

The President's face was white with anger. 'Why didn't you tell us before? Why bother with all this DNA-altering nonsense?'

The Doctor put on his most earnest expression. 'Because ionisation is extremely dangerous! You'll be creating an enormous electrical field, disrupting anything within thousands of kilometres. Your ships will be able to transmit the killing charge but there will be no escape for them!'

'We know that,' said the President solemnly. 'And we have all decided that the sacrifice is worth it.'

The Doctor kneaded his forehead with his knuckles. 'No no no! Can't you see? There's no need for further loss of life! I can reprogram them!'

President Vargeld's eyes had a sheen of bloodlust. 'Can you destroy them?'

The Doctor met his gaze. 'Even if I could, I wouldn't. Even manufactured life is still life.'

'What if there was no other choice? Them, or us?'

The Doctor squared up to Vargeld. 'There is always a choice. If ifs and buts were candy and nuts –'

'Silence!' barked the President.

The Doctor grimaced. How could he have compared this man to a brother? Only one thing connected them: loss, a universal emotion common to all life forms. The Doctor had more in common with the Ixtricite than the Yquatine leader. 'You're sacrificing your people for no reason whatsoever.'

President Vargeld turned away, ignoring him.

The senators gathered around the console at the far end of the chamber.

The Doctor sank back down in his chair. The idiots. He wasn't going to give up. He'd let them plan their attack and then he'd have another go at convincing them. Maybe some of the other senators would listen...

He became aware of a presence before him. He looked up. Senator Zendaak was standing in front of him, arms folded. 'Want to come Omnethoth hunting?'

Chapter Nineteen
'Escape? No, thank you very much!'

There had been installations on Muath ever since the twenty-eighth century during the original colonisation of the Minerva System. Over the decades, the small moon had gone through many changes of ownership and usage, and the original envirodomes had been upgraded and replaced many times, mostly by choice, but sometimes through necessity. During the Anthaurk conflict Muath had been an important staging post, from which Space Alliance ships had struck out against Anthaurk attacks on Yquatine. After the war, the moon had languished unused for a few decades until various industrial concerns had taken it over, and then it had been turned into a residential area and theme park. This has prospered for fifty years, after which its popularity had begun to wane and it began to lose money, with people moving back to Yquatine or off to other planets.

In the early years of the twenty-ninth century the University of Yquatine had set up a research facility for scientific studies requiring low gravity and isolation such as the more microscopic, infectious reaches of xenobiology. Now, however, the university no longer owned the whole installation. Various industrial concerns once more had vested interests, using it for their more dangerous lines of research.

Powell Industries had recently purchased a plot on Muath, and, being of a rather strict financial outlook, had decided to use prison labour for the difficult, dangerous work of erecting the outer shell of their envirodomes.

Prison labour was cheaper than robotic labour. It wasn't quite slavery – the prisoners were paid, and were glad of the work, and, like Sorswo, glad of the change of scene – but it struck Fitz as a very old-fashioned way of going about things. Surely Powell

Industries could plonk their domes down with no help from humans. Dakrius, who had accompanied them to Muath, had told Fitz the reason – money, or lack of it – and this had reassured him.

The future wasn't a place of infinite choice, freedom and convenience. It was a place of injustice, pain, penny-pinching and inconvenience. At least, where the human race was concerned – you never heard of this sort of thing from the Ixtricite, on whom Fitz had done some research while in the Centre. There were no Ixtricite prisoners, or even criminals: they kept themselves to themselves on their crystal world. In a moment of paranoid terror Fitz had imagined that they were responsible for the coming tragedy, which was going to happen tomorrow and which he was going to avoid. But no, it was the Anthaurk, wasn't it? Fitz remembered the way they treated him in Il-Eruk's Tavern all that time ago.

There were thirty workers including Sorswo and Fitz, only six of them human, and the accommodation dome was cramped. The work was hard – welding, positioning, fetching and carrying – but Fitz was glad of it. It took his mind off things and allowed him to plan his escape. But, as far as he could work out, escape was impossible. Thanks to the nanochips Dakrius was able to monitor their positions constantly on a portable unit strapped to his stony wrist, and while they were outside all conversations were monitored through their suit receivers.

There was also the fact that nobody wanted to escape, least of all Sorswo.

In the depths of the first night they spent on Muath, Fitz had enjoyed a hushed conversation with Sorswo which had gone something like this:

'Sorswo… wake up!'

'Huh… Fitz? What is it?'

'I wanna talk.'

'What about?'

'I think we should try to work out how to escape.'

Indrawn shocked breath. 'Escape? No, thank you very much!'

'Why not?'

Sorswo's eyes had gleamed in the darkness. 'I'm out of here in a few months anyway. Why bother trying to escape? We're bound to fail and that would be goodbye to my remission.'

Fitz gnashed his teeth. 'So you won't help me?'

'No.' His voice took on a sonorous ring of finality. 'Let us never speak of this matter again.'

And so it had been with all the other prisoners. They didn't want to risk their parole. Miserable, short-sighted, mooching mice that they were.

So Fitz was stuck on the moon with no way off. What if the attackers struck Muath, too? Then he would be out of the frying pan into the fire. Or, at best, out of the fire into the frying pan.

Either way, it wasn't a very comforting thought.

There was one ray of hope: maybe the Doctor had escaped. He usually did. And maybe Compassion had gone back to him. Surely they would come and look for him. The Doctor wouldn't leave him behind. Or would he? One cold thought often filled him with dread: what if they'd gone on their travels, leaving Fitz smack bang in the middle of a war? That thought sent him into black moods, and he tried to entertain it as little as possible.

It was the day before Treaty Day, or rather the night before – Fitz found it hard to keep track of time on Muath. He was out with Sorswo, applying sealant to one of the finished Powell Industries envirodomes. A feeling of dread had seeped into his bones. The attack was going to happen, within hours. He kept looking up at the blue-green globe of Yquatine, hanging in the sky overhead.

Had he, the Doctor and Compassion arrived there yet? Was the earlier version of him buying gooey food off a giant insect? Were they in Lou Lombardo's pie shop? He tried to remember the exact sequence of events leading up to the moment the Yquatine sky had darkened with the invading ships, but it was all confused in his mind.

Sorswo's voice crackled in the earpiece of his helmet. 'Why do you keep staring at Yquatine? Homesick already?'

Fitz was seized with a sudden impulse to tell his friend everything. He fought it down. Too bloody late now anyway. Why hadn't he warned anyone? Didn't want to harm the timelines. What utter bollocks! Millions were going to die – Il-Eruk, Zabulong, Val, President Vargeld and his goons – and he could have prevented it. You could have done something, Fitz Kreiner. You could have made a difference, but what did you do? You tried to run away, and failed. You got pissed out of your face. You ran away with the President's girlfriend only to be caught and that's why you're here now, you stupid bastard.

Arielle. She was probably still on Yquatine now, still in a coma. She may even be dead. Fitz hoped she was. He couldn't stand the thought of her face staring up at the sky as the black ships polluted the air with their filth, screaming as the first spots of acid rain hit her skin –

Fitz fell to his knees, pressing his eyes shut, his gloved hands clawing at the dome of his helmet. He screamed in frustration and confusion, letting out all his pain, all his fear. How had he come to this? Why was the universe doing this to him? What had he done to deserve this?

Hands on his shoulders, a voice crackling in his ear, the concern evident even through the small speaker. 'Hey, friend, what's the matter?'

Fitz couldn't wipe the tears away, nor the snot that had begun to trickle from his nose. ''S all right,' he said, his voice thick and numb, his throat aching. 'I get a little claustrophobic in these suits –'

'Shh!' The sound was a harsh burst of static. 'Don't let Dakrius hear that or he'll send you straight back to the Centre!'

Fitz bit his bottom lip. 'Course, yeah.' The thought of being sent back to Yquatine right now brought him back to his senses and he got to his feet, allowing Sorswo to help him, his qualm over.

Get a grip, Fitz. Don't give in to insanity. Was he prone to it? Would he end up like his mother? Would madness be a welcome release? Was that how it been for his mother?

So easy to give in, to abdicate responsibility for yourself.

As he stood, these dark thoughts swimming through his mind, something flashed on the horizon off to his right. He blinked, looked again. There, in the distance, was a silver shape, bright against the darkness of space.

He pointed. 'Look.'

Sorswo looked. 'Well, I say.'

It was a spacesuited figure, a few miles distant, standing on a low scarp of grey rock which bordered the horizon. As they both stared, the figure ducked down – sunlight flashing off its visor – and was gone.

'That was odd,' muttered Sorswo. 'Section Leader, sir!'

Dakrius's voice crackled in Fitz's helmet. 'What is it, Sorswo?'

'Is everyone accounted for?'

Dakrius confirmed that they were. 'Why do you ask?'

'We saw someone, on the horizon.'

Dakrius sounded indifferent. 'Probably someone from the university.'

'That's kilometres away,' said Sorswo. 'On the other side of the moon! It might be someone in trouble.'

Dakrius sighed. 'OK, finish up at the dome and then take the buggy.' Satisfaction crept into his harsh, grating tones. 'I'll be watching you, don't worry.'

A few minutes later, Fitz and Sorswo were rolling across the lunar landscape in the small buggy used to ferry prisoners and materials between domes.

This was clearly their one chance to escape, though Fitz dared not voice the thought. Dakrius was monitoring their conversation.

They climbed the escarpment. It sloped down gently on the other side. Footprints could clearly be seen, leading down the slope, towards a range of small mountains.

They drove the buggy to the edge of this. There was a small passageway into the mountains.

Sorswo described the conditions to Dakrius.

Silence, then: 'Proceed, but be careful.'

Sorswo shot Fitz a rueful glance from beneath his faceplate. The look said it all: we're criminals, we're expendable.

They dismounted from the buggy and Sorswo led the way along the passage. Walls of rock reared up on either side at wild angles, there was little light. Fitz switched on his helmet lamp.

They walked for what seemed like ages.

They came out into a clearing – a deep, bowl-floored crater with walls hundreds of feet high.

Fitz and Sorswo both cried out in exclamation at what they saw on the floor of the crater.

'What is it?' came Dakrius's voice.

How to describe the thing? It crouched in the bottom of the crater, like a giant, sprawling black flower or a mutated spider. The central mass was a pulsating abdomen the size of a house. Trailing out from it were hundreds of thin, black, hairlike roots or legs which shuddered and trembled as if alive.

And standing in front of the thing was the figure in the spacesuit, one hand behind its back. Its faceplate was black, as if it had been coated from the inside.

'There's someone here, and some sort of growth,' began Sorswo. 'It's –'

The figure took its hand from behind its back. It was holding a gun, with which it shot Sorswo.

He was blasted against the wall of the crater, a smoking hole in the fabric of his suit.

Fitz sank to his knees as Sorswo's dying screams and Dakrius's urgent enquiries reverberated inside his helmet. He reached up and, although it was forbidden, shut the speaker off.

Silence.

His ears ringing, Fitz gazed up dumbly as the figure approached him, the blaster hanging from a gloved hand.

Fitz tensed, waiting for the killing shot.

But it never came.

Instead, the figure holstered the weapon, reached up and

started undoing the catches on its helmet.

Fitz watched mesmerised as the figure removed its helmet.

He couldn't find the voice to scream as the face beneath was revealed.

There before him, golden hair floating in the low gravity like a mermaid's in the deep ocean, eyes gleaming black, was Arielle.

Part Four

As Long as Your Luck Holds Out

Chapter Twenty
'I wouldn't stand too close if I were you'

The Doctor stood on the flight deck of the Anthaurk battle cruiser *Argusia* and tried not to feel put out by the décor. It wasn't easy: the Anthaurk were hefty, powerful, military-minded creatures and their ships were built to match. Everything was made of some tubular material which glistened like innards. The backs of the pilot's and navigator's seats reared up in front of him like tombstones. In front of them was a control panel packed with big levers and glowing green displays. The ceiling was a good twenty feet above him, crammed with snaking cables, ducts and lighting arrays which looked like clusters of Anthaurk eyeballs. The whole area was washed in a disturbing blood-red light. The Doctor looked down at the back of his own hand. It looked pink, lurid, the nails shining pearly white.

Ahead, an oval-shaped viewscreen showed a virtual representation of what was outside, overlaid with tactical grids and readouts. Around the sides of the flight deck, Anthaurk sat or stood at their command posts, intent on their tasks. Their uniforms – some sort of leather, no doubt made from whatever unfortunate beasts trod the plains of New Anthaur – obviously hadn't been changed or cleaned for a while. The Doctor briefly considered having another crack at the paper on differing hygiene standards between species he'd started one rainy afternoon during his exile on Earth. Maybe he would, if he got out of this current situation in one piece.

The Doctor looked up at Zendaak, who was standing at his left, arms folded, red eyes inscrutable. 'You know it really is good of you to go to all this trouble.'

Zendaak didn't seem to have heard the Doctor. Instead he issued an order to modify their course and maximise speed.

They had left Aloysius Station without the consent of the President or the Senate, and were now a few hours from Yquatine. They may just be able to catch up with the specially prepared attack fleet. Unless they did, the crews of all twelve ships were doomed.

Zendaak's question came out of the blue. 'Why do want to save the Omnethoth, Doctor?'

'Well,' said the Doctor, 'because I like to believe all life is sacred.'

Zendaak sneered, revealing sharp teeth. 'Ah yes, your liberal, life-respecting stance. But even accepting that all life is sacred, the Omnethoth are manufactured, not naturally evolved. They have no place in the overall scheme of things. Wanting to save them is like wanting to save a lethal virus manufactured in the bio-war labs.'

'Interesting point,' said the Doctor, glad that Zendaak had opened up. He enjoyed a good conversation. 'The Omnethoth have the potential for good. I can alter their DNA so that they'll be peaceful, benign creatures. I'll be giving the universe a new species, creating a new form of life. And that rather appeals to me.' Out of the roots of evil could come great good, et cetera. It was like thumbing your nose at the universal process, not that it could possibly care. 'But most importantly I want to prevent the ionisation attack, which would cause unnecessary deaths.'

Zendaak nodded thoughtfully. 'You're sure you can adapt the Omnethoth?'

The Doctor waved a hand. 'Oh, yes. Piece of cake. All we have to do is get hold of one. And are you sure you know what to do when the time comes?'

Zendaak nodded. 'We have been over the procedure a number of times.'

'It's important we get it right. And, while we're on the subject, why are you helping me?'

Zendaak looked down at the Doctor. 'I want no part in the madness of the ionisation of Yquatine. In helping you I hope to prove Anthaurk innocence beyond all doubt.'

The Doctor smiled. 'A noble motive.'

Zendaak appeared not to notice the sarcasm in his voice.

Maybe, the Doctor wondered as he stared at the Anthaurk's ballooning muscles on his thighs and upper arms, the three-clawed hand, the blunt, snakelike head, just maybe Zendaak's motives were altruistic. Maybe he really did want to help. After all, he had pulled all the Anthaurk ships out of the attack, which had angered President Vargeld, until Zendaak had agreed on the compromise measure of the Anthaurk fleet forming part of the protective cordon around Aloysius should the Omnethoth retaliate.

There was something else. Something the Doctor suddenly remembered. A memory of being smothered in choking blackness, breath surging from his straining lungs. Of his mind taking a back seat as something ancient and crude had taken over, using his voice to communicate its obscene, bombastic threat. Of collapsing, chest aching, the gas creature gathering like a cloud above him, preparing to unleash its deadly rainfall... And then strong arms lifting him to safety. Anthaurk arms. Zendaak's arms.

The Doctor reached out and touched Zendaak's shoulder, which was at the level of the crown of his own head. 'You saved my life! And I never even thanked you.'

Zendaak's great head turned and dipped, red eyes staring down at the Doctor. 'There is no need to thank me.'

The Doctor looked into the Anthaurk's widely spaced eyes, staring from the black scales like fire from inside a cave. 'Well, thank you anyway.' He smiled and shrugged. 'Slightly curious as to why, though.'

Zendaak pointed with one arm at the forward screens. They showed a virtual image of the surrounding space, the attack fleet a flotilla of red dots approaching a fuzzy green area that represented the Omnethoth domain, which had once been Yquatine and its moon. 'You revealed the true nature of that,' he hissed. 'Proved it has nothing to do with us.'

Fair enough. If unchecked, the Omnethoth infestation would certainly destroy New Anthaurk; that was proof enough of Anthaurk innocence.

But could he trust the creatures? Could he trust Zendaak? The Doctor looked around the bridge at the other Anthaurk at their stations. There were about a dozen of them, tall, powerful reptiles armed to the teeth and willing to die for their commander. He had no other choice but to trust them, at least for now. Play along with them. He had a suspicion that they would expect him to deliver the Omnethoth to them as a potential weapon. He'd better make sure that the changes he made to their genetic code were irreversible.

The Doctor forced himself to concentrate on the screen. 'How much longer before we reach the Omnethoth?'

'Another hour.'

Couldn't they go any faster? The Doctor tried to conceal his impatience, with only partial success.

Fitz backed away from Arielle, shuffling along the gritty surface of Muath on his backside, his mouth moving but nothing coming out.

This was the last straw. He could feel his mind trying to cope with it all, his left eyelid twitching of its own accord, his heart pounding. What the hell was she doing here? He couldn't take his eyes off her face – her eyes like black orbs, her mouth stretched back across her face like elastic. How could she *breathe*?

There was nowhere to run. His oxygen tank was bumping and scraping against the ridged wall of the crater that curved solidly to either side of him. Arielle stood, legs either side of his feet, her mouth opening in a wide O, surely wider than it was meant to. Her beauty distorted, warped, as if reflected in a broken mirror. Why hadn't she shot him, killed him like she'd killed Sorswo? Maybe there was something left of her, some trace of personality. 'Arielle,' said Fitz, his voice cracking. 'Whatever's happened to you, I can help. You're ill…'

His voice tailed off as he saw wisps of dark, black gas issue from her mouth.

Now he realised why she hadn't killed him. Whatever had taken her over was now going to do the same to him.

Suddenly she was yanked backwards and spun round by a black-clad figure which seemed to have come from nowhere. The figure wrested the gun from Arielle's hand, and, before Fitz could intervene, fired at her.

Arielle sailed through the air and landed on her back by the side of the spider-flower thing. She lay there, not moving, wisps of gas twirling round her head, her golden hair splayed over the grey rock. Fitz went to stumble after her, but then he caught sight of her assailant.

'Hello, Fitz.'

The voice wasn't coming from his earpiece: it was inside his mind. And it was familiar. Standing before him was a woman with pale skin and ginger hair in a black cloak. She wasn't wearing a spacesuit. She wouldn't be able to breathe.

She didn't need to breathe. She was Compassion.

Now he could go mad. Now he could give in, start laughing and never stop, let the starshine pour into his addled mind…

But that was not going to happen. No way. No way because he was far too angry.

He went over to Arielle. She was lying face up, eyes open, wisps of black gas running from her open mouth. 'You've killed her!'

Compassion came over to join him, looking down at Arielle with obvious disinterest. 'She's just stunned.'

There was something odd about her, a look in her eyes he hadn't seen before. 'You… you bloody… thing.' His voice was thick with sobs of anger. 'You tried to kill me. You abandoned me.'

She frowned in annoyance. 'I have just saved your life. Or hadn't you noticed?'

Fitz refused to respond to her sarcasm, letting his anger pour out in a torrent of words. 'You left me on a doomed planet and I've been in sodding prison for a month and why the *hell* couldn't you have turned up earlier?'

'If you only knew what I've been through to get here.' A sigh. 'You wouldn't understand.'

'Oh, fine!' cried Fitz, aware that his voice was cracking. 'Yeah, I wouldn't understand because I'm only human and you're, you're... I don't know what or who you are any more. Hey!'

She was ignoring him, was walking over to the spider-flower thing.

Fitz watched her through his spit-flecked faceplate and fumed. He opened his mouth for another tirade - but why bother? What notice would she take of him? And, more to the point, did he really want to annoy the one person who could rescue him? He fought down his anger. There would be time to have it out with Compassion later, he hoped. Right now he had better play along with her.

He went to stand beside her. Damned if he was going to apologise for his outburst, though. 'What do you think it is?'

Compassion was running her hands over the black skin. Close up, Fitz could see that it was covered in tiny pores and wrinkles.

'It's alive, in a sense,' muttered Compassion. 'This torus is an organic power generator, a giant living battery. It's been growing, for the past month or so, tended by our friend over there.' She waved a dismissive hand at the prone form of Arielle and stood back, hands on hips. 'By now it must have stored up a colossal energy charge.'

Fitz stood back, gazing warily at the legs and tendrils of the thing. They were pulsing, tensing, as if in time with a giant heartbeat. He shuddered. It made him itch all over. What had Arielle to do with this? 'What's it for?' he wondered aloud.

Compassion licked her lips. 'It's a transmitter.'

Images of aerials and pylons flickered through Fitz's head. Nothing like this thing. 'For what?'

Compassion smiled grimly. 'It's a good job I turned up.'

She placed her hands on the skin of the transmitter and closed her eyes.

'What are you doing?'

'I have to destroy it. It's a transmitter for a teleport carrier beam. When it activates it will bring those black ships we saw.'

She said it so casually that it took a few seconds to sink in. A teleport beam... those black ships... raining acid death on to Yquatine...

Fitz stared at the transmitter. So this was it. The beginning of the invasion. How long had this thing crouched obscenely here, growing, pulsing, waiting to summon the invasion fleet? A dreadful thought struck him. 'What if you set it off accidentally?'

Compassion glared at him. 'Out of the question. I'm going to flood it with Artron energy, burn out its sensory network. I wouldn't stand too close if I were you.'

Fitz found himself taking a few steps back, turned to look at Arielle, only to see that she wasn't there any more. He glanced wildly around. There – a silver blur vanishing around the back of the machine. He ran after her, loping in the low gravity.

Round the back of the transmitter, Arielle had sunk her arm into a flowerlike opening. The black skin of the transmitter started to ripple. Fitz stared at it helplessly for a second, then he lunged forward, grabbed Arielle around her waist and pulled. She was caught fast, up to the elbow in the guts of the thing. Fitz pulled harder. Suddenly she came free and fell against him.

They stumbled backward together. Arielle's hands were scrabbling at her throat and Fitz turned her round.

Her eyes were back to normal – and bulging out of her head.

Compassion appeared by his side. 'We're too late. It's activated.'

Fitz shoved the convulsing form of Arielle at her. 'Take her in! She'll die!'

Compassion stood impassively as Arielle fell, clutching at her black robes.

'Oh, Christ, do it!'

Compassion shrugged, there was a white flash and Arielle was gone.

'Is she OK?' gasped Fitz.

Compassion seemed to consider for a second. 'Not by any definition of the word.'

A shadow passed over them. Fitz looked up. The sky was full of dark oval shapes.

It had started. It was Treaty Day. The circle was complete. Somewhen about now, an earlier version of him was standing on Yendip Esplanade with an earlier version of Compassion watching the sky of Yquatine fill up with death.

Compassion was staring up at them, an absent look on her face.

Fitz, terrified of the threat of acid rain, all but threw himself at her. 'Let me in!'

Her smile was playful but her eyes were cold, dead things. He shuddered. Was she going to leave him here to die? Suddenly there was a flash of light, a falling sensation and he was inside the console chamber.

He reached up and undid the catches of his helmet. The cool air of the console chamber felt like heaven. He looked around the chamber. 'Where's Arielle?'

'Somewhere safe,' came Compassion's voice from all around him.

Fitz looked up at the roofspace scanner. The sky was full of the black ships and they were pouring out spined missiles which were plunging into the surface of Muath.

Fitz ran up to the console, gripping on to the railing. 'Compassion, dematerialise! We've got to find the Doctor!'

A sound came from all around him which was something like a sigh, something like an autumn wind rattling through bare branches.

Fitz put his helmet down on the grating next to the console. 'Compassion?'

Two words, small and packed with frustration. 'I can't.'

Damn her! 'You found me, didn't you?'

The chamber darkened and there were flashes of blue from below. Fitz touched his throat nervously, remembering how she'd cut off the air supply and almost killed him.

Compassion's voice came again, thick and low, as though she'd been crying. It struck Fitz then how calm Compassion sounded when you were outside her, and how unhinged she sounded when you were inside.

'I can't dematerialise or I would randomise into the vortex. No control. No control.'

Evidently she hadn't mastered the Randomiser. 'So how did you find me?'

'I was trapped in the vortex. Feels like I've been everywhere, everywhen. Eventually I found a way past the Randomiser. I anchored myself to your biodata signature. Used it as a focus. But the Randomiser kept pulling me back. Had to keep rematerialising, getting nearer each time. Took years, decades – I don't *know* how long.'

Fitz sank to his knees. He didn't realise how she'd suffered. But he still had to know. 'Why did you abandon me in the first place?'

'Wanted to get rid of the Randomiser and test my new powers.' A pause. 'Failed.'

Fitz smoothed his beard, thinking. 'Well, so, erm, we can't take off, so what are we gonna do?'

'Use conventional means.'

An image of the shuttle, crouching buglike on its support struts. 'There's a shuttle –'

'I see it,' whispered Compassion.

Fitz looked up at the roofscape. Everywhere, the black stuff. Compassion was presumably OK, but how long would the shuttle last?

'We'll make it,' said Compassion. Was she reading his mind? 'I can run pretty fast when I want to.'

Dakrius twisted the dial of his comm unit. 'Kreiner? Sorswo?' Nothing.

Sorswo's last words rang in his head. 'Some sort of growth.' Then a burst of static, then nothing. This had all the hallmarks of an escape attempt. He cursed himself for being so trusting. Kreiner was probably the main culprit – political prisoners were always the worst. But Sorswo? He was due for release soon and Dakrius knew escape was the last thing on his mind. And where was there to escape to? Only the three domes, linked by tubular corridors, which comprised the habitation areas, the mess, the workshop and storage areas and Dakrius's office. The Powell constructions loomed over all, but they wouldn't be habitable for days yet. There was the shuttle, stationed on its launch pad some way from the domes, but that was under constant surveillance and he had the only enabler key.

Dakrius left his office and walked through the silent workshop. It had been end of shift when Sorswo and Kreiner had set off in the buggy. All the other workers would be in the mess, probably wondering where the pair were. They had better not have crashed that buggy. It was an expensive piece of equipment.

Dakrius paced up and down, twisting the dial on his comms unit. Nothing.

He was going to have to go after them in the other buggy. He shambled along the tubular corridor, his bulk shaking the sides. He liked being up here, where he weighed less. Yquatine's gravity was twice that of Adamantine and it played hell with his joints and digestion.

He entered the mess hall, and silently pointed to two prisoners. No point alarming all of them. Last thing he wanted was a riot on his hands.

* * *

A few minutes later the two prisoners, Melebele and Jayd, had suited up and were sitting in the buggy in front of Dakrius. Melebele was a tall, strong Rorclaavix; if there was anything nasty out there Dakrius would be glad of his help. Jayd was a human, a petty pilferer who'd been in and out of institutions all his life, and an expert with machines, which was why Dakrius had chosen him to drive the buggy and repair the one Kreiner and Sorswo had taken, if need be.

The Adamantean's spacesuit was specially adapted, adding to his bulk – in it he looked like a giant and unwieldy robot. He knew that with his weight on the buggy it would take longer to get to the scene of the incident, but he wanted to be there in person. He left Torris and Muller in charge. He hoped they could cope. Humans often had problems with discipline.

They started out, the buggy crawling across the bumpy grey surface of Muath, Dakrius's patient, methodical mind ticking over the possibilities. Escape seemed the most likely. The more he thought about it, the more suspect Sorswo's manner seemed. Perhaps the man had been lulling him into a false sense of security.

So intent was Dakrius on the motives of his charges that he didn't notice the sky darken above him until a grumble of astonishment from Melebele and a cry of alarm from Jayd crackled simultaneously in his helmet receiver.

'Sir!' Jayd's voice. 'Look – look up there!'

Dakrius looked up as a shadow slipped over the buggy. He squinted, trying to make it out. The stars were being occluded by the passage of – what? Something huge and black. Ships?

He spoke into his helmet mike. 'Take us back.'

Jayd began to take the buggy in a wide arc, sending up a wall of fine dust which hung for a moment before falling slowly back down. Just before the arc was complete, something thumped into the soft ground in front of them. Jayd jammed on the brakes and Dakrius fell forward in his harness.

Melebele had already got out and was walking towards the thing.

'I gave no order!' barked Dakrius, unbuckling his harness and stepping on to the surface. His feet sank a good few centimetres into the dust.

He stood next to Melebele. The Rorclaavix wasn't particularly bright – he'd been caught mugging Luvian tourists in broad daylight – and beneath the dome of his helmet his furred face was alight with dopey interest. 'What you think it is, sir?'

Dakrius examined the object as closely as he dared, twice arm's length. It looked like a bomb of very strange design, covered in spines and grey tubes. As Dakrius watched, a thick black gas began to leak out from the tubes and expand in the thin atmosphere. From all around him Dakrius could see plumes of grey dust where similar objects were falling.

He shoved Melebele towards the buggy. 'Get back in right now.'

Melebele did as he was told, and Dakrius followed, clambering into the buggy and strapping himself in. 'Take us back to the domes, Jayd.'

Jayd had kept the electric motor idling and on Dakrius's command the buggy lurched into life. It was tough on Sorswo and Kreiner, but Dakrius's first duty was to the other prisoners.

All around, the black spiny missiles were falling and disgorging their thick black contents. Dakrius cursed. A wall of the stuff was curling around the domes, sliding up over their silvery outer skin. It seemed alive, like a hunter seeking out its prey.

Melebele's gruff voice. 'Domes under attack now, sir.'

'I can see that,' said Dakrius angrily. He couldn't risk taking them into that stuff. Fortunately, the shuttle stood some distance from the domes – a safety measure Dakrius was now heartily glad of. 'Jayd, take us to the shuttle. We've got no choice but to abandon base.'

They made good speed towards the shuttle. Dakrius glanced back at the domes. They were now completely enveloped in the black stuff. He didn't want to think what it was doing to his charges and other officers. Choking them? Burning them? The sky was dark with the ships, cutting off light from the sun. Jayd had switched on the buggy's lights, their beams bouncing crazily on the grey sand. Dakrius was surprised the Anthaurk – for it had to be they – were bothering with such a nontarget as Muath. Perhaps they were after some of the secret research rumoured to be taking place at the university installation.

They were a hundred metres or so from the shuttle when the buggy jerked to a halt.

'What is it?'

'Power's cut out,' said Jayd. 'Some sort of system fault.'

'We'll have to run.' Dakrius scrambled out, Melebele close on his heels. All around them surged the black gas, twice the height of an Adamantean, closing around them like a sphincter. It was almost upon the shuttle.

Jayd was unclipping his harness when something fell out of the sky, smashing into the side of the buggy, sending it spinning end over end towards the stuff.

Dakrius took a step towards it, a cry on his stone lips.

Jayd's screams rang in his ears. He could see the man frantically trying to undo his harness. Must be stuck. Jayd began to curse.

And Melebele was running after him. 'I rescue!' panted the husky Rorclaavix voice.

Dakrius raised his arms over his head. 'No! Come back, you fool!'

The buggy spun once more and was swallowed up by the black stuff.

'Jayd!' cried Dakrius.

'It's eating into my – Shit!' Jayd's cursing changed to thick, choking screams, as if something was being forced down his throat. And then, thankfully, silence.

'Melebele, I order you to come back – that stuff's corrosive!'

No reply. With a roar, the Rorclaavix ran headlong into the rolling black wall. Dakrius cut the intercom. There was no hope for Melebele now.

And for him? He whirled round. The blackness had cut off his route to the shuttle. He was as good as dead.

Dakrius looked at the enabler key, which he'd got out in readiness. He'd never use it now.

With frightening suddenness, the black stuff was upon him, and he could see nothing but darkness. His suit warned him that its integrity was compromised, that he should seek immediate assistance, and then the computer voice fizzled away as the corrosive gas got to it.

Dakrius sank to his knees. So, he was going to die. And it was going to be painful. He would probably take longer to dissolve than the flesh-and-blood human and Rorclaavix. His silicon-based body would resist the acid for longer.

He got to his feet again. He could run for it, make it to the shuttle, but even as he took one step he realised that he had no idea in which direction the shuttle lay. He sank to his knees again, a tickling feeling creeping over his body, an acrid taste forcing its way down his throat.

Such was the beginning of the end for Dakrius.

In the tumult of pain that followed, he saw many visions. His ancestors, staking claim to the barren rock that would become Adamantine, his homeworld. His office in the Centre, with its never-ending parade of papers and the recalcitrant computer. And a tall human woman in a black cape who bent to him, her face full of compassion, her hand grasping his, taking the enabler key from him.

Compassion took the enabler key from the dying Adamantean and without pause turned and walked towards where she sensed the shuttle lay on its launch pad. The entrance ramp was already buckling under the assault of the corrosive cloud. She tripped lightly up the steps, pressed the enabler key against the lock and the door slid open. She slipped inside, sealed the airlocks and went forward to the flight deck. The controls were simple to master. It was a small interplanetary shuttle with limited field facilities, minimal weaponry, some warp facility. Better not let Fitz out until they were clear of Muath: didn't want him around being all emotional and getting crushed by the g-force. With deft movements Compassion took the shuttle up and through the black cloud, using full power, the acceleration pressing her back into her seat.

Suddenly, they were through the cloud, and the screen showed the black gulf of space.

Fitz was pacing around her console chamber, in some agitation, demanding to see Arielle. She told him she was safe but that didn't seem to satisfy him. Compassion didn't think it would be a good idea if he saw her in her current condition, so she ejected Fitz from herself and plonked him in the copilot's seat.

'Dammit, Compassion!' cried Fitz. He was still in his spacesuit, but he'd taken his helmet off; it was rolling around her console chamber.

'Look,' said Compassion, pointing at the screen.

Fitz gasped. Compassion had to admit, it was an impressive and disturbing sight. There were hundreds – thousands – of oval ships, in a thick cordon around Muath. And they were heading towards Yquatine.

While Fitz gaped, she did a quick systems check. Things didn't look good. The black stuff had eaten through the engine cowling. They were losing power.

Fitz was babbling, about Arielle, about the Doctor, his face streaked with tears. Compassion remembered when she'd tried to suffocate him, to force him to remove the Randomiser. She felt she ought to apologise for it sooner or later, but now wasn't the time.

'Fitz,' she said, and, when he didn't pay her any attention, she said it louder. 'Fitz!'

He was breathing heavily, his face was pale and it looked like he'd put on some weight. What was that he'd said? He'd been in prison? Well, they'd have plenty of time to talk. 'We've lost power, we're drifting.' She rose from her seat. 'I'm going to see if I can repair the engines.'

A grey-gloved hand touched the darkness of her cloak. 'Take me back inside you.' Fitz's pale-blue eyes were pleading, his lips trembling. 'Take me to Arielle.'

Compassion sighed. She wouldn't get any peace unless she did as he asked. 'All right. I will.'

Chapter Twenty-One
'The cellular damage is irreversible'

Arielle woke up from a dream of suffocating blackness to the feeling of a hundred wet mouths sucking at her body. She tried to scream, but her throat hurt, as though someone had tried to strangle her.

Strangle her? The last thing she remembered was being on the *St Julian* with Fitz. Then – then she'd had… a headache?

After that, nothing. Until now. Where was she?

Now she'd got used to the sucking sensation, she found it soothing. She tried to focus on her surroundings, make sense of things. She was lying down, she could ascertain that much. Her whole body hurt. It felt as if her bones were coated in tiny shards of glass. Above her, something wide and blue and dark like the sky at night. Dark shapes crowded at the edge of her vision. She couldn't see properly, so she struggled to sit up, but the pain was too much, her joints grinding and her head splitting with white light; so she sank back down on to the sucking mouths.

She reached out with the palms of her hands, which stung as if she'd been grasping a bouquet of nettles. They touched a wet, slippery surface, like a porous skin bathed in… oil? sweat?

She brought her hand up to her face. It was red. Red with blood. Not her own blood –

The blood of millions, dying in agony, eaten away and that was good – good – good

Then she found the voice to scream, though the effort tore at her throat and sent slivers of fire through her limbs. She relapsed into a state of numbness, of shock. She remembered something black with shivering skin and a mouth in her mind which had spoken to her. It had told her its name: Omnethoth. It had made her –

All solid mortals will be dissolved.

She shied away from the black thing, pushing it right down inside herself, stifling its inhuman voice.

Then all was still.

It took her a while to notice another voice, a quiet, soothing voice in her mind. It was saying one word, over and over again.

'Hush. Hush. Hush.'

Arielle concentrated on the voice. It calmed her, gave her something to focus on. She spoke, the words coming slowly, painfully. 'Who are you? Where am I?'

The voice spoke to her from deep within her own self. 'I am Compassion. And you are safe. It's gone now. You are going to be all right.'

Compassion. Safe. All right. Arielle looked at her hand. There was no blood.

Wearily, Arielle sank back into the mouths. She was so very tired.

'Sleep now. You're going to be all right.'

The pain ebbed away slowly and Arielle sank into a warm, soothing sleep.

'That's a damn lie,' said Fitz, wiping the tears from his eyes, not caring if Compassion saw. 'She's not going to be all right, not going to be all right at all.'

'You can't fault my bedside manner, though, can you?'

Fitz swore wearily. 'There's a time for humour, Compassion. It isn't now.'

'Sorry.'

She actually sounded like she meant it, but he wasn't going to give her the satisfaction of letting her know that.

He knelt by Arielle's side, holding her hand. It was cold and dry and it felt as brittle as burnt paper. The skin was almost transparent. She was lying, naked, on a giant spongy leaf Compassion had grown for her in her forest – her deep, secret place of nature and emotion. The leaf pulsed gently around

Arielle, infusing painkillers through her skin into her body. That was all Compassion could do. Make it as painless as possible. Live up to her name in actions if not in actual emotion.

Because Arielle was dying.

Compassion had told him why. She had been possessed by spores of the Omnethoth, the thing that controlled the transmitter, the thing that had brought about the destruction of Yquatine. Their very essence had invaded her cells, making her one of them. They had made her build the transmitter, birthing it from her own cells, nurturing it. It sent signals to the dormant Omnethoth colonisation clouds spread throughout the universe, activating them. They had worked to produce the invasion fleet, the thousands of black ships that the transmitter had teleported to Yquatine. Now the transmitter's work was done, the Omnethoth spores had withdrawn from Arielle, taking their essence away and leaving behind a devastated body. Arielle was disintegrating before Fitz's eyes.

He remembered what had happened on the *St Julian*. Arielle's eyes completely black. Arielle in a coma. They had taken her then, these Omnethoth. It could have been him. He railed against the unfairness of it all. Why couldn't it have been him? At least he was used to being taken over by alien entities.

'Arielle?' whispered Fitz. 'Can you hear me?'

She gave no sign that she could. Her eyes remained closed. Short, gasping breaths escaped from between her desiccated lips.

If he hadn't come back in time one month, if he hadn't worked in Il-Eruk's, if he had never met Arielle, then she'd still be alive. And maybe the Omnethoth attack wouldn't have happened. His head reeled as he tried to work it out, and he came to a shattering conclusion. His coming back in time had set in train the sequence of events leading to the end of Yquatine. He'd been so bloody careful, not warning anyone, going out of his way to avoid Lou Lombardo, but it had all been for nothing. He'd walked right into it, like a trap. Was it because he was tainted by Faction Paradox? Was this some intricate, temporal sick joke? Fitz couldn't shake the feeling that it was all somehow his fault. That inbuilt Kreiner guilt again.

'Arielle?'

She was hardly breathing now.

Fitz let go of her hand, turned away. He couldn't stand this. 'How much longer?'

Compassion's impassive tones. 'Not long.'

Fitz screwed himself up to say *kill her, put her out of her misery*, but he couldn't do it. He couldn't let go of hope. 'Isn't there anything else you can do for her?'

'A massive infusion of Artron energy might reverse the process. But I don't know how to control it, Fitz. I'm too young. It could kill her – or worse.'

Fitz looked around at the forest. It was like a hotchpotch of all the forests in every horror movie he had ever seen. The strange thing was, he could see quite clearly, although there was no obvious light source. The nearest trunks were gnarled, the bark ancient and black, crooked branches thrust as if in supplication to the 'sky' above, which was like an upturned bowl of blue glass, cloudless, starless. The leaves on the trees were dark-green spiked things, like tiny daggers. Beyond the first row of trees the trunks proliferated, until they became one solid mass of gloom.

And, in the middle of the haunted forest, this oasis of life. Arielle, on her green leaf, Fitz kneeling on the short purple grass willing her to live.

It had to be worth a try. 'Do it, Compassion. It's her only chance.'

A sigh whispered through the trees. Something glowed within their depths, a golden sprite. It danced nearer, nearer, zigzagging through the branches and trunks.

Fitz crouched near Arielle again, leaning on the porous pale-green tongue of leaf, placing his hand in hers. 'It's gonna be all right,' he whispered, mainly to calm himself.

The golden sprite danced out of the woods, a fairy sparkle, a magic spell. Compassion was murmuring wordless soothing sounds at the edge of his hearing.

The golden sparkle settled over Arielle, spreading out over her body. For a second, Arielle's skin glowed with health, and she was young again, young and beautiful, her perfect face smiling in sleep.

Fitz's heart leapt –

– and then the glow vanished, and Arielle was ravaged and desiccated and dying.

Fitz's heart was thumping fit to burst. He pressed her hand to his chest. A sob escaped his lips.

'The cellular damage is irreversible. All the energy in the universe wouldn't be enough to save her.'

Fitz let Arielle's hand drop. He turned away, walked into the forest. 'Take me outside,' he said.

There was a flash of light and –

– he was sitting in the copilot's seat next to Compassion. He stared at the blackness of space through the forward window. He could make out only a few distant stars. If he stared long enough he could forget he was sitting inside a shuttle, and could believe he was floating in space, drifting between the stars, a bodiless entity.

Compassion spoke. 'Fitz, I am sorry.'

Fitz looked away from the window, rubbed his eyes. He turned to look at Compassion. 'For abandoning me on Yquatine?'

She nodded.

'For trying to kill me?'

She nodded again.

'For not being able to save Arielle?'

Compassion hung her head. But her voice carried threat. 'Don't push it.'

Fair enough, thought Fitz. At least she was still human enough to realise that trying to kill your companions was just not on. He stared at the blackness of space once more, trying to push all thoughts of Arielle from his mind. Something was bothering him. If Compassion hadn't turned up to save him, if she hadn't interfered with the transmitter, then maybe the possessed Arielle wouldn't have activated it. It was an uncomfortable thought. He tried to put it into words, though Compassion was probably the last person – person? – you would ask for reassurance. 'Compassion, if you hadn't attacked the transmitter, would it have activated?'

Compassion smiled, which Fitz thought highly inappropriate. 'It was due to be activated shortly. Had I not arrived, you would be dead, remember?' She rolled her eyes. 'Have a little faith, Fitz.'

The phrase was so Doctor-esque it brought Fitz up with a start. 'What about the Doctor? Couldn't you have traced his biodata when you were in the vortex?'

'The Doctor's biodata is complicated, spread out through time like seeds in a storm, impossible to track. You were easy to find, which is why I came to you first, even though I wanted to find the Doctor.'

Thanks a bunch, thought Fitz. 'So, where is he now?'

Compassion's eyes gleamed. 'He's in this time zone. I can feel him. On Aloysius Station. I've set us on course but it'll take a couple of days in this pile of junk, even with the repairs I've managed to make.'

She obviously saw the little shuttle as a far inferior travel machine to herself. But at least it worked. Just. Fitz relaxed a little. The Doctor must have escaped from Yquatine. He'd probably saved hundreds of people as well. Could Fitz allow himself to hope that the Doctor was alive? Compassion may think she was right, but Fitz was afraid of having his hopes dashed, afraid of the grief he would feel if it turned out the Doctor was dead. Only when the Doctor was standing there before him would he allow himself to believe.

'I hope we find him,' said Fitz with feeling. 'I hope he's OK.'

'So do I,' said Compassion.

There was a tone in her voice that made Fitz stare at her. 'Look, you're not blaming him for all this, are you?'

Her eyes blazed. 'Who fitted this thing to me? Who cursed me to travel for decades in the vortex?' She sighed. 'Who's the only person who can remove it?'

Her questions were clearly rhetorical, so Fitz lapsed into thoughts of Arielle. 'How is Arielle doing?'

Compassion's fingers danced on the keypad in front of her. 'She's asking for you.'

Fitz all but lunged at her. 'Well, take me to her, then!'

Arielle's eyes were open, her lips trembling to form a word, to speak a name. 'Fitz?'

He moved so his face was above hers. 'I'm here.'

'What happened to me?'

Fitz held her hand. There was no point in lying. 'I'm so sorry, Arielle. It must have been on the *St Julian*. You got infected with something and I couldn't help you because I was in prison.'

'Prison?'

Fitz nodded, swallowing hard. 'The President chucked me in prison. He thought I'd caused your illness.'

The once full lips, now parched and cracked, formed a smile. 'Bastard.'

Fitz smiled back. 'Yeah, you were well shot of that smarmy git.'

A look of terror passed over her face. 'Hold me.'

Fitz climbed on the leaf beside her, cradling her body in his arms. She felt light, as if she was made of polystyrene.

'Not long now.' Compassion's voice, intrusive.

'A little privacy, please?' snapped Fitz.

Silence. He couldn't be sure she wasn't watching, but he didn't care.

Arielle was trying to speak again. 'It wasn't me,' she whispered.

'What?'

She struggled to hold Fitz. 'If it wasn't me, would have been… someone else. Just my… bad luck.'

He lay there on the spongy leaf, her hair over his face, feeling her fighting to breathe, feeling the life ebb away from her. It was true. If the Omnethoth hadn't got Arielle then some other poor sucker on the *St Julian* would have copped it, maybe even him. Just an accident, just bad luck. Sod's law. Life's like that. No such thing as fair or unfair, depends on your point of view. Road accidents, disease, famine, plague, whatever – all part of the grand scheme of things and you just have to put up with it, or go under. Life is unfair – kill yourself or get over it.

But travelling with the Doctor had made him realise that you could make a difference, that you could cock a snook at the universe and get away with it. You could save lives, work miracles, defeat the baddies and win the girl. You could – but you very often never did. In all the victories of his life, there had been defeats and disappointments. He'd helped save the creatures of the Dominion, but he had lost Kerstin, who was presumably still moping about in Sweden. Looking at it the other way round, it didn't seem so bad, but there wasn't even the smallest slice of solace to balance against the death of Arielle. Yquatine was destroyed, Compassion was unable to use her TARDIS powers, and the Doctor was out of reach.

Arielle's death was like the punchline of an enormously long and cruel joke which had seen him abandoned, arrested, imprisoned and now unable to save the life of someone he cared about.

Arielle clung to him, like a ghost or a drowning nymph, waiting to be plucked away into the silent depths of the ocean. She was struggling to speak, and he put his ear close to hers. He couldn't hear what she was saying so he whispered gently to her. 'I love you.'

She was struggling to speak. Fitz's insides were like knots of ice.

'Tell my brother – tell Boris...' Her eyes widened, there was a soft, sad sigh and her clinging arms fell limp.

Fitz let her go, let her body relax into the leaf. Almost immediately she began to fade away as if she was made of smoke, dissolving into the leaf. Fitz slid off the soft, porous surface and stood watching as with a soft sucking sound the leaf folded itself up and retracted into the ground, leaving no sign of its presence but a fairy ring in the purple grass.

Fitz stared at it for a while, feeling too numb for tears. He raised his eyes and looked at the forest, with its dark trunks and gnarled branches and spiky leaves.

It looked positively inviting.

Perhaps if he walked for long enough he'd lose himself.

Chapter Twenty-Two
'People of the Minerva System...'

Blank screen. Then an image – a male, bland-featured even by human standards:

'–ockman of Minerva News Network bringing you the latest on the catastrophic events taking place on Yquatine.'

The image expanded to include another human, a female with long dark hair. Like the male, she had a fixed stare and stiff-shouldered stance. The shadow of fear was in her eyes:

'Good evening, I'm Lyria Holst and later on I'll be talking to some of the tragically few survivors about how they feel in these darkest of days.'

The male spoke again:

'But first a word from President Vargeld who miraculously – and thankfully – escaped the destruction of his homeworld.'

The image changed to a head-and-shoulders shot of Vargeld, in front of the flag of the Minerva Space Alliance. He spoke, the tone of his voice low and unsteady with emotion: 'People of the Minerva System, there is little I can say that will lessen the shock, fear and grief you, like me, are all feeling. My thoughts are with the millions dead, and those who have survived. We have all lost families, partners... We have lost more than we can comprehend at this present time. But there is solace in that we are not alone in our grief, that we all bear the brunt of the sorrow that shrouds our hearts. And out of this sorrow will grow a greater determination to face the uncertain future.'

A pause.

He continued, his voice taking on a higher, more urgent tone:

'Now is the time for action. And action is being taken to counter the danger that is spreading out from Yquatine and threatens to engulf the entire System.'

Cutaway to a shot of ships positioning themselves around the stricken planet. The President continued in voice-over:

'This time, we will not fail. These ships are armed with weapons designed to deliver an ionisation field to the Omnethoth. A field that will break up their molecular structure and destroy them.'

The image changed back to that of Vargeld, eyes gleaming in defiance:

'When – not if but *when* – the Omnethoth are defeated, we will all have to work together to rebuild the shattered heart of our beloved System. Once again, my thoughts are with you all.'

The image changed again to the two MNN newsreaders. The female – Lyria Holst – was speaking: 'The nature of the Omnethoth – an ancient weapons system which somehow reactivated itself – was revealed by an out-System scientist known only as the Doctor.'

An image of another male human, this one with curly light-brown hair, standing in a corridor presumably of Aloysius Station, speaking quickly and urgently: 'Yes, soon the Omnethoth surrounding Yquatine will be ready to manufacture whole fleets of assault ships. They'll spread out to occupy the entire System, unless…'

Unseen interviewer's voice: 'Unless the attack fleet gets there first?'

A quick, nervous smile, blazing eye contact with the camera. 'Quite… Now if you'll just excuse me…'

The image wobbled as if the cameraman had been shoved out of the way and then returned to the two newsreaders. The male spoke: 'No one knows who he is or where he came from but we are all thankful for his help in the war against the Omnethoth.'

A switch was pressed and the screen went blank.

The Grand Gynarch wheeled her chair around to face the six members of the Inner Circle Elite, seated on stone blocks in a chamber deep within the Imperial Palace. Her hips had given way a few weeks ago and she was confined to a motorised chair. It wouldn't be long until she followed the great line of Gynarchs into the coils of the Six Hundred. Already the youngest of her children was being groomed and oiled for the role of Gynarch. Young, supple, fierce-hearted Zizeenia. A worthy successor.

'As you know, the Doctor is on a mission with Commander Zendaak to retrieve a sample of the Omnethoth weapon. With this, we shall be able to conquer the System, and beyond.'

The Elite nodded, remained silent.

The Grand Gynarch waved a hand at the silent screen, and it activated again. 'Whether or not the attack on the Omnethoth fails, it is time for us to move.'

The screen now showed a view of Aloysius Station, like a silver claw hanging in space. Ranged around it was a ring of Anthaurk battleships.

'Our fleet is guarding Aloysius against any Omnethoth incursion. The main fleets of Adamantine, Zolion, Ixtrice and the others are still stationed on their homeworlds and would take hours to reach Aloysius. With many ships of the Minerva Space Alliance fleet destroyed in the first attack on the Omnethoth, their forces are in disarray and the time is ripe for us to press home our advantage.'

She scanned their faces quickly for any sign of dissent. There was none, which was good. She had never got the chance to interrogate the dissident M'Pash before her strange disappearance and, though she supposed she'd never find out where the dissent had started, she was always on the alert for a fresh outbreak.

'It is time we issued our ultimatum.'

Six pairs of eyes stared back at her. She could sense their unease. She shifted in her motorised chair, wincing at the dull pain. 'I smell questions. Do not be afraid. We stand before a great moment in history – I will not let protocol get in the way.'

Zuklor, the oldest and wisest of the Elite, stood up. 'Grand Gynarch, with respect, it is not certain that the Omnethoth are going to be destroyed. The ionisation attack may fail.' There was the faintest trace of fear in his dry old voice. Fear was always an ugly sound. 'The Omnethoth could yet spread out, as they threatened. They could consume New Anthaur.'

The other Elite remained staring unblinkingly at their leader, showing no sign of agreement or disagreement with Zuklor.

The Grand Gynarch rested both hands on top of her blackwood staff. 'And what would you advise?'

'We must prepare for evacuation, not war.'

The Grand Gynarch crashed her staff into the stone floor three times, ignoring the pain. The sound echoed around the stone chamber. Zuklor was male, he was old, he possessed neither the fire of a warrior nor the blood-thirst of the Gynarchs. Was he the source of M'Pash's dissent? 'Enough! If the Omnethoth are to prosper and our planet is doomed, then that is even more reason to fight! This may be our last chance for glory. Better to die fighting than to flee to yet another world! Imagine trying to build up another New Anthaur – the decades of work it would take! The spirit of the people would be crushed utterly. They are behind me! They would rather fight and die than flee!'

She had half risen from her chair, and slumped back down again.

Zuklor sat back down on his stone block, head bowed respectfully. 'I am sorry –'

She cut short his weak words with a thump of her staff and an angry hiss. 'Enough talk.' Her mouth curved in a wide grin. 'In the words of that weakling Vargeld, now is the time for action. Whatever happens, we fight.'

The flames in their holders on the walls of the chamber guttered and flickered as if in a sudden gust of wind.

The Doctor had witnessed the deaths of many stars. Most died slowly of old age, cooling and dying gradually. More rarely, others went out in the biggest, most spectacular blaze of glory this side of the Big Bang – a supernova. The Doctor had seen – at a safe distance and behind shielding – a dying sun flare with the brightness of an entire galaxy, flinging heavy elements far into space, creating the stardust that floated in the interstellar voids between the galaxies. From this far-flung matter, new stars would eventually form. New star systems, new life. Out of death comes life. It was the way of things. It was the upside of the universal process – in an indifferent universe, death is equal to life, or, rather, *part* of life. The bones in the ground feed the soil. The exploding star seeds other stars. The fallen leaves nourish the new trees. Winter gives way to spring. An endless cycle of life and death, indifferent and uncaring yet paradoxically because of this allowing care and love to flourish in the life that was thrown up, green and new and questioning, to solve the riddles of existence.

The sombre beauty of the grand scheme of things always comforted the Doctor. Even without him, the process would carry on, in this universe and the next. It was a shame that no one else seemed to be able or even willing to try to see this – maybe Compassion would appreciate it, if she was still out there somewhere. A worthy companion-TARDIS to share in the immensity of things.

If he ever met her again. If she would forgive him.

He shied away from such thoughts, turning his mind to the Senate and President Vargeld with his closed, hostile mind. A sense of detachment might help them come to terms, accept things as they were. Give them the necessary sense of objectivity so that they could carry on with things.

Despite this, the fate of Yquatine filled his hearts with sorrow.

On the screen of the *Argusia*, he could see the attack fleet positioning itself around Yquatine. Zendaak and the Doctor were too late – they had never really had any chance of catching up – and the fleet were about to deliver their fatal charge. Nothing would come of the destruction of the

Omnethoth. Yquatine would become a misshapen, scarred lump in space, an ugly tombstone for the millions dead. Life would shun such a place for millennia, perhaps for ever.

'Cruel, cruel, cruel mistress,' the Doctor said to himself, the words soft and whispering. 'Dark princess, caring naught for the fate of her subjects.'

An Anthaurk swivelled round to face Zendaak. 'Commander, they're getting ready.'

Zendaak turned slowly to the Doctor. 'You still want to proceed? The anti-ionisation shields we have installed are untested.'

The Doctor nodded. 'We haven't got any choice.'

Zendaak raised an arm and pointed at the screen, at the green blob that represented Yquatine. 'Take us in.'

Throughout the Minerva System, every screen on every media unit was tuned to the MNN broadcast. The station would attain record audience figures as viewers on the remaining nine planets tuned in to watch the final battle.

The twelve ships positioned themselves equidistantly around the equator of Yquatine at an altitude of twelve thousand kilometres. Below them, the surface of the planet churned and heaved, a mind-warping morass of darkness. There was no doubt, it was expanding, swelling out into space. Preparing to seed the System with its spores. The twelve ships shut down their engines and routed power to their ionisation weapons. Twelve lances of blue fire plunged down into the thundercloud surface of the Omnethoth mass.

Several billion beings watched. Several million hot beverages cooled unnoticed on tabletops.

And, similarly unnoticed, a cloaked Anthaurk battleship shot at incredible speed past the orbit of the twelve ships and hurtled down towards the surface of Yquatine.

The *Argusia*.

The attack fleet couldn't deliver a charge sufficiently big

enough to envelop the entire Omnethoth in one go; they had to reposition themselves at different points above the globe of Yquatine. The fleet having deployed around the equator, the Doctor had instructed Zendaak to take the *Argusia* through the Omnethoth-clouded atmosphere above the south pole, as far away from the discharges as possible.

Now the Doctor stood, clad in the spacesuit he'd brought along (no chance of fitting into even the smallest of Anthaurk suits), on the bridge of the *Argusia*. Even though they were away from the discharges all shields were up to ward off the acid attacks of the Omnethoth. They didn't have much time.

A claw on his shoulder, twisting him round. Zendaak's face, eyes of red fire. 'Now!'

The Doctor nodded and followed Zendaak from the flight deck beyond which ran a long, low corridor, his mind ticking over the calculations. The Omnethoth would be too distracted with being frazzled to worry about attacking the ship. Not too frazzled for him to be able to take a sample, though.

They came to the outer airlock door, which resembled a crusty star-shaped shield. The Doctor went to check a certain piece of equipment he'd insisted Zendaak install for him on a shelf outside the airlock, and nodded in satisfaction. Then, as he checked the seals on his helmet, he glanced up at Zendaak. Now was the time to find out about trust. 'You know what to do?'

Zendaak nodded, his hand resting on the airlock control nodule.

'Then open the door.'

The inner airlock door ground open. Without hesitation the Doctor stepped into the chamber and the door closed behind him.

Strips of red light skirted the walls of the boxlike room. Ahead, another door similar to the first, with a big spiked wheel in the centre. The Doctor walked over to a panel by the side of the door and pressed a control lever. The airlock began to depressurise and he checked the seals on his helmet and his oxygen reserves once more – you could never be too careful.

Soon the airlock was devoid of air. The only sound was the rasp of the Doctor's own breath inside his helmet. He grabbed the spiked wheel of the outer door and began to turn it. Almost immediately, dark splurges of Omnethoth gas leapt in through the gap. The Doctor spun the wheel the other way, and the door thumped closed.

He turned to face the thing that was forming in the centre of the airlock. Though the Omnethoth were a gestalt entity, with each particle operating as part of a greater whole, they tended to work in attack units, such as the one the Doctor had brought back from Muath. His intention was similar here – to take an attack unit inside him, tinker with its DNA, turn it from an attack unit into a something less aggressive, like a tea-and-cake unit.

The Doctor reached out with his mind, to the mind particles of the Omnethoth cloud.

He gasped in shock.

Something was wrong.

The creature was closed to him, a barrier of anger and fear preventing him from reaching it. The Doctor tried harder, sweat breaking out on his brow. Why was it so scared? They were hundreds of miles from the source of the ionisation – it hadn't reached this part of the cloud. Then he realised. They were a gestalt entity, of course: the fear of the units under attack was being communicated to the rest of the cloud.

The Doctor backed against the wall.

The unit was bunching to attack. One touch, and his suit would be ruptured and he'd suffocate in the vacuum.

The Doctor skirted around the smoky shape towards the inner door. Working quickly, he bypassed the safety controls and the inner door began to open.

There was a roar as air began to fill the vacuum. The Omnethoth was broken up by the jet of air and the Doctor hung on to the handle as he was buffeted about. Heaving himself along the ridges on the door towards the gap, he saw Zendaak dive in, thrusting his arm towards the Doctor.

The Doctor felt his arm almost wrench from its socket as he was pulled to safety.

Once outside the airlock Zendaak slammed the door closed, a few wisps of Omnethoth cloud gusting out from the sides. Not enough to do any damage, the Doctor hoped – but you could never be sure. He grabbed the equipment Zendaak had prepared – a miniature vacuum cleaner – and with deft movements hoovered up the floating wisps of Omnethoth.

That done, he handed the vacuum cleaner to Zendaak. 'I'd get that ejected into space pronto,' he said, taking off his helmet, 'before they convert to acid and eat their way out.'

Zendaak handed the unit to a waiting guard, who hurried off, holding it at arm's length.

The Doctor took off his helmet and ruffled his hair. 'That's the second time you've saved my life.'

Zendaak stood over him, seven feet of frowning orange and black reptile. 'What happened?'

'I wasn't able to, er, ingest it. It was a bit shook up. I need a properly equipped laboratory, controlled conditions... Oh no.'

Zendaak was pointing a gun at him. 'You will find that there are plenty of well-equipped laboratories on New Anthaur.'

The Doctor wiped the sweat from his forehead. He'd been half expecting this. 'Don't tell me, you want to take the Omnethoth back to your homeworld and you want me to reprogram them so they obey only you.'

Zendaak's wide head dipped in a snakelike nod.

The Doctor spread his arms in a gesture of exasperation. 'Madness! Unutterable madness!'

Zendaak growled, grabbed one of the Doctor's arms and sent him spinning down the corridor towards the flight deck.

The Doctor collided with a bulkhead and collapsed, winded.

Zendaak stood over him. 'Not madness. The glory of the Anthaurk race!'

The Doctor rolled over, groaning, clutching his arm. He was yanked to his feet and propelled back to the flight deck.

The screen showed a mass of confusion. They were still flying through the Omnethoth cloud.

The Anthaurk lieutenant handed a datachip to Zendaak. 'Sir, a message from the Grand Gynarch!'

Zendaak read the communication. 'Change of plan. We're going to rendezvous with the Grand Gynarch at Aloysius – which will soon be under Anthaurk rule.'

The Doctor closed his eyes and muttered an Ancient Gallifreyan curse. Would some races never learn?

The moment he opened his eyes, all the lights went off and he was in total darkness. He backed away towards the wall, wondering where the escape pods were. Then dim red emergency lighting came on, revealing a tableau of Anthaurk milling about in confusion.

'What is happening?' hissed Zendaak.

'We're not going anywhere,' said the Anthaurk lieutenant. 'The shield has failed. The ionisation field has knocked out our power systems. All we have is the battery cell backup, enough for basic life support.'

The Doctor ran forward, familiarising himself with the controls. It was true. The ionisation had reached the south pole and had fatally damaged the *Argusia*. So much for the bolted-on Anthaurk technology. He should never have trusted it, any more than he should have trusted the Anthaurk themselves. Along with the attack fleet, they were paralysed – and surrounded by dying Omnethoth.

The screen showed a swirling fractal vortex of chaos as the dying creatures flailed and writhed in the electrical energy that danced around the planet. Occasionally the ship shuddered as a discharge of energy passed through it.

'He's right,' cried the Doctor. 'We're trapped.'

He turned to Zendaak. The creature was actually smiling. 'So it ends here,' he hissed.

The Doctor turned back to the screen, his face set in a mask of determination. 'Not if I can help it.'

Chapter Twenty-Three
'I suggest you surrender immediately'

It was one of the few remaining bottles of Château Yquatine in the entire universe. It stood on the table, the blue glass shining like the towers of the Palace of Yquatine once had.

President Vargeld would never see the palace again, never have time to get used to it, settle in. With a pang he thought: Where is home now?

He raised his glass. The flame of the solitary candle on the table was magnified in the red liquid so that it looked like a setting sun. 'To the captains and crews of the attack squadron.'

Krukon, Fandel, Okotile, Juvingeld and Tibis raised their glasses and returned the toast. It was a token gesture for the Adamantean and the Kukutsi, as they could not drink the wine. However, they had all felt that they needed to make some gesture. Rhombus-Alpha revolved above, its light dimmed in respect. A silence fell, which none of them felt like breaking. All eyes were on the holo of Yquatine that occupied the centre of the makeshift Senate chamber. It was a crackling ball of energy, as though thunderstorms raged across every centimetre of its surface. Already, glimpses of the true surface of the planet could be seen – bare, scorched rock. No sign of the beautiful cities of Yendip, Farleath and Orlisby. No sign of the oceans. What had the Omnethoth done – boiled them away into space?

President Vargeld put down his glass. He didn't feel like celebrating. It was a hollow victory, against a senseless, faceless, implacable enemy. No, 'enemy' wasn't the right word. 'Force' seemed more appropriate. The Doctor was right: the universal process – as he'd called it – was indifferent, uncaring. Yquatine would for ever be a monument to the unfairness of things.

And a tomb for Arielle.

Stefan Vargeld suddenly felt very tired. He didn't want to go to bed in case he dreamed of Arielle, and woke up thinking she was still alive; but his body was crying out for sleep.

'Well, gentlemen.' He sighed. 'Our scout fleets will keep an eye on things for us. I suggest we all take some rest. God knows we've earned it.'

Weary nods. They all filed from the Senate chamber towards their quarters.

Fandel walked beside the President. 'I wonder what happened to Zendaak and the Doctor.'

President Vargeld couldn't find it within himself to care. 'If they were caught up in the ionisation then they'll have gone the same way as the attack squadron.'

'Pity,' said Fandel. And then, with feeling, 'I was dying to ask him for the name of his tailor!'

Their eyes met. There was a desperate cast to Fandel's expression, his pale pudgy face slack, his eyes haunted. Clearly he wanted to share even the most pathetic of jollities, needed some sign that everything was normal.

President Vargeld forced himself to smile. It felt like trying to make himself vomit. 'Yeah.' He patted Fandel's stout shoulder, unable to say anything else. Fandel grasped his hand, shook it, and scurried off down the corridor.

The President turned away and headed towards his quarters. At least Fandel still had a homeworld, with tailors and shops and banks and taverns and parks and lakes and people. Would Luvia become the new heart of the System? Was the quaint little world up to the task?

Was he up to the task of pulling it all together, now that the Omnethoth had been defeated?

He didn't know. All he knew was that he was tired but scared to sleep, and that he ached for Arielle.

As the artificial night of the station fell, the duty officers of Spacedock Three drank coffee and chatted to while away the hours. Their cylindrical tower overlooked the entire spacedock: the hangars, maintenance bays and launch pads. Monitors allowed a 360-degree view around the station. They showed the ring of Anthaurk ships, which remained even though the Omnethoth threat had been nullified.

'What are they still doing there?' muttered Jalbert. It worried him. They hadn't responded to any of his hailings. Perhaps they were all asleep like every other sane being in the sector.

About halfway through the night there was a bleep and a voice announced that a shuttle was approaching the station.

The officers sprang into life. 'Status report?' enquired Guvin, a dark-skinned young lad from Oomingmak.

The calm computer voice cut in. 'Small municipal shuttle, badly damaged, motive power nil, drifting, no life signs.'

'Lock tractor beam when in range,' ordered Jalbert.

A few hours later, the small shuttle came within scanner and tractor-beam range.

'Wonder if those Anthaurk ships'll do anything,' mused Guvin. 'Maybe they'll blast it.'

But they took no notice of the tiny ship and it was drawn safely into dock, guided by the invisible hand of the tractor beam.

'Guess we should go down and check it out,' said Guvin.

Jalbert frowned. The guy was always trying to find other things to do. Never wanting to stay in one place. Jalbert had worked most of his life on the spaceyards of Beatrix, had spent his years governed by endless safety rules and security regulations. Guvin had been a sledder, gathering meat for the freezefarms of Oomingmak. There was something of the wild snowy wastes glinting in his dark eyes. A restless young lad. 'No. That's not our job. Besides, you heard the 'puter – no life signs. Just floating junk.'

Guvin's face, usually sullen and unsmiling, took on an even more frosty expression. 'Yes, sir.'

An idea struck Jalbert. 'Besides which, anything could be on board – even some of that Omnethoth stuff.'

Guvin raised heavy eyebrows.

Jalbert grinned. 'Not so keen on going down there now, eh?' He accessed the comms network and informed the duty trooper squad of the situation.

Their job done, Jalbert dialled them more coffee. It had been a busy day, and the shuttle was hopefully the last –

'Hey!' cried Guvin. 'Look at that!'

Jalbert spilled coffee on his lap, leapt to his feet brushing it away. 'What –'

Then he saw the screens.

The ring of Anthaurk battle cruisers was closing slowly on the station.

'Warning: incoming vessels, weapons ports fully armed.'

Jalbert swore. 'Sound the general alarm.'

Guvin hit the alarm button without hesitation.

The Doctor sat cross-legged on the floor of the Anthaurk battle cruiser, a mess of cables in his lap.

He shoved them to the floor with a sigh of frustration. It was useless. There was no power to reroute. They were stuck. He stood, shaking his head. 'It looks like we're doomed.'

Zendaak cursed.

'What about the escape pods?' said the Doctor.

Zendaak folded his arms. 'There are no escape pods on an Anthaurk battle cruiser,' he said with obvious pride.

The Doctor raised his hands. 'Don't tell me, better to die in the glory of battle than to run away.'

Zendaak nodded. 'I had no idea you had an appreciation of our philosophy, Doctor.'

'Appreciation?' exploded the Doctor. 'All I feel is disgust. You should be helping the System regain its feet after the Omnethoth disaster!'

Zendaak bore down on the Doctor, eyes gleaming. 'No, Doctor, that is not the Anthaurk way! The Anthaurk way is glory. With the heart of the System taken out, it is time for us to seize control.'

The Doctor drew himself up to his full height, shouting hoarsely. 'Well that's good, as we're all about to die! You'll never live to see your victory!'

A zealous expression crept over Zendaak's wide face. 'I may die, but in my death I can be assured of Anthaurk supremacy.'

The Doctor rolled his eyes. And so it went on. Once warlike, always warlike. The Omnethoth invasion hadn't united the System: if anything it had spurred the Anthaurk on. Maybe, if Yquatine still stood, there would be a basis for negotiation. But, in the chaotic aftermath of the Omnethoth, it was every species for itself. Survival of the fittest and nastiest – in this case, the Anthaurk.

The cycle of life. Sometimes it reassured the Doctor, sometimes it appalled him.

The deck lurched beneath their feet as another explosion rocked the ship. The Doctor ducked as the control console burst open in a shower of sparks. The screen cut out.

It couldn't be long now.

There was only one chance, but it was a long shot.

He shoved past Zendaak.

He ran along the corridor to the airlock. 'Oh, no!' he cried, both hands plunging into his mass of brown curls.

The inner airlock door hung open. Inside, there was no sign of the Omnethoth attack unit.

A scream from behind him. He whirled round to see snakes of black gas wrapping themselves around Zendaak, choking the life from him. The attack unit had smeared itself over the walls and ceiling of the corridor and dropped on Zendaak as he passed beneath.

The Doctor pressed himself to the floor, shuffling past Zendaak, watching in horror as the Anthaurk commander fell to his knees, his form wreathed in black Omnethoth matter, an arm occasionally shooting out, claws splayed wide.

Zendaak fell face down, and the Omnethoth attack unit slid away. The Doctor's lips curled in disgust. His face had been burnt away, leaving behind a steaming skull, jawbone hanging open in a death's-head grin.

Zendaak may have been belligerent, driven and blinkered, but he'd saved the Doctor's life on two occasions. He was an intelligent creature. There might have been some basis for negotiation. Too late now.

As for the Omnethoth –

The attack unit billowed upwards, spreading its smoky arms wide, its black centre bulging towards the Doctor.

No basis for negotiation here.

The Doctor backed away towards the flight deck. A seventh sense made him whirl round – and there was another attack unit, its limbs curling towards him. Screams from the flight deck told him that there were more of the creatures on the *Argusia*. How they'd got on board he had no idea. Perhaps there were weaknesses in the hull through which they had insinuated themselves. Perhaps the Omnethoth he'd trapped in the airlock had reproduced.

It really didn't matter, anyway, because he was trapped.

The deck shuddered beneath him and he fell to his knees.

A smoky tentacle caressed his face.

The Doctor screamed.

Compassion opened the hatch of the shuttle, and stepped down on to the boarding ladder. The spacedock was deserted: just a few handling droids standing idle, a couple of other ships, but no troopers. That was good, that was how she'd planned things. They wouldn't have detected her presence on the shuttle. She wouldn't have registered as a life sign.

She descended, opened herself up and deposited Fitz on the oil-stained grating in front of her. He'd found a bathroom she never knew she had, and had scrubbed himself until his skin positively glowed with pink, perky health. He'd then found a wardrobe she never knew she had, and kitted himself out in black leather trousers and a baggy black shirt. As he came out of her he grabbed her shoulder for support.

'Aloysius Station,' said Compassion. 'We made it.'

'Great,' said Fitz. 'Now let's find the Doctor and get out of here.'
He strode away across the spacedock towards the exit, his
booted feet ringing on the floor.

Compassion followed more slowly. Something was stirring
within her forest, a slow wind rustling the branches. She could
feel an emptiness deep inside. Only now was she beginning to
realise what it meant.

As she caught up with Fitz alarms cut in.

'Do you think that's for us?' yelled Fitz over the noise. 'It
usually is.'

Compassion briefly scanned Aloysius's AI network. 'No, the
station's about to come under attack from the Anthaurk.'

Fitz stopped dead and groaned. 'How long have we been
here? Two minutes. That must be a record.' Despite his chirpy
manner, there were dark rings around his eyes. He'd been
crying a lot over Arielle. He must have really loved her. Stupid
thing to do. At least she, Compassion, was free of such
emotional millstones.

Fitz was looking impatient. 'The Doctor?' he said.

Compassion nodded. 'Let me concentrate.'

She reached out with her mind, searching for the Doctor's
biodata trace.

There was nothing. No trace. That was what the empty feeling
had meant, what her forest had been trying to tell her. The
Doctor was dead.

She opened her eyes, looked away from Fitz. Started off up the
stairs that led from the spacedock.

'Hey!' Fitz caught up with her, grabbing her arm. She shook
him off, but he stood in her path, blocking her way. She sighed.
She hated having to cope with his feelings sometimes.

'Are you going to bloody well tell me or not?'

She fixed him a look she knew would unnerve him. Strange
feelings were pulsing through her systems, as though they

were missing the Doctor. A TARDIS bonds with its tenant. What would happen now that bond was broken? 'He's gone, Fitz. He's dead.'

She pushed past him, continued up the stairs. No clear plan at the moment, just walking.

'How do you know? He might be in danger somewhere – in a Time Lord coma or something!'

She whirled round to face him. 'Even if he was in danger, even if I could detect exactly where he was, I wouldn't be able to do anything about it. He could be surfing into a black hole and I would just have to stand and watch!'

A look of gloom clouded Fitz's face. 'The Randomiser.'

Compassion nodded. 'Ironic, isn't it? They very thing he fitted to me prevents me from saving him. If he wasn't dead, that is.'

Fitz winced. 'So what do we do now? It's all over,' he said, fatalistic as ever.

The floor heaved underneath them, and a second later they heard the dull crack of an explosion. The scream of the station's atmosphere rushing out into a vacuum followed, and the air around them began to shift uneasily.

Compassion flexed her fingers. 'No. It's far from over.'

President Vargeld was woken by the screaming of alarms. He was out of bed and dressed in minutes, his body performing the actions automatically, his mind still caught up in a dream of Arielle.

Still couldn't believe she was gone; maybe she was still alive somewhere; she could have escaped from Muath –

Shaking his head as if trying to dislodge such futile hopes, he entered the command centre of the station, a circular two-tier room manned by technicians and communications officers.

The station chief, Keri Eperdu, saluted as he approached.

'Status report,' barked the President.

Eperdu was a tall, dark-skinned woman from the tropical Amerd Archipelago on Yquatine. A home she would never see again, the President realised. She looked tired and her voice was hollow. 'The Anthuark ships, sir. They're preparing to attack.'

No time to react. He'd been waiting for this. 'Alert all troopers. Contact every available Alliance ship in the sector.'

'Incoming transmission.'

'On screen.'

The circular screen on the far side of the room flickered into life. Staring out was the image of the ancient Anthaurk leader, the Grand Gynarch.

'President Vargeld,' she hissed slowly. 'You are surrounded. We have drafted a new treaty, an agreement which replaces the now sadly irrelevant Treaty of Yquatine.'

'Nice to see you've been keeping busy,' said President Vargeld, exchanging a wry glance with Eperdu. 'Order your ships to stand down.'

'I will not!' hissed the Grand Gynarch. 'You will agree to the terms of this treaty, or be destroyed!'

President Vargeld swallowed hard, cursing the unswerving callousness of the Anthaurk leader. Millions dead, and she had taken the opportunity of the lull after victory to make her counterstrike. 'What terms?'

'Rule of the Senate is to pass to the Anthaurk Inner Circle. New Anthaur will be the centre of the System.'

The President almost laughed aloud. 'How can you hope to maintain such an agreement? Every other sentient being in the System will resist you.'

'You have no choice. I suggest you surrender immediately or we will bombard this station until it is totally destroyed.'

'She is right. We have no choice.' Eperdu's eyes were on him. Their message was plain. No more fighting, no more death.

This was the worst part of being President. Taking the long view, making sacrifices for the future. He turned back to the screen. 'No surrender. Cut the connection.' Technicians obeyed and the screen went blank. 'Raise all shields, maximum power. Activate the defence grid. Contact the rest of the fleet, tell them to rendezvous at Aloysius a.s.a.p. in full battle readiness.' Many Alliance ships had been destroyed in the first abortive attack on the Omnethoth and the Space Alliance lay in disarray, the fleet scattered between Yquatine and Aloysius, licking its wounds. But there were still enough of them to fight. He was almost glad of the challenge.

'Sir.' Eperdu's voice showed signs of panic. 'The shields won't hold out for long under continual plasma barrage.'

'I know,' said President Vargeld. 'But we have to make a stand. How long before the others ships get here?'

Eperdu consulted one of the technicians. 'Two hours.'

'And how long before the shields fail?'

Eperdu shrugged. 'Hard to say. Depends on where they hit us first.'

There was a distant booming sound and the command centre floor shook beneath their feet.

'It's started,' whispered Eperdu.

'We'll just have to sit it out.'

A technician passed a datachip to Eperdu. She shook her head. 'Sir, that's not an option. There are still a couple of hundred Anthaurk on board – pitched battles are breaking out everywhere.'

Enemies within, enemies without. The President felt a thrill of fear and excitement run through him. 'Then we fight,' he said. 'Order all troopers to attack and kill the Anthaurk on sight.' He grabbed a blaster from a rack on the wall.

Eperdu was staring at him as if he was mad. 'What are you doing?'

The captain going down with his ship? Not giving up without a fight? Trying to prove himself?

Throwing his life away because without Arielle nothing mattered any more?

'Trying to save lives.'

'President Vargeld,' said Eperdu, 'with respect, the only way to save lives is to surrender to the Anthaurk. We may be able to negotiate terms with them.'

'Never,' said the President, and, without looking back, he ran from the command centre.

Chapter Twenty-Four
'Child of the universe'

Fitz followed Compassion through the corridors of Aloysius Station, a feeling of hopelessness welling up inside him. Yquatine had fallen, Arielle was dead, the Doctor was dead, the station was under attack and they couldn't dematerialise for fear of being trapped in the space-time vortex.

The outlook wasn't good.

The blaring alarms weren't helping, either, hurting his ears, preventing him from thinking, and helping along the bubbling feeling of panic that threatened to erupt from within.

They were trying to make their way back to the spacedock to find a ship. They had found their way barred by troops, and so they were trying for a spacedock on the other side of the station. This involved crossing the crowded central section of the station, full of mourners and refugees, all milling in panic.

They entered a large communal area. The place was full of people and beings trying to sleep or waking up, slowly realising that they were under attack.

There was an explosion from somewhere below and the floor shook beneath their feet.

Fitz clung on to Compassion. 'Can't we land anywhere that isn't about to be totally marmalised by evil aliens?'

No reply.

Her face had the look of a predator. Fitz followed the line of her stare.

A man with thinning auburn hair and chubby features was scrambling to his feet. He was wearing a spangly silver shirt.

Lou Lombardo, the pie vendor. The man he'd dreaded bumping into in his month on Yquatine. It was all right now, though – Fitz had passed the point in time when he'd first met Lombardo.

'Hey!' cried Fitz, waving frantically.

The sound of blaster fire. Tall, helmeted figures ran into the far end of the hall. They were wide at the shoulder, narrow at the waist, and sported big boots and big guns.

'Oh, nuts,' muttered Fitz.

They began to fire indiscriminately into the crowd.

Fitz found himself being dragged away from Compassion. He fought to stay with her, but the pressure of the crowd was too great. The last he saw of her was her red-haired head as she pushed through the crowds towards Lombardo, who was scrambling as frantically as everyone else for the exits.

'Compassion!' yelled Fitz.

She paid no heed. A bolt of blaster fire sizzled over his head, making a big hole in the wall. The woman in front of him screamed and started to claw the Adamantean in front of her in panic, staining the alien's stone skin with her own blood.

Sod Compassion. She might be immune to blaster fire but Fitz certainly wasn't. So he did what he was best at. He ran – or rather pushed, shoved and scrambled – for his life.

Compassion batted the screaming humans aside as if they were flies. She didn't take her eyes from her target. He was blissfully unaware of what was approaching him. Inside her, gears and cables started to churn and flail.

The fat man cannoned into her, sucking in great gulps of air. She held him by the arms, ignoring his screams of pain and fear.

Yes. It was definitely him. The one from whom the Doctor had obtained the Randomiser.

Something whizzed past her ear. She raised her head. A line of Anthaurk commandos were picking their way across a carpet of dead bodies towards her. Casually, she took the screaming Lombardo inside herself and ran out of the hall, a part of herself looking inwards towards the cowering man.

* * *

Lou Lombardo stood on the metal floor of the console chamber, staring about himself with a look of dawning realisation.

'You – you're the Doctor's new TARDIS, aren't you?'

The Doctor had been foolish to be so free with such information. They were supposed to be fugitives, after all.

Compassion spoke, making her voice as loud and sinister as she could. 'I am.'

He bent at the knees, arms going up to cover his head. 'N-nice to meet you,' he stammered.

'You know what I have brought you here for.' Lombardo shook his head. 'Look at the console. The black box. You recognise it.' It wasn't a question.

He walked over to the console, one hand picking at the other nervously. She saw him examine the Randomiser, muttering under his breath.

'Thanks to you, I am damaged. I cannot perform properly with that thing embedded within me. You must remove it!'

He looked up the at the console. 'I – I can't! I'm no engineer, I'm just a salesman!'

Compassion swooped her internal viewpoint right down into his face, around his body. Who was he? Was he even human? The Doctor had never mentioned him before. She scanned him. He was human. A physical coward, like Fitz, but she could detect reserves of cunning and resilience. A con man, an entrepreneur, but certainly no Time Lord agent.

Compassion sent cables snaking down from the ceiling, wrapping around Lombardo's podgy body.

'Tell me how you obtained the Randomiser. Tell me!'

Lombardo's jowls shook as he struggled against his bonds. 'I bought it from a fence, honest. I don't know his name. In my line of business it doesn't pay to ask too many questions.' He strained against the cables. 'Let me go!'

'No.' Rage surged through Compassion. She felt herself losing control, felt the TARDIS taking over. Like an animal in pain it was lashing out. She squeezed harder, harder, watching as Lombardo clawed at the cables around his chest and neck. She was going to punish him for what he'd allowed the Doctor to do to her.

She was going to *kill* him? As she'd tried to kill Fitz?

What had she become?

Compassion was suddenly afraid. Was she going mad? Was her new self developing a dual personality – half the old Compassion, half the new TARDIS being? Had the Randomiser cleaved her in two? She looked outside herself. She was curled up in a dark, cramped space behind a wall panel. She could hear the distant sounds of battle. Fitz. She should be helping him. She closed her external eyes.

Lombardo. He was still alive. She wanted to let him go. She was the universe's newest creation, and stomping about killing things was not her style.

She marshalled her energies, fought down her rage. The cables went slack and retracted, like snakes skulking back to their lairs. Lombardo slumped to the grating.

She stared at his body for a while as he gasped for air, marvelling at its fragility, and the obstinacy of the mind within that could go on living, knowing that there were hundreds of things that could go wrong with the body.

She supposed that was what being human was all about. Going on, despite the odds, despite the facts, despite the total insignificance of one life in relation to the universal scheme of things.

But Compassion wasn't human any more. She was the first of a new breed. She was significant. She mattered. The universe was going to have to take notice of her.

'I'm a child of the universe,' she whispered. 'I'm special, so special, I got to have some of your attention, so give it to me.'

Lombardo gasped and wheezed. 'What was that?'

'Nothing,' said Compassion. 'Nothing of interest to you.'

Then she let him go.

Lou Lombardo found himself on his hands and knees on the cold floor of Aloysius Station, facing a crack in the wall. He shook his head, and peered into the crack.

Eyes gleamed at him. The eyes of the Doctor's creature.

His mind a whirl of terror and confusion, Lou Lombardo scrambled to his feet. He ran one way up the corridor, skidding to a halt as the sound of blaster fire broke out ahead.

Turning on his heel, he ran back the other way, giving the crack in the wall a wide berth.

He vowed that he would never, ever, have anything to do with time-travel technology again. From now on – if he survived the Anthaurk onslaught – it was back to pies, pasties, sausage rolls, samosas, cream cakes and soft drinks for Lou Lombardo.

Compassion watched him go, and emerged from her hiding place. There was the distant boom of an explosion. A quick scan revealed that Aloysius Station was sustaining extensive damage: its shield capacity was down by 40 per cent and the superstructure was being hit by concentrated bursts of plasma fire from the Anthaurk ships. Inside, several squads of Anthaurk commandos were murdering their way through the station's mostly civilian population.

Aloysius wouldn't survive much longer. It was time somebody did something about it.

Compassion smiled to herself. Maybe she was that somebody.

She set off down the corridor, a plan forming in her mind.

Fitz was lost, afraid, and fully expected to be blasted to bits any second. He had to find Compassion, had to get out of this place. But it was beginning to feel as if he'd been running for a long time now. Surely his luck had run out, and it was going to end here, in pain, in fire, in –

He skidded round a corner and hit something hard. Something that dragged him into cover behind a bulkhead door. Hot breath hissing into his ear. 'What the hell are you doing?'

It was a soldier – human, thank God – young, blonde-haired. She reminded Fitz a little of Sam. Only Sam didn't have a scar across her cheek and would never wear a uniform or carry a blaster.

She grabbed his shoulder and shoved him back the way he came. 'Get the hell out of here!'

'Where "the hell" can I go? I've just come from an area swarming with Anthaurk. I'm afraid to say we're losing, baby.'

That didn't seem to be news to her. 'Yeah, well they caught us napping.' She looked him up and down, a cool, appraising glance. 'Can you use one of these?'

Fitz grabbed at the blaster she tossed to him, fumbling it and almost dropping it. 'Yeah, sure.' He smiled at her.

She didn't smile back. Instead she dragged Fitz over to a nearby section of collapsed wall. Every now and then the floor beneath him shook. How long before Aloysius burst open and let the coldness of space in? He felt dazed, as if this was a dream.

'You saw our situation?' said the trooper earnestly.

In the dash for cover Fitz had caught a wild glimpse of a wreckage-strewn open area crisscrossed with walkways. There were about a dozen troopers, ranged in a ragged formation under the cover of various bits of collapsed infrastructure. They were laying down covering fire to suppress a squad of Anthaurk who were sheltering behind a mobile shield thing. Between the two forces was a doorway in the wall, from which the occasional blaster bolt streaked out towards the Anthaurk.

'Yeah, I saw,' he shouted over the incessant sizzle of blaster fire.

'We gotta take out that Anthaurk unit. Watch me.'

Fitz's guts were churning and he felt the urgent need to visit the lavatory. He crouched as close to the floor as he could get as the trooper flung herself upwards and over the collapsed wall, loosed off a round of blaster fire and ducked back down, face flushed, blue eyes fixing him with a stare of expectation.

She clearly expected him to do the same. 'What's your name?' he asked.

A minute frown. 'Trooper Jones.'

Fitz boggled. 'Not – not Samantha by any chance?'

'Is this relevant?' She shoved him. 'Get up and fire that damn blaster.'

Fitz closed his eyes, breathed in as far as he could, and with one panicky lunge threw himself upwards, both hands around the heavy blaster, arms swinging across the charred rubble. He pressed the trigger, feeling it throb and pulse as beams of energy shot from the business end. Then he threw himself back into cover, and opened his eyes.

'Did you hit anything?'

Fitz shook his head. 'Didn't see.'

She was in his face in an instant, spittle flecking his skin. 'This isn't a game. The President's in there.'

'The President?' Fitz had assumed he'd died on Yquatine along with Il-Eruk and everyone else. So he was still alive. He'd almost got Fitz killed. Fitz ached to get his hands on him. Did he know what had happened to Arielle?

Trooper Jones was talking. 'We can't let the Anthaurk get to him. They've already killed Fandel. If the President goes, the whole System will fall to the Anthaurk.'

There was a lull in the shooting. Fitz peered over the rubble.

'Oh, no,' groaned Jones. 'Mr President, no.'

There, framed in the doorway, was President Vargeld, hands raised over his head.

Another groan from Jones. 'He's surrendering.'

Fitz was just relieved that the shooting was over.

Vargeld's voice rang out, loud and clear. 'Everyone put down your weapons. There will be no more shooting today.'

Fitz threw his blaster to the floor.

Jones did the same, with a sigh. 'Lindsey,' she said, with the tiniest of smiles.

'Fitz,' said Fitz, with larger smile. He was just being friendly, he told himself. Arielle's death had killed his libido and, as for his heart, it didn't even feel as if it was there any more. 'So, what happens now?'

Her voice was small, afraid. 'Don't know.'

Anthaurk commandos were pouring in from every direction. Fitz watched as the President was led away. Something was bothering him. The Stefan Vargeld he'd briefly met was a complete bastard. Surrender seemed totally out of character. Maybe it was a tactical thing, maybe he was bluffing.

Fitz trudged back down the corridor with Jones and the other troopers, Anthaurk commandos marshalling them onward. The humans looked exhausted, their faces slack with disbelief. Shell shock. Their planet destroyed, and now this?

'Vargeld's betrayed us,' muttered a thick-set trooper to Fitz's left.

Fitz swallowed, smiling nervously at Jones. Any moment now he expected her, or one of them, to say that they'd rather die than accept Anthaurk rule. Surely they weren't that stupid? Surely?

Perhaps it was true. His luck had run out, and it was going to end here, in pain, in fire, in defeat.

The Grand Gynarch felt a warm glow of satisfaction spread through her tired body. She could feel the blood pulsing beneath her skin, jetting along her narrow veins, swelling her wizened old heart. She hadn't felt this alive for many cycles. After a century of waiting, victory was hers.

The President and the other surviving members of the Senate stood against the circular window of the makeshift Senate chamber. Krukon stood as still as a statue, eyes fixed on her. Tibis had fought and killed several Anthaurk; his robes were in tatters and his golden fur matted with dark blood. Okotile crouched on the floor, his black carapace singed with blaster fire. Juvingeld pawed the ground, horned head looking this way and that nervously. Fandel was dead, roasted by Anthaurk blaster fire. As for the Ixtricite, it had transmitted itself back to its homeworld. The President looked suitably cowed and abashed. Ready to bow to Anthaurk rule.

The chamber was packed with Anthaurk commandos, rifles hefted across their chests.

The Grand Gynarch occupied the centre of the chamber, flanked by the six members of the Inner Circle Elite, the young Zizeenia at her side. She knew that her successor must be feeling the same sense of triumph.

The Grand Gynarch knew that their victory would be short-lived unless they acted quickly. The Adamantean battle fleet had arrived – all it would take was one word from Krukon for them to attack the Anthaurk fleet. A pity Zendaak wasn't here, and an even greater pity the plan to capture the Omnethoth had failed. With that, there would be no doubt of Anthaurk supremacy.

But that wasn't going to happen. The President had surrendered. He was going to sign over rule of the System to the Anthaurk. A thrill of delicious anticipation ran through the Grand Gynarch's frail frame and she motored her chair forward until she was directly in front of the beaten President. 'You were wise to surrender, human. You have prevented further loss of life.'

The President cocked his head, an oddly indifferent expression. 'What makes you think you've won? You're still outnumbered by all the other species in the System.'

The Grand Gynarch produced the document from the pouch on the side of her chair. 'Once you have signed this, we will have won.'

The President took the document from her, appeared to read it. He raised his eyebrows. 'Senators,' he said, 'this "treaty", if we sign it, will allow the Anthaurk to rule the System. They will have control of the trade routes, all economic policy, and set the taxation levels on all planets of the System. Do you think we should sign it?'

They all shook their heads and voiced their unanimous decision not to sign. Tibis even said that he would rather die than sign such a treaty.

'You must,' hissed the Grand Gynarch. 'Our ships are poised to destroy this station.'

'Make one move to fire upon us and my fleet will destroy yours!' bellowed Krukon.

'We are prepared to make that sacrifice,' said the Grand Gynarch.

'So, it's a stand-off,' said the President, laying the treaty down on the lectern. 'Seems the only way out of it is if I sign this.' He took out a pen from his inside pocket.

There was absolute silence in the Senate chamber. The President sighed. 'I really don't want to have to do this,' he said. 'None of the Senate will back me up. If I sign, there will be system-wide resistance. There are hundreds of other species in the System. Do you really think they're going to subscribe to your rule?'

The Grand Gynarch bridled. 'The might of the Anthaurk –'

The President snapped his fingers in her face. 'Is as nothing compared with the might of the Adamantean, the Luvian, the Kukutsi – and, as for the Ixtricite, no one really knows what they've got on their crystal planet! Think, Gynarch, think of the consequences. You can't go rampaging about, asserting your will. Rejoin the Alliance, we can all work together.'

'Never.'

The President picked up the treaty and returned it to the Grand Gynarch unsigned. 'I'm not signing this. If I do, you will destroy this station, including myself and the Senate. What then? There will be another war, you are outnumbered, you will lose. You can't be that stupid!'

'Listen to him, Mother.'

The Grand Gynarch turned to see Zizeenia by her side, her young eyes imploring.

The Inner Circle Elite all nodded as one, and Zuklor spoke. 'We are in agreement. We must commence negotiations with the Senate.'

The weak, cowardly fools! 'No! We either rule – or we die!'

The President hunched down in front of the Grand Gynarch. 'You are a throwback to the old ways of the Anthaurk. You're obsolete. The time when the Anthaurk needed to wage war has long since passed. You must now live in peace with the other races of the Minerva System.' He turned to Zizeenia and smiled. 'A new leader is required, one who is young enough to be able to learn.'

The Grand Gynarch's vision was hazy. Her limbs ached. The President's words brought forth hatred and bile.

'I can see no future for your race unless you co-operate with others. Unless you learn the word "compromise".'

That word! The Grand Gynarch hissed her hatred. 'For a century the Anthaurk have paid lip service to human ideals! Now – no more!'

The President spoke earnestly. 'We need to draft a new treaty, one that encompasses all races in the System, one that embraces peace. Will you help us?'

He was addressing Zizeenia and the Inner Circle.

'We will help you,' said Zuklor. 'It is the only way we can survive.'

The Grand Gynarch spun round in her chair. 'We must not listen to these lies! We can rule!'

The Inner Circle were shaking their heads.

'M'Pash was right,' said Zuklor. 'Peace is the way forward now. We need to evolve.'

'She certainly was right,' said the President, smiling broadly.

The Grand Gynarch frowned. How could the President know of M'Pash?

'The Inner Circle has decided. It is time for a new leader,' said Zuklor. Now his eyes gleamed with triumph and his voice rang with conviction. He didn't sound foolish or cowardly any more. 'It is time for a new Grand Gynarch.'

Zizeenia bowed to the Inner Circle. Anger coursed through the Grand Gynarch's old frame. Had they got to her, poisoned her with their views?

There were tears in Zizeenia's eyes as she turned to face the Grand Gynarch. 'You know what I have to do, Mother?'

The Grand Gynarch nodded wearily, the anger draining out of her. Her world, her universe, was falling apart around her. The Inner Circle speaking of peace? Her own flesh and blood not wanting to go out in a blaze of glory? She couldn't stand against them, not on her own. She was too old, too tired. If peace was going to be the Anthaurk future, she wanted no part of it. She wanted to die.

'Yes, child,' she said, darting a look of bile at Zuklor. He stared back impassively. 'You alone are forgiven.'

The Grand Gynarch closed her eyes as she felt her daughter's hands around her throat, the claws squeezing until finally there was no more pain and the Grand Gynarch was floating into the divine, glistening coils of the Six Hundred.

Chapter Twenty-Five
'All in a day's work, eh?'

I'm not insane.

President Vargeld stared up at the dome of darkness above him. It was watching him, he was sure. Watching him, and, worse, laughing at him. He shuddered, looking down between his feet into the churning blue-black void beneath the grating. What was the stuff? He seemed to catch glimpses of forms – alien, twisted forms, machines, worlds, *lives*: a man and a woman laughing and holding hands, a six-legged insect champing its mandibles into the side of a trumpeting mammoth, a world of stark angles where frightful clusters of eyes stared blankly into a churning void –

He tore his gaze away with a groan. Madness capered below him and even if he looked straight ahead he could still sense it flickering and chattering away, wanting him to look back, join in.

But, when he looked straight ahead, he could see the thing that was almost worse than the madness below because it looked designed, looked like it was *made for* something, something evil, wrong. He forced himself to look at it. At the angular, sick-looking column in the middle of the chamber, the tube-covered plinth supporting it and the crystalline structure above.

What was it for? Was it there at all or was he –

Please, I'm not insane.

Where was this place? He walked along the metal walkway towards the console. Its surface was an insane confusion of dials, their surfaces smoky and black, and spiky switches, with little black wires sticking out everywhere.

He reached out tentatively. There was a buzz of energy, a

tingle in his fingertips which somehow seemed to say: Watch it – I could hurt you, and hurt you bad.

He turned away. If this was a machine, it had been designed by a madman.

There was a door at the end of the walkway. He hadn't noticed it before. He ran up to it, hoping it was a way out of this madhouse; but, however much he pushed it or pulled at its scarred metal handle, it wouldn't budge.

He turned around, his back against the door, trying to control his breath.

I'm not insane.

For a start, there was no history of madness in the Vargeld family. Then there was his last medical, only a few months ago. A-OK, tip-top health, slight signs of stress but that was understandable in his position. OK, he'd cracked up over the death of Arielle but he'd loved the woman. Loved her.

He began to shake with unwanted laughter which turned into sobs of fear and confusion. He fought to control his emotions, hugging himself, staring up at the smooth darkness above, not letting the madness below have the slightest glimpse of him.

That was the worst part.

Arielle was dead. He was sure of that.

But she had been the one who had brought him here, to this shrine of madness.

During the Anthaurk attack, Vargeld and Fandel had been forced to retreat into one of the loading bays. They had sheltered behind a goods container as a squad of Anthaurk kept up a continual barrage of blaster fire from the maintenance gallery which ran across the middle of the loading bay.

The container was shuddering under the impacts, burning up, melting. President Vargeld could feel the heat of it against his back, and the air was thick with black smoke. They didn't have long. There was no way out. The President was calm, almost detached. Yquatine was gone, Arielle was gone; it seemed only natural that he should be next. At least, if there was an afterlife – something he'd never seriously considered before this moment – then he'd see her again. Kiss her again. Hold her again. He was reconciled to his imminent death.

Fandel, on the other hand, clearly wasn't. The Luvian kept up a ceaseless babble of imprecations and yells of fear. President Vargeld phased him out, trying to muster a sense of finality. Only the pressure of Fandel's fingers on his arm and the shouted words, 'I'm going to run for it!' shook the President from his reverie.

'No!' he cried, making a grab for Fandel's retreating figure. But it was too late – Fandel squirmed around the side of the container and ran into the middle of the loading bay, beneath the serried ranks of loaders.

President Vargeld stayed hidden, cursing Fandel's cowardice. He could hear him begging the Anthaurk to remember the treaty, to have mercy.

President Vargeld was unable to resist peering out from around the side of the container, and was just in time to see three orange beams of energy arc towards Fandel, his Luvian finery going up in a roaring ball of flame. Soon, all that was left of him was a charred husk.

Harsh Anthaurk voices called him to emerge from hiding, promising that they would spare him. He laughed at their clumsy tactics. If he stepped out he'd meet the same fate as Fandel.

And if he stayed here they'd keep firing until the container became so hot he'd either choke to death or be forced to come out. Or until Aloysius caved in under the Anthaurk onslaught.

He checked his blaster, calculating. Perhaps if he ran across to the next container, he'd be able to take one of them out. Maybe he could hold them off. Maybe he didn't have to die.

As he deliberated, he heard a sudden crackle of energy and Anthaurk voices screaming in pain. Both sounds died away and as President Vargeld tried to work out what had happened, he heard a familiar voice. 'Stefan?'

He crouched there, blaster in hand, and stared at the gantries above, not believing what he had just heard.

There it was again, cutting straight to his heart like a knife. 'Stefan, are you there?'

He stifled a sob, and emerged from hiding.

She – she was walking down the stairs from the maintenance gallery, the smoking bodies of the Anthaurk behind her.

She – she was wearing the red dress she'd had on the night he'd proposed to her. And she was carrying a plasma pulse rifle.

He let his blaster clatter to the floor. He was unable to move, unable to take his eyes away from her, away from Arielle.

She walked right up to him, a quirky little smile on her lips. So many thoughts flashed through his head: after the first time they'd met on Treaty Day a year ago, he'd played music all night and danced around the palace like a loon, feeling as though he could live for ever; the image of her naked, her eyes closed and mouth open and his name on her lips (hearing it had made him cry); her cold eyes the last time they had met.

Now she was here, as real as Fandel's smoking corpse, the smell of which was curling up his nose.

Arielle, back from the dead. He didn't care how she'd got here, for now, and he ran to her, feeling her body fill his arms, mumbling her name into her hair, breathing in the smell of her. Except there was no smell. He remembered that seeming odd.

They disengaged and looked at each other. 'Stefan, it's good to see you again.'

There were a hundred things he wanted to say. How did she escape from Muath? What had she been doing there? Had she been taken over by the Omnethoth? Perhaps she was still possessed. But all he could do was smile and say, 'It's good to see you again, too.'

But there was something about her eyes…

'Stefan, you must surrender to the Anthaurk. It's the only way.'

He shook his head. 'No way. I would rather die.'

She looked angry, offended. 'Think of all the lives you'll save!'

Stefan shrugged. 'There are, what, about five hundred souls on this station? Do you think, after what happened to Yquatine, that I care? There is no way I am going to give in, and why are you so interested?'

She ignored his question. 'So there's absolutely no way you're going to surrender.'

'No.'

'Very well, then.' She smiled and spread her arms wide. 'Come to me.'

He'd had no choice in the matter. He stumbled towards her and there was a flash of light which split his head in two.

And then he'd found himself here, in this church of madness.

But I'm not insane.

It was Arielle. It had been her, right down to the last detail.

It had been her.

There was a loud click, the sound of footsteps. Fitz woke with a start and looked up as the cell door opened, expecting to see the huge form of an Anthaurk commando.

But instead there stood Compassion.

'Oh, hello,' he said, yawning and stretching. 'Wondered where you'd got to.'

Compassion's dark eyes flickered down to the blonde head of Trooper Jones, nestled in Fitz's lap.

He waved a dismissive hand. 'We didn't have any cards,' he said by way of explanation. Let her think what she liked. All they had done was talk until sleep had overcome them both.

'The battle', said Compassion with a smile of extreme smugness, 'is over. President Vargeld is currently negotiating terms with the new Grand Gynarch.'

Fitz yawned again. Just couldn't seem to become awake. Maybe it was his age – all downhill once past thirty, wasn't it? 'The Anthaurk had won, last I heard.'

Compassion stepped into the room, flinging her black cape around her like some vaudeville villain. The other troopers had stirred from their slumbers and were regarding her with expressions of dopey amazement and confusion.

'There is now a peace, of sorts,' she announced. 'You are all free to go.'

The troopers all got to their feet. Fitz shifted his legs, rousing Jones, who swore and lifted her head from his lap. There was a wicked grin on her face. 'You make a bony pillow, Kreiner.'

Then she was up and gone with the rest of them.

Fitz stood opposite Compassion. He yawned again. Then he burst into tears. She watched him, tapping her booted foot on the tiled floor.

Fitz rubbed the tears from his eyes, feeling embarrassed, and a little worried. 'Sorry,' he mumbled. 'Don't know where that came from.'

They looked at each other. Fitz wondered if her eyes were really eyes, in the organic sense. How did she cope with having a universe both inside and outside of her? How did she manage to keep an eye on both? How was she able to walk without falling arse over tit?

'Finished?' she said at length.

'I bloody hope we're not,' said Fitz, making to go out of the cell. Now everything seemed to be wrapped up, it was high time they got going.

Compassion grabbed his shoulder. 'Where are you going?'

He turned to face her, felt another qualm coming on, suppressed it. 'I don't know. I mean, the Doctor's dead; you can't take off without being sent on an endless magical mystery tour; and –' he waved a hand – 'this is our home, now.'

Compassion had folded her arms and started pacing about the room. '*Your* home. I have other plans.'

Fitz rolled his eyes. Not this again – the 'mere human you don't understand' stuff. There was nothing mere about being human, but he couldn't be bothered to rise to the bait. 'What plans?'

A look he would never forget – the look a girl would give you if you'd just shagged her mother and given all her clothes to Mencap.

Fitz backed away. 'How – how were the Anthaurk defeated, anyway? At least tell me that!'

Compassion sighed. 'It wasn't easy. I impersonated Arielle, kidnapped the President, impersonated him, and then surrendered. It was the only way to ensure peace. I tried to convince the Grand Gynarch that she couldn't take over the System just like that. She wasn't having any of it but fortunately her successor is a bit more progressive. They've got a long way to go but I think I've just averted a major war.'

Fitz boggled. 'All in a day's work, eh?' He remembered the President's surrender, how out of character that had seemed. Made sense now.

And then it hit him. Compassion had impersonated Arielle. Had used it to trick President Vargeld. Whatever his faults, the guy had loved her. Fitz could easily imagine how it would feel to see Arielle alive again.

'What's the matter?' said Compassion impatiently.

'Oh, nothing,' said Fitz. 'Look, whatever you do, please, please, do not ever turn into Arielle in front of me. I don't think I could take it.'

'Funny,' said Compassion, a smile creeping over her lips. 'That's almost exactly what President Vargeld said.'

The coffee was slightly bitter with a smoky aftertaste, which lingered long in the mouth. It was the best he had ever tasted.

President Vargeld sat on the edge of his bed in his quarters, the coffee mug cradled in his hands, and told himself that he could handle it. He could handle the facts.

Arielle hadn't been Arielle. She had been a *thing* called 'Compassion' – the lady friend the Doctor had mentioned. Only this was no lady. As far as he could tell she was some droid with internal dimensions that were larger than the outer shell. Impossible, sure, but he'd seen the evidence. She could change her shape. She'd taken on Arielle's appearance so she could get to him, get him out of the way so she could impersonate him.

Thank the stars she had abandoned her Arielle disguise. She'd changed before his eyes, to prove her story – from Yquatine woman to Anthaurk to a rather stern-looking pale-skinned girl with ginger hair. The change wasn't easy and had seemed to cause Compassion some pain.

He'd seen it with his own eyes. So he had to believe it. Still, it was difficult to accept. He'd asked her about the Doctor, but at the mention of his name she'd closed up, and strode off in a huff.

Leaving him with more questions than answers.

And in a few minutes he was due to meet the new Grand Gynarch to start to piece together the broken shards of the Minerva System.

Was he up to it? He'd been too blinded by grief, rage, maybe even madness, to see that surrender to the Anthaurk was simply the first step on the road to peace. He'd been immature, selfish, unfit to be President. And Compassion had made peace, had solved the problem using his appearance. Everyone would think it was him. He was going to be hailed as a hero, when in fact he'd almost started another war.

Stefan Vargeld, Marquis of Yquatine and President of the Minerva System, put his head in his hands, squeezing hard, as if he could somehow physically hold his mind together.

The plate was groaning with golden chips crowded round a hefty steak-and-kidney pie with a crimped border, glistening in the soft light of the restaurant.

Things had almost returned to normal on Aloysius Station. The Anthaurk had all gone back home, apart from their leaders, who were in negotiations with the Senate. Repairs were being carried out to the battered and blasted superstructure of Aloysius Station. There was a palpable atmosphere of relief, a delicate, brittle feeling that the end was in sight. People were openly weeping for the loss of Yquatine and the crime rate was sky-high – typical if diametrically opposed manifestations of grief – but the hostilities were over. For now.

Fitz picked up a chip and popped it into his mouth. His stomach growled in anticipation.

Opposite him sat Lou Lombardo, who kept darting nervous glances at Compassion, sitting bolt upright and glowering to Fitz's right.

They had talked briefly about what to do next. They really had no choice. The longer they remained in one place and time, the easier it would be for their enemies to find them. Sooner or later – probably sooner, judging by Compassion's hunted expression – they were going to have to Randomise themselves into the vortex. Then, that would be it – no more Doctor, just Fitz and Compassion zooming on crazy unpredictable adventures through time and space.

But without the Doctor there seemed to be little point to it. Fitz had more or less decided to stay here, help with the reconstruction of the System. Compassion could go her own way.

He popped another chip in his mouth. When was the best moment to tell her? How would she react?

'The trouble with the pies in this place', said Lombardo, his large frame hunching over the table, 'is that they're not fussy about their suppliers. Now I only use – er, used to use – SynthoCorp.'

Fitz was glad of the chance to think of something else. 'Doesn't sound like they manufacture real meat.'

Lombardo frowned. 'What do you mean?'

'You know – real meat. From cows, pigs?'

Lombardo stared at him oddly. 'No, lad, almost all meat's artificial these days. Grown in vats. Eliminates the possibility of infections and animal cruelty. No carcinogens, either.' He smiled and patted his stomach. 'Pork, lamb, beef, chicken, all artificial. And it tastes great!'

Fitz had to admit it, the 'steak-and-kidney' pie he was gobbling down like there was no tomorrow – and he still couldn't shake the feeling that there wouldn't be – was the finest he had ever tasted. 'Yeah,' he said through a mouthful of crust and gravy. 'This is lush!'

'Be quiet!' Compassion held up both hands.

Fitz noticed how lined and old-looking her palms were. 'What is it?'

'Something's coming.' She rose from the table, sending her chair scraping back over the tiles. 'Something bad.'

Fitz dropped the chip he was holding. 'Oh, farts. Not again!'

Lombardo's moon face was a mask of incomprehension.

'I'll explain later,' said Fitz. 'Yow!'

Compassion had grabbed his arm and he was dragged from the table. 'Where are you taking me?'

'Spacedock One,' yelled Compassion. 'We've got to get there before anyone else does.'

Fitz gripped the railing on the observation bay in Spacedock One. Compassion wasn't saying anything, which was highly annoying. He heard footsteps behind him. He turned to see President Vargeld, followed by a phalanx of troopers. The guy didn't look very happy. Fitz gave him a little wave. Ignored. Fitz winced. Bad move. The President could still have him locked up but apparently this latest crisis was taking priority.

There were others with President Vargeld: a tall Adamantean, a deerlike creature, a bipedal tiger in tattered robes. Oh, and a giant beetle thing, a bit like the creature he'd bought that yukky food from when he'd first arrived on Yquatine – earlier that morning, a month ago. Fitz tried to stop his mind from boggling at the thought. 'Compassion, for the last time, what the BH is going on?'

A remote expression, a faint smile. 'You'll see.'

All Fitz knew was that a ship of some sort was heading right for the doors of the spacedock. As he watched, they slid open like a giant robotic mouth.

And there, blotting out the stars, was the unmistakable, sleek, ovoid shape of an Omnethoth ship.

'Oh, hell!' cried Fitz. 'Why didn't you tell me?'

On the floor of the dock, a row of gunlike things had been set up, cables snaking off towards the walls. Fitz heard the President shout an order into his comms unit.

Compassion shoved Fitz aside, made for the President. 'No!' she screamed.

The passion and urgency in her voice made Fitz's jaw drop.

The troopers drew their weapons but President Vargeld ordered them to stand down. He looked uneasy. 'You again.'

'Don't use the ionisers,' snapped Compassion.

President Vargeld pointed at the Omnethoth ship, which had floated right inside the dock, the space doors sliding silently closed behind it. 'Give me one good reason why I should spare it.'

'Look!' cried Fitz. Something was happening to the Omnethoth ship. It was changing, rainbow colours washing over its surface like oil in sunlight. A hole appeared halfway along its back, and something emerged.

It was beautiful. A cloud being, its body a gently undulating mass of cotton-wool blue, pink tendrils waving gently. Another followed, and then another, then another. Fitz gasped in wonder as they floated about the spacedock like giant jellyfish.

The ship descended to the floor. A hatch opened in the side and someone stepped out.

Fitz almost fell to the floor with shock and relief.

The someone was waving up at them, a big smile on his handsome but rather tired-looking face.

Fitz waved back weakly. 'It's the Doctor!'

Compassion raised her eyebrows and tutted. 'Well, duh.'

Chapter Twenty-Six
'That's fine, then'

Much as Fitz admired the Doctor, he badly wanted to tell him something. Tell him that, while he'd been off on his jolly jaunt solving the Omnethoth problem, he, Fitz, had spent a month in prison, all hope lost and certain to die. He was also fighting with the ever-present guilt, remembering how before his imprisonment, he'd planned to run away with Arielle. Well, the Doctor need never know about that.

Compassion looked extremely annoyed with the Doctor, impaling him with her most evil stare, but he seemed oblivious.

He was enjoying himself. It was explanation time.

'So you see, they were almost upon me when I realised what they wanted. They wanted me to rescue them – they knew I could reprogram them. They, ahem, thought I was a Master.'

The Doctor had an attentive audience – President Vargeld, the senators, Fitz and Compassion all stood on the observation gallery, as the reprogrammed Omnethoth wheeled and arced in the spacedock.

'They're now totally tame, and pose no threat to anyone,' said the Doctor, waving indulgently at the creatures.

The President's face curled into an expression of pure disgust. He raised his arm and spoke into his comms unit. 'Destroy them.'

The Doctor lunged forward. 'No!'

But it was too late. The ionisation weapons sparked into life, and within seconds all that was left of the tamed Omnethoth was a pall of dirty grey smoke, which sank slowly to the floor of the spacedock.

The Doctor's face was white with anger, his voice choked with emotion. 'There was no need for that!'

President Vargeld stepped right up to the Doctor. 'Yes, there was, Doctor. Those things killed millions of people. We cannot tolerate their existence – even if you have reprogrammed them. Some madman might steal them, remake them into weapons. Or they might reprogram themselves. How can we even know for sure that you're not working for them?'

The Doctor waved a dismissive hand. 'Oh, this is stupid!'

'There is going to be a full enquiry into your backgrounds,' said the President. He walked up to Fitz. 'And don't think I've forgotten about you and Arielle. There's still a lot I don't know about what you were doing with her.'

Fitz met the Doctor's eyes. The Doctor flicked his gaze towards Compassion. Compassion nodded. The Doctor mouthed a phrase silently. *Time to go.*

Fitz thought of Arielle, folded up in the giant leaf within Compassion. He would never see her again; he'd never got to kiss her, let alone make love to her. And neither would anyone else. She was free now, a victim of the universe.

Anger made Fitz brave. 'Wouldn't you like to know!' cried Fitz, giving President Vargeld a shove which sent him sprawling into the troopers.

Fitz dived towards Compassion as she opened herself up.

The Minerva System had been the life's dream of two thousand pioneering idealists. Julian de Yquatine and his followers had dreamed, planned and built it.

And now it was shattered, broken, a fallen paradise. Something evil had struck out from the past and brought it down.

The Doctor ached to stay and help resolve matters. But it was time to go. They'd been in one place – and time, near enough – for too long, easily long enough for the Time Lords to get a fix on them.

They had to leave the System to its uncertain fate. To the chilling indifference of the universal process.

And, with a pang of sorrow, he realised he didn't have time to say goodbye to Lou Lombardo. Oh well. They'd meet again, somewhen. Probably.

With a wave at President Vargeld, the Doctor stepped into Compassion. He wished the best for Vargeld, he really did, and he forgave him his suspicions. After all, Compassion was difficult to explain.

He found himself in front of the console, right in front of the Randomiser he'd installed. He winced at the sight of it. And then he stared up at the crystal column.

Would she forgive him?

Compassion faced President Vargeld, the Senate and the troopers, Fitz and the Doctor safe within her. Well, within her at any rate.

The troopers were looking around the observation gallery, disbelief evident on their faces.

'They're inside her, you idiots!' cried the President.

They stared at him as if he was mad. He certainly looked mad: his eyes were button-bright blue, his face unshaven. Maybe his time inside her had unhinged him.

Inside her, the Doctor was standing at her console like a priest before an altar. He was shouting at her to dematerialise.

But that meant giving herself up to the whim of the Randomiser, the yawning eternity of the vortex.

The Doctor looked so small, so puny. Fitz was lolling about on one of the walkways. He was even more delicate than the Doctor. His mind had come close to being broken. Did she need such beings? Could she not exist on her own?

The Doctor called again for her to dematerialise.

President Vargeld ordered the troopers to surround her, but not to shoot. He walked right up to her. 'No one here knows that you saved the day in my name,' he whispered. 'So let's keep it that way, huh?'

Compassion nodded. 'All right.'

'Now are you going to let me have the Doctor and Fitz back? There are some serious questions I need them to answer.'

Compassion shook her head. 'Sorry, Mr President.' She reached out and took his hand. 'Good luck with everything. Sorry about Arielle.'

A shadow of pain flitted across his face.

Compassion waved goodbye, and then FEAR.

Fitz landed face down on the grating in the console chamber.

The Doctor was at the console. 'Dematerialise!' he yelled.

The floor lurched beneath Fitz, and the roofspace showed a dizzying golden whirlpool. The vortex.

The Doctor sagged over the console.

Fitz held his breath. Would Compassion force the Doctor to remove the Randomiser? He stood up, leaning on the railing.

The Doctor looked weary. 'I went to all that trouble to save a few Omnethoth. All for nothing.'

Fitz remembered the acid rain dissolving the buildings of Yendip, the grotesque shape of the transmitter. Arielle, her broken body fading to nothing. He was glad the Omnethoth had been wiped out. 'You can't blame the President, Doctor. How would you feel if your home planet was destroyed?'

The Doctor shot him a dark, unsmiling glare, his face lit up blue by the time-stuff below. Then he turned to the console. 'Compassion?'

There was a rumble, like distant thunder.

Here it comes, thought Fitz, bracing himself against the railing.

Compassion spoke. 'Doctor. Remove the Randomiser.'

The Doctor shook his head. 'I can't. It's part of you now. It would cause you even more pain to remove it.'

Another rumble, louder this time. 'Do not lie!'

'I'm telling the truth, I swear to you!' He glanced desperately at Fitz. 'And even if I could remove it I wouldn't because it's still our best hope of evading the Time Lords.'

The rumbling faded away. 'Doctor.' Compassion's voice was full of pain. 'You hurt me.'

The Doctor nodded sadly. 'I know. And this won't help, but it was for your own good.'

The light faded and the stuff below began to churn. 'Do not patronise me, Doctor!'

Fitz swallowed, a nervous hand at his throat. He wouldn't put it past her to cut off the air supply again.

The Doctor looked scared, his face upturned to the ceiling, his voice imploring. 'Compassion, if you hadn't run away I would have been able to help you integrate the Randomiser circuit!'

The time stuff below boiled in anger. Fitz could feel the grating shuddering beneath his feet.

Her voice became a booming echo. 'I was trapped in the vortex for decades thanks to you. And you say this was for my own good?'

The Doctor dropped to his knees, arms outspread. 'Compassion!' he roared over the thunderous echoes. 'I'm sorry!'

'Sorry?' Her voice escalated to a howling scream.

Fitz ran up to the console, wishing there was a face he could talk to, shout at, not this grotesque mushroom of black metal. 'Give him a chance, Compassion! We're all on the same side, supposedly.'

All at once there was silence, and all was still.

The Doctor stood up. 'Compassion?' He adjusted a dial on the console. 'She's retreated within herself,' he said, averting his face from Fitz.

Fitz let out a sigh of relief, and looked nervously around the console chamber. 'I think you ought to know that she threatened to kill me to force me to remove that thing.'

The Doctor shot him a look of pure horror. 'No!'

'It's all right,' said Fitz, 'I hope. I don't think she knew she was doing it. The Randomiser's really buggered her up, you know.'

They both stared at the black box on the console. 'It's all my fault,' muttered the Doctor. 'She'll never forgive me. I'm going to have to leave her to fulfil her own destiny.'

Fitz stared up at the dark roofspace. 'It might not come to that.'

'We'll just have to wait until she comes out of herself,' said the Doctor, pacing up and down before the console. 'Now what's all this stuff about being trapped in the vortex?'

Fitz suddenly realised he had a heck of a lot to tell the Doctor. He thought back to Il-Eruk's tavern, Arielle, the *St Julian*, the Internment Centre, Muath – while his experiences had taken a month, the Doctor had been around for only a few days. Where to begin? 'Yeah, erm, well, when the Omnethoth attack started we jumped back a month, and she abandoned me. The Randomiser wouldn't let her come back to Yquatine, and it took her quite a long time to track my biodata.'

The Doctor tapped his lips with a bony finger. 'And during that time you met Arielle?'

Fitz blinked. He didn't want to think of Arielle, not now. 'Yeah,' he said dully. 'I met Arielle.'

The Doctor rubbed his hands together. 'Yes, well, we have got a lot of catching up to do.'

Fitz closed his eyes and sighed.

Suddenly the temperature dropped, and a voice came from all around them. Compassion's voice, an ice-queen breath, a brittle thing of frost. 'You are forgiven, Doctor.'

Fitz shivered. 'Well, that is a relief.'

The Doctor smiled, but his eyes were sad. 'Thank you, Compassion.'

There was a deep, heavy sigh, which surged around them like the sound of the sea. Fitz was sure he could feel a light breeze tickling his face. 'I accept that what you did was for the best.' The Doctor visibly relaxed at the contrition in her voice. 'But you must never do anything like that again, Doctor. You mustn't interfere with my systems without telling me. As Fitz said, we are all on the same side.'

'Yes, of course,' said the Doctor, stepping up to Compassion and adjusting a few dials and switches. 'We're in the vortex now, drifting,' he mumbled. 'Probably best if we let Compassion decide when she's going to materialise.'

'Definitely best,' said Compassion.

The breeze faded. And was it just Fitz's imagination, or was it a shade lighter, a tad warmer now, as if Compassion was trying to make them more comfortable?

'So,' said Fitz, a smile spreading across his face. 'We have no idea where the hell we're going next.'

'No,' said the Doctor, returning his smile. 'And neither do the Time Lords, Faction Paradox, the Daleks, the Cybermen, the bloke down the road or his cat!'

Fitz realised with a shock that he felt really quite pleased. The moment he'd seen the Doctor emerge from the Omnethoth ship, all his plans to stay behind in the Minerva System had vanished just like that. Then he realised with an even greater shock that this Goth wet dream called Compassion was now home. She was like a scary new girlfriend with dark secrets you stuck with because you were afraid of the alternatives. Also like a haunted house in which you were forced to shelter.

Some home.

Fitz yawned and stretched. 'That's fine, then.'

The Doctor came over to Fitz. There was an unsettling look of feverish enthusiasm on his face. 'I think you'd better tell me everything that happened to you on Yquatine. I'm especially interested in what you got up to with Arielle. If my facts are right, she was the carrier of the Omnethoth spores.'

The last thing he wanted to do was explain about Arielle. 'She was – she was…' He sighed. He was tired and he wanted to be alone. 'Oh, Doctor,' Fitz groaned, 'right now, I need a bath, a pot of coffee and a few hours in bed, more than anything else in the universe.'

Fitz could see further questions in the Doctor's eyes, ready to burst from his lips. But instead he nodded, smiled and reached out, patting Fitz's shoulder. 'Yes yes, of course you do.' He looked up at the ceiling. 'I've got a few things I need to discuss with Compassion anyway.'

Fitz patted the Doctor's hand. It was, after all, bloody great to see him again, pain that he sometimes was. Great to be back in the mad flight through time and space, destination unknown. Who knew what fresh hells they would face when they next landed?

The thought of more action filled his limbs with aching tiredness. 'See you later.'

The Doctor nodded absently. He had already turned away, examining the dials and displays on Compassion's console.

Yawning hard enough to crack his jaw, Fitz walked from the console chamber and trudged down the wood-panelled corridor towards his room on the dark side of Compassion.

The Eighth Doctor's adventures continue in COLDHEART by Trevor Baxendale, ISBN 0 563 55595 5, published March 2000.

PRESENTING

DOCTOR WHO

ALL-NEW AUDIO DRAMAS

Big Finish Productions is proud to present all-new *Doctor Who* adventures on audio!

Featuring original music and sound-effects, these full-cast plays are available on double cassette in high street stores, and on limited-edition double CD from all good specialist stores, or via mail order.

Available from March 2000
THE MARIAN CONSPIRACY

A four-part story by Jacqueline Rayner.
Starring **Colin Baker** as the Doctor
and introducing **Maggie Stables** as Dr Evelyn Smythe.

Tracking a nexus point in time, the Doctor meets Dr Evelyn Smythe, a history lecturer whose own history seems to be rapidly vanishing.

The Doctor must travel back to Tudor times to stabilise the nexus and save Evelyn's life. But there he meets the Queen of England – and must use all his skills of diplomacy to avoid ending up on the headman's block...

If you wish to order the CD version, please photocopy this form or provide all the details on paper. Delivery within 28 days of release. Send to: PO Box 1127, Maidenhead, Berkshire. SL6 3LN.
Big Finish Hotline 01628 828283.

Also available: THE SIRENS OF TIME starring Peter Davison, Colin Baker & Sylvester McCoy
PHANTASMAGORIA starring Peter Davison & Mark Strickson
WHISPERS OF TERROR starring Colin Baker & Nicola Bryant
THE LAND OF THE DEAD starring Peter Davison & Sarah Sutton
THE FEARMONGER starring Sylvester McCoy & Spohie Aldred

Please send me   [ ] copies of *The Marian Conspiracy* @ £13.99 (£15.50 non-UK orders)
                   [ ] copies of *The Fearmonger* @ £13.99 (£15.50 non-UK orders)
                   [ ] copies of *The Land of the Dead* @ £13.99 (£15.50 non-UK orders)
                   [ ] copies of *Whispers of Terror* @ £13.99 (£15.50 non-UK orders)
                   [ ] copies of *Phantasmagoria* @ £13.99 (£15.50 non-UK orders)
                   [ ] copies of *The Sirens of Time* @ £13.99 (£15.50 non-UK orders) – prices inclusive of postage and
packing. Payment can be accepted by credit card or by personal cheques, payable to Big Finish Productions Ltd.

Name..

Address...

Postcode..

VISA/Mastercard number...

Expiry date...Signature...

For more details visit our website at **http://www.doctorwho.co.uk**